PRAISE FOR JACK L. CHALKER'S SOUL RIDER SERIES

"A well-told, satisfyingly intricate story."

—*New York Daily News*

"A plot summary of this first of the Soul Rider series is impossible. There are countless groups and people in conflict, apparently heading for Armageddon, and no one and no thing is ever quite what it seems. There are twists and surprises in every chapter. Just as important, the characters, from the young Anchor girl, Cassie, to the world class wizard, Mervyn, are fully developed and fascinating. You find yourself not only wondering what is going to happen next but actually caring."

—*The Milwaukee Journal*

NOW READ THE THIRD VOLUME IN THIS EXCITING SERIES

MASTERS OF FLUX & ANCHOR

Look for all these TOR books by Jack L. Chalker

SOUL

BOOK THREE:

RIDER

MASTERS OF FLUX & ANCHOR

BY

JACK L. CHALKER

TOR

A TOM DOHERTY ASSOCIATES BOOK

SOUL RIDER III: MASTERS OF FLUX AND ANCHOR

Copyright © 1985 by Jack L. Chalker

First printing: January 1985
Second printing: June 1985
Third printing: November 1985

A TOR Book

Published by Tom Doherty Associates
49 West 24 Street
New York, N.Y. 10010

ISBN: 0-812-53281-3
CAN. ED.: 0-812-53282-1

Printed in the United States

0   9   8   7   6   5

For Tim Sullivan,
in the hope and expectation that
he will hit the big time,
a giant spectacle with a dash of *byap!*

1

POWER AND INFLUENCE

If evil looks ordinary, even mundane, until it is too late, then Zelligman Ivan looked more ordinary than most. He was a small, thin man of apparent middle age, with a long, drawn face that had a chin far too large, a beak-like nose, two beady little brown eyes, and short gray hair. His beard was a close-cropped goatee only slightly less gray than his hair, and his thin, short moustache was both small and gray enough to be invisible from any distance. He wore the clothing of a respectable Anchor, a brown corduroy suit and string tie, with faded brown dress boots and a peculiar formal round hat, and he sat on a horse upright and unmoving. Overall, Zelligman Ivan riding through Flux was a comical sight, but there was nothing at all comical about the man himself.

They watched him come, as only those who live in Flux and are driven mad by it can watch, and they licked their lips. They were mad and they were deadly, but they were not stupid. Stupid people do not last long in Flux. Any man riding alone in Flux could read the strings, the multi-

colored bands of energy that were the roads through the
reddish, crackling nothingness of the void. And anyone
riding alone had to be a wizard, for without power you
were quickly dead. This, too, they took into account, but
again it didn't bother them severely. There were wizards
and there were wizards.

Ivan had no idea they were there until they struck.
Sounds traveled only a short distance in Flux before being
smothered, and visibility was always quite limited, as in a
thick fog. Suddenly from all around him rose horrible
shapes, gigantic shapes that reached upwards of ten meters
or more. Growling, drooling, snarling monsters that looked
frighteningly real. His horse stopped and reared back in
panic, and it took all his effort for a moment to keep from
being thrown, but he managed to calm the frightened
animal and look around at the threatening horde of hissing
and slobbering horrors.

He smiled.

Ivan knew that these were mere projections, a false
wizard's convincing and threatening show of his or her
own imagination without real threat. He had a rifle in his
saddle but did not draw it, instead waiting for the attackers
to tire of this and show themselves.

They moved in on him slowly, warily, but with determination. A dugger cult, he saw, fifteen or twenty of
them; all misshapen by their own inner fears. All were
naked, howling savages, so deformed that it was impossible to tell their sex or their original looks, save one, who
was dressed in tattered hides. That would be the leader.
They all left no doubt that their intent was more than to
rob; they were quite ready to pounce on him and eat both
him and his horse.

He traced a small circle with his hand, and the advancing creatures stopped. He watched them strain against
nothing, an invisible barrier he had simply decreed into
existence. Some gave up and turned to retreat, but found
an identical barrier to their rear.

Ivan surveyed them imperiously, then pointed at the leader. "You!" he called out, in a thin, nasal voice that nonetheless had the confident ring of command in it. "Come forward!"

The leader looked nervous, but realized that he was trapped and had to deal with a new situation. He approached the invisible barrier and seemed almost surprised to see that it gave way for him—but when the others tried to follow, they were stopped cold.

Close in, the leader showed himself to be a creature with a round, ugly face that had all the right features in distorted positions. The eyes were huge and bulging, and the mouth sagged on one side, revealing sharp, pointed teeth. The leader stopped before Ivan.

"Can you speak?" the man on the horse asked calmly.

"Oh, yes, sir," the cult leader responded. "Gody speak real good."

"I'm sure," Ivan commented aloud, mostly to himself. He noticed that the dugger held a small object in his hands, almost fondling it. "You're not frightened of me?"

"Gody fears none!" the creature responded. "Gody true wizard with *this*!" He held up the object and looked at it, and from it sprang a powerful beam of pure energy, racing straight at the rider.

Ivan had been prepared for it. He held up his hand and casually deflected the ray; and suddenly, it was gone. Gody looked concerned, then puzzled.

"I know those toys," the rider said scornfully, "although goodness knows where *you* picked one up." They were, in fact, small Flux power amplifiers created from the models of the huge ones built years ago by his old associate, but they were strictly rationed and carefully controlled. "They are adequate for some things, but they have a weakness."

Gody looked down at the little cube, not quite understanding why it didn't work. Suddenly the top flew off, and a huge number of paper streamers flew out in all directions. The dugger chief yowled in fury.

"They are just machines," Ivan explained patiently. "A good wizard has no more trouble with them than with guns and knives."

Gody knew when he was licked. "Sorry, sorry, Master. Will not trouble you further. . . ."

Ivan thought for a moment. "You're not really hungry, if you had that box, so this was just for the principle of it. Tell me—do you know this area of Flux well?"

The dugger looked confused, but at the moment was willing to go along with whatever the wizard said. "Yes, Master. Know from Anchor to Hellgate to Anchor again. Can read strings, can Gody, with. . . ." He looked down sadly at the box.

"I will restore your little toy," Ivan told him.

"Oh, thank you, Master! Kind Master!"

"I will give you even greater power than you have dreamed of. But for this, you must perform a task for me."

Gody was very interested now. "Anything, Master! Name it, Gody do!"

"Very well. Attend me. I will give you powerful spells, and yet another toy. The task I set for you is very dangerous, so you must do it exactly as I say. I will tell you how to capture a powerful wizard. You are to do so, and then take the wizard where I say. I will know when you have done this, and I will give you power."

"Tell! Gody and his people will do as you command!"

"I know you will," Ivan responded. "My spells will guarantee it. If you serve me well, there are great rewards for you. I may have other tasks for even greater rewards. But if you do this wrong, you and your people will die horribly. You understand?"

"Gody understand, Master, oh, yes. But—what you doing out here, such powerful wizard?"

"Fishing," replied Zelligman Ivan. "And I caught what I was after."

2

DYNAMICS OF DISTURBANCE

''In the old days, folks knew they were at war as soon as the first attack was launched,'' remarked Mervyn, high wizard of World, chairman of the Nine Who Guard. ''Now, it seems like we damn near lost the war before we even know we've been shot in the back.'' He nudged his brown horse a bit to increase the pace.

His companion was a strikingly beautiful woman, dressed all in the black of stringers, and wearing a gunbelt with two large and menacing black revolvers perched one per hip. She was very tall and slim, but a flex of her muscles showed strength in both arms and legs that few men could match. Her skin was a smooth chocolate brown, her eyes large and jet black, her hair and brows a striking silvery white that provided both a startling beauty and a stunning contrast. Unlike most female stringers, she wore her hair long, letting its silver gleam down her back halfway to her very trim waist. Her horse, too, was of the blackest black, but the mane of the large beast was the same silver as her hair. Clearly she was a stringer wizard of some power, and, therefore, one to be avoided by all sane people.

"Surely it is not as bad as all that," she responded to the old man's comments. "Any plot unmasked before it is completed is a failure."

"Perhaps. I hope you're right. But a plot is only a failure when it fails. You're good, and you've got much talent and experience, but I fear you are very young, my dear. I am over seven hundred now. Seven hundred years of fight."

She looked at the small, frail-looking man in the green robe and sandals, the wizened bearded face and long, scraggly strands of white hair flanking a bald pate making him look every bit as old as he claimed to be, and shrugged. "A winning fight," she noted.

He shrugged. "I can win a thousand times. Ten thousand. *They* only need to win it all once. I'm getting very old for this, maybe too old."

"You only look that way because you like the image," she taunted. "You could look and feel like anything or anybody you wanted, as can I—and I don't have half your power over Flux."

"Yes you do. In fact, I'd say your potential is as great as anyone's I have ever known, but that's true of most genuine wizards. If you can handle the Flux, you can handle it easily and in any way you want. It's the *mind* that makes the difference—intelligence, experience, and knowledge, which are the keys to anything. Your mind, for example, keeps you from such totality of control. Not your intelligence, certainly, but the way you see yourself and your place on World. You are content in the Guild and with what it offers; you are not one to sit for ages in study and practice as I have, perfecting your talents. You inherited your looks and your power from your mother, but there is too much of the father in your soul."

She chuckled. "He was never more than a false wizard, a conjuror of illusions with no substance. But he feared no wizard and killed the strongest. That tells me more about where real humanity lies than creating my own little world and playing goddess so long that I get to believe my own publicity.''

He shrugged and changed the subject. "Have you encountered any Soul Riders in your travels?''

She nodded. "Yes, three in fact. They seem to stick close, one to a cluster, or, perhaps, one to a Hellgate.''

"No, one to an Anchor. Twenty-eight in all, in fact. Tell me—what did you think of them?''

"Very little, really. They rode inside wizards of varying types, with no clear preference so far as I could see. The hosts gave off curious double auras, and were difficult to truly focus on with magic, but the wizards did not seem extraordinary or even very ambitious.''

"Ambition comes when the masters of the Soul Rider command it, and not before. I've studied one closely in my cluster the past century, and there is no question that the Soul Rider is as much a tool of something or someone else as the host is of the Soul Rider itself.''

"I shouldn't want one, then. Bad enough to have something influencing your life. Worse to know that they, too, are but puppets of yet another. Who? The goddess of the Church, or something greater?''

"Greater, I think, and lesser as well. The Riders are creatures of pure energy, minds without bodies, that's for certain. Their number and their deeds are too well ordered and well reasoned to be random, yet they are individualistic enough that I cannot see them as conjured beings. More than once I've touched their thoughts, and touched briefly as well the orders from their masters, but it only compounds the mystery. The mathematics of it is both very simple and very complex, as all of the messages consist of only two distinct parts. There is only on and off, open and close, yet the messages are impossibly complex and impossible, too, to translate or decipher.''

"On and off," she mused. "Sounds like a machine.''

"That was my very thought. If machines could think, this is what it would be like. That has driven me to despair, that thought. If the gods are machines, then where are they? Who built them? And to what purpose?"

"Perhaps to no other purpose than keeping the Hellgates closed," she suggested.

"I have thought of that, but it brings up unpleasant implications. If that is their sole purpose, then their mission is to keep us down at all cost, to make certain we do not interfere. We are learning now at a great rate, Sondra. The Codex has given us much, and sooner or later we will find the missing books, those which give the answers to the really big questions. What then? Will they turn on us as the enemy and slap us down to barbarism as they might well have done before?"

"Don't worry so much. Those books probably don't even exist anymore."

"They exist," he said gravely. "Years ago one of the Seven, Coydt van Haas by name, had collected enough of them to do wonders. With them he built the great amplifiers that increased an ordinary wizard's power a thousand-fold. With them he created a demented revenge, and resurrected long-dead beliefs and attitudes. With them he revealed enough to destroy the foundation of a revolution. And that was only a smattering of what those books must contain."

"My father killed Coydt almost twenty years ago," she pointed out. "If they exist, they're in the hands of the Seven."

"No. I know just where they are, and who has them, but it does neither me nor anybody else much good. They are in the hands of the New Eden Brotherhood, and they are hidden and guarded well. Occasionally scraps are fed out to keep their alliance firm with wizards they need, but that's about all."

She made an expression as if smelling a foul odor.

"*Those* maniacs. Why do we stand for it? Half of World would unite to crush them."

"Indeed. You find the Brotherhood distasteful, then?"

She looked over at him strangely. "Not merely distasteful—repugnant. Do you mean you *approve* of it? Women treated as subhumans, as animals?"

"I neither approve nor disapprove, but I wonder how strong your dislike would be if the sexual situation were reversed? No, don't get so angry—hear me out first. World is dominated by those with the power, both political and Flux power. You said it yourself—wizards who act like gods get to believe they really are. Three out of five of the most powerful wizards are female. I can name you a half a dozen that simply reverse the Brotherhood's philosophy, but ninety percent specialize in dominating, limiting, and oppressing their populations, although not in sexual ways. Some are more benevolent than others, but all are no more than variations on what the Brotherhood has done, perhaps substituting some other group for women as the oppressed, or being democratic about it and oppressing everyone. Are *they* as repugnant to you? Or do you even think about them that way?"

"But the Brotherhood is not in Flux; it's in Anchor!"

"And what difference does that make? Not too many generations ago a small cadre of women in the Church decided who among the young population would be sold as slaves in Flux, and carefully and completely controlled everyone left. Their control was more subtle, but no less authoritarian or complete. When it was finally rotting and begged replacement, it was a woman who did it, and the control was no less complete for having nobler motives. The Reformed Church was out to do what it said—reform the existing church to eliminate corruption. It did not question the order of things."

"But you have put your finger on an important difference," she noted. "I agree that Flux is one thing, because either you have the power or you must depend on one that does, but Anchor held at least the possibility of change, of revolution. When that is taken away, when Flux comes to Anchor, there is no hope.''

He smiled. ''And for two thousand years Anchor was more stable and less revolutionary than Flux. The people of Anchor were very unhappy at the system, yet they endured it and did not question it to any threatening degree. See how easily the newly recombined Church has reestablished authority? The people are not happy, but their religion teaches that unhappiness, pain, and suffering is their lot until they attain Heaven. The women of the Brotherhood are happy and contented with no thoughts of Heaven.''

''Because they have been brainwashed and Flux-changed into it!''

''Ah, yes. Yet some people take drugs to chemically induce a happiness they cannot otherwise achieve; others drink to excess for the same reason. Still others throw themselves into religious frenzies in a bout of self-intoxication. All are seeking happiness. But happiness, even Heaven, is the absence of further progress. When one is happy, one wants no more than that, and will spend his life in a search to keep the brain's pleasure center permanently on. It is the essence of humanity. We learn, we progress, by our unending quest for eternal happiness—yet should we achieve it, it all stops.''

Sondra shook her head as if to clear it. ''You make the world seem ugly and upside down.''

''The world *is* ugly, but only viewpoints on it are upside down, not the world itself. All I am saying is that people pursue happiness in order to obtain it, then try to force it on everyone else. That's the way of things. I do not like the Brotherhood, but I also do not like most of World. That's why I tend to keep apart from it as much as possible. When I was forced into active long-term participation in it, during the reign of the Empire, I found myself acting just as ugly and ruthless as the other wizards. I didn't like it.''

"You'll not eliminate my hatred of the Brotherhood with cold logic, even of the irrefutable sort," she told him.

"I know," he sighed. "That's why people still fight wars."

World had changed much in only twenty years, but it was arguable whether it was for the better or worse. The way, Mervyn thought, the position on that question depended on just what you wanted.

Cass had broken the grip of the old Church by splitting it in two, and uniting opportunistic Fluxlords and Anchors chafing at the old system to create an empire that had at its height spanned more than half of World. In the end, though, the Empire spread itself too thin. Internal jealousies and love of power cracked the empire in various places. While Mervyn and others of the most powerful wizards attempted a unified governmental authority, in the end the glue that held the Empire together and drove it onward had been the will of one woman: Cass, Sister Kasdi the warrior-saint. And so the enemies of Empire, led by Coydt van Haas, had set a trap for her, a trap she escaped—but at a great price.

Coydt had been stronger; he had, in fact, defeated her in a test of wills, and only a shotgun blast from a cynical stringer seeking revenge had allowed her to triumph, her self-confidence shaken. But in his death throes, Coydt had achieved his aim, for he removed from her all of the spells that bound her, that made her the saintly leader, leaving her open to more human feelings, desires, and needs. Already wilting under the enormous weight of her responsibilities, she had taken her drive from the fact that she could enjoy no alternatives. With those spells removed, the choice of going back to that miserable life was impossible. She had retreated to a Fluxland with her daughter, Spirit, who had been cursed to neither speak nor understand, and to be forever forbidden all tools and artifacts.

With them had gone her grandson, Jeffron, whom Cass and the agents of Mervyn would raise.

And with the "death" of Sister Kasdi and the withdrawal of Cass, the Empire had quickly crumbled. The conciliatory leader of the old, original Church met with the highest priestesses of the Reformed Church, and after much argument and tribulation they hammered out a concordat which reestablished a single Church once more under a single set of doctrines that incorporated the fundamental changes of the Reformers with the basics for which the old Church had fought. None could lead the Church, or become a High Priestess of a temple, or minister directly to the people, without the Vows of Sanctity undertaken by binding spell. Those involved in other aspects of the Church, such as administration and research, were not so encumbered unless they wished to be. The Church had become far less corrupt, but had strengthened its grip, for it extended to parts of Flux as well as to Anchor.

Hope, the Fluxland created by Kasdi as the source of the Reformed Church, had slowly dissolved without her force of will. Work on compiling all of the ancient writings and attempting to interpret them, a project called the Codex, had been moved to Holy Anchor, where a Queen of Heaven elected by the temple High Priestesses ruled as chief administrator.

Much had been learned from the Codex, but researchers were bound by spells to reveal nothing except through the Church, which kept tight controls. Much of the work was suppressed, either as heretical or as too dangerous and disruptive. Science, however, began to be encouraged in Anchor, where understanding of the devices that maintained them was now deemed crucial. Many of the key scientific works, though, were missing from the Codex, and scientists who went off on tangents not approved by the Church found themselves stepped on rather hard. The Church was interested in the practical. Still, the last twenty years had brought revolutionary changes.

With the understanding of Flux energy as just one form of all other energy, a form that could be modified, redirected, and controlled, many of the Anchors were in the process of being wired for full electrical power, not just the capital cities as in the old days. Wireless telecommunication based on the temple intercoms was also under development, linking all parts of an Anchor instantaneously. But no one had yet discovered a way to communicate Anchor to Anchor, for the Flux squashed and suppressed all forms of electronic broadcast signal. The standard of living for the average man and woman of Anchor had improved substantially, but these new developments put them ever more securely under the absolute control of the Church.

The breakup of the Empire had worried the Nine Who Guard most of all, for it left the mysterious Hellgates insufficiently guarded. They coped as best they could, using the Flux power amplifiers built by Coydt van Haas to create virtual walls around the Flux entrances to the gates, walls maintained by priestess-wizards under saintly vows, and by the defenses of the Hellgates themselves. The weak point was the other entrance, the one that allowed someone in each Anchor temple to travel directly to the gate itself, bypassing the defenses. There was no real answer, for new energy weapons could dissolve concrete as easily as anything else, so the Nine had decided to be content with an incorruptible Church devoted to eternal vigilance. It was true that forces had previously defended the Gates from entry via Flux, but not only Cass and Spirit but even Coydt had managed to bypass them.

Of course, not all Anchors were under Church control, and only a small part of Flux; but the Seven Who Wait, also known as the Seven Who Come Before, needed access to all the Hellgates at once to open them as they were determined one day to do. Control by the Nine of just one was sufficient to keep them from their work. Mervyn knew this, but had called a meeting anyway, an unprecedented one, to discuss the problems.

All Nine were there, which was the fact without precedent. They met in a tiny Flux pocket so secure that none could even guess its presence, let alone penetrate it, and they listened intently to the old wizard's comments.

"We have become too complacent of late," he chided them. "While we have sat and done little, the enemy has been actively on the march with their characteristic subtlety and with uncharacteristic precision and coordination. A new empire has been created under our very noses, one in the hands of our enemy."

He spread out a map of World showing the Anchors in their characteristic clusters. "This is a copy of an ancient map, but it will do for our purposes. The letters are in the ancient tongue, but mostly correlate with the names the Anchors have today."

Krupe, the fat, bald wizard in brown satin robes, looked down at the map and frowned. "Curious. If we use the ancient language, there's almost the full old alphabet represented there," he noted. "Funny I never really saw that before." He stared again at the map.

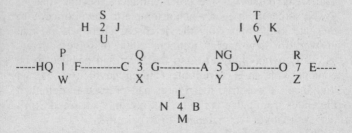

"The dotted line is the equator, the numbers are the Hellgates," Mervyn explained needlessly. "As to the alphabetical list, I saw that long ago, but it is in a haphazard order and seems to mean little except to denote the first letter of the old language versions of the names. 'HQ' is often an ancient abbreviation for 'headquarters,' and is appropriate, since that is Holy Anchor today. Why Tezgroph should be designated by 'NG' is something we may never know, as I have found no correlation of those two letters with any standard abbreviation. Still, there is World as we know it. All the rest is Flux.''

"So? As you say, it is common knowledge,'' remarked the dark and enigmatic Serrio, one of the two of the Nine not assigned to guard a specific Gate and cluster but free-roaming, to add extra strength where needed. "I could draw it in my sleep. Why show us this?''

"Patience. The nonstandard symbols might have been strange to some of us. However, I draw your attention to the fact that the northern, eastern, and western clusters are firmly under our, and Church, control. The center and south are not, including my own.''

The small, exotic wizard Kyubioshi shrugged. "It is not necessary for us to control all seven, as you know. As for the rest, they are a mixture, a hodge-podge of independent Anchors, some under Church control, some under the control of odd groups and factions, as are the Fluxlands inside and between. We agreed long ago, at the breakup of the Empire, that this was to be desired.''

"Indeed,'' Mervyn agreed. "However, my agents recently have completed a massive task that might have been impossible in earlier times. In compiling a structure of ruling Fluxlands and Anchor leaders on a cluster-by-cluster basis, we find *civil* control in the Anchors in the hands of just one or two individuals. As always, the government is totally subservient to the Church, but only outwardly. These governments have alliances with Fluxlords, allegedly also supportive of the Church. In tracing the relationships, an effort that has cost many lives, I might add, we came up with some startling information. Ultimate civil power in each cluster seems to reside in a centralized source—one for each cluster. In most cases this central source cannot be traced, but I have traced two, both in the north. Do the names Varishnikar Stomsk and Gifford Haldayne mean nothing to you?''

There was a collective gasp. Both were long-time members of the Seven, and their arch-enemies.

Mervyn looked satisfied with their reaction. "Even over in the west, the former Queen of Heaven, Romua Togloss, retains enormous power and loyalty. We have long suspected her of being one of the Seven, as there is some evidence in the old genealogies that she is in fact Rosa Haldayne, Gifford's sister." He looked at each one's eyes in turn. "Anyone seen Gabaye or Tokiabi lately? Anyone know who took Coydt's place in the Seven?"

There was no answer.

"I believe," the old wizard said carefully, "that certainly four, if not more, of the clusters are in such a position that the existing order could be overthrown in a moment, on orders from the shadowy authority who controls them."

"But they couldn't hold them. We proved that years ago," the tall, stately Hjistoliran noted.

"They don't have to. Once all seven are under their influence, they need only wait until it is time and strike at once, quickly. They can hold long enough for all seven to take the temples and reach the Gates. You can see their enormous influence now. What scientific project takes precedence over all others in the eyes of Church and state?"

They thought a moment. "Inter-Anchor communications," the tiny, green Talanane said. "Oh, my!"

Mervyn nodded. "And they'll get it, too, if it is possible—and it almost certainly is, or no other safeguards against the Seven are really needed."

"Do you believe that they already control all seven, then?" Krupe asked him.

"No. The south is the key, in many ways. The New Eden Brotherhood is not merely a revolt by the have-nots against the Church and World, it is in every sense of the word a religious movement and an expansionist one. Within two years after the collapse of the Empire it had abrogated its treaties and made alliances with very powerful Fluxlords. Within five, it had overrun Anchor Bakha and secured the Fluxlands between. They have developed new and devastating weaponry that can be used in Anchor, and I believe Anchor Nantzee is in imminent danger of falling, giving them the factories and heavy industry to really expand their program.''

"But where are they getting all of this knowledge, all of this new and revolutionary weaponry?'' the rock-like Makapuua asked him. ''From the Seven?''

''No. If the Seven had such weaponry and knowledge it would have used it long ago. Coydt had amassed a massive amount of ancient writings over the years, and had whole teams of his people working on them. From those writings he created the Flux amplifiers, and it is from those writings that weapons such as this are springing. Small items of use to Fluxlords are being parcelled out to secure their complete cooperation, but most of it they are keeping for themselves. I daresay the Seven would like to get their hands on those books as much as we would. But, like Matson's shotgun, science is proving more powerful than sorcery.''

''Then they must be attacked and stopped at once,'' Krupe put in. ''They must be contained or eliminated.''

Mervyn stared at him. ''How? The leaders keep to Anchor, where we are powerless, and they are so paranoid and secretive that they are nearly impossible to infiltrate on a high level. What forces can stop them, when they have weapons that in an instant can return an entire army to its Flux components? They are driven and they are ruthless. Bakha was determined to resist them, and it did so to its last ounce of strength. It cost them fully ninety percent of their population. Anchor Logh, or New Eden as they call it, no longer has a population problem. Half of it now lives in Bakha. Far worse, from our point of view, is that they have the same goal as the others—inter-Anchor communications. And they are unencumbered by the Church's restrictions on research. And they barter just enough with unscrupulous Fluxlords to get what they need by magic. Above all, they are pragmatists.''

''But at the cost of some of their best minds,'' MacDonna pointed out, ''considering what they do to their women.''

''Quite so,'' Mervyn agreed, ''but that is far less a handicap if you have the blueprints for what you need set out in front of you, lacking only the industrial capability to create what you need. Somehow, when they're ready, the Seven will be able to talk their way through to that Gate. Bet on it. The south is even now being handled for the Seven by Zelligman Ivan, one of the best. Like any good snake, he can manage to wiggle through the smallest of cracks. Right now he's thinking of ways to get himself in close to the New Eden leadership. Not inside, but enough to ask a favor when needed.''

''But this is terrible!'' Talanane exclaimed. ''What you are saying is that the doom we have so long fought is not only coming but is inevitable!''

''Not inevitable. Nothing is inevitable until it is accomplished and proven so by hindsight. What I *am* saying is that we have been badly finessed, outmaneuvered, and outthought. The true danger is not imminent. I would say it is years away, perhaps many years. Finally, though, conditions that have always been right for us are turning right for them. It had to happen, sooner or later. In a way, it's our fault, for the old system served us well and we helped destabilize it. Perhaps not. If indeed the former Queen of Heaven is Haldayne's sister, they already had control of the old Church. Perhaps we made it harder, not easier.''

There was an almost collective sigh of resignation. ''Then what can we do?'' Krupe asked hesitantly.

''We can forget about the other clusters, the ones totally under control, except for what we're doing now, and suggest to the Church that it strengthen its guard at the temples. We should concentrate our own efforts on securing the center, for if we hold just one Gate we hold them all. Pool our forces. Four of us on the western cluster—Anchors Qwantzee, Chahleh, Gorgh, and Ecksreh, four others on the eastern center—Anchors Tezgroph, Yonkeh, Abhel and Doltah. I don't care if we have to sit, one on top of each temple entrance itself. Plan it out among you. But one must be held at all cost. They can move, but they cannot sustain a move for very long.''

''And you?'' MacDonna asked him. ''Where will you be?''

''I'll be down there with Zelligman, watching him and everything else like a hawk. And if Anchor Logh starts talking even the most idiotic nonsense to Anchor Bakha, you all will be the second to know.'' His mind was already very much focused on Zelligman Ivan, wondering just what the man was up to now. . . .

3

A LITTLE FAVOR

They never had a name for the small Fluxland Mervyn had created for them north of Anchor Logh, but they never needed one. To Cass it was just "home," and to Spirit—well, names wouldn't mean much to Spirit.

It was a pretty place, a garden with a nice stream and waterfall and plenty of flowers and fresh fruit and vegetables growing wild. Spirit wouldn't eat cooked food, but little Jeffy had to have some, even though he stayed on his mother's breast for a very long time.

Spirit was a tall, beautiful, slender woman with long auburn hair and a creamy tan complexion. She lived more or less in a world of her own, unable to speak or understand anyone, unable to use or make use of any human-made tools or artifacts. While Coydt van Haas had originally used the kidnapping and spell on Spirit as a way to hurt Cass, and to divert her from his bigger plans until it was too late to stop him, the spell had been broken once, while Coydt was turning their home of Anchor Logh into a male sex fantasy. But she had been so revolted by her old friends' and family's acquiescence to this weird new order of things that she had chosen once again and for all time to return to what she'd been in Flux.

And the Soul Rider continued in her. The strange energy creature lived in some kind of symbiotic relationship with its host, and could only be perceived by powerful wizards like Cass and Mervyn, and then only as a doubled aura.

Spirit was an eternal child, but she had a child, Jeffron, who early on needed his grandmother's care. Cass felt useful and secure during that period, after forty years of stress in which she had almost, but not quite, revolutionized World. But she found her patience short and thin, and soon had to depend on those people Mervyn had sent—strange half-animal creatures of Flux and his imagination, creatures who'd once been human—to handle the routine chores.

Little Jeffy was a tiger and a delight, too, but it was clear that this Fluxland, so perfect for his mother, was not a place where he could grow and develop and learn. Ultimately, Mervyn suggested sending the boy to school in an Anchor up north, with later training part-time in Globbus, the Fluxland which trained and developed half the wizards of World. Cass had to agree. For Jeffy had the power, as his parents and grandmother had had before him, and only time would tell how strong he might become. He would be home for frequent visits, of course.

Spirit was sad at this, but seemed to understand why it had to be, and overall took it better than her pragmatic mother. For Cass, the boy's departure simply left her with nothing to fill the days and nights; with no purpose at all.

She brooded. She loved Spirit more than anything, but her daughter's condition made it impossible to get close to her, and was a constant reminder to her of her past.

Cass had been depressed most of her life, but action and events had always served to divert her mind. Now there was nothing, and she sank into a total gloom. Although she was famous over all the world, she considered herself worse than a failure, and made a good case for that judgment. She'd failed at romance, she'd done worse than fail as a parent—she'd exposed her child to the condition she was now in—and her actions had cost so many lives, eventually including the life of her father, the one human being she'd loved above all others. She had led an army that had taken half the planet, something no one else had ever dreamed of doing, yet the Empire stalled and collapsed in ruins when she could no longer lead it, and the old and new Church had reconciled in a way that might have been more honest but was certainly no more progressive.

She'd wanted to travel World, not conquer it, as a girl, but that was next to impossible now. There wasn't much fun in seeing the remains of what she'd built, in finding out that the changes had, after all, been mostly cosmetic. She felt as if she belonged nowhere, a ball adrift after plowing through a perfectly ordered display. Her failure at romance was the one thing she felt desperately.

She took to having long, elaborate fantasies in the gardens, lying there naked and half-dreaming. She was fifty but looked twenty-five, and she had had sex only once in her life. Not that she couldn't have it now, for she was a powerful wizard and all the binding spells limiting her were gone. Yet she feared failure and rejection more than ever, and feared hurting anyone else.

She imagined herself as a voluptuous sex bomb, and knew that she could change herself into that image at any time, but she didn't have the guts to do so. She imagined herself as a man, and thought that had possibilities. She'd always been a tomboy, always looked like a boy, dressed like a boy, and did a man's job, and she was proud of that. She'd spent so much time acting as a boy she just about thought of herself as one. She liked the perfect female form, such as Spirit's, but it just wasn't *her*, and what attracted her in the men she *did* find attractive was an aura of strength, of competence, of being in control. Few men she'd met fit that description, and certainly if she took on a male form that quality, to her mind, would be lacking as well. She'd never liked living lies, yet she saw her whole life that way and wasn't about to create another.

Because she'd conquered half a world, creating and running a Fluxland, which she could learn to do through Mervyn, didn't really appeal to her, either. The trouble was, the way her fantasies were, it'd wind up being too much like Coydt's version of Anchor Logh.

She was tempted by drugs, but was immune to them. Yet she did drink, quite a lot. It was pleasant to be drunk and know that one could banish an upset stomach and a hangover with a wave of the hand. She visited Mervyn's Fluxland of Pericles and found in its vast and ancient library many spells for exciting the pleasure centers, and these helped. They stopped her brooding, anyway.

Mervyn kept trying to get her interested in something— the Codex she'd begun to assemble of all the ancient writings, politics, and teaching at Globbus—but nothing really appealed to her after a while. She just drifted aimlessly, wallowing in her guilt and self-pity, feeling her life was over and wasted but unable to bring herself to terminate it.

She thought often of Suzl, made over by binding spell into a gorgeous sex object, and wondered who'd gotten the better of the deal. Coydt had cursed Suzl to everlasting slavery, it was true, but no worse a one than citizens of most Fluxlands endured. And there were compensations. She'd been cursed to eternal beauty, to eternal sex appeal, and, most mercifully, to ignorance so that she would be happy. She had pitied Suzl for that, but Coydt had cursed Cass as well by removing from her every binding spell, setting her aimlessly adrift and showing the lie of all she had built up. One was free, and powerful, the other weak and a slave—and who was the happier?

Damn Coydt van Haas! He had worked such exquisite,

such perfect evil upon World and then died so that he paid nothing for those deeds. He was at peace, and his victims continued to suffer.

And yet, Cass was still wanted. The Church would richly reward anyone who got rid of her. Its leaders feared her return as a renewed and this time perhaps fatal blow to the social structure. All the wizards she'd defeated who still survived wanted her—boiled, fried, or any other way—as did relatives of those thousands killed in her useless wars. None of this worried her. Between Mervyn's powers and her own, home was secure. One could not even find it without an invitation, for no strings led to or from it. And she was a powerful wizard in Flux and a formidable opponent with gun or knife or sword in Anchor.

Yet Coydt had beaten her, and broken her self-confidence forever. She could never be sure anymore just who was the stronger, and that made her reluctant to use her powers.

She had lost all track of time, for it wasn't relevant. Time was measured only in the growth of Jeffron, who now visited less and less frequently. He was a strapping one hundred eighty-two centimeters tall, lean, and muscular now, with coal-black hair and his mother's green eyes. He was smart and powerful, but seemed rather aimless and impetuous, the sort of young man who knows he looks good and can get whatever he wants, but hasn't decided what yet; willing to try almost anything once, but never satisfied. She loved him, and worried about him, but feared to give him any advice or direction. Who was she to screw up yet another life?

One day Mervyn sent word that a stringer named Sondra wished to meet both Cass and Spirit. Cass wasn't used to visitors and wondered what new trick Mervyn had up his sleeve to pry her from her seclusion, but he explained that Jeff had had enough of learning for a while and wanted to see the world. Sondra was willing to take him along as a wizard-dugger, and she had a long route in the northern

Flux, far from Anchor. Cass decided she did very much want to meet this person.

When she arrived, Sondra proved to be a shock. She was stunningly beautiful, and the silver hair and eyebrows against the chocolate skin was even more stunning. Irreverently, Cass wondered if Sondra's pubic hairs were also silver, and finally decided they had to be. Flux magic had been used to color-coordinate horse and rider; even the saddle and butt of her shotgun were black embossed with silver.

Cass, who usually went nude, had dressed for the occasion in a rumpled shirt, faded jeans with holes in them, and a very old and worn pair of boots. She felt overawed and inadequate. This was no stringer like those she'd seen before—most of the female stringers were flat and bald—and she couldn't resist the comment.

"You are a wizard, I see."

Sondra smiled and nodded, dismounting and letting her horse graze. "Yes. Mervyn says I blew my chance at greatness by going with the Guild, but I'm strong enough for my needs."

I'll bet you are, honey, Cass thought jealously, but aloud she said, "Well, I'm very strong and it didn't get me anywhere. I can see why Jeff would be eager to ride your strings, though."

The stringer laughed. "I like the effect. People remember me, and it's good for business. A little intimidating, too, I hope. If you knew what I *really* looked like, or the horse, either, you'd wonder why I ever left home."

It was a nice comment, although Cass didn't really believe it. Except maybe about the horse. Still, Sondra might be good for Jeff. Might teach him some humility, too, if she knew her stringers. Sondra had the same inner strength she admired in men, a toughness and resourcefulness that shone through any disguise. She knew she could come to like, even admire, Sondra, if she weren't so damned awesomely beautiful.

"Mervyn says that your routes are all way up north, past Anchor. How'd you happen to meet Jeff?"

"It was a set-up. I was brushing up on some technique at Globbus and Mervyn spotted me and suggested it. I took pains to look Jeff up—apparently he'd been talking about going out on a train lately anyway—and I liked him. If he learns some self-control, instead of going off half cocked at everything, he's going to be quite a man."

That was the right thing to say to a grandmother.

"Well, I can't see any way of preventing him from doing anything he wants to do. What is he, now? Seventeen?"

Sondra looked surprised. "Twenty."

Cass felt ancient. "Mind if I ask how old you are?"

"Thirty-four, and I don't mind a bit. But I've been riding string since shortly after Jeff was born. It's still a dangerous profession, but less so for a full wizard. Most of the stringers are false wizards, you know."

Cass nodded. False wizards could conjure up anything as convincingly as a true wizard could—only it wasn't real. Most stringers didn't need the full power; there were just enough like Sondra to make most folks nervous attacking any stringer at all. "Uh—you say you're from up north. You ever run into an old retired stringer named Matson?"

"He's my father," Sondra said softly.

Cass's mouth dropped. "*You're* the little girl with the talent who was interested in the Guild?"

"I suppose that's how he'd have said it. That's why I'm here, really. Spirit is, after all, my half-sister, and I've heard a lot about you that doesn't make the rounds of history or gossip."

"I'll bet," she said sourly, recovering somewhat from her surprise. "So Jeff's actually your half-nephew, or something like that. Does he know?"

"No. I'm saving it for when he tries to put the make on me the first time on the trail. But if you think I should—"

"No, no! It's perfect! It'll take him down three pegs! Come on—I'll find Spirit, and then we'll talk a while."

They spent the day just talking and roaming around the small garden. Spirit didn't know who the stranger was, but was obviously as impressed by her appearance as Cass had been. Sondra was distressed by the woman's spell-enforced condition—although Spirit seemed happy enough—and she examined the spell. She had been doing some work with more advanced sorcercy, but this one was a beauty, so complex and riddled with traps that she could well understand why no one had broken it. No one but one.

For Suzl, supercharged briefly by the energy flowing directly out of the Hellgate, had managed somehow to do it, aided by the mysterious creature that guarded the gate. But no one else had ever been able to achieve that energy level, and no one else had ever directly contacted one of the mysterious spirits—and Suzl hadn't known why.

Sondra felt relaxed and with family, but she was difficult to get to know or understand, as were so many stringers. She loved her work, that was clear, and was very good at it.

"You never think of settling down, having kids?" Cass asked her.

"No, not really. This may sound a little cruel or selfish, but I don't want the stuff that comes with kids. I was never very good with them, and they tie you down for years and limit your freedom. Some people are cut out for it and some aren't. I'm surprised you never found somebody else and had more, though. Seems to me you could just pick a good-looking wizard and have at it."

"No, I don't think so. Not now, anyway. I have to admit that there's a temptation to try and replace some of the lives I've cost, maybe to really experience the joys and pains of raising a child, but I can't bring myself to take that kind of responsibility anymore. We're totally different, Sondra, but in one way we're the same—we're wizards, different from other people. Wizards don't get sick, they never die of natural causes, and they live until some accident or attack kills them. Life's not the same with us.''

''I know. That's probably why there are so few wizard children. We once did as much of a trace as we could on Mom's family, and found she was related to most of the best-known wizards on World. They're mostly related, too, in one way or another. There's probably no more than fifty or a hundred families that have it.''

''Not me—I was an Anchor girl.''

''But you have it in the blood somewhere. It's passed down, sometimes full, sometimes diluted, sometimes skipping a generation or two, but it's there.''

Cass walked her back to the garden entrance, where the great horse still grazed. Sondra hugged her and mounted the horse, and Cass walked with them to the Fluxland border, which would open only to Cass or Mervyn or a few trusted aides of Pericles from either side. Cass walked through the barrier and into the void, and Sondra followed.

''You take care of him, Sondra—and yourself, too!''

''Don't worry—and thanks. I'll be back.'' And with that, the strange, dark, beautiful woman rode off into the void.

Cass sighed and watched her vanish, then turned to the garden once more.

She felt a sudden, tremendous shock and jolt, then collapsed in a heap.

Sounds were deadened in the void, but Sondra heard the sharp *crack* of some kind of weapon and immediately turned and rushed back, drawing her shotgun at the same time.

They were on her in a moment—horrid, drooling, yowling creatures of a dugger cult. She pushed them away and continued, and when others jumped up she fired both barrels of hard shot into the throng.

She didn't see Cass anywhere. Had she been somehow

killed or taken, or had she made it back inside? Sondra
halted, and her great horse reared on its hind legs and
came down again. Now she charged straight at the densest
part of the group, and before her swept a fierce wall of
flame that caught those who could not retreat. There was
another sudden loud *crack*, and a blue-white ray lashed out
and missed her and her horse by several meters. She
turned in the direction from which the ray had come and
saw an ugly dugger dressed in tattered furs and jewelry
made from human bones fumbling with a large device on a
tripod.

She sent out a line of force that struck the projector and
caused the dugger using it to cry out and fall back. She
was about to close on the thing and make it tell what this
was all about when she was suddenly struck by nausea and
dizziness. She reined up short and looked back and saw
immediately what was happening.

The Fluxland was dissolving!

She abandoned all thought of the duggers for the moment and stared at the phenomenon. A Fluxland was just a
thought, a tiny world created out of a wizard's imagination
and held together by the force of that will. Mervyn had
created this place, but it was modified and fine-tuned by
Cass, and now she knew that Cass was either dead or so
nullified that not the tiniest thought or will concerning this
Fluxland remained. Mervyn's structure should still have
held, but it was under some sort of psychic assault from
outside as well, taking advantage of Cass' incapacity.

She couldn't tell exactly where the assault was coming
from, but she knew in an instant that its power was more
than a match for hers. The beautiful setting was visible
now; the trees, plants, and flowers seemed to be dissolving,
like a watercolor in the rain.

She thought of Spirit, alone and with no substantial
power, and headed into the decomposing mess.

She found the bodies, eventually, of several of Mervyn's
people, but of Spirit or Cass there was no trace. Angry at

whoever had done this, knowing that she had to track them down now and make them pay, she nonetheless set off for Pericles. Not only had they harmed kin, but the only way they could have found the place was by following *her* there. Well, they'd made an enemy who would give her life to apprehend them, but who was smart enough to know when she needed reinforcements.

4

WELCOME TO HAPPINESS

The men stood around the still, small body of the woman and examined it as if it were some sort of specimen. One was Zelligman Ivan, ever his dapper self, while a second was a tall, beefy-looking man with a thick black moustache and the uniform of an officer in the New Eden forces. Looming over the figures was the black cubical shape of a full-blown Flux amplifier.

"Something is troubling you, old comrade," Ivan noted. "You stare at her as if she will suddenly rise and strike you down."

"She looks so tiny, so frail, so—*vulnerable*," the other man noted. "Not at all like one who toppled the old Church and gave us a real run for our money."

"Not to mention beating you in a head-to-head fight," Ivan retorted. "I fail to see why she makes such an impression. You have met before."

"Long ago and before we knew what we had," the big man pointed out. "She is the only one who ever bested me."

"And now you wish revenge?"

"No, no. That's not it. I have an innate respect for power. For those who have it and those who have the guts to use it. In a sense, that's *us* lying there, Zelligman. Somehow—I just don't know how to put it so you'd understand—it seems *wrong* to do this, particularly this way. To lose a fair fight is one thing, but there's something in this business that threatens us as well. These machines make us obsolete. Anyone with the tiniest bit of the power can best the strongest of us with one of those."

And Ivan *did* understand. World was a rough and brutal place, but it was based on power—power inherited and the skill and will to develop and use it. There was a certain honor and comfort in the system despite that, one which the amplifiers violated.

The little wizard sighed. "World as we know it is in its final days anyway, Gifford. You know that. New Eden is our tool and our weapon. Don't despair so much yet, my friend. It will take great knowledge, skill, and finesse to do what must be done here. This is using a cannon to trim a gnat's wings without killing it."

What they were attempting was in fact that sort of operation, and it had never been tried before. Ivan mounted the console command chair of the amplifier and trained the beam focus to its narrowest point, then concentrated on the still figure as Gifford Haldayne stood behind him looking nervous.

The first problem was the removal and memory storage of the spells Cass had on her. Many of these were protective in nature and self-imposed; others were placed there by ones with skills perhaps equal to or superior to Ivan's own, such as Mervyn. The amplifier certainly helped, but while the spells were far clearer and easier for him to read and understand, it required intense concentration, since the amplifier quite literally gave him a million times more details and information than he needed. It was simply not designed for this close work.

Ultimately, though, he sighed, sat back, and sipped a drink. "She is now devoid of spells of protections," he told Haldayne. "It would have been impossible to do without this machine. Impossible. They were that good. Now we can go in and, I hope, make the very small fine tuning adjustments required."

"I don't see why we just can't turn her into a Fluxgirl and be done with it," Haldayne groused.

"Subtlety was never your strong suit," Ivan said impatiently. "She is more than the sum of her parts. She is a symbol of strength and a role model. She must believe that everything that happens, every choice she makes from now on, is a free one, for that is the only way to convince others as well. The political shocks from it will then be enormous, as opposed to the heavy-handed way you propose in which she'll simply be a casualty and therefore a martyr."

"I still don't see how you can do it. We have never understood her, and these things can only go so far. You're not even a woman. How can you make those little turns in her mind?"

"I won't. She will do it for me." He sighed and put the helmet back on. *Talk to me*, he whispered to her through the medium of Flux. *Tell me your regrets, your fears, your inner angers and desires.*

It took several hours, but the pattern fell into place with greater ease than he'd expected. She felt tremendous guilt for those who'd died in her name, and some large resentment for the Nine who forced her into that position. She had a curious love-hate reaction to Matson, whom she at once loved and wanted dearly and yet could never forgive for walking away. Matson's image was greatly intermixed with her near-worship of her late father, and some of the attributes she found most attractive in Matson were really those of a father-figure.

It was, in fact, long and complex, but really rather easy. It was far more difficult to replace all the spells he'd removed exactly so, so that no one, absolutely no one, could tell that anything had been done to her at all.

Cass did not come to until they were well within the Anchor gates. When she awoke, she found herself in the back of a wagon, bound with handcuffs and light, thin, but very secure leg irons. She was stark naked, but that didn't bother her nearly as much as the restraints.

She was able to turn a bit and look out the back of the wagon. With the hand and leg restraints, escape was out of the question, so they'd decided to give her a view. She realized with a shock that she wasn't just in any Anchor, but in Anchor Logh—or what had been Anchor Logh. Now it was New Eden, a land she associated with fanaticism, slavery, and terror. It seemed almost odd to her that it still looked tranquil and pastoral.

A man came back, seeing that she was awake, and sat down beside her. He was a big, gruff-looking man of apparent middle age, thick but gray hair, a well worn face that spoke of great trials in his life yet seemed to have in it a hint of softness, even kindness. His eyebrows were almost as thick as his drooping moustache; the brows remained black, but the moustache was tinged with gray at the ends. His eyes were a deep brown, and they held compassion, not the steely fanaticism she expected to see. He wore a uniform of shiny black with no insignia.

"Welcome home," he said casually. He reached back and undid the gag, slipping it off, then offered her some water, which she took. Finally, she said, "So this *is* Anchor Logh!"

"New Eden. You wouldn't recognize it now that it's been so changed."

"I've seen enough—out the back."

He nodded. "There are three divisions of labor here, as we like to say. The men administer, plan, take all the responsibility. The bulk of the women live communally in sisterhoods, performing the basic work that makes things

SOUL RIDER: MASTERS OF FLUX AND ANCHOR   41

go. Some women, however, are special, and serve more intimate purposes. Don't worry about yourself—you are in a very special category.''

She didn't like that. ''I found the system repulsive at the start, and I don't find the refined version any better.''

''Huh! Listen to the High and Mighty one! Women made the old Church and the old order, and it stagnated and strangled people. Me, I was once a sergeant of a palace guard in Flux, run by a woman wizard who believed she was the center of all creation. Women did all the bossing there, and men did all the dirty work. Me and my men did all the guarding and enforcement, but under women officers who also commanded us in other ways. You could be castrated if you didn't perform to their satisfaction, on the walls or in the bed. They loved it, because we had all that strength but could only use it at their direction because of that old bitch's magic. You were around then, building your high and mighty empire, but you thought Makasur was just fine. You even stayed over there a couple of nights and said what a really fine place it was. You remember that?''

She felt a little sick. ''No, I don't. There were so many places. . . .''

''Yeah. But it's damn strange to take that moral tone when you saw the same thing happening to men and thought it was a wonderful place.''

''I—I didn't know.'' She was irritated at being placed on the defensive when she was in such a position, but her guilt at what she'd justified to herself as expedient always haunted her after. She had no doubt that the man spoke the truth, for there were hundreds of variations on Makasur in the campaigns. ''But does doing it to others, to innocents, out of revenge make it right? Or does it justify such places in your mind?'' -

''I can't deny that revenge played a big part in founding this place, but it's more than that now. A lot more. Among the ancient writings that fell into our hands were the holy books of our ancestors. Not the stuff the Church dishes out, but the system it replaced. This is God's will, His way of returning the human race to the right path, to purging humanity of all that went unholy. Hell *did* rebel, and it won. Now we are here to make it right again.''

She realized from long experience as a religious leader that the man's tone was matter-of-fact and definite. He really believed what he said.

''I'm sorry,'' she responded. ''I don't believe in my own old holy writings anymore. I'm certainly not ready for something like yours.''

''We will convince you, too,'' he told her flatly.

''You can do many things to me, but you can't work your Flux changes on me as you do the others. Surely you know that.''

''You underestimate us. Do you think you're the first world-class wizard we have dealt with? Wizardry is a horror we will one day eliminate from the face of World. The books showed us the ways, and they work. We wanted you particularly and for a very long time, you know. Not for your looks, certainly, although you are, I admit, quite a bit more appealing than your pictures. You're not just anyone. You are a symbol, recognized and recognizable, now as before. Wizards know your power, and your very presence in our system will demonstrate ours, generating fear in them and respect as well. This enhances our security and insures their cooperation with us when we need them. Word will grow and spread of this far beyond our little cluster. The Church will not fall because of it, but it will rattle a great deal. We were ready for you a while ago, but until now your capture had not been possible.''

''H—How did they do it, if I may ask?''

''You may indeed. A simple ray projector of our creation that uses Flux energy to concentrate enormous power on every cell of the body, but without destroying any of those cells. You might call it a near-electrocution. It is instantaneous through the whole nervous system, so there is no time to counter it. A very powerful but evil wizard has been trying to get in our good graces for quite a while. We told him that you were a prize that would make us think more kindly toward him, and he delivered you. Zelligman Ivan is his name.''

She started. ''But he's one of the Seven!''

''We are not stupid. This land was founded by Coydt van Haas, remember. We know what Haas was, and who and what Zelligman Ivan is and what he wants. I said the Church was a perversion, not something out of whole cloth. We know what Hell is, and we know from whence its influence flows. He is as powerless as you in our Anchors. He may gain a lot of friendliness from us so long as his power suits our needs, but neither he nor his agents will get near a Hellgate. Not from our side.''

She didn't know whether to feel relieved or not. At least now she could understand the cold pragmatism of the Nine in allowing this abomination of Anchors to exist. If they guarded their end as zealously as the Church did, it was not worth the thousands of lives to retake and clean up this place.

And where did that leave *her*? She shivered slightly, and he saw it and read her thoughts.

''Don't worry. God's object now is to provide happiness and contentment. You will have both.''

As a blade of grass is happy, even when it is cut, for it knows no other way, she thought sourly.

They pulled into a nondescript building in some town not far from the Anchor gate, and she was lifted down and walked with this strange man into the building and up a flight of stairs. It was slow going with the leg bracelets, but she was determined not to falter or fall. They placed her in a room that was no less a cell for being clean and comfortable. All restraints were then removed, but she had no illusions that she was not under constant surveillance.

In all, she found the place surprising. Electric lights here, in the boondocks! Some kind of powered air filtration system that kept things dry and comfortable at all times. She knew she was in for a great ordeal, but she had been through ordeals no human had ever before endured and she was still here. Suicide did not really occur to her; if she'd been the sort, she would have done it years ago.

There was a tap of drinkable water in the cell, and the first food they delivered was quite an excellent meal. She knew it was probably drugged, but considering the air system and the water it hardly seemed worth starving to death to avoid it.

She worried about Spirit, but she knew that Mervyn and Jeff would take care of her, at least see her through the tough times. It would be rough on Jeff, and she hoped he wouldn't try to rescue her. Not here. She was not convinced that they could make her become what they wanted, and she knew she would look for escape if she could, but she knew she would probably die in the effort. Oddly, that idea did not disturb her, and she fell fast asleep.

If they'd put anything in the food, water, or air she certainly couldn't tell. The next day they introduced her to the collar, a very nasty little device. Although it clipped on, it was very securely locked and appeared seamless. It was tight around the neck, but not so tight that it would interfere with eating or breathing. What it did was deliver the most horrible, painful shock she had ever known every time anyone pushed a button, and black-clad men pushed the button frequently. It was a textbook conditioning technique; not something that would induce permanent changes, but would give them control of her behavior, that was certain. She tried to stand it for a while, but the pain was simply too excruciating. After a bit, anyone would do anything to avoid it, and anything meant doing exactly what they said exactly when they said. Even the smallest infraction was punished.

For someone who was as intelligent and strong-willed as she was, it was incredible how easy it was to break her. Every mistake, every little error, got a jolt from the collar.

It took less than a week for Cass to realize that the only way to avoid such pain was to begin to think the way they wished. Even though she knew what was happening, it proved impossible to resist, and this helped destroy her self-confidence all the more.

The men who administered the system were highly skilled experts and they were very patient. It was impossible to fool them for long, and they proceeded in a methodical manner, never advancing until they were positive an earlier plateau had been reached.

At the start it was reduction and disorientation. No set schedules, no set feedings, no sight of the outside, and no prolonged or regular sleeps. The total disruption of the biological clock, the total absence of time sense, and sleep deprivation and consequent eternal fatigue coupled with the shock collar were as effective on her as on the thousands before her. She was human; that was all they needed.

There were the lectures, which she was expected to memorize, lectures given again and again, asleep and awake, and on which she was constantly quizzed, with any hesitancy or wrong answer producing a jolt. The only way to avoid it was to quite literally incorporate what was being said into her thoughts.

Not that she didn't try to fight it, but short of committing suicide there was simply no way to do it for long. The techniques used were thousands of years old and they worked almost every time. The old Church had found them quite effective.

Eventually, she found herself waking up automatically when the light came on, getting up, washing herself at the basin, brushing her hair, and waiting for the guards. All of the thoughts in her mind were consumed by the whole of the Revealed Truth upon which she would be endlessly and dispassionately quizzed. When all of your waking thoughts are directed to the same texts, you tend to begin to believe them.

World circled an enormous planet shrouded in poison

gasses, held to this orbit by natural forces. In the beginning, God had created the heavens and World and also created out of Flux all that was. Ultimately, He had created the first man in His own image and set him in a paradise called Eden, which was World in the first days. When the first man was lonely, God created the first woman as his opposite and complement. A true, divinely ordained social structure was in that way created.

But God wanted them tested, and allowed Hell the Tempter into Eden, and the demons failed to tempt the man but succeeded in getting the woman to disobey God's commandments, and then she was able to get the man to do the same. Because of this, God dissolved Eden into Flux and created World as it is known today. It was commanded that woman be the subordinate to man, as she was more easily corrupted; that because the woman alone could bear and rear the children the man would be the provider and the protector, the woman the nurturer and keeper of the home and family. Being created out of man rather than God, the woman had no innate soul of her own but could attain heaven by a proper life and service to a man, becoming an adjunct to his soul. To do so, she must follow God's plan and keep to the divine role assigned to her, one of subordination and service, as she had demonstrated in Eden that power and authority were not proper for her. Still, any woman who served God, obeyed His divine rules, and joyfully accepted and dedicated herself to service could attain divine bliss.

For thousands of years this society had existed, until finally the demons of Hell had cracked it, driven as they were to test all of God's creations. Misguided men allowed women too much power and freedom and this corrupted them. The men were overthrown for this, as God's punishment for their own weakness, and a corrupt perversion of society replaced it, one in which women set up an exclusive and false Church and used it to dominate and run all of human society. It was a period of misery and stagnation for human kind, in which all of the ancient knowledge was lost or hidden and all of society was devoted only to maintaining the status quo.

Now God had allowed, after all this time, some of the ancient knowledge and writings to reappear in the hands of men—the men of New Eden. God had delivered into their hands the means of deliverance from the blasphemous system that had oppressed World and the means to once again set up the true path according to Divine Will. This was New Eden.

After a while—she could not know how long—the initial treatment stopped. She was allowed to sleep and was given time to think and relax, but the collar stayed on and the tests always continued. Now, though, there were more structured sessions with a variety of people. She was taught the proper methods of dress and makeup and expected to make herself not merely presentable but as attractive as possible before leaving her room. She had always believed herself plain and unattractive, but they showed her all sorts of ways to enhance her looks. She did not even then see herself as a sex goddess, but she found the reflections in her mirror more attractive now and she liked it. Something deep down began to stir in her, something she'd never really suspected was there. She craved to be attractive, to get those looks from men, to be seen as someone sexy and desirable.

The sessions, too, challenged her, turning her inward. The Church was a sham; it could not be reformed, as she had thought, for it was innately corrupt and bankrupt. She had long ago lost her faith but there had been no alternatives; now she had one, and it seemed to fill a tremendous inner need to embrace it and believe it. She had been appalled by the corruption and stagnancy of the old Church, yet in reforming it she had killed tens of thousands and reached an empty end. She had sacrificed her life, her friends, even her daughter to a hollow idol, a Church that served nothing but the narrow political ends of nine powerful, amoral wizards.

Carefully they took her back to the original, innocent Cassie of Anchor Logh, dreaming of romance but trying to be content with a mediocre career that would replace it.

She fought it, fought it all the way, but her own internal counters to their arguments and philosophy were hollow, too, dead ends of unhappiness, loneliness, despair. She was in turmoil, unable to really think straight or counter any of it. In the end, it came down to alternatives. Accept this, totally and completely, or—what? More unending misery, loneliness, and despair? The carefully measured pressure built up inside her, based upon the groundwork laid, unknown to her, by Ivan and Haldayne in Flux.

Ultimately, one evening, something finally slipped in her mind. All arguments fled, all questions faded, and she prostrated herself and prayed to the God of New Eden to grant her happiness and peace.

Then they introduced her to Adam Tilghman, the same craggy-faced former sergeant she'd talked to when first awakening in New Eden. Somehow she'd seen something she'd liked in him even then, and the more she saw of him the more she liked him.

Human contact with anyone other than Tilghman was kept to an absolute minimum and was always done in silence by both sides. Tilghman alone became her sole source of conversation, punishment, and praise. He tended to be apologetic for the shock technique, yet he defended it as the only way to break through decades of conditioning without physical harm. "We are still feeling our way, and searching for the true grace of God," he told her.

The more time she spent with him, the more she looked forward to the next. In many ways, on both a conscious and subconscious level, he reminded her of her father— kind, wise, tough, strong, self-confident—a man sure of himself and secure within his own mind. In other ways, he was much like Matson—world-wise and somewhat weary, sure of power and radiating authority and confidence. He was the Chief Judge, the most powerful man in New Eden, and he was interested in *her*, interested enough to transfer much of his office and schedule to this outlying area.

After a while, he began to take her out of the place where she'd been secluded for how long she couldn't pinpoint. He was set up in a small house just outside the nearby village, and she relished the relative freedom of movement and the looks of the men and other women when it was obvious that she was with the Chief Judge. She had begun to fantasize just what it would be like to be the wife of the Chief Judge. She was aware that this part, too, was still a trial period for her, and that everyone was watching her, but she was beginning to realize that she didn't feel particularly demeaned or uncomfortable now. She began to feel that God had given her one last chance at redemption and personal happiness. No matter what doubts she might have had about the overall scheme of things, it was no longer right to think about society or broad roles and major causes. She'd done it herself, lived for others, her whole life up to now. From now on, she decided, someone else must save the world. She was going to do whatever *she* felt like doing, whatever gave her what she personally needed.

She had fallen in love with Adam Tilghman, and when you didn't resist the system, didn't think about it but just lived it, it was so easy and so peaceful. If the system wasn't perfect, well, neither was it a horror chamber, at least not for her.

Tilghman himself almost apologetically admitted that New Eden was not yet the society the faith demanded, and that many of the original men who'd taken over the Anchor were slow to accept change. He was confident, though, that change was inevitable, that even now a new society was emerging that reflected the ideals of the faith. Eventually there would be a society without want, without fear, in which people could live out God's tenets of living. He did not deny that there was a lot of oppression of women, but said that she would see the changes being made. He, supported by the younger generations raised in the faith, would see to that.

The faith took hold in her, not so much as a result of the conditioning sessions as because it gave her something to believe in that answered most of her questions and provided an easy way out of her guilt. It rang true when compared to many of the Church-suppressed documents in the Codex; it was far older than the Church, and it absolved her of guilt. She had been the product of an "unnatural" society; she could not be blamed for its results. With that acceptance she began to rationalize virtually everything she had detested about New Eden's society. The fact that Tilghman and the new faith both recognized their own failings and imperfections and pledged changes held great promise. Although she saw the hand of God in the death of Coydt now, she realized that his evil had corrupted many, but by no means all, of his lieutenants and that excising such evil would take time and care.

Tilghman was a big part of this realization. She had faith in him, believed in him and knew his sincerity of vision. His strength, intellect, and determination gave her a whole new reason to live and to hope; a product of oppression who wanted to build a more perfect world for all, not just be another petty Fluxlord.

It was not a sudden thing, no matter what the conditioning process, but rather gradual. One day she woke up and simply realized that Tilghman was right, that he offered the only positive vision in a stagnant and evil world. It was in every way a deep, emotional, religious experience which she was convinced came from Heaven itself. She bowed down and prayed that she be allowed to participate in this vision, and vowed she would try to attain perfection as a woman in God's eyes. She knew war, and hated it. Henceforth she would be passive. She had known sex, once, but never love. She would seek love. She had always been ashamed of her looks; now she would try to emphasize what God had given her and be proud to be feminine. She had given birth but denied herself motherhood; now she would seek that. She had competed all her life; now she would seek consensus.

When she told him of all this, he seemed greatly pleased, but he grew serious. "Cassie—I know you're telling the truth, and I know you think you love me. If you didn't know, I think I'm in love with you, too."

That remark sent feelings through her she never knew before.

He sighed. "Cassie, if we marry there will always be those who doubt and remember the old days. They wouldn't trust you, and that would weaken me. If you truly love me and wish to be my wife, would you be willing to make the ultimate sacrifice?"

She was taken aback. "I—I don't know what you mean, Adam."

"I mean to marry in Flux, and make the oath binding. To trust me so thoroughly that you will place yourself completely in my hands and accept whatever spells are offered you."

She hesitated a moment. Flux. . . .

"Yes, Adam, I'll do it. I want this so *very* much. Let me wipe the slate clean and be born anew, as your wife, your lover, and the mother of your children to come."

"Then we will do it tomorrow, at midday. And all who witness it will know and be content." He knew he was taking a calculated risk in allowing her into Flux, but it was the final step. She wouldn't know it, but there would be an amplifier out there anyway, sealing them off from the rest of Flux and preventing escape. Ivan and his own people had done a great job, but this was the ultimate, and final, test.

"There is nothing for me out there anymore, if there ever was," she told him. "I will take any binding spell you wish to prove it."

He smiled, and drew her to him and kissed her, for the

first time. She did not flinch or hesitate, and it became prolonged and more passionate and she felt herself getting terribly aroused.

And it felt good.

The next day they were picked up by a fancy carriage and taken to the Gate, which proved to be less than a half-hour's ride away. There were witnesses there, who'd been conducting one sort of business or another with New Eden, and all were invited to the apparently impromptu ceremony. Some were wizards from nearby Fluxlands, and not all were in the employ or under the complete control of New Eden. That was the way they'd wanted it. If the gamble worked and the timing was just right, word would soon be spread all over World, with confirmation by unimpeachable sources. Not by coincidence, the crowd included one Zelligman Ivan himself, who had been around for weeks killing time just to see the end result of his handiwork for himself. And, of course, insure his investment and collect his rewards.

The book on Cass said that she was subject to emotional rushes and that during that period she was pretty much willing to do almost anything. Mervyn had chosen such a point to get her to lead the Reformed Church movement and to take spells against ever being so receptive again. Coydt had removed those restraints; now, they gambled that she was at a similar point.

She was smiling as they faced the void, and they held hands and stepped into it. With them went the witnesses and a powerful Fluxlord named Constantine who would perform the spell. She seemed at that moment to have eyes only for Tilghman, but she did look around briefly at the void and at the witnesses, and there seemed a little flicker, a bit of hesitancy, in her eyes.

"Cassie," Tilghman said seriously, "I will take you as my wife, and swear that I will treat you according to God's will, that I will love, protect, provide, and cherish you always, 'til death. But it must be done freely, and you must place your faith and trust in God and in me. Will you?''

"I will, Adam," she responded, looking up at him. "I swear that I will love, honor, and obey you so long as we both shall live."

"If you love and trust me, then take the spell that is offered and bind yourself with it."

Constantine fed the spell, but clearly it was more complex than even he could actually divine. It was a spell such as Coydt had spun, in the impossible mathematics no human mind could follow.

She looked again at the crowd, and then at Adam Tilghman, and then out into the featureless void, and many held their breaths wondering just what she would do.

She accepted the spell, even though she had no idea what it contained, and bound herself with it.

Immediately she seemed to glow and shimmer, and there were dramatic if subtle changes in her. She was shorter, barely a hundred and forty-seven centimeters and perhaps forty-one kilograms. Her figure, which had always been slight, even boyish, filled out, with perfectly proportioned, firm breasts; a body tapering dramatically down to an extremely narrow waist, then out to large but ideally proportioned hips. Her skin remained bronze but became creamy smooth, without blemish of any sort, and her reddish-brown hair became waist-length and seemed interwoven with strands of gold. She was still recognizable to those who'd known her, but her boyish face had been subtly altered as well to erase all traces of the maleness in it; the lips had been thickened and sensuously shaped, the eyes very soft and seemingly huge, with long lashes and thin, feminine eyebrows. There was no body hair, save pubic hair, beyond the face.

All the women of New Eden bore an identifying tattoo on their left rump, and this, too, was there, although with the usual addition. "CASSIE TILGHMAN," it read, and underneath in much smaller print, "AL6-466-080N."

They kissed, and walked back into Anchor, where she was given a small case with clothing and jewelry in it, and a makeup and mirror kit. She gasped when she first saw herself in the mirror, and seemed pleased.

She wasn't quite sure how she felt inside. Certainly no different than she'd felt when accepting Adam's proposal, yet she remembered who she had been and, she thought, all that had happened. And yet, as she put on the silver fine-mesh garment, the decorative belt that secured it and hung on her hips, and the glittering silver high-heeled shoes, as well as the sparkling earrings, necklace, and bracelets she found and admired, she realized she couldn't read the small words engraved on the bracelet—and, curiously, it didn't seem to matter.

She basked in the looks she was getting from all the men, and felt very happy and at peace. The essential content of the spell, however, was not apparent to her, and would not be for some time; but it was set forth in a basic text of New Eden she would never read.

"In New Eden," it said, "the mind rules the body of the male; the body rules the mind of the female."

But most men did not have spells to enforce that holy rule. Fluxgirls did, and now, by her own choice, Cassie was a Fluxgirl, bound by a spell as tight as any and one she could never break.

The Brotherhood had been formed by Coydt van Haas as part of a project for the Seven, to undermine the credibility of the Reformed Church and show its vulnerability. For that task he'd recruited determined men from all over the planet, most of whom were tough and ruthless when they had to be but were, nevertheless, also highly intelligent and experienced. They also had one other thing in common with Coydt: they had all at one time or another been victimized, exploited, enslaved, or, as in Coydt's own case, mutilated by women in matriarchal societies.

In the end, Coydt had died not from sorcery but from the shotgun of the stringer Matson, out for revenge. But Matson, understanding that these desperate men would fight to the death and take a civilian population with it, also made a deal with them to relinquish Anchor Logh to New Eden without massive bloodshed. The deal that they accepted, though, was one to contain them, predicated both on a strong Empire to enforce it and on the impression of the invaders as a gang of murderous thugs. Both proved unfounded.

Coydt had brought with him his valuable collection of ancient writings and devices, and the team of experts who deciphered, attempted to interpret, and created practical applications from the vast amount of material in that collection. These were not merely the written works of the Codex, but included small machines that drew their power from unknown sources and provided illustrations and instructions. They did not understand how the devices they made from these sources worked, but they learned how to build them and found that, once built, they worked as advertised.

The initial year of their conquest was one of unremitting brutality, particularly towards women. Massive purges were conducted of the Anchor's indigenous population; the rest were indoctrinated into the new system by all of the new devices and a lot of old methods some of the conquerors had learned the hard way, on the receiving end. They had little Flux power themselves, but as much as they hated it they also coveted it, and were not above trading some gadget or scrap of knowledge useful to a wizard in exchange for services. The devices in particular were very clever, such as the small booster of Flux power that could be carried in one's hand or on a belt. Yet any attempt to open it to see how it worked caused it to fuse into a mass of goo; transforming it so it wouldn't do that also rendered it useless. All wore out after a while, and had to be replaced. The Brotherhood had created a marketable niche for itself, limited only by its inability to do more than small-scale manufacturing without wizards to transmute required materials. Anchor Logh had been primarily agricultural.

By the end of five years in power, the Brotherhood felt secure, and had also seen the Empire crumble and its guardians desert it. That time was also well spent in learning the complexities of running a government. The ancient holy books found by Coydt had given them a mission and a justification for it all, but it said little about practical administration.

Men ran the government and the religious institutions, fought wars, protected property, planned, studied, engineered, and administrated. That left women to do the basic work. Seventy percent of Anchor Logh's males had been killed in the takeover or the purges that followed. Those women not taken by party—meaning Brotherhood—leaders or the thirty percent of the men who went along with the new system were, therefore, reindoctrinated and in many cases transformed in Flux into a new underclass of dim, docile women to do that work.

The girls of the Brotherhood, the wives of the party men, were all broken of will and remade in Flux into the sexual fantasies of the men. They were expected to always be these male fantasies, to think of themselves that way, but they also were expected to prepare the meals, make the clothes and jewelry and other luxury items, keep the houses neat and spotless, bear and tend to the children of the conquerors—boys until age five, girls through puberty—and all of the other domestic needs. They also were the hostesses, the planners of parties and receptions; in communal groups they serviced the workplaces of the men, prepared and served the institutional food and cleaned and kept up the offices and official buildings. This level of organization took a lot of work and required intelligence in planning and execution. They were made safe by law with severe punishments for offenders so that they could walk the streets alone, night and day, without fear. A credit system was developed allowing them to purchase necessities for home and duties, with the bill going to the husband, of course. Luxuries had to be bought for them by their men. Much of the wives' lives was rather dull and routine, yet intelligence was needed.

Flux had provided the means to keep them where New Eden needed them. The body, which became uniformly attractive and sexy, literally would rule the mind. Emotion would always override reason, and physical needs were absolutely predominant, not something that could be ignored. Their minds were directed inward. Their attention spans were limited, so that thinking or brooding about things beyond their control, or the complexities of politics, finance, the world outside their immediate family and community, technological discoveries, and the like simply bored them after a little bit. They were practical and pragmatic; the things that interested them were the things that applied directly to their day-to-day life, such as housekeeping, sewing and design, clothing and makeup, hairstyles, child care, cooking and cleaning, and sexual techniques, which they sometimes practiced on one another. Beyond this, conversation centered entirely on relationships—husbands, children, friends—whether it was bragging, complaining, comparing, or simply gossiping. Still, the ultimate insurance of power is ignorance on the part of those without. The spell-imposed inability to read, write, or count beyond their fingers and toes guaranteed forever that the women of New Eden would be subordinate, dependent and never a threat.

Polygamy was allowed, even encouraged, primarily because there were far more women than men. Many of the Judges and top officers had many wives, for the law said you could have as many as you could support, but the Chief Judge, in particular, had always been too busy to even think of it. He confessed, however, to being very lonely at the top, but never before found anyone he could consider marrying. He took marriage far more seriously than most of the others.

In the seventh year, using new weaponry, they attacked their vulnerable neighboring Anchor, Bakha. Knowing what had happened to Anchor Logh, the Bakhans had fought furiously and well, the women alongside the men, but to no avail. The new ray-type weapons, which could be tuned to vaporize human beings while leaving all else untouched, just about wiped out the entire population of over a million. Wizards who had helped the Brotherhood get its men and equipment through Flux were well rewarded, and a new government was set up there, staffed with younger officers, in which polygamy was not only encouraged, but required. Bakha contained vital raw materials, but it was Anchor Nantzee, to the far west, that contained the factories. That was their next logical move, but it took a very long time to consolidate Bakha and get it running again with new personnel.

Cassie was near the center of power and decision, but such things simply didn't interest her anymore. She had returned with Tilghman to the capital, a very different place than it had been in her youth, with only the ancient temple, with its shiny no-maintenance facade and seven towering spires, really recognizable. Much of the old city had been demolished, and in its stead had risen large buildings for research and administration, others for the central market and general services. Most of the workers lived in large, spacious apartment buildings where quarters were as limited or grand as the man's job and social rank, which also determined which building you lived in. For the top, though, there were now a series of grand structures around Temple Square, luxurious homes which had previously been seen only as dwellings for Fluxlords. The largest and grandest of these, facing the temple entrance itself across the park, was Tilghman's.

She was awed by it even before stepping inside, and

once inside she saw that the ornate carpeting, the huge rooms all tastefully furnished, the art and statuary—female nudes, mostly, she noted with some amusement—were all of a kind only a Fluxlord could have. "You are mistress of this place," he told her proudly. "The serving girls are all unmarried daughters of prominent men, and they will address you as 'Mistress' or 'Madame.' Other wives must do their turn in the public buildings, but this is your sole responsibility. It will not be easy. There are a lot of official parties and receptions that must be held here." But she was so in awe of the place that she hardly heard him.

The staff included a huge number of young girls, mostly between the ages of ten and fifteen. They would be married off, of course, but others would take their places. These girls were, in fact, the new generation that had been born into the system and knew no other. They were ignorant that any other way existed; their education had been entirely tailored to the roles they were expected to fill. They knew the skills Cassie had to learn, and she threw herself into the job enthusiastically.

The work was exhausting and time-consuming, and for a place that size it never ended, but Cassie earned the respect of the staff by being willing to try herself any and all tasks she asked of them, and to keep at it no matter how hot or dirty it was until she could do it with the best of them. She found none of it drudgery, and took great pride in the results.

Adam had proven *very* well endowed, and very, very good, although she was, in fact, virtually a virgin. She quickly learned what he wanted most, and learned new tricks from the other girls. She felt insatiable, as if making up for all those years of deprivation, which, of course, she was.

In a few weeks, Tilghman had held what he called a "diplomatic reception," actually a party for both rewarded party functionaries and for representatives from places, both Flux and Anchor, with which they did business. In truth, it was to show her off.

It was a gala affair, with music and dancing, but later on that evening, while she was over checking on the small pastries and drinks, a young woman approached her. She was a knockout by any standards, short, pert, incredibly cute and very, very sexy, with breasts that had to measure over a hundred and five centimeters. Cassie had always wondered how such women bore the weight, and how they kept from chafing in this braless society. Still, there was something oddly familiar about the girl. . . .

"Cassie?" the stranger asked, in a soft and sexy soprano.

"Yes?" She was somewhat startled to be approached so familiarly by a stranger.

"Don'tcha *rec'nize* me? Even after all this time I kinda hoped y'might. 'Course, you never seen me lookin' like this," she continued, displaying a pronounced and sexy lisp. "I'm Suzl. Suzl Weiz."

Cassie's mouth opened, and then they were embracing and crying and hugging again. Finally they broke, and Cassie looked at her old friend. "Look at *you!*"

"Look at *you*," Suzl retorted. "Oh, Cassie, you are *gorgeous!*"

She felt warm at the compliment. "You only say that because you know how impossibly beautiful you are! All that was fat is now in your breasts and it looks wonderful there!" They laughed at that.

"Cassie, when I came I didn't know what to 'spect, but it's really not a bad life here. It ain't perfect but it's the best I ever had. I hope it's the same for you, too. You *glow* with beauty."

"I truly *am* happy, Suzl," she responded, and realized that it was somewhat true. "The old days, the old times— they happened to someone else. I can hardly even remember them now, except that they were mostly sad, miserable times."

"Suzl unnerstands. If I bring back the bad times, I'll go and stay way aways from you."

"Oh, *no*! We just *must* be friends! You have much to teach me about life here. I need a friend bad."

Suzl smiled. "Well, O.K. then. Oh, Cassie, we'll get t'make friends all over again! It's gon' be *great*! You'n me."

"Do you have any children?"

Suzl smirked. "Ten."

"Ten!" She was filled with envy and admiration.

They were about to continue when one of the young serving girls came up. "Pardon, Mistress, but your husband sends for you."

And that was it; all other thoughts and wants simply fled. Suzl understood; she was subject to the same thing. Cassie hurried across the hall to Adam, approached, dropped to one knee and bowed her head, waiting to hear what he would say to her.

It was a small price to pay for being a wife instead of a drone.

At the end of the evening, when all had gone and the basic cleanup had finished, Adam, tired by a very long day, had gone quickly to sleep. Cassie, however, lay in bed in the dark and thought for a while.

All the ghosts of the past were there, but she shut them out. She had no desire to be a man, to take on that responsibility and those worries. She had gone that route, and it had brought her only misery, deprivation, loneliness, and despair. She wanted it no more, did not desire it in the least. There were compromises to be made in this life, but they were, on reflection, no worse than other compromises everyone had to make.

What had her life been? First an ugly duckling tomboy, then a dugger—property, really—who was used by the major powers of World and saw her lover die in their arguments. One who was then used by those same powers, who convinced her it was her destiny to mount a revolution and become a saint. Years in which she had deprived herself of everything, while killing those who did not bend to her and overlooking the sins of those who went along, even depriving herself of her own daughter's growing up and exposing the innocent child to evil and a life of savagery. Spirit could have still been here now, normal and married and happy, had she not been corrupted by her own mother's stubborn defiance and chosen savagery over this. And for what? The Reformed Church that mother had built had been false to the core; the Empire she'd founded had crumbled quickly into disarray, leaving most no better off than before, and at the cost of thousands dead to build it.

No collar or spells had converted her, in the end. They had only served to show her how ugly and futile it had all been. No more. She *liked* being a wife, she *liked* someone else to do the thinking for a change, she *liked* being sexy and have men's eyes twinkle as she swayed by, she *liked* the idea that she might have a second chance to be a mother in every sense of the word. She liked being the center of attention rather than the center of power. To Hell with the past and all its damage! She was going to live in the present now, and that was that.

It was too late to wonder if she had done right, so she dismissed the question from her mind. A binding spell could never be undone, and could be transferred only by the efforts of a wizard more powerful than the accepter. And Coydt van Haas was dead, thank Heaven!

5

SOUL RIDER'S SONG

"We can't just sit here and twiddle our thumbs!" Jeff protested. "We have to *do* something!"

Sondra had sent word to him, summoning him quickly from Globbus to Pericles.

"What do you think we ought to do, sonny boy?" the stringer snapped back. "Mobilize half of World? They'd laugh at you. Go back and forth through every inch of the void? You could fly within fifty meters of her a hundred times and never see her."

Jeff was a large, muscular young man with wild hair and a thick, if unkempt, full black beard. "It's easy for you! It's not your mother and grandmother who might be dying out there someplace!"

That hurt, and required an answer. "Jeff—I was saving this for a better time, but I'm your aunt. Spirit's my sister."

He stared at her. "Don't feed me that shit. Cass only had one kid."

"That's true, but Spirit and I have the same father."

He was suddenly fascinated. "You mean—you're one of Matson's kids?"

She nodded. "So, you see, I've got a stake in this, too. A personal stake as well as a professional obligation. The only thing I can figure out is that they always shadowed Mervyn, and when they saw I was going off in the right direction they took a chance on me."

"Yeah, well, it seems to me—"

"Look, Jeff," she interrupted, "let's get a few things straight. First of all, I could have handled the duggers and that whatever-it-was machine, but so could your grandmother. Those duggers couldn't have stalked Mervyn and me, made the right choices, and organized to do what they did. Somebody else put them up to it, and that somebody did their thinking for them. And that someone was powerful enough to literally collapse and undo the whole Fluxland, while keeping me at bay almost as an afterthought. And I'm a pretty strong wizard."

He calmed down a little. "Yeah—but who? Where do we start?"

"With Zelligman Ivan," Mervyn's voice told them, and they turned to see the old wizard enter.

"Mervyn!" Sondra exclaimed. "Thank Heaven they found you!"

" 'Bout time you got here," Jeff grumped.

"I was up north trying to get some coordinated action against New Eden," the old man said. "A messenger came a few hours ago and I rushed down here as quickly as I could. I'm not cut out for turning into birds anymore. I'm bushed."

"You said something about Ivan?" Sondra reminded him.

He nodded and sank into a chair. "Yes. He's been working this cluster and has been up to all sorts of mischief for a year or more."

"Then *that's* who I was thinking of facing down back there?"

"Most likely. And a good thing you didn't, my dear. You're no match for him, nor are most people. He's not like the Haldaynes or Coydt van Haas; he generally likes to be in the background and get others to do his dirty work. But when he's cornered, he's among the best there is. Lots of folks might lie in wait for Cass, if they could find her, but only Ivan would try for a clean sweep."

Jeff felt distinctly unhappy about all this. "Where do you think he's taken them?"

"I doubt if he has your mother. If he does, he won't keep her. Soul Riders bother them, and they've never really beaten one. As for Cass, she's strong—very strong—and the threat to Spirit will feed her emotions and therefore her power and will. He won't want to chance tangling with that sort of power. I'd say he's taken her to Anchor."

"Then you think she's alive? We'll go after her—"

Mervyn held up his hand and Jeff sat back down in his chair. "No, it's not that simple. I *think* she's alive, yes, because he had no need to go to all this time and trouble just to kill her. Now, Sondra, before we proceed, I want all the details of the visit and the attack. *All* of them. Leave nothing out, no matter how trivial or inconsequential it might be."

As Jeff fidgeted and fumed, she did as instructed. When she finished, Mervyn just sat there a moment, deep in thought. Finally he said, "Well, if it is any consolation at all, the projector you describe is not intended as a lethal weapon. Its builders intended it essentially to negate powerful wizards. It seems to both knock you cold and cut you off from any Flux power or feeling. The effects last from a few minutes to a few hours, but that's neither here nor there. It's long enough for a powerful wizard to spirit someone from the middle of the void to an Anchor, certainly."

"Who would build such a thing?" Jeff asked.

"New Eden, of course. They hate wizards, but they need them for some of the things they do. This sounds like a payoff of some sort, I fear. Or, perhaps, a wizard's attempt to curry New Eden's favor.''

"Huh?'' Jeff was startled. "What would *those* guys want with Grandma?''

"They have always had a paranoia about her. She thumbed her nose at them twenty years ago and many have never forgotten it. She was born and raised there, and they were responsible for killing her father, whom she practically worshipped. She's a powerful wizard with powerful friends who's led conventional armies. They think she's the biggest threat to them going.''

"Then they want to execute her!'' Jeff almost shouted. "We've got to go get her!''

Mervyn frowned. "Must you yell so? No, I sincerely doubt that. It wouldn't fit their curious mind-set. They will seek to turn her, to change her into one of their own. It would earn them powerful friends, a great deal of fear and respect, and be the ultimate food for their egos.''

"They—they can't really *do* it, can they?'' Sondra asked nervously. "I mean, I didn't speak with her for long, but she didn't look like somebody they could do that to without Flux power, and she's strong there.''

"You have no idea how devastating modern brainwashing techniques, as they're called, can be on *any* mind. Every weakness is defined and exploited, and I'm afraid Cass has quite a number. And if they can't wear her down enough to take a binding spell, well, she's powerful, perhaps as strong as Zelligman, but if she had to face not only Zelligman but a half dozen other Fluxlords at the same time. . . . Yes, I'd say that at least *they* think they can do it, or they would never have tried it.''

"Then we have to go in there! Rescue her!''

Mervyn sighed. "Jeff, aside from you, there is no one with more respect and love for Cass than I, mixed in with some not inconsiderable guilt on my part. I have just been in Anchors Abehl and Yonkeh, and I must go yet to Anchor Gorgh and perhaps further. Part of those efforts were to defend the Gates, but I'm also trying to organize support for some move on New Eden before it's too late. And I'm having almost no luck at it, I fear. They're scared, Jeff, and that gives New Eden a free hand. And they have a perfect right to be scared."

It was Sondra's turn to be surprised. "They're *that* powerful?"

"They are. Where do you think those amplifiers they used twenty years ago to take over Anchor Logh came from? Coydt had them built, in bits and pieces, in various industrial Anchors, then duplicated them in Flux. That ray weapon they used is the least of their arsenal, most of which we can't possibly understand. Coydt somehow discovered, amassed, or perhaps even inherited or stole a wealth of ancient writings describing exactly how to build and use these sorts of things. And he assembled a brilliant technical staff to study and experiment with them. Coydt's forces were dangerous before, but now that they've an Anchor to use for their trials and experiments, a place where everything is always consistent and under natural laws, they've learned so much about these ancient devices that they have a monopoly on terror. New Eden's bosses inherited them all, and have encouraged them in every way, as well as recruiting bright young men from all over World to come and help. When you're offered a job studying and deciphering a scientific revolution, and doing so in a setting where you're surrounded by beautiful, sexy women who only want to serve you—well, they've got the best."

"Somehow I can't imagine Grandma as a sexy plaything."

"Neither could she," Sondra said. "That, I think, is part of her problem of late, although who am I to know for sure?"

"Very astute," Mervyn approved. "Sometimes you can be too close to someone to really know and understand them. But, you see, Jeff, nobody's going to go after New Eden until it scares them directly. The other Anchors and far-off Fluxlands see them as simply another land, a cross of Flux and Anchor perhaps, but that's about it. To take a land defended with weapons so powerful, the cost would be enormous—and they lost enough of their people in the wars for the Empire. I've failed to convince them that they will lose more than their lives if they don't move.''

"And just days ago you were telling me what *fine* folks they were in New Eden," Sondra noted acidly. Jeff didn't hear.

"O.K., so maybe an army can't get in—but what about a small number? One or two folks, maybe. It's been done before.''

"It was done years ago, yes, but that was different. It's extremely well policed now. The populace is conditioned, men as well as women, to be supportive. If their security devices did not match their weaponry, don't you think I would have made a raid by now? Oh, it's been tried by the best, but if anyone has pulled it off we don't know it. You've never been under those kinds of conditions, Jeff. None of us have. I have some indirect channels of intelligence through the Fluxlords who do business with them, but nothing else.''

"They still use stringers," Sondra pointed out, thinking of alternatives.

"Yes, but it's all unloaded right on the apron. Stringers do not go in because their loyalties are suspect. And if they did, it wouldn't be you, Sondra. They'd *love* to get a crack at converting you.''

"Are you telling me we just *leave* Grandma in the hands of those bastards?''

"For now, we have no choice. We just pick our opportunities and watch for them, but I can't see how we can do anything now. No, it's Spirit we have to be concerned about. I fear that she is out there, confused and all alone in the Flux, with very limited powers. She can follow strings if she's lucky, but she won't know where they lead until she gets there, and the closest main string is Logh to

Abehl. We're covering that. I have a huge reward posted and there are hundreds searching now."

"And I put out the call to the stringers on the routes," Sondra added. "If she's following a commercial string like the one you say, they'll find her."

Jeff stared at Sondra. "You knew that all the time? Why didn't you *tell* me?"

"You never let me get a sentence in edgewise. I admit I'm concerned about Cass, and there's nothing I'd like better than shattering New Eden, but Mervyn is right. First things first. Spirit needs us."

Jeff looked at them. "I—I'd like to go out and join in the search. I know what the odds are of me finding anything, but *I'd* feel better about it, and at least I'd be close by if somebody did happen on her."

Mervyn nodded. "Sure. I'll give you directions to a search camp."

"One thing puzzles me, though, in all this," Sondra put in. "Why totally destroy that Fluxland? There was no threat left."

"Two reasons that I can think of," Mervyn replied. "In a sense, it's a message to me, a direct challenge of sorts. Zelligman wants me to know that he's ready for me. He must have used one of the amplifiers to break it down so quickly and completely. He's basically warning me to stay away or be crushed. The other reason, of course, is that it puts the Soul Rider on the run and probably away from him. Zelligman thinks he is using New Eden, but it's actually New Eden that's using him. I wish he'd realize that they are as much his enemy as ours, but he's a devious bastard, like all the rest of them, and very patient. Whatever he and his associates are up to, it's something very, very unpleasant, you can bet on that."

The world ended for Spirit with shocking suddenness. She had just come from seeing that beautiful woman visitor, who seemed very kind, and she was walking down the small hill to the stream bank for a drink when it hit.

She felt a wave of dizziness and nausea, and then the whole land seemed to begin to melt. Somewhere in the distance she could hear screams of agony, and her first thought was to find her mother, not only because she was suddenly confused, disoriented, and frightened, but also because her mother maintained this land, and she feared whose screams they might be.

It had been twenty years since she'd felt and seen evil, but she had no sense of time and it made no difference. She *knew* that, at last, their enemies had come for them, and that they were attacking with tremendous force and power, a power she no longer had and could not match, but one which she could at least keep from herself. She had given her own powers away years ago, but the same spell that limited her existence protected her from others.

The place was too much of a mess now to even *find* her mother, and the feelings of nausea and dizziness continued unabated. She realized it was hopeless, and decided that her only defense was to escape and wait it out. She was very strong and very athletic, but she could be overpowered by sheer brute strength.

There was no wall, she saw, just the void beyond. She made for it, picking a spot at random and jumping through, then running as fast as she could for several minutes. The odds were with her; only an army totally surrounding the land or a massive new Flux barrier could stop her. The attackers here were few, and, although she didn't know it, were in their own brand of trouble from Sondra.

After a while she slowed down, then stopped and simply sat on the soft, spongy, featureless ground of the void. It had been a long time since she'd been out in it, and she sat there, suddenly entranced by the beautiful display of electrical discharges that made the place shimmer. She could always see wonders others could not, that she knew, and this might well be one of them.

Still, she would have to consider her next move. She was fine now, and had few requirements, but she would need a source of food and water. In the old days, she could just wish them into being when needed, but while she had the wizard's sight she knew she had no control. She could receive, but not send.

She was worried about her mother and the pretty lady, but there was nothing she could do about it. Whoever had done this was strong and mean, and could have her for breakfast. There was a linking spell connecting her mother to her, but although it had always been there and she'd taken it for granted all this time, it wasn't there now. That scared her, for she feared her mother might well be dead.

And that left Spirit entirely on her own. It wouldn't have bothered her if she still had the power, but it bothered her now. There were lots of places, good and bad, on World, but she didn't know where any of them were and which were the good ones. There was nothing to do but to walk until she found a string, and follow it wherever it led.

She felt the Soul Rider stir inside her head. It had always been there, this invisible, incomprehensible companion. She knew it had been in her mother until she was born, but had then chosen to be born with her. She had never feared it, and had pretty much taken it for granted.

She began walking, and covered what seemed to be a good distance, without ever crossing a string. She grew tired, and thirsty, and finally stopped and stretched out in the void. She always slept when she felt like it, and did so now. There was nothing to be done for the thirst.

The Soul Rider stirred again as she slept, and assessed the situation. It could aid her body, minimize the harm, but the point was that, without someone with the power, it couldn't make what she needed. It felt frustrated, for it knew all the spells but had no way to carry them out.

Spirit might be discovered tomorrow, but it could sense

no one nearby, not now, and while there was a red string nearby, indicating a main trail to somewhere, there was no telling exactly where it led. To direct her into the hands of the very people who had done this was not in Spirit's, or the Rider's, best interest.

The line, the link that connected it to its unseen master, was open and functioning. Certainly what had happened had been monitored and recorded, it thought. Why was I directed to this poor woman if only to watch her die? They may be searching now, but they may have done so complete a job that no one even knows about it, and won't for weeks. It was often that long, or longer, between visitors to the Fluxland.

The Soul Rider, for the first time in many lifetimes of hosts, was confused enough to transmit a request for instructions, rather than simply waiting for a command to come.

And, to its surprise, there was a reply, in the complex binary code that was its language.

Probabilities indicate the unlikelihood of regaining the established protector, the message said. *Therefore a pragmatic, although radical, course is called for. Therefore, direct contact is authorized in the following manner*. It went on to feed the proper strings of instruction, and the Soul Rider recorded it and was amazed by its simplicity and excited by its potential. Never before had a Soul Rider been permitted to make direct contact with a human intelligence, although it altered and influenced human behavior. It understood that this exception was being made because they wanted Spirit the way she was for some reason, and because Spirit could not communicate anything except the most basic information to another, by pantomime.

Coydt's spell had altered the internal language by which Spirit's brain processed information. The new language the Soul Rider had always known was mathematical in nature, but now it was clear through the strings that it was a simplified variant of its own. Until now, it had not been permitted to recognize this, although it was more than logical. It knew her every thought and feeling.

It sent out a tentative probe, and Spirit woke up with a start, very puzzled. She could have sworn, although it was impossible, that someone was calling her name.

Spirit? Do not be afraid. . . .

It *was* something—but it wasn't sound, and it wasn't a voice. She was—thinking it—but it wasn't her! Or was it? Had the experience driven her mad?

It is real, Spirit. I must use your own mind to communicate, so when I must talk, you cannot. But I understand your thoughts. I have always understood them.

"Who are you?"

I am a spirit of Flux and Anchor. Many call me the Soul Rider.

She didn't know whether to believe her own thoughts or not. She was confused, a bit afraid, and yet very excited. It was the first time she had been able to talk to anyone in a long, long time. If she was just crazy, well—what difference did it make?

The excitement turned to anger and frustration. "Why has it taken so long for you to speak? Don't you know how desperate I was to talk with someone, anyone?"

I was not permitted to know how. I begged for a way to help you, and received the knowledge.

"Who—gives you permission? How?"

I do not know. None of us knows. We have no choice in what we do but to follow orders.

"But not this time?"

No. Not this time. My masters believe you are of some future service to them.

"What happened back there?"

One of the Seven, aided by a dugger cult, attacked your mother as she was outside, rendered her inoperative, and carried her away. Your home was destroyed by that same one of the Seven, using one of the great amplifiers of Flux power. That is all I know.

"Is my mother—dead?"

No. I receive data sufficient to indicate that they intend to render her harmless in a way that is different than but at least as restricting as what you must bear.

She didn't like the sound of that. "Will it work?"

Unknown, but the probability is that it will. The Seven would not take on a top wizard, a Soul Rider, and a construct of one of the Nine unless they were very certain of themselves. The mere fact that it was done puts the probability of success over the eighty percentile mark.

"I—I don't understand numbers any more."

It will work.

"Oh." She felt genuine sorrow, and tears came to her eyes, but she knew it was useless to dwell on things she could neither understand nor control. She let the sorrow pass, then said, "Then I am alone now."

You are not alone, nor am I. We will never be alone again. Allow me to control your body commands, and we will find food and drink.

"You can do that?"

There is a stringer trail nearby, a main one running between Anchors and major Fluxlands. Such trails have pockets the stringers create for themselves so that they might have food and water if need be. We will find one.

It was a curious sensation. She got up and began to walk, and she had no control over it at all. She had never feared the Soul Rider, nor did she now, but the whole thing was unnerving. They came to the string in a short while, and she stood there while the Rider probed.

They are searching for you.

"They? Who's 'they?' Friends or enemies?"

Unknown. It is a relative concept, anyway. Do you wish to be discovered?

"Without knowing who's who?"

Then we will avoid them. Come, we will move away from the string and follow it in parallel. The nearest pocket is barely within my range, but we can get there fairly quickly. You can run, you know, at the speed of a trotting horse.

"*I know. I was just thinking about my son.*"

I know your thoughts, remember. When you have fed and watered, we will seek out one of the Nine who will be able to help.

This is the land where dwells the chairman of the Nine, Mervyn.

"*I—I think I was there once.*"

More than once. But it is dangerous to enter. Agents are watching the sole entrance and charting the comings and goings. It is most certainly how they found you in the first place. They have things that could hurt or kill you. I cannot read the composition of those inside the Fluxland from this distance, but certainly there are friends, powerful friends, inside.

She hesitated. "*Do they—want me?*"

The only minds open to me are minds which I have entered. I can calculate probabilities, but even here that is impossible. They may, or they may not. The odds go both ways.

She didn't know what to do. "*What do you recommend?*"

I have no directive. It is a question of what you want and feel. If we try, and are not captured, they will know you are safe. Your loved one will be reassured.

She thought about it. "*But if I go in, I will stay in. They will fear for me, and I will be kept from all harm. I have a nightmare of being captured and put on display. This would be little different, even if it is my son and my friends.*"

Is it so different from what you had?

"*Yes. I didn't have you. Alone, there would be no*

choice, but I only stayed back there for my mother's sake, knowing she needed to be with me and knowing, too, that going out with her would mark her for her enemies no matter what her disguise. There's no reason for it anymore. I want to be free, to roam, as my nature tells me."

Again I receive no countermanding data. Whatever danger you will help prevent is not imminent. But some will not give up the search.

"We'll worry about that when they catch me. I think after this long time I'm due some fun, away from this, away from all the mess around here."

Hold! The stringer who visited you just before the end emerges from the Fluxland. She turns north.

Spirit thought a moment. *"Can we keep pace with her? Until we're out of immediate danger, that is?"*

I believe so. She seems in no hurry.

"She goes back to work, then. Tell me—do you think I could make her understand? Do you think she'd turn me over, or go along?"

Unknown. Do you wish to take the chance?

"It's worth a try. They'd catch me otherwise. I know that."

The Soul Rider gave some thought to the problem. It was in its own way as limited as, and by, its host, yet it had powers to influence others in Flux or Anchor. That was its job. It was beginning to like being half a person, having something other than a vicarious life, and its masters were not interfering. Perhaps, it thought to itself, it was some sort of experiment. In many ways, its powers were empathic. It could transmit and control emotional reactions in others, and by that shape their choices. It had done that, on directive, with countless hosts, and with Cass and Spirit and many of those with whom they came in contact, such as Suzl and Matson, but it had always done so by directive.

But there was no reason now why it couldn't do a little

bit on initiative. Its stake in its host had just increased massively.

Spirit broke into the inhuman sprint that her incredible body was capable of, and began paralleling Sondra in the void.

6

WHAT YOU NEED

Cassie had had several good months to get to know her old homeland and New Eden once more. She insisted on doing all the shopping for the household, and this took her back and forth in the capital and allowed her to see what this new life was all about.

Adam had been away more than home of late; there seemed to be big doings in the capital and big plans afoot. The atmosphere was charged, but there seemed no threat to New Eden—if anything, it was the other way around—and so she dismissed it from her mind. It was a warm, pleasant day, the household was in order, and while there was always something to do this was not the day to do it. She had packed a small basket with fruit and cheese and some good local white wine, and she went out and across the street to the park and sat and waited for Suzl.

Temple Square was still a park, but they had planted a lot of nice trees and shrubs and put a large mechanical playground in the center. Now, as usual on nice days, a number of girls were there looking over hordes of kids playing, and she watched them idly. One day soon *she* would make use of that place. Although it didn't show as yet, she knew she was over three months pregnant.

She looked over at the temple, still the dominant structure in the town and the Anchor, its gleaming, shiny facade and seven steeples reflecting the bright colors of what she'd been brought up to believe was Heaven. New Eden knew better, knowing and teaching that it was merely a planet like World, but far larger, its massive gravity causing World to forever circle it. Light, but no heat, came from it. Where the heat *did* come from was still a subject for speculation, and not something that greatly concerned her. They were working on things like that in the temple now, which had become the center of New Eden's progressive scientific research: out of there had come the rural electrification, the indoor bathroom and shower, the electric polishers and even the electric oven. She still hadn't adjusted to that one, and continued to look for the wood bucket.

She stared at the steeples, and felt an eerie sensation run through her. It seemed almost as if something flowed to and from them in a steady stream, something that was indistinct but tangible. Suddenly something seemed to focus directly on her, reach out to her. . . . She gasped and shivered in the warmth, and stood straight up, but it was gone.

"Felt it too, huh?" came Suzl's voice behind her.

She turned, frowning. "It was—*eerie*. I could almost swear"—she paused, looking for the words—"that it was looking straight *inside* me."

Suzl looked at her very strangely. Finally she said, "Well, forget it for now. It's a totally *gorgeous* day, and I thank you for letting me get out in it."

"Huh?" Cassie was still a little disturbed by the sensation.

"If the Chief Judge's wife hadn't called for me, this little one would be slavin' in the big brain's kitchens today. Now, 'cause it's a duty day and the kids are bein' sat, I can take it easy. C'mon, doll, let's *go* someplace.''

Cassie nodded, and the two walked back over to the big house. Although only a fraction taller than Cassie, Suzl towered over her old friend now because she wore sandals with platform soles and high heels. Although Cassie almost always wore shoes with very high heels, today she'd decided to go barefoot. Neither wore more than the minimum amount of jewelry and brief panties, Suzl's a reddish fur and Cassie's a silvery material.

The bicycle had been around World as long as anyone could remember, but supplies of them in Anchor Logh had been quite limited, because they did not manufacture them there and had to trade for them. Still, there had been a few on the farm when they had been growing up, and Cassie had been delighted to find that she could still ride one, even after all these years, and even more delighted to find that her position allowed her access to them. She often did her shopping this way, and found it a lot of fun. They were quite common now, even among children, since Anchor Bakha had not only made them but had had a very large supply warehoused when it was conquered. A good thing, too, for she found she now could manage only a basic child's bike.

''Where'll we go?'' Suzl asked Cassie.

''I—I been thinking of going home just once. Just to see.''

Suzl looked a little nervous at a journey, even a short one, but she finally decided. ''Oh, why not. Nobody'd ever give *me* p'mission t'go so far alone, but nobody'll screw 'round with the Chief's wife.''

''Adam knows. I been nagging him for weeks and he finally gave in.''

They pedaled slowly, keeping close to the curb. Suzl was right—as they cleared the center of the city they began being challenged, but none of the authorities were willing to take the risk of running in the Chief Judge's wife on suspicion that she didn't have permission to go wherever she was going. The two were shy, humble, deferential and all the rest, but as soon as Cassie was recognized it was almost the other way around. It wasn't hard to verify who she was. Most girls only had their first names tattooed, but the nearly nude Cassie's I.D. clearly read "Tilghman."

They cleared the city and went out on the main road, now smoothly paved, and found little traffic. The wind on their bodies felt good, and they were giggling and laughing like children all the way. Suzl wore her hair short, but Cassie's did present something of a nuisance, one that she was happy to accept. It felt *good* to be out, like this, with Suzl once more. It had only been in the last few weeks that Cassie realized just how much she had missed Suzl. She had changed a lot, and not only physically, but deep down the old Suzl was still there and kept coming through.

The farm was not far from town, and the landscape approaching it hadn't changed much. The first entrance road had also been paved, and was now lined, as had been the main road, with poles and electrical wires, but it still looked like an old friend. It still ran through the pasture, and it was still, as always, littered with horse manure and the droppings of other animals.

Cassie had found herself depending more and more on Suzl's company to alleviate the loneliness. The two had much in common, and always had, even now to being equally pregnant, but Suzl had all those duties and a number of children still at home and had little time. Cassie had, however, found herself at times fantasizing about the "new" Suzl, and it bothered her a little. It didn't seem natural to get turned on by thoughts of those oversized breasts and that cute, shapely form.

The road curved as it came to a wooded area that had always been there, before going into the small mini-village on this side of the huge communal farm. They drifted to a stop at the curve. "Just beyond was my father's blacksmith shop. I found out he's now buried here, and I'd like to visit him, at least this once.''

Suzl made no objection, and they pedaled on. Where the old blacksmith's shop had stood there was now only an overgrown clearing. The wooden building, it seemed, had burned down long ago. They found a farm supervisor, and when he learned who she was he took them to the graveyard that had been carved out of the pastureland. There were no stones, but small plates had been placed in the ground with the names. The man patiently checked until he found it, and Suzl took him off and flirted with him, allowing Cassie a little time alone.

Cassie had picked a few flowers growing wild by the side of the road, and now she placed them on the plate, then knelt on one knee and bowed her head. Tears welled up inside of her, and she started to sob. Finally, through it all, she whispered, ''I'm so sorry, Daddy. In the end I just couldn't be the son you wanted. I tried so *hard*.''

A tiny gust of wind came up, and seemed to whisper back to her, *That's all right. At least you tried, and that's more than most can say.*

But it was probably just imagination, or the wind.

She rejoined Suzl, and they managed to get rid of the man by thanking him profusely and apologizing that they had been allowed little time to come and go. Then both got back on their bikes and headed up the road, but Suzl again stopped near the clearing for the smithy, and Cassie looked at her, puzzled.

Suzl looked around, and saw no one nearby except a few cows. ''Come on into the woods a little,'' she said. ''It's time we talked.''

Wondering what was going on, she followed, walking her bike into the woods and out of sight of anyone around. There was a small clearing in the middle, and there they stopped, resting their bikes against the trees, and spread a blanket from the basket on the ground.

Suzl reclined lazily on the blanket, and Cassie just stared at her. A very subtle change seemed to come over her old friend, something not physical but something *sensed*. Finally Suzl closed her eyes, then opened them again. "It's pretty hard to break out of it once you've done it for so long," Suzl said. She still had the lisp and the soft, sexy voice, but there was, somehow, a slightly harder edge to it. "Don't looked so shocked. They didn't destroy my mind, just kinda rearranged it a little. The 'portant parts took, but some of the old girl's still there. I just don't like to bring her out much is all. Went to a lotta trouble to keep her and then I find it's better not thinkin'. Saved it 'cause I figured I'd want out, but I never did and it ain't no good for girls t'think 'round here 'cause it's easier not to. Better and happier, too. I figure you got the same problem."

Cassie sighed, smiled, and sat down. "Yes, Suzl, you're right. You come in feeling you can leave when you want, and then you kind of fall into it. It's so *seductive*. No responsibilities, no cares, no worries. Like a little child again, only with all the sex. I'm also really in love, Suzl, but the difference between what Adam dreams of and what's really here just gets to me sometimes. But—you had Coydt's spell. How'd you manage to save *anything* of your old self?"

"I knew what Coydt had in mind, sort of. I couldn't change it, I had no choice in it. But I could *add on* to the spell, and I did. One of the things I added was, well, a *power*. Turns out it don't work with men—I'm jelly in the hands of a man—but it works on me. Suzl can't change the way she is, the way she'll be for the rest of her life, but she can bury the ghosts, bury the dreams. Wipe 'em out. It makes things so—*easy*. You don't think, you just experience, sort of. I left things that'd bring me out, but it takes a big shock and you were it, honey."

"I—I'm not sure I'd like that. Oh, Suzl, I'm not sure of *anything* anymore! All I ever wanted to do was be a vet, grow up here, and maybe get married and have kids. Daddy saw me as the son he never had, though, and I was a plain, flat-chested girl with a real deep voice and the looks of a boy anyway. So I sort of grew up a boy with a boy's work and not a boy's fun. I—I even ogled the girls. I—I loved to look at girls' bodies. They were pretty. Boys, well—they were like me.''

Suzl nodded, but did not interrupt.

"So then came the Paring Rite," Cassie continued, "and there I was sold into slavery in Flux, just like you. And it all seemed to change, somehow. Matson had *strength*, the kind I'd never have. And I had the Flux power, 'though I didn't really know it, to make him make love to me. But he never loved me, Suzl. He *liked* me, that's all. I kidded myself that it was otherwise, but I really knew it wasn't, and when I thought he was dead it all just—left. I punished myself into bein' a saint for all those years, but I wasn't really the head of anything. The Nine ran the Empire, and they told me where to go and what to do, and I was happy with that, but everybody from Daddy to you seemed proud of me, and it seemed like I was doing the right thing. All I wound up doing was destroying everybody close to me. Spirit, you, Anchor Logh itself, even my own Daddy, suffered or died because of me. And for nothing. The Empire was built on them buildin' up a saint who'd stay a saint, and suddenly I wasn't. Then I thought at least I could raise my grandson, but I really didn't know how. I was useless, worn out, tired, and I didn't have the guts to kill myself.''

Suzl sighed. "And that's why you took the binding spell? To punish yourself? Get rid of the guilt?''

"I don't know. All I knew was that I didn't have to make any decisions, and for the first time in my entire life people were relating to me not as an 'it' or a 'he' but as a girl. I'd never really had that before in a way I couldn't fight it, and it felt, well, *good*. When I stood there in Flux and looked out at the void, that's all I could see—void.

There was nothing for me out there. Nothing. Something just sort of *snapped*. For the first time I had a big decision to make about myself, entirely by myself. I wanted to be somebody else, and there it was.''

"Poor Cassie," Suzl sighed. "The first real 'portant d'cision she ever really had to make all on her own in her whole life, and it was to never hav'ta make another one 'cept what she'll wear today and what she'll cook for dinner. And it's forever, 'cause the spell they use is Coydt's old spell and he's long gone, gone, gone.''

"I know, but this is where I *belong*, Suzl.''

"Nope. Old Merv and his ghost buddies just got it wrong, is all. Old Suzl, now, *she* should'a been the boss, and you should'a married her when she was a he. Some folks, guys or girls, are cut out to run things, and most are not. It's no shame in that. Suzl unnerstands. She didn't wanna be you, but she got turned into what you always thought you wanted to be. So now you're it, and you're *still* not sure.''

"Oh, Suzl- -you're so wise and *sweet*! I've missed you so much!''

"You know you're stuck. Oh, I know you can shift into wife mode, but you can't stop thinkin' and wonderin'. Lemme tell ya what Suzl is, 'cause that's what Cassie is—for a long, long time. We're Fluxgirls, you'n me. We never get old and we never get sick. I once tried to work a slicer machine and cut my thumb almost off. It healed before I could 'member it was hurt. Couple days, tops. Look—all them kids and no stretch marks!''

It was true, Cassie realized. She just hadn't noticed it before.

"Now I'll tell you what Suzl is. She can't 'member, can't even '*magine*, havin' a prick, or wantin' it anyplace except inside her as much and as long as possible. I'm just smart 'nuff now to know that I'm a lot dumber than I used to be. I can't keep two things in my head at the same time and I forget a lot. My 'motions are stronger than my head.

I'm so passive I get chills just looking at a butter knife. Once I saw two guys fightin' in the street and it made me sick. In a 'mergency, I panic, scream, and freeze. The idea we're out here alone kinda scares me silly. I can't do *nothin'* without beggin' p'mission. I can cook, sew some, and scrub and clean a place like crazy. They keep tryin' to show me how to change a light bulb and I can't do it. Animals bigger'n a pussycat scare me. I don't even unnerstand what readin' and writin's 'bout, and I don't really wanna. I *like* bein' pregnant and tendin' babies. I need men to have sex with me and tell me what to do, but I still think girls are the most perfect things nature ever invented. My body's all I got, and I *love* it; I want to feel *good*. I'm selfish. I got no interest in whatever men do when they're not home. It jus' goes in one ear and out the other and I smile and say, 'Yes, dear.' I'm more a pet than a person, but I can't handle it any other way. And I'm gonna be that way, prob'ly, long after the Brotherhood is gone. And you 'n me are two of a kind. What you see on the outside is just 'zackly what we are. Ain't nothin' more inside. You jus' ain't lived it long 'nuff yet to know. You're a perfect body and nothin' more, and you can't never be nothin' more.''

Cassie sighed. "I guess you're right." She was seeing herself after twenty years of this, and it unnerved her a bit. "When you said you had ten kids I had to count on my fingers to see how many that was. And I had to take that guy's word for it that it was my Daddy's grave. I *believed* him, too, 'tho it don't make much difference, I guess.''

"On the outside we're sweet sixteens, but on the inside we're five years old. It's hard for me to keep this talk goin' now. The longer you are this way the more you *wanna* be this way. This ain't no spell anymore, it's *me*—an' I *like* it.''

"Suzl—why are you telling me this?"

" 'Cause Suzl's got the power, like I told you. Not just over herself. It's hard to 'member, but I think it was to

give me some power over men. Didn't work. Don't work
on men. Don't work good on nobody, less'n they want it.
But you got hang-ups. All that guilt. Don't even know
why you don't wear heels 'round Suzl.''

She *did* know, but she couldn't act on it. ''It's because I
love you, Suzl. I always loved and depended on you. I
missed you so much! Not the kind of love I have for
Adam, more personal. Different—but real.''

Suzl sat up and lifted up her huge breasts. ''You want
these? Take 'em. Want the longest, sexiest, strongest tongue
ever inside you? I wanna do it, but I can't 'less you tell
me. Take any or all of me. I can't resist and don't wanna.''

Cassie didn't know how to respond.

''Look, Cassie, you got to accept what you *are* and be
what you *are*. Maybe you ain't what y'thought y'were
gonna be, but it's what y'are that matters. I'm slippin'
back now; I really can't hold on no longer. So come to
Suzl. Suzl's got the power to make it *easy*.''

Cassie moved over next to Suzl, and Suzl moved around
and started massaging her back. It felt wonderful.

''Let go, Cassie. Trust Suzl to make it all right,'' Suzl
whispered in her ear.

And she was right, Cassie realized. There was no going
back; there was only being the best at what she now was.
''I trust you, Suzl,'' she responded sincerely.

Suzl's eyes closed, and she continued the massage, but
now something, some energy, seemed to flow from her
hands and into Cassie's body. It was electric; it aroused
every area of her body. She lost herself in the glow of the
feeling, and that feeling replaced all else. There was no
thought, just sensuality, yet she was awake, and her defenses did not activate.

''There's only now, there's no then,'' Suzl crooned as
she rubbed. ''Look at yourself. See yourself.''

Suddenly she *did* see herself, in her mind's eye, or in
Suzl's.

''See Cassie. That's Cassie, that's all Cassie is, or ever

was, or ever will be. Outside is inside, inside is outside. Cassie was always this way, Cassie will always *be* this way, and Cassie likes it. Thinkin' is for others, not for Cassie. Cassie's built to please, to give pleasure, and for nothin' else. It's 'nuff, it's all she wants, all she ever was or ever will be. No holdin' back. Cassie's not brains, Cassie's *feelin'*. Feelin' good's the only thing in her life. That what makes her feel good is good, that which don't is bad. You was born the day you was claimed, there was nothin' before. Lookin' good is feelin' good. Nothin' on the inside that ain't on the outside. No worries, no problems, no past, only now. Dreams of pleasure, life of pleasure, no worries, no thinking, jus' let it *flow* and be what you *feel*.''

She kept crooning and rubbing and it all flowed in. A tremendous peace filled her, and she felt wonderful and content. Pleasure and service were all there was, and it was enough. The massage ended now, and she lay back on the blanket and let Suzl do *wonderful* things to her charged body. It went on and on and there was no passage of time.

Finally they lay there, side by side, exhausted, holding hands. The orgasms faded, but their glow remained. She opened her eyes and turned to stare at Suzl, beautiful Suzl, wonderful Suzl, her oldest and dearest friend and lover. Suzl looked at her and smiled, and then up at the sky through the trees. The sky was darkening rapidly. Suzl jumped up.

''Hey! We gotta go! It'll be dark soon! I got kids to fetch!''

Cassie was jolted into action. They quickly packed up, munched some of the uneaten food, and got on their bikes. They went back out to the farm road and sped up to the main highway, then right towards the city, their only thought to get back as quickly as possible. They had duties and responsibilities, and that was the only thing in their minds.

*   *   *

Suzl hurried into her house. She could hear some of the kids playing, but she knew the girls who were on babysitting today wouldn't leave them until she returned.

Her husband was home, and she hugged and kissed him and apologized for looking so bad.

"Oh, that's all right," he soothed, and petted her hair. "How did it go?"

"Oh, Cassie was *so* unhappy, my darling. Suzl made her happy. Suzl gave her peace."

"And the rest?"

"Cassie loves me, and I always loved Cassie. She'd do most anything for me."

"That's good. That's really good." It had taken him years to discover some of Suzl's peculiar talents, but he'd made good use of them. It was about time his wife got out of all that miserable work for others, and it was about time he achieved a social rank to equal his military one.

7

AN INFORMAL DINNER

The single chime awoke Cassie from an erotic dream. She almost always had erotic dreams, usually involving her stretched out and helpless on a bed while hordes of godlike men and girls with enormous sexual equipment ravished her constantly.

She sat up, yawned, and stretched, then looked over on the other side and was surprised to see that Adam wasn't there. It puzzled her for a moment, and then she remembered he'd told her he had some early meetings and that she didn't have to awaken for him. She *liked* to wake up and wait on him, get him and his things ready, but he knew best.

She *did* know she had a lot of work to do today, because tonight Adam was having an informal working dinner, whatever that was. It meant that the house had to be absolutely spotless and the dinner perfectly prepared, and that meant a lot of work.

She went down the hall, went to the bathroom—she was doing that a lot lately—then showered. She dried herself off and, as always, looked at herself in the full-length mirror.

Unlike a lot of the girls, her body had adjusted as the baby had grown inside her. She ate a lot more, including some funny things that tasted good now but didn't sound right together, but she still felt well. Although only into her eighth month, her tummy bulged, because she was so tiny and the baby was so big, she guessed. Still, she seemed to find a lot of extra energy when most girls said they were tired, and she still looked real sexy, and her balance was fine. She liked the fact that her breasts had swelled, and the nipples were so sensitive that almost anything brushing against them gave her a chill. That was why, even though some fashions were now permitted top to bottom, she was going to stick to the old wardrobe.

She felt normal, right, and happy. She was vaguely aware that once she had been miserable and unhappy, although she couldn't remember why and didn't want to, but that only made things all the more perfect now. She wouldn't change a thing.

She went through her early morning routine pretty much without thinking, usually just humming or whistling some little tune she'd heard someplace and doing what had to be done. Girls didn't have to think. That's one reason she was glad she was a girl and not a man. Girls got to dress up and look pretty and sexy and make out and make babies and all the good stuff. She sometimes felt sorry for the men. They had to work all day and worry about all sorts of things and have no fun at all. The only fun they got was out of one part of their body and if they jerked off they made a mess.

Suzl arrived in time for breakfast in the kitchen, taking off a full-length fur coat and revealing that she was wearing nothing under it but fur-lined soft boots. Cassie had on some cute little slippers to warm her cold feet, but otherwise was similarly undressed. It was chilly outside, but there wasn't much in the wardrobe for anybody with their tummies. Later on, before the company came, they'd have to dress, but it hardly seemed worth it now. They tried to hug and bumped their swollen bellies and laughed and giggled and went in to breakfast.

"Ready for t'night?" Suzl asked her.

"Is the girl kiddin'? The whole place needs a clean and scrub, and the dinner must be cooked." It was the sole and only important thing in her life or mind, then or that day.

They did the dishes, and shortly were at work. The rest of the staff arrived one by one from various routine duties and pitched in, and later on two of Suzl's daughters arrived: Tandy, who was seven or eight—Suzl couldn't remember— and Christy, who was ten or so and was approaching the age of maturity. Already she had incipient breasts and was wearing heels and jewelry and makeup, and the younger one, imitating big sister and Mommie, had at least given it an honest try.

The girls all joyfully scrubbed and cleaned and polished and giggled and played silly games as they worked, Cassie and Suzl right along with the rest of them, and when they were through the place was absolutely spotless, and they surveyed and inspected their work with pride.

As was tradition, another small group composed of the wives of the evening's guests cooked and prepared the food, and set the tables. Many by now were accomplished chefs, although they couldn't read a recipe.

Satisfied, and with the hour growing late, the staff took over the final preparation as the wives all scurried back home to shower and make up and dress. Cassie went upstairs and pulled out the silver mesh garment she'd been married in. After showering and making up all over again, she put it on, covered herself in her most lavish jewelry— even adding a tiara that Adam had given her not long before—and found some silvery sandals with eight centimeter heels, some nice perfume, and, as an afterthought, some extra-long lashes. She studied herself in the mirror, and decided that she was stunningly gorgeous. She even liked the way her usually firm breasts rocked as she walked and sagged just a bit. It was sexy.

Adam came home to clean up and change, and when he saw her he couldn't help but smile and whistle. "Darling, you are the most stunning creature on God's World."

A shiver of joy went through her and she almost squealed in delight. He hugged and kissed her, then told her to go down and check that the dinner was coming along and to stand by to greet the guests.

They began arriving before Adam was down, and she received them and directed the men to the smoking lounge and the girls to the sitting room. Adam didn't smoke and drank only a little wine and then only on occasions like this, but he allowed smoking in the lounge for those who had to. Girls, of course, did not smoke, although Cassie and Suzl found they both fantasized occasionally about smoking gigantic cigars.

Cassie's head girl, Mina, who was sixteen and waiting for her father's permission to marry, came to them separately and announced that dinner was served. Mina was wearing the newest allowed style, having proven quite a seamstress, and looked radiantly beautiful. Cassie would be sorry to lose her, but she knew that the girl had to follow the destiny of all girls. Apparently the only problem was that the big shot who wanted her had three other wives, and that bothered Mina's monogamous father a little.

The dinner went quite well, served by the staff. All eight of the other Judges were there, with their wives—or, in a few cases, head wife—and also present were eight others, of whom Cassie knew only three, and one only because he was something of a household name. She knew Suzl's Colonel Weiz, of course, looking very handsome in his full-dress uniform, and she knew Onregon Sligh, the chief of Research and Development, the man who made the electric hair dryer possible. He was a fat, gruff, middle-aged, swarthy man with a thick head of wooly snow-white hair and a deep, gravelly voice. And it was impossible to avoid looking at General Gunderson Champion, New Eden's Chief of Staff. Pure blond and with deep blue eyes, the exceedingly handsome general looked and sounded the image of a god come to life and was the subject of many wives' fantasies. They all kept looking dreamily at him and sighing. The general, of course, hardly noticed; he was used to it.

Conversation, of course, was limited to compliments and general niceties and banalities, but Cassie could see how proud Suzl was that her husband was here in such company. There were a few toasts, mostly to the girls, and then Adam Tilghman rose and all the others did likewise.

"Ladies, you will excuse us," he said in a businesslike tone. "Colonel Weiz, I'd like to talk to you privately before we convene the meeting. The rest of you gentlemen can take your after-dinner drinks in the lounge, and I'll be with you very shortly."

Weiz looked surprised and Suzl shrugged when he looked questioningly at her, but he left and followed the Chief Judge into the study. The wives, of course, assisted in the clean-up. Although most of the men at the table had let themselves age into a look of mature authority, all were high-ranked enough to either have Flux wives or wives made young again in Flux. Not a single one looked or acted much older than sixteen-year-old Mina.

Suzl, however, was plainly a little nervous. "Do you know what this is all 'bout?" she asked Cassie anxiously.

Cassie shrugged. "Nope. That's men-talk. I don't ask or even want to *know* his business, and you know I wouldn't understand it if he *did* tell me."

In the study, Weiz was equally nervous. An audience with the Chief Judge was quite rare, and usually unpleasant, and Tilghman, up close, was as tough and hard-looking as from a distance.

"Have a seat, Colonel. I've been meaning to talk to you

for some time, but I've been quite busy with this thing, you know.''

Weiz tried to hide his nervousness. A mere colonel in the company of the entire Directorate, the Chiefs of Staff, and Sligh was already enough to swell him, and he could only fear that a blow was inevitable.

"Do you know why you're here?" Tilghman asked him.

"No, sir.''

"I owe you something of a debt regarding my wife.''

He felt suddenly chilled. "Your wife, sir?''

"Yes. Oh, don't bother to hide it. I know you've got a wife with many talents and an absolute passion for further-ing her husband's career.''

He felt like crawling in a hole but said nothing.

"This may sound crazy, Colonel, but I'm in love with my wife. She had, as you know, the kind of past that would destroy anybody, man or woman, and most of it was unhappy. I could see that we could never get it all out, that it would keep coming back, and I had a constant fear of it. I am, after all, responsible in a way for the death of her father. Once your wife worked her little trick, all that conflict inside her just seemed to die out. Somehow you hit the right balance point, and she's happy and at peace. Not as bright as I might like, but I realized that any more mental ability than what she has would bring back the pain and guilt and memories. We all have to make compro-mises in this life, I guess. Still, I would have liked to have been informed *before* anything was done rather than find out about it afterward.''

Weiz didn't know whether to be pleased or scared, and was a little of both. "They were friends—before, long ago,'' he explained, although he knew Tilghman knew that. "It won't work unless somebody wants it, and then only to the degree that they want it, so we weren't pulling anything, sir.''

"My ass you weren't! Can it be broken?''

He shrugged. "If she wants it broken, she can. My

wife, who knows her better than anyone else, says she wants it just the way it is. If she clings to it, nothing can break it.''

"That's all I wanted to know. Colonel, you've never gotten any further because you've never had a combat command. You were one of the originals, and your conditioning techniques are sheer genius, but if you're to go any further you know you'll need a command. Do you want one? Do you honestly think you're up to it?''

The fact was, Weiz had avoided such a command most of his life, and was frightened of combat and its risks, but he was in no position to turn it down. "I'll gladly take one, sir, and serve in any capacity you direct. I assume such a command is imminent?''

"What in Heaven do you think this meeting's about? We're going after Nantzee, Colonel. We *must* have it. We need the people, too, particularly those with industrial skills and experience, so it can't be like the Bakha slaughter. It's going to be tricky. Are you willing to have a go?''

"Yes, sir." The idea petrified him, but to have said "no" would have meant the end of him and he knew it. Retirement—and that meant just plain growing old—with no more Flux rejuvenations. Well, the back door approach to advancement hadn't fooled the old man, but if he could survive this and do a decent job, he knew, he might well be sitting on the Directorate one day, living the high life and embarrassing juniors.

"Very well." Tilghman got up. "You and your lovely wife may leave now, and if you'll be so kind as to stop by the lounge and ask Dr. Sligh to come in, with my apologies to the others? Don't worry, Colonel. Your orders will come in a matter of days.''

He was startled. "That soon, sir?''

"I'd start packing tonight. Light.''

And, with that, he was dismissed.

*   *   *

Jeff returned to Pericles from the north feeling less depressed than he thought he would. Although he didn't like the fact that she was exposed to danger, he found his mother more cheerful and alive and full of life than he'd ever seen her before. He was somewhat angry at Sondra—initially for not immediately sending Spirit home when they found each other, then for taking so long to get word back. But the two strange half-sisters seemed to belong together, and there was something in his mother's eyes that he'd never seen before. He couldn't quite put his finger on it, but where there had always been a childlike, innocent quality there now seemed a thoughtfulness and deliberateness that was difficult to understand and a little bit frightening. What could one such as she be plotting and planning?

Mervyn listened with interest to his account. "This is something very new," he told the young man. "Something different is happening once more. I'm very afraid, son, that your family seems destined to fall into things that others do not. Beware your own self. I've seen this sort of phenomenon run in families before, when a Soul Rider was involved, although not nearly as dramatically as your line."

That interested him. "You mean—there are others like us?"

"No, not like you. As I said, your family seems to be unique in the extent of its doings and its tremendous reach, not to mention how complex the spells. But, yes—there are many other families in which a Soul Rider is involved, all of whom have great power. Some don't know it, because they never leave Anchor. Some wind up heads of Fluxlands. But they are all there. Rather dull, though, when compared with our lot."

"Thanks a lot. I think we could all stand a little more dullness."

"But it is not to be. I thought you were going to stay with the train up there for a while and see some of the adventurous north."

"Too chilly. Besides, it was different with just me and Sondra. Now I find out she's my *aunt*, for heaven's sake, and she's taken my mother in tow; I'd just get in the way."

"Uh huh. Poor boy crushed by romantic fantasy. I thought so. So now what will you do?"

"Oh, I kind of hoped I'd be of some use around here for a while. The way you've been talking, things are going to start popping around here any second."

"And so they will, my boy," Mervyn told him gravely. "So they will. You have the power, and some formal training, but very little self-control, I fear. Still, only your heritage makes me hesitant to accept your services. You folks, as I said, always seem to make your own trouble and inflict it on everybody else."

"Well, if you think it's a curse, it's going to come anyway, so I can't lose any sleep over it. At least that Soul Rider's over a thousand kilometers from here."

"I know, I know. Don't worry so much, son. Have a seat and relax." He paused a moment, trying to find a bit of strength for person-to-person intensity. He never was very good at this sort of thing. "I have news of your grandmother."

"You do!" He frowned suddenly. "Bad news, I take it."

"In a way. I was correct in all things. Zelligman Ivan was clearing away the one distinct threat to him—the woman who routed Haldayne from this cluster and helped destroy his predecessor here—as well as currying favor with New Eden. He delivered her to them. A young Fluxlord named Richards was witness to the result. She allowed herself, *in Flux*, to be transformed into one of their kind of women and then married Adam Tilghman, the strongest mind and will of New Eden."

"*What!* I don't believe you! She would never—"

"Yes she would, and did," Mervyn responded calmly. "You know only the loving grandmother and the warrior legends. We forget sometimes that those are *human beings* under all that guff. You think nothing of stalking a comely young lady and taking her to bed, but none of us can really imagine our *parents* doing such a thing or acting in such a manner. Family and authority figures are rarely taken as they are—real people with real hurts and wants and needs. Your grandmother considers herself a total failure, a killer of thousands. For over forty years there's been nobody except possibly me whom she could relate to, human-to-human, and not as a legend, an institution, or a parent— and she blames me for part of her problems.''

Jeff was absolutely crushed. He simply couldn't believe it. ''They brainwashed her, that's all.''

''Undoubtedly, but it didn't take. She has more automatic protection than I do, and while I admit my body may be killed I consider my mind invulnerable to external pressure. If she took that binding spell it's because she *wanted* to.''

''But she always *hated* them and everything they stood for!''

''Ah, yes, but we're not dealing with a machine here. This is a person. She is paying off her guilt in a way that is physically painless. She's had a life like no other, one of greatness, but it is for others to see and understand that. For every great thing she accomplished, she died inside, and benefited not a whit. No, if suicide runs in families, then you're immune. What your grandmother and mother endured would have destroyed lesser people quickly. It just finally caught up to Cass.''

Jeff sat there quietly for a moment, trying to understand what Mervyn was saying. On an intellectual level he followed it, but on a personal one he would never understand it. ''So what you're saying is that the pressures of her life finally caught up to her, and she had a breakdown, and now she's found a way out without shooting herself in the head.''

''That's about it. It does, however, cause a severe headache for me. Don't underestimate Tilghman. He'll use her as a symbol. Her conversion has already spread terror among the local Fluxlords, who can't jump fast enough to get on the New Eden bandwagon. Just tonight your grandmother is hostess to a dinner gathering of the uppermost echelons of New Eden. I don't need to be there to know what they're talking about. New Eden, with the intervening Fluxlords in line, is about to move on Anchor Nantzee, the most highly industrialized Anchor in the cluster and one of the top four on World. Bakha gives him the raw materials, and Logh is the breadbasket. Mareh, with its hordes of sheep and textile mills, is least important to him, but if Nantzee goes it'll fall into his hands almost for the asking. His cult will control an entire cluster, and the vast bulk of Flux in between. It's the start of a new Empire, and this time a very ugly one that might engulf us all.''

"Then this is where I guess I'd better be. Uh—sir?"

"Yes?"

"How do you *know* there's this dinner party going on tonight? I thought you said New Eden was air-tight."

"No, it's not air-tight. What I told you was that what you were proposing was impossible. It is far easier to get information than to act on it. I, my boy, am off to Anchor Nantzee in a matter of hours, with a few stops at some nervous Fluxlands.''

"Surely the Nine could take them out!"

"Possibly. Certainly, so long as they have to move forces through Flux. But the Nine will not take them out. The Nine does not interfere as a group unless it is to directly thwart a dangerous act by the Seven. Had Coydt lived and been in control, we *would* have stopped it, but he's long dead. New Eden hates the Seven as much or more than we do. I tried to get that distinction across to Sondra, but failed. If they take the cluster they will do as good or better a job of defending our Gate as we would. Old Zelligman is running around trying to break in, but he's frustrated. On a personal level, I spent a good deal of time trying to talk them into some action, and failed miserably. I'm on my own in this, for humanitarian reasons and because I don't like messes like this in my neighborhood. And to quiet you once and for all I should tell you that a majority of the Nine, like a majority of the Seven, are female.''

Jeff shook his head in wonder. ''Then how could they . . . ?''

''Because they are committed to a higher duty. And, in a pinch, so am I. But I'm not pinched. Unless I've missed something very, very important, the Gates are not at risk here. The terrible thing about New Eden is that it is the legacy we have reaped from the past two thousand years. The men who built it and formed it are our children. They are the children of an overbearing, dictatorial matriarchy in Anchor and the abuse of power by wizards in Flux. Coydt, and your mother and grandmother, are all victims in different ways. We let the matriarchal church go on and on in our complacency and did not stop it, and now the hate has combined with power, and is striking out. You see, we didn't tell them or teach them that enslavement or dictatorship by a privileged class based on a random inheritance of power or a restrictive religion was wrong. We *condoned* it, as maintaining the status quo. *We* weren't affected—oh, no! *We* were the powerful wizards. All of the leaders of New Eden grew up as slaves of the system, but we didn't teach them an alternative system. So now the slaves are masters of Flux and Anchor—and they are retaining the system, merely turning the ruling class on its head. We taught them to hate, to oppress, to be ruthless. And we were very, very good teachers. . . .''

Onregon Sligh entered and sat down in a chair, nodding to the Chief Judge. ''Adam?''

''Doctor. I want to know ahead of time if we're ready. I've read your reports, but I want it directly from you.''

''I don't feel there's going to be any great difficulty

with the takeover. It's quite risky, but I think you'll make it on sheer gall.''

"That isn't what I mean and you know it. Do you know how to do what we have talked about for so long?''

"I believe I do. We have enough amplifiers now to do it with half the cluster, but I do wish you'd wait until we have Mareh. Not only is that amplifier shield around the Gate an unknown quantity—we don't know if the signals will pass through or around it and our field tests have given contradictory results—but the process requires eight wizards, and they will be smart enough to realize what we're up to in time to stop it. That'll put eight wizards with amplifiers right at our throat.''

"Would you need less if we had Mareh?''

"No, the same. But we'd eliminate the potential problem with the shield at the Gate. It would be irrelevant. And doing it now, to half a cluster, would tip off the whole of World. The Fluxlords would be up in arms over their very survival.''

"Could they undo it?''

"I don't believe so. I believe that the ancients who designed the machines did so for just this purpose and no other. Once it's complete, it's *done*. But, remember, we don't know what sort of file they designed for so vast an area. They were not a secretive lot. The filing system is rather straightforward. If we had thought of the full implications of the category 'Landscape Architecture' rather than dismissing it as a euphemism for gardening, we'd have seen it long before. No guarantees, though. But the filing system is not the language of those programs. An inconceivable number of atoms goes into making up just you, yourself. Not even a wizard can duplicate a human being; he can only modify it. Now consider the number of atoms that goes into making up the whole of an Anchor— New Eden, for example—and all that it contains. All arranged just so in exactly the right order to make what you see. Now consider that a program, a small metallic cube that would fit in my hand, contains that information for a much greater mass. Far greater. I can read the label, and I can read the instructions—but no mind alive today or in the foreseeable future could grasp the mathematics in that cube. It had to be manufactured by another machine, and that by another machine, and so forth down the line until you get to where a man designed one. Men tell it what to do, what to make, but I doubt if the men who built it knew how it stored that information.''

Adam Tilghman nodded thoughtfully. "So we'll never know what we're getting, and we just have to trust that the ancients numbered things in order. All right, I'll accept that. But we must have a test, and soon. I don't fear the Flux armies. By the time the alarm is raised we'll be at Mareh's gates, and they'll have to come through the cluster to get at us and fight on *our* terms. I am, however, fascinated by the idea of it. What do you think will happen to the Fluxlands in the way?''

"The forms of those lands will be overtaken and overrun by the program. The people and other living creatures who live there will, however, most likely freeze as they are.''

"Hmmm . . . Yet there will be no wizard's powers binding them. They will rebel, and be violent opponents of any Fluxlords entering. I think we can use that to good advantage, until we're ready to directly incorporate them under our system.'' He reached back and pulled a long, tasseled rope in back of him.

"Yes, but you don't address the major problem. Where will we get eight wizards strong enough who are also willing to operate the machines?''

"Doctor, you are the most brilliant mind of our age in science, possibly of many ages, but you'll never think like a commander or a politician. Has it not occurred to you that we have in our midst a number of sufficiently powerful wizards who will obediently climb up into those things and do exactly what we tell them?''

At that moment the doors to the study opened; Cassie entered and scampered over to Tilghman, kneeling before him. "Yes, my husband?"

Adam Tilghman grinned at Sligh, who sat there, mouth open. "You can tell the other gentlemen to come in now, Cassie. And—Cassie?"

"Yes, my lord?"

"Think about packing. We're going on a little trip soon."

8

PLAYING HARDBALL DIPLOMACY

Cassie had felt only excitement at the prospect of a trip. The doctors were not at all concerned about it, since Fluxwives were absolutely perfect baby machines. Short of injury or death, she would deliver normally and with no complications exactly on schedule, trip or not. This, in fact, had been the convincing factor for Tilghman, for he wanted her along both for political reasons and because he considered it intolerable that a child of his might be born while he was away.

It was a large wagon train, heavily defended with over four hundred soldiers, many armed with strange-looking weapons, as well as several wizards in New Eden's employ and, to ease commercial problems, a tough-looking stringer in charge of leading them.

It was only when the void loomed in front of her that she grew suddenly fearful, and turned and clutched Adam. He put his arm around her and said, soothingly, "It's all right." They passed into Flux without hesitation, and she felt a sudden chill run through her as her defenses automatically activated. Suzl's spell faded away and she came to face reality as if waking from a soft and pleasant dream. It was this her subconscious had feared and known would happen, but now that it had she found she didn't mind it so much.

The front of their wagon resembled a coach, with plush seats and a canvas covering that could be brought up and around to seal them off from the outside world. The driver sat higher, atop the wagon and essentially out of sight, only the long reins reaching upward betraying his presence. Aft was almost a small apartment, with a bed, a food storage and preparation center, a fold-out table and a couple of fold-down chairs, even a small wardrobe cabinet, all nicely carpeted. Side casks dispensed fresh water, mixed fruit juice, and wine. It was a kind of luxury few had known on the trail.

She looked up at Adam and let out a short gasp. The unmistakable aura of Flux power was within him, something she could feel and sense rather than see.

"Yes," he told her, "I am what they call a wizard, too, and a pretty good one, I think. My father lost to a better one, and until all this came along I was right-hand man, so to speak, to my father's murderer. She was strong, and always surrounded herself with other strong women wizards."

She frowned. "Then why do you hate wizardry so?"

"Because it is a poison. It makes men into animals, where only the strongest gets to rule and make the rules. Even Coydt van Haas wasn't born bad—wizardry made him that way, and his own power corrupted him and fed his hatred until it consumed him. Uh—do I disturb you mentioning him?"

She shook her head negatively. "No, my husband. The webs are clear from my mind, it is true, but it is no longer important. What I am now is all that is important."

He stared down at her. "And what are you now, Cassie?"

"Your wife. The mother-to-be of your children."

He had hoped something like this would happen, but nothing was ever certain and this least of all. "You're getting back into politics now, you know."

She nodded. "Suzl said I was destined to be the wife of a great leader, not a great leader myself. I feel—wanted, and needed. I hope this is so."

"Oh, it is, Cassie, it is. Things won't always be the way they are now. Men and women have different roles in life, but these extremes won't last. They can't. The scriptures say nothing about dull wives, they only define roles and duties. It'll just take some patience, I'm afraid. Hatred and the memories of hurt run deep, and revenge and short-term satisfactions of our baser natures are easier for most to accept. Champion, for example, was created by a cruel, vain witch as a sexual plaything. By reversing things, he's content and continually reassured about himself. He'll oppose every change, and he'll have to be carefully handled. He's a brilliant general, but like all brilliant generals he's a terribly dangerous man who interprets scripture in a rigid and deeply personal way."

The holy book used by New Eden in its churches was a fragmentary one, culled from a number of books whose whole had been lost somewhere in the past. Still, even in wildly differing texts, there had been much agreement. There was one God who was everywhere, and who had created World and the first man, whose name had been Adam. Woman had been made by God from man, to ease his loneliness and bear and rear his children. But Eve had been corrupted by Hell and had dragged man down with her, and so the woman would always require a man's judgment and must defer to him. Another fragment had told of marriage, service, and duty to husband through the story of someone named Ruth. The ancient heroes were all male; the ancient heroines were all victims or mothers of great men. It presented a concrete and logical view to the leaders of New Eden. Still, their past oppressions had been

at the hands of women, so when in power they had
overreacted.

Adam Tilghman had read concrete evidence of the all-
pervasive Church's falsity in the ancient scriptural frag-
ments that had indicated an older and to him far more
logical way. Yet, "I want a nation of Ruths, not zombies,"
he told her sincerely. "When we are secure we will move
that way, and you shall be in the lead."

"Where you go, so shall I," she said, and liked it.

She looked out into the void, and saw both old friend
and bitter enemy there. She tried to conjure up the simplest
of spells, and found that she had forgotten how, nor could
she read the few spells on those who came near. She could
see the strings, and thought them pretty, but she had no
idea where they might lead. Still, her binding spells, not
only to Adam but those for defense as well, were in
perfect working order, and she felt she had nothing to fear
from the void.

New Eden had seemed to her grotesque on the surface,
but particularly out here she realized that it was no worse
than many Fluxlands and better than most. Adam, in
particular, was different from the rest of them, who were
spending the rest of their lives working out their hatreds
and revenges. Adam Tilghman had been called a ruthless
monster, but she knew that this simply wasn't so. There
was no generalized hatred in him, only vision and purpose,
a vision and purpose that required decisive and even ruthless action at times, for he would eventually have to
impose that purpose and vision on others. She understood,
vaguely, that this trip was his mission to save lives on both
sides, not take them.

The journey to Nantzee was about fifteen hundred
kilometers, and they made very good time despite brief
stops at various Fluxlands along the way. These stops were
courtesy calls, as it were—politically necessary, but accomplished in the shortest time possible. These stops, brief as
they were, were another revelation to Cassie. She had seen

hundreds, perhaps more, of these little "countries" which existed in reality by the force of will of the local Flux wizard with the most power, but, somehow, she'd never quite looked at them this critically before.

Almost invariably, the active deity, worshipped by the population, was the wizard in charge. The people there thought the way the wizard decreed, they acted the way the wizard wanted, and in many cases were caricatures of real human beings, turned into creatures to fit a dream landscape. For perhaps the first time she looked at them not as something taken for granted but from Adam's viewpoint, and they were indeed repulsive to her in that regard. Oppression, it seemed, did not exist when you were not one of the oppressed. Oh, you knew it academically, but you accepted it. New Eden, by comparison, seemed to look better and better even from her place in that society.

Adam was right, she decided. This sort of power corrupted absolutely, no matter who possessed. She had run a Fluxland as a religious center, but she had been just as autocratic and just as godlike in her own way—only she had rationalized all of it at that time. Even after, she had accepted the Fluxlands as normal and the Fluxlords as equals.

It was no longer a wonder to her that the system had created the excesses of New Eden; rather, she wondered that it had created so few. One did not upset such a system easily, and not without cost, but Adam's determination that the system must be upset and his dedication to that eventual goal made him far more of a revolutionary than World had ever seen before, and she loved him for it and understood it perfectly.

Additionally, she found that her own presence was quite a shock to the Fluxlords and others they met. She smiled and was the deferential wife but she answered their questions. Yes, she was the same Cass/Kasdi who built the empire. No, she had not been forced into this position, but had taken it voluntarily and now believed in it. They could read the spells for themselves and see their voluntary nature. She had not been transformed, she had been *converted*. It shook them up, the men as much as the women.

Although a fast stringer train or a military march could make eighty kilometers a day or more, the fifty that they made, considering the size of their party and all the stops, was considered nothing less than a miracle. As they went, her belly and breasts continued to swell, but her body continued to cope with whatever changing conditions it faced. As Suzl had pointed out, the Fluxgirls had been *designed* for baby-making.

They carried six girls from the household staff with them to help her, particularly for after the child was born, but she found she liked the way the men seemed more and more solicitous of her and how kindly and helpful they became, even the hardest of them. It had not been this way with Spirit, where much had been done to conceal her condition and the attitude had been an entirely impatient one: get it over with and get the kid away from her so she could go about her job.

As they approached Anchor Nantzee, they began to run into large masses of men in New Eden's black uniforms, many setting up large machines or practicing the various arts of war. After the peace and serenity of the trip to date, it was a sudden, shocking reminder that this journey was no diplomatic jaunt but rather a stratagem in an impending war. She had seen, and even organized, too many such massings, and she had hoped never to see another. The sheer manpower, all military professionals, coupled with the huge assortment of strange and new weaponry told her that Anchor Nantzee would indeed fall. Its only choice was whether to do so bloodily or with minimal loss of life.

Tilghman spent many hours in conference with military leaders, including the hard-to-miss General Champion, going over maps and charts and playing with little toy armies.

She did not want to know the plans; she wanted no more part in military bloodletting.

Adam was visibly tired, but rested very little, and they soon went forward, out onto the Anchor apron, and approached the ancient gates of the Anchor, the high stone walls and fortifications looking very much like those of Anchor Logh. She had been in Nantzee, but never through the front gate. Adam had told her to dress her grandest, and she had, although she was surprised when only their wagon passed through the armored double gate into Anchor, leaving the entourage behind on the apron and in Flux.

Although superficially the same, Anchor Nantzee was quite different from Anchor Logh. This was hilly, even mountainous country, with great folded mountains running as far as the eye could see, cut only occasionally by river gorges, evergreens and other hardy trees running all the way to their summits. The main highway from the gate led after a kilometer to the first of these narrow gorges and to a small town at the bottom of the pass. Above, clearly visible, complex fortifications had been carved into and out of the surrounding very high ground. Any army that got through the gate would have to get through this trap as well. It looked formidable indeed to her.

It was cooler here, too, than in the constant warmth of Flux or Anchor Logh, and there was a slight breeze, but she decided against a coat or wrap. After her Flux appearances she fully understood her purpose here, and she was determined to carry it out if lives could be saved.

Large tents had been set up in a park-like area just outside the town, and they headed there. Various flags flew from the tents, although she recognized none of them. They could have represented leaders of various boroughs of the Anchor, or quite a bit more than that. She quickly learned, though, that the hammer and tongs symbol represented Nantzee itself, and she knew that the starburst represented the Church.

"Be honest, tell only the truth, conceal nothing,"

Tilghman instructed her. "Don't think or mull over any answers, just say what you feel." Those, she decided, were the easiest instructions ever given to her.

Mervyn moved through the small crowd of people feeling more like he was at a social function than at a conference of war. He nibbled idly on a sandwich and looked over the crowd, then frowned and spotted someone whose face he simply never thought he'd see in person—particularly not in a situation like this. He blinked and stared hard, then realized that the prim, aristocratic fellow with the goatee had to be who he'd first thought he was. Nobody else would look like that on purpose. Slowly, he made his way closer.

Zelligman Ivan looked over and spotted the figure of the old man in flowing satin robes coming towards him, and he stood up and smiled as the other reached his lone table. "Please! Have a seat and welcome!" Ivan said warmly. "The wine is not the best, but one takes what one can get under the circumstances."

Mervyn pulled over a folding chair and sat down, putting his sandwich on the table. Ivan poured a drink from a wine bottle and handed it to him.

"So we meet at last," the old wizard said. "I must admit, Zelligman, that you are the last person I would have expected to see here."

The other nodded. "I know. Not really my territory, but, damn it, it's where the action is. Those psychotic thugs have the whole file, the top ancient technology along with the instructions. No matter what our differences, Mervyn, we have that in common. That's our common heritage over there being perverted and used like a bludgeon by reactionary idiots."

The old man nodded. "I agree, although you certainly have been a busy little bee with them. I owe you more than one for that, Zelligman."

Ivan shrugged. "It was truly nothing personal. What are

a few lives compared to what might be gained? No, don't go moralizing on me, old man! You've been responsible for more than your share of innocents yourself, and you still sleep well at night. They were paranoid about her being so close, and they were paranoid about what they perceived as your base so close to their front door. I made an offer to ease their paranoia, and they took it.''

''And the price? Some advanced communications equipment, perhaps?''

Zelligman Ivan sighed. ''You should know that they are even less enamored of that idea than you are. I hardly expect that from them—they are primitive, animalistic thugs, but their leaders are not that stupid. No, we expect that such a device will be naturally available when they secure this cluster, as they almost certainly will. They will need a method of communications to keep their little empire secure. No, the price was supposed to be a copy of Toby Haller's journal.''

Mervyn looked suddenly ashen, as if having a seizure, and it took him a moment to recover his composure. ''But that's a myth! Your father and mine both would have sold their souls for it, but after all this time it simply cannot exist!''

''I am certain it does. Coydt found it—or, rather, a copy of it on one of the small storage modules—quite by accident, in the midst of a mass of mostly junk that was also on the module. He would never allow anyone else to read it, or know much of its contents, but he definitely did have it, and he definitely did read it. Indeed, it was after that that he began to act very oddly and very much on his own. He began to question our very goals, and, in fact, began sounding more like you than one of us, but he was very strong and he knew too much and he had too much. We didn't dare touch him until we knew where his library was and how to secure it intact, and by the time we knew—it was too late.''

''But the journal! You're suggesting New Eden has it?''

"I *know* they have it, and I know, too, that the Chief Judges have all read it and quite a bit more of the ancient nontechnical writings. Much of their odd theology comes from those writings, but it's the journal that has fed their moral self-righteous mission. You know its reputation—that it would shatter World to its foundations and drive the strong mad."

Mervyn *did* know. Quite a number of legends were associated with the journal, that one paramount among them. The journal, it was said, was the only true record surviving from the ancient days that held the true answers to World. Written in longhand by one of the first of the truly powerful wizards of Flux, it was said to reveal all the basic secrets of the universe, written as it was by one driven from Anchor but still of the old civilization. The original had been reported almost everywhere on World, including the Cold Wastes of the void, two thousand kilometers from Anchors and Hellgates, where magic was weak or nonexistent and no known creatures could live for long. Most now considered it merely a fable, a nonexistent book created by some imaginative or insane mind in ages long gone.

"If such a book really exists," Mervyn said, "surely you have agents within New Eden capable of securing at least a copy of it."

"It exists. Ask old man Tilghman when you meet him. *He's* read it. But it's not in the temple, I'll tell you that, and its audience is very limited. I suspect the old man himself has it somewhere, but where is a different story. I can hardly risk my people on such a blind chase."

"Well, they promised it to you, and you delivered. What happened?"

"They backed off. This general of theirs, Gunderson Champion, promised it to me. He's never read it, but it doesn't interest him much. You can't conquer masses of territory or kill thousands with it, so it's irrelevant to him. He simply couldn't deliver, though. The judges pulled a switch and I got mostly theological garbage. Gave me the thing at Tilghman's wedding and I rushed off with it. Sat through ten days of crap before I realized they'd given me a ringer. I wish I knew when. To think it might actually have been right there, and I didn't know it!''

Mervyn had regained complete control. ''Tilghman's wedding? To Cass? You were there?''

''I was. A most interesting and unexpected experience. I half expected to lose the book right then, as soon as I realized that she could have broken off and escaped. But she didn't, to my great relief. She was almost enough for Coydt, who was as far ahead of me as I am of the worm in Flux power. I'll never understand it. I could read her protective spells. I was already looking for an exit and fast.''

''You of all people should know that the human mind is the most complex of all things. I *think* I understand, but I'm not really certain.''

''Well, perhaps you can ask her. I understand the old man's brought her with him, and her ready to drop his child any time now.''

''I've heard so. It will be interesting to see.'' He sighed. ''But you still haven't explained what you are doing *here*.''

''Gathering information, the same as you are. Tilghman's up to something more than just taking over Nantzee. Something big. I want to know what before it can possibly hurt me.''

Mervyn nodded. He, too, had heard rumors to that effect, but had not been able to track anything down. The deployment of so many Flux power amplifiers—for an attack on an Anchor—was curious. The vanishing of a large number of Fluxgirls from Anchor Logh in the past month and a half or so was equally curious. One or two amplifiers would be sufficient to protect the troops and equipment in Flux; the Fluxgirls chosen were all former wizards with plenty of power but they could no longer use it. He had to admit that he, too, was both curious and nervous.

"So, Zelligman, since we're being so civil, will you answer me a simple question I have been wondering about for centuries?"

"Of course, if I can."

"Why?"

"Why what?"

"Why do you want to open those Gates? What is the percentage?"

Zelligman Ivan sat back and lit a thin cigar. "You know the answer. You've stood at least once at the Gate lock of one or another Hellgate and heard the message."

"An inhuman, horrible voice from the prehistoric past recorded there promising that if we don't resist it will make us gods."

"I grant the inhuman, but question the horrible. It's no monster—it's a mechanical voice, a synthesized voice, that's all. It was that which panicked our ancestors into sealing those Gates, except for the power we need. And so for twenty-six hundred years we've been sitting here, in a stagnant, brutal, primitive society, quaking at the sound of the boogey man's voice. For what? Five percent of us live for centuries as tinpot godlings, while ninety-five percent toil and live short, miserable lives of poverty under the control of a reactionary Church and state. Ancient knowledge is suppressed or destroyed, and we are mired in social, technological, and spiritual mud forever. So you spend your life saving this system, only to find that its heirs are the New Eden Brotherhood. Have you considered the implications of a World entirely under the New Eden Brotherhood? Their system is only the tip of the depravity that exists."

Mervyn nodded. "I very much agree with that last. In fact, I more or less grant your points. The problem is, your alternative is to abandon all hope in favor of instant suicide. Let's not forget, Zelligman, that our ancestors, who had all that rich knowledge and technology, *knew* who or what was on the other end of that voice, and they chose to build the barricades, cut down the power, and reduce us to this state rather than greet that voice with open arms."

"I doubt if it was that clear-cut, my old enemy. I have lived for almost six hundred years, and I think you are even older than I. In all that time, I've never seen any evidence that humanity would find unanimity on any weighty issue without totalitarian control, nor severe variations in human nature. We do *not* know that they chose to build the barricades. We only know that the *winners* chose to do so, and that they then chased all of our forefathers— yours and mine, certainly—into Flux and built their walls against them as well. Tell me—how does Anchor Nantzee decide in their crisis?"

"You know as well as I. The Church and many major groups want a fight to the death, even if it means a repeat of Bakha. The government and many of the guild and commune leaders want an accommodation."

Zelligman Ivan grinned. "See?"

The conference was to meet in a small, secure tent set up for the purpose. Mervyn had arranged to be present, although he was aware that he represented the losing side in all this. Ivan was not invited, but the old wizard knew that his counterpart would have no difficulty in learning exactly what went on. In spite of Ivan's "doublecross" by New Eden, Mervyn was well aware that they owed the prime sorceror for services rendered and that Ivan was, therefore, in far less danger than he was.

There were formalities, of course, even in a situation like this. In fact, it seemed that the greater the crisis the more emphasis people placed on ceremony and correctness. When one's world was falling apart, such things were needed to keep some level of sanity.

And so Mervyn stood there with High Priestess Gowann, Coordinator Dixon, who represented the government, Haagen

Sertz, head of the trade unions guild, and General Yakota, head of the Anchor militia, and watched the luxurious wagon pull in and up. The driver was a top sergeant in the New Eden forces, but he concerned himself mostly with handling the team and, from his lofty perch, surveying what he saw for security. In back were two black-uniformed footmen, heavily armed and suspicious of everyone and everything. Steps were removed from an undercarriage and then the passengers, Adam Tilghman and his wife, made their appearance.

Cassie's appearance was still a shock to Mervyn, although he knew just what she would look like. What startled him was not the golden garb with all the jewels, nor her smaller size or her obviously advanced pregnancy, but her manner and demeanor. There was a softness and delicacy to her that was most strange, and yet she radiated the same professionalism she always had. There was no doubt in anyone's mind that she understood exactly what was going on, and that, far from being brainwashed, she had indeed committed herself to the other side. It was just such a demoralizing effect that Adam Tilghman had counted on.

The man himself exuded confidence; his tall, muscular figure, gray hair, and face appearing carved from stone and hard experience, made him all the more fearsome. He wore only a plain black uniform and boots, with no insignia of any kind, no medals, no badges of office. Such a one was powerful enough not to need such things.

The Chief Judge and his wife greeted everyone formally and in turn, and when Cassie reached Mervyn there was a look of recognition in her eyes but nothing in her manner to indicate that it was anything special. Tilghman had wanted a period of informality before they sat down, however, and they found themselves the center of attention. Mervyn ignored Tilghman and concentrated on remaining close to Cassie.

"Hello, Cassie," he said hesitantly.

She nodded. "Mervyn."

"Want to talk about it?"

"If you wish, sir."

He felt instantly uncomfortable, and the chill was notice-able to all. "We are just trying to understand."

Cassie replied, "This girl might humbly suggest, sir, that you are shocked but not surprised. You invented Cassie, and used her, and you don't like the fact that she has become someone else of her own choice."

Since that was partly true, he felt a bit embarrassed. "And you think your new life, your new system, is better for everyone?"

"Better for me, sir. Few people get to choose their masters, or change them. I have rejected you and chose another."

She still had that knack for getting to the heart of things. What had Ivan said? Five percent versus ninety-five percent? And even among those five, there were few masters and many servants. At least he thought he understood now, better than he had before. He *was* a master, the top rank of World, and he would always be one. She had ruled half a world, but *he*, indirectly but firmly, had ruled her. One had the power one was born with, but how and how well that power was used depended on personality. Politics, too, depended on personality most of all. It was the old classic, the killer instinct. She had the power and the knowledge, but lacked the will. That instinct wasn't in her, which was why she'd failed against Coydt. Mervyn had manipulated her into positions of power and had fur-nished that will, that killer instinct.

Coydt had understood, which was why he'd removed from her those spells that supported Mervyn's manipulation. So long as she was forced to live her life the way the old wizard had arranged, she was forced to act in the Nine's best interest. Removing it removed her as a threat, and removed Mervyn's leverage. With all the power, but with no killer instinct, all she had built for him had collapsed, and she, too, had collapsed. Without his will, his instinct, she had withdrawn from human society, feeling depressed and without purpose. And he had let her drift, because she was no longer useful or relevant to his broader purposes and goals.

What she might have become if left alone would always haunt her. The Church had wrenched her at just eighteen from her home and family and cast her into slavery in Flux. She had survived, found some love and much comradeship, and developed a new direction as a chief dugger. Then that too was taken from her by Matson's apparent death. Emotionally devastated, Mervyn had used her state to force her into the leadership of a reformed Church and used her as the nucleus for an expanding Empire, but in a position where even acknowledging her own daughter was forbidden. In the end, Matson had spurned her, Mervyn had lost his control over her, and she was left, bereft of purpose, left to wonder what might have been. Even the Soul Rider that had used her and influenced much of her life's directions had cast her off when it, for its own mysterious purposes, found her less useful than someone else.

Adam Tilghman had the killer instinct, all right. Just looking at the man was seeing power personified—a power not created by Flux, but one that was within him and was him. She had sensed it, then seized upon it as at least a tiny measure of purpose and salvation. No matter if New Eden was an unpleasant alternative—it was the only alternative she'd ever really had offered, and she committed herself to it body and soul.

"If I may ask—how is Spirit?"

He was startled by the change in subject. "The same. Better, in fact. She's with a stringer train." He hesitated a moment. "She is with her half-sister. Jeff is working for me at the moment."

She nodded. "Better than I hoped."

"Cassie—are you happy?"

She hesitated a moment. "I am not sure I know what 'happy' means. I am content, sir."

He sighed, and let her talk to others, where she gave all the right answers and was far more friendly. Yes, she knew the Church was a lie now. No, she didn't go along with every single thing in New Eden's system, but it would improve once it felt secure. Political and military matters she professed little interest in, and always deferred to Tilghman.

Now they went in to start the conference. Cassie did not remain for it, but left for the wagon.

Dixon got right to the point. He was a small, nervous man who was clearly uncomfortable. "Judge Tilghman, what are your intentions toward us? Are we to be wiped out?"

Blunt enough. Tilghman liked that in a man. "I certainly hope not. If that were our intention, we would not be sitting here now. Let me make our position plain. We have access to many of the secrets of our ancient ancestors. We know how to revolutionize and raise ourselves up and, eventually, all of World. What we don't have is the industrial capacity to produce what we need except in Flux, and we feel a dependency on Flux—and the release of our secrets there—would bring terror to World. As with any powerful knowledge, it can be used for good or evil. Our two Anchors give us plentiful food and raw materials, but we lack industrial capacity which you have in abundance. It's as simple as that."

"Um, perhaps not, sir," Sertz put in. "There's no reason for a destructive fight. We can and will make what you wish—for our own security's sake."

"I wish it were that simple," Tilghman responded. "As I pointed out, the knowledge we have could, in the wrong hands, produce a society so horrible none of us could imagine it. Our own people have been guilty of excesses with just a small part of it, and it is a constant battle to reform those excesses, a battle I wage daily. If this sort of thing were to fall into the hands of powerful Fluxlords, or the Church, or the cabals known as the Seven and the Nine, it would be devastating. You must understand our higher duty to all the citizens of World. We cannot manufacture any of this unless we control every step of that production, and the places in which it is produced. Absolutely control them.''

"But you'll win nothing here your way," Sertz pointed out. "Factories are the easiest things to destroy, but even if you took them intact you couldn't run them without skilled workers. Such things as steam under pressure and blast furnaces are not run with a crew that can learn by doing. These are skilled crafts and trades that take much time and experience to do well. It took your people ten years to master Bakha's bicycle factory, an extremely simple operation compared to any of ours. I suggest, sir, that we are here not so much out of your mercy but because you know this, too."

"I'll agree with part of that, but I will also state the facts. We *will* control this Anchor. If we must hire and import experts from other clusters to rebuild and retrain, then we must. We are patient. Your alternatives are simple. You can categorically reject any accommodation and suffer the fate of Bakha. This will inconvenience us, but all of you and your children and your children's children will be dead. Forever. Or, you can merge with us, join us as partners—junior partners at the start, but full later on—and we can create a standard of living here undreamed of before, and one with eventually no dependence on Flux.''

"And the Church?" the High Priestess interjected.

"Madame, you and your *ladies* and whatever you wish to take with you are free to go. We will guarantee safe passage to anywhere outside of New Eden's sphere that you wish. But your Church has been the primary cause of keeping human beings in the dirt for too many centuries. It has no place here." He paused a moment. "In fact, we make this offer to you all. We will agree to an orderly evacuation of all who wish to leave this Anchor. We will even arrange for temporary shelter and safety for them through Flux and to various other Anchors to the north, or they may remain just inside Flux, under our protection, until this matter is resolved and then make their own decisions on whether to return or go. We wish no more slaughter of the innocents.''

They buzzed and whispered over that for a few seconds, and there was clearly a strong argument between the High Priestess and Dixon. Mervyn sat silently through it all. He had already done all his arguing and all his pleading, and there was nothing left to do but see it through.

Finally, there seemed some measure of acquiescence, although hardly agreement.

"Judge Tilghman," Dixon said carefully, "we appreciate the gesture and we accept your generous offer. Hopefully, some time will be allowed to get this message to everyone and give them their options."

"Ten days from today," the leader of New Eden said firmly. "Not one minute longer. At dawn, ten days from now, it will be cast."

They argued for more time, but he would not budge. "An army takes a lot of organization and resources to sustain in the field. I'll not keep them out there any longer than necessary."

Dixon sighed and nodded. "Very well. You are doubtlessly aware that the Borough and Commune Council, by a majority vote, determined that massive bloodshed should be avoided at all costs. That means that the majority is willing to surrender to you, but that some will fight. We can't stop that."

"The guilds are also divided," Sertz told him. "The journeyman's association knows that you need them, and so it's willing to go along, but much of the rank and file will be opposed and will fight."

"The militia is subject to the orders of the Council," General Yakota added. "As such, despite bitter arguments, there will be no organized resistance. I cannot, however, control a group of armed and trained civil militia in every instance. There will be resistance, and these hills will not be easy to take."

Tilghman nodded and thought for a moment. "Then what we have is a problem of separating the majority from the minority. Might I suggest this, then? Those of the majority—all of them—will proceed from Anchor into Flux by the two gates within ten days, under our complete protection and with adequate provisions assured. At this stage we are still partly dependent on Flux, and so we might as well use it. Our amplifiers can feed and provide for the short time necessary. Anyone remaining in Nantzee after this period will be considered an enemy and will be dealt with. When the Anchor is secured, all may return to their homes and lives."

"Be reasonable!" Dixon implored him. "Do you realize you might be talking about as many as three quarters of a million men, women, and children?"

"I do and I'm prepared for it. Just such an alternative was brought up in the preliminary meetings and is fully provided for—a contingency that many did not believe would exist. We could handle a million—for a short period, a week or ten days. Up to a month with strain."

This seemed to greatly please all but the High Priestess— and the one observer present.

Mervyn felt suddenly very uneasy, and spoke up for the first time. "I advise against it. Surrender if you must, or fight if you must, but don't put your population at the mercy of Flux. To evacuate essentially an entire Anchor with only the clothes on its people's backs! Incredible!"

Both Sertz and Dixon looked over at the old wizard. "What else can we do? Accept the eight hundred thousand dead of Bakha? Kill half or more of our population because of a few hotheads within it?"

"But they have the population as hostage!"

"Exactly," Tilghman agreed. "Therefore, the militia

must not only supervise the evacuation but also guard the factories and industrial might of the Anchor. There will be a terrible price for sabotage. Some of our officers can be brought in now and supervise these details to minimize any problems." He sighed and got up. "You have made the correct decision, the only decision that insures us both a long and increasingly productive future. Staff at both gates will assist in every way. I'll return now to notify the commands. Thank you very much. You will not regret your wisdom." And, with that, he walked out of the tent.

"Better than we dared hope," Dixon sighed.

Mervyn stood. "This is the darkest day in the history of World. I firmly believe that you who rejoice in your deliverance now will live long enough to see your names cursed for all time." And with that, he walked out, followed by the grim-faced High Priestess. Both had known what was coming, but had hoped against hope that it could be avoided.

"They fold like sheep, eager to welcome the butcher," she said bitterly.

"Tilghman is a far more brilliant tactician than I gave him credit for being," Mervyn replied. "The scars of Bakha, whose population they needed the least, have justly terrified the rest, and their weapons are formidable. And now he's got the victim turning over a huge portion of the population to him as hostage to a painless takeover. I do admit, Reverend Mother, that I feel fear for the first time in many long centuries. You will leave, I take it?"

"What choice did they give us? But I'll not surrender my people to their sexist gunmen. We will evacuate to the temple and out through the Gate. A small volunteer crew will remain, and we will flood the lowest level with concrete. The entrance will remain solidly blocked."

He nodded. "I hope that's sufficient. I will also make use of it, so expect me on the tenth day as well."

She looked up at him in surprise. "You are staying that long? Why?"

"Because I want to see just what they have in mind. I looked into Tilghman's eyes and I saw a combination of brilliance, audacity, and arrogance that I've never seen before. More, he knows I'm here and a real threat to him. With Ivan and who knows who else about, it's safest for me to exit through the back door, as it were."

"Don't delay. I will be the last to leave, but you must. be there on the tenth day by nightfall. I will not have a barbarian horde invading and controlling my temple!"

9

GALL AND GUTS

The mass evacuation of an Anchor had never been attempted before, and it was a mammoth and massive undertaking. Additionally, the fear the majority of Anchorfolk felt for Flux had to be counterbalanced by the fear of the invading army and certain death. Some who were not rebellious still would not go, of course, including many of the aged and many simply too stubborn to give in, but the majority did in fact agree to move.

Wizards in the employ of New Eden handled large Flux amplifiers, creating semblances of normal terrain in large pockets. Many of those fleeing Anchor Nantzee tried to take carts and animals and other belongings with them, but troops receiving them just inside Flux stripped them of anything they could not carry themselves.

Both Tilghman and Champion were in high spirits as they watched it progress, and even the general had to admit a certain admiration for the way the Chief Judge had pulled it off. There would still be fighting, some of it potentially fierce, and there would still be a lot of split-second timing to bring it to fruition, but this first and hardest step had been surmounted.

Tilghman set up a command post just inside Flux, where he felt more secure, and held a number of meetings. One of the first was with Onregon Sligh, the obese chief of Research and Development. Sligh was obviously not in the best of condition for long rides and strenuous activity, but he was doing what he could.

"I've given some consideration to what we discussed back at the house," Tilghman told him. "With this operation going so well, I am inclined to give you your way. Mareh is chilly rolling hills with a base of animal husbandry, open range, and textiles. They can't move south without getting into the Cold Wastes, and we will now control all routes within the cluster to and from there, and thus their lifeline. I expect they will fall faster and easier than this one. I think we can afford to wait."

Sligh looked relieved. "You won't regret it. At least we can be ready to go only days after Mareh is secured, which puts the timing up to you."

"What about our situation here? Are we ready?"

"It's never been done on this scale, you know, although all of our experiments and calculations indicate success. It's a least common denominator approach, though. I see no reason for failure or apprehension. The amplifiers are set up both east and west of Anchor, away from the Gates. It will be necessary to process them in batches of a few thousand at a time, but that should be no problem. We've set up one hundred pockets down both sides of the Anchor in a checkerboard pattern, each holding between seven and ten thousand. We must begin immediately, though. We can't sustain such crowds of frightened people while we wait for the last to come out of Anchor. The Flux squares of our checkerboard, however, give us some measure of isolation. I would like to start immediately with the farthest squares."

Tilghman nodded. "Very well. The proper orders will

be given immediately. You're certain that the programming is correct?''

"As certain as I can be. This is tricky. You might also realize that we will have to move directly on Mareh, before news of this gets out.''

He nodded. "I know. Champion's already on that end, but we've still got this one to do yet.''

Sligh rose tiredly, but still managed a chuckle. "Adam, this is so audacious, so insane, it's simply *got* to work. You have the damndest mind I've ever encountered.''

Adam Tilghman shrugged. "What did you call it? Gall and guts, I think. That's how you win.''

Troops moved the miserable population through Flux, through restful-looking pockets which had water and some basic foods, then back again. Anchor Nantzee was somewhat heart-shaped, with its entrance gates at the north and south, as opposed to Anchor Logh's east-west orientation and potato-like boundaries.

When the marching refugees were near the brink of exhaustion, troops moved in and began to separate them. Resistance was strong, but the tired marchers were no match for fresh, well-armed soldiers who showed just how brutal they could be. Families were split as men and women were led to different grassy pockets, totally dependent on their captors for food, water, and rest.

Sligh had used his master amplifier to duplicate itself many times; he had more than enough of the big machines for his purpose, and without moving them far. Sligh, however, was the first to admit that he was on new ground. It was one thing to feed one of the ancient modules in the machines to activate and carry out those instructions; it was quite another to attempt, as he was now, the actual mass transmission of a wizard's complex spell that had to be both a group and an individualized phenomenon. It had been tried, successfully, on small groups of the pitiful survivors of Anchor Bakha, but never on this scale.

The amplifiers went on, concentrating on a single "square" containing by the soldiers' count eighty-four hundred and twelve women ranging in age from small children to advanced middle-age. The youngest were removed with the explanation that it was necessary to run them all through a sterilization procedure to eliminate the possibility of disease from the overcrowded conditions but that this procedure might well harm children below the age of five. They were positioned so that the children could be easily returned to them "in a matter of an hour." There was again much resistance to this, but even the kindly soldiers turned very nasty very quickly when argued with.

The spell was a variation of Coydt's, the only complex one that they understood well enough to modify. Basically, it imposed the physiological rules of New Eden on all the women, which was in and of itself very limiting and genetically firm as well. The specific features were based upon the original's appearance, but shaped and idealized to make them extremely attractive. They were now small, physically weak, at the mercy of their bodies, and also illiterate and unable to master mathematics, a guarantee that their status could never change. Beyond this, an overlay was created compelling *acceptance* of all this. They actually felt that their new form and limitations were right and proper, and were anxious to be taught the new system. It worked better than the originators had hoped. Where a milling and frightened throng of diverse women had been, there were now eighty-four hundred and twelve Fluxgirls, just waiting to be classified as tattooed.

The men were trickier, for this was where much research and major modifications of the spell were made. Each kept his own sense of identity, but had an overlay impressed on them to totally and completely accept the new system without question, to unthinkingly obey the orders of all superiors, and to enthusiastically learn and embrace the new order. As a reward, they, too, now were all tall, muscular, and darkly handsome.

There were deviations and aberrations in both squares, of course, and on these, perhaps four or five percent of the whole, a check was run by the amplifier program and they were either modified to fit the "norm" or were, if this proved impossible, quite simply eliminated.

While refugees were still pouring from the gates, the process continued, a square at a time, and Champion's army swelled with sudden new recruits. There would be no need for years of indoctrination and terror in the newly conquered Anchor; the population was simply being converted wholesale.

And, with the exception of specialized units, and officers, the soldiers who would take the Anchor from those who remained and fought would be their own former friends and neighbors.

The first of the specialized teams went in the night after the agreement had been made. Using odd-shaped devices the ancient writings had called "gliders" and a boost from Flux, teams soared over Anchor walls and landed, fully armed and ready with the most sophisticated gear, near almost all the major factories and installations in Anchor Nantzee. Stun rays were used to counter any opposition within, and they held and secured key positions in a single night. Most of the casualties were due to bad landings and accidents, not hostile action. When the rebels came to blow up the plants, they would find it very difficult to do.

A few had been wired already, and were gingerly defused.

Other advanced teams of veterans came in over the walls during the ten-day truce period, to occupy and hold vital passes and the high ground. These met some scattered resistance, but managed to establish a sizeable presence. One such team, ordered to take a key town that sprawled on a hill overlooking the junction of major roads, was led by Colonel Weiz.

Weiz had been terrified getting to this point, and had only allowed himself the luxury of relaxing a bit now that they had pushed into Anchor so far with no incidents. The place was, in fact, eerily deserted, the farms quiet except for the milling about of confused animals, the small towns ghostly and unnerving. He was also very well aware that his troops, all professionals, resented his appointment as their commander over their own junior officers and were just waiting for him to make a mistake. Although a colonel, he commanded only a captain's company; they weren't risking a really major operation.

They pulled up as they neared their objective, the town standing as quiet as the others, overlooking a crucial break in the mountains where two major rivers joined. Neither of the rivers were deep enough to be navigable, but alongside them were canals and a major roadway. An enemy holding this position for any length of time would cut the main road from the south gate to the industrially vital capital. Taken and held by determined defenders, they could deny vital reinforcements to the teams holding the important points in the capital until a major assault could be mounted to destroy the industry and deny the conquerors the spoils of their victory. Anchor Nantzee *looked* deserted, but there were almost two hundred thousand people unaccounted for, and a number of anti-New Eden outsiders as well. Each military detachment had a list with drawings of those outsiders, with orders to capture and hold if found.

Weiz halted the detail and motioned for his lieutenants to come forward. Although frightened and inexperienced, he was not ignorant of military tactics. "Too bad we don't have some artillery," he said, looking at the quiet scene. "I know we couldn't spare the time and trouble to haul it along, but a few guns on top of those bluffs would control everything."

One of the lieutenants nodded. "Yes, sir. But if I was the enemy, I'd do just what you said. We know there's a lot of militia stuff gone, including cannon and rocket launchers. They've had plenty of time to dig in and conceal, and it's their turf."

Weiz surveyed the quiet scene through binoculars. "So you think they're up there, huh?"

"Yes, sir. I'd bet on it. Let's just say that if they aren't we're not going to lose a man in this operation anywhere."

Weiz sighed. "Very well. Send squads forward to scout out the opposing hill positions there. We'll save the town for last, because if they're dug in there we'll need every man we have to get them out."

They camped and let the horses graze and checked their weapons and ammunition as they waited for the squads to report back. About forty minutes passed by when they heard some automatic rifle fire being exchanged in the vicinity of one of the three hills overlooking the crucial junction. They were immediately up and at the ready, but the small battle didn't last long and things settled down once more.

It took almost two hours for the first squad to report back. This one had gone to the second of the three hills and had heard but not seen the firefight. "They're there, all right," a grizzled sergeant told them. "Some force too, I'd say, and dug in solid. A number of machine gun positions—these three, here, here, and here on the map—and one, possibly more, rocket launchers concealed by this line of trees. I didn't see any cannon, but I wouldn't doubt that they're there. Not a big force, by the sound of 'em, but it looks like they got caves dug into them mountains."

Weiz nodded, growing increasingly nervous. He looked back and wondered if he had enough men for this. "Could we hit them with the ray projectors?"

The sergeant shook his head. "No, sir. Not from here, anyways. You'd have to be almost down at the river junction to do that, and I don't see how we'd get men and equipment down there without tipping our hand. We'll have to end around, get as close as we can on the other side, then go over the top. Pepper 'em with grenades and hard fire to force 'em back into their hidey-hole, then go down and blow it."

Weiz sighed. "How many men do you think you'd need?"

The sergeant and his lieutenant exchanged glances. "I'd like the whole company, sir," said the officer.

Weiz thought a moment. "Well, let's see what the others report when they get back. If we need everything, we ought to take the easiest first. We can assume they're in the town in force now, and probably dug in along the bottom there."

The remnants of the second squad took another hour to report. They had lost four of their seven men. The other ridge had a line of heavy artillery right on top, with a circle of dug-in emplacements a kilometer down surrounding and protecting the artillery. This was no easy task, either.

Weiz looked at them. "Suggestions?"

"I'd take the artillery post, sir," one of the lieutenants said. "It'll give us the high ground. From there we can set up the ray and use it against the rocket positions in support of our assault. Command two of the three and the town will be in a vise."

The colonel sighed. It was everything he had feared. "All right—draw up your plans and we'll go over them. If we can, I'd like to get us as much in position tonight as possible, so we can attack at first light. However, I want to send a man back for reinforcements—just in case."

Getting into position in unfamiliar terrain and in the dark was difficult, and thanks to the earlier firefight the enemy was expecting them. It was a fierce and bloody assault, mostly uphill. The first two attempts left twenty dead and another fourteen wounded—a third of his force, more or less, out of action. They had cleared three key machine gun emplacements and still outnumbered the defenders, but this simply freed the commander on top to fire his cannon down at point-blank range.

Still, they finally succeeded, on the fifth assault, when they at last got to the top of the hill and in hand-to-hand combat took the position. Weiz had not had to personally take part, but now, sitting atop the hill and counting his men, he was clearly worried. He'd lost one of his lieutenants, two of his best noncoms, and half his force killed or wounded badly enough that they were now useless. The surviving lieutenant, a veteran of Bakha who'd risen from the ranks and whose name was Taglia, was not as easily worried.

"We've taken the hill, sir, and command one of the three positions. Our ray will reach the other positions, making a downward assault much easier. I think we should go as soon as the men are rested enough to do it."

Weiz looked at those men and saw weary, bloodied soldiers in no real shape to proceed. "Look at them, Lieutenant. Do you think they could do this all over again? And how many would we be then? Twenty? We need everybody we have just to take that position, and that'll allow the ones below to take this one. No, let's do what damage we can with the ray and lick our wounds."

"Sir—if we don't take that second hill we can't hold this one any more than *they* could."

"I'll not argue, Lieutenant! We're staying put!"

They brought up the projector, a complex device that looked like a large fixed machine gun with shades and mirrors, and assembled it quickly. "We can't hope to kill 'em at this distance," the gunner warned. "All it'll do is knock 'em cold for a while."

Still, he ordered it powered up and they began spraying the opposite hill with a wide beam. After a few minutes they had to stop to allow the central element in the projector to cool. Ten minutes into the pause, they were raked by rocket fire from the hill they'd just sprayed. Several men were killed outright, and everyone else could only duck for cover.

The lieutenant crawled up to the cowering Weiz. "See? They just duck back in the cave and when we have to pause they come out and pound us! If we don't attack now they'll push us right out of here!''

The colonel felt frustrated, confused, and frightened. He was a clinical psychologist, a specialist in drug and conditioning research, who'd been recruited long ago by Coydt van Haas. As such, he had turned Anchor Logh into the kind of vision the early New Eden leaders had desired, and he'd been rewarded handsomely for it. He had been high enough, in fact, to protect his own daughters from his handiwork, then disguise that fact through Suzl's hypnotic conditioning powers. In fact, he'd had everything New Eden could offer except the top social ranking that could only come with a combat command. Now he'd gotten into it, but he had no way of getting out clean. Perhaps he hadn't deliberately been given the toughest job in the operation, but he had it all the same. Toughest, hell— impossible!

"We can't take this much longer!" he shouted over the rockets' roar. "I'm going to order a withdrawal! We simply need more men!"

"No, sir!" Taglia shouted back. "We can do it! All of us together! Take that position and the town's ours!"

"I gave you an order, Lieutenant! We are withdrawing—now!"

A number of the other men crept closer and listened intently to the exchange.

"Sir, I will not insult the men who've died by withdrawing when I know we can succeed! We're going to take that hill, with or without your permission!"

"I gave you a direct order, Lieutenant! This is mutiny!"

"No, sir, this is cowardice in the face of the enemy! I am assuming command! Huddle here, come with us, or go anywhere you want. You are relieved!" He looked over at the techs. "Get that damned thing turned back on and give that hill all you've got for as long as you can! We're going to work our way around. I'm leaving five men here to fire off some random artillery shots. When we're in position

I'll fire a flare and you give 'em everything you've got, even if you burn that bastard up! You hear?''

The techs grinned and reached up and turned on the ray. In a few moments, the firing, except for some random small arms fire from below, stopped. They got up and picked up their weapons. Taglia looked down at Weiz. ''Are you coming, or not?''

''You're all committing suicide!'' he screamed.

They left him there on the mountain, still screaming orders that no one would obey.

Taglia lost twenty-two more men, but he took the hill in under four hours.

The last of Mervyn's spies had reported in, and he knew what he had to know. Now he rode a tired horse almost to death, racing along the road to the capital. It was early afternoon on the ninth day, and time was running out. By nightfall, a victorious army would march through both gates, and secure the walls of Anchor.

He knew he had stayed too long, and he'd had more than one gunfight to get out of tight situations. He had been a victim of overconfidence, the bane of all powerful wizards and the death of many great ones. He had thought from the first that, in a pinch, he could simply get over the wall and return to Flux that way, but now he'd found that impossible. A Flux wall had been created in a devilishly clever way, to maximize efficiency. The consistency of Flux around Anchor had been changed, so that he had no power in it and moved through it like a swimmer in a mass of mud. He had no idea how far the barrier extended, but there were constant patrols and Flux monitoring would be easy with those machines. He couldn't afford to find out.

Black-uniformed patrols had chased him, and he was exhausted by the effort of the last few days and the chase itself. Although he took on the appearance of a very old man, he was in truth biologically strong and as healthy as many of the twenty-year-olds who chased him, but he was not used to this sort of thing. He knew, though, that his worst fears had been realized. Now he was out of ammunition and on a very tired animal, but he was closing in on the outskirts of the capital itself. There was a small patrol chasing him, barely visible behind him now, but he knew he could outrun them without trouble.

Suddenly his horse shuddered and keeled over, throwing him from his saddle. He was flying through the air before he knew what happened, and then he hit the ground with a hard and painful crash. He tried to recover and run as quickly as possible, but no amount of adrenaline would enable his right leg to carry him. It was certainly broken, perhaps in more than one place, and the pain was tremendous.

He crawled as best he could to the shelter of some bushes and waited. The patrol was soon in view and closing on the body of his horse, lying in the middle of the road.

The five-man patrol drew up beside the animal, then fanned out. It took only a minute for them to find him.

The corporal leading the patrol took a clipboard from his saddlebag and flipped quickly through the pages. He stopped, nodded, and came over to the fallen wizard. "You are Mervyn the wizard?"

"What use is there denying it?" he managed. "My leg is badly broken."

"I have no painkillers or medical supplies. You'll have to ride in on one of our horses to the city, where there's a field hospital set up."

He nodded, but cried out in terrible pain as strong hands lifted him and put him atop a horse. It was the most horrible pain he could remember, but he knew he would survive it.

Survive it, but in the hands of the enemy.

He entered the city, and even through his pain he found it ironic that they had set up their small medical facility in a clinic just across the square from the temple. *So near and yet so far*, he thought sourly. Although they set his leg and poured a temporary cast for it, he knew that there was no way he could make it across that way on his own. It was ironic, since there really was no strong force surrounding the temple at this point—they were too busy holding the important areas. The only thing he managed to do was take advantage of their painkillers to get a little sleep.

The next morning was the tenth day. Around midday, he had a visitor, one whom he recognized despite the shiny black uniform and boots with the insignia designating the man a major in the New Eden army.

"So, Zelligman, you've found the easy way out, I see? You look rather—undistinguished—without the goatee."

Zelligman Ivan knelt down and kept his voice low. "A handy disguise. A major is too low to be questioned but high enough to get through the lines. But, in the end, old friend, I'm in almost the same fix as you. They are quite well organized, and freedom of movement is increasingly limited. I am on their list as you are, and I suspect I will not bluff my way out a gate come this evening."

Mervyn had to chuckle, although it hurt. "So at least everything is balanced. One of the Seven dies by firing squad next to one of the Nine."

"Not necessarily. This place is lightly staffed now and rank-conscious. Do you think you could stand on that cast?"

"Stand, perhaps, but not walk."

"Crutches, then. You've already used them to relieve yourself today."

"I'll manage."

"Very well. In the latrine there I have placed a straight razor and shears. Go in, while I divert others, then make yourself unrecognizable by getting rid of that hair. I will bluff you out of here. There are only a few people, mostly medical personnel."

"Yes? And then what?"

"We will go together to the temple by the back way

which I know is open but guarded by your people. I rescue you, you rescue me, and we go our own ways after."

Mervyn had to grin. "Done! At least if we're shot this way it'll save a lot of embarrassment!" He hesitated a moment. "This is no trick, is it?"

"I swear to you that it is not. Believe me, if I had another way even this certain I would leave you here to be shot. Nothing personal, you understand."

It was crazy enough to work.

The latrine was easy to reach, and the scissors worked wonders on his beard and long hair. It was messy, but it would do. Shaving with the big straight razor and just water was painful, but not as painful as the leg—or bullets flying into his midsection. When he was through, he looked disapprovingly at a face that resembled a funeral director's with a bad haircut—and looked nothing like his own. The leg he could not disguise, but they were on the ground floor. Overconfidence worked both ways.

Ivan, despite some disparaging comments about his old foe's appearance, was as smooth as ever, pulling rank and introducing Mervyn as "Colonel Damion, the commander of the glider assault force." The real Colonel Damion was, in fact, still back in Flux someplace, but his name was known more than his face to these young soldiers, and Mervyn played his own part, griping about breaking his leg in his own gadget.

Once around the corner and into the back alley, though, things became trickier. Ivan had a small two-seater pony cart there, and Mervyn managed very painfully to get in. They rode slowly and tensely down the alley towards the alley entrance to the temple, an entrance few really knew about but one common, in one form or another, to all the temples. Ivan, of course, would know the secrets of all the temples inside and out.

They were, in fact, almost to the entrance, a pair of hinged doors in back of a former grocery shop, when they were challenged by two black-clad soldiers. Ivan greeted them warmly, then shot both of them quickly with a mean-looking handgun. He fired again, this time at the lock on the hinged doors, and it shattered. He pulled up the doors and helped Mervyn through and down the stairs as the sound of running feet came behind them. He closed the doors and found a light switch. Turning it on revealed a very ordinary-looking cellar. "Quickly! How do we get in?"

"We don't. Unless somebody is watching us and knows that I'm really Mervyn, we're sunk."

One of the hinged doors was suddenly pulled open, and an object dropped in. Ivan lunged for it and tossed it back, showing extreme speed and precision.

Two more came down, and he wasn't quick enough. Both burst into foul-smelling gas and smoke, obscuring everything.

"You in there!" a voice commanded. "Come out now or we'll toss in grenades next! You have ten seconds!"

Behind them, a wall moved slightly, and two female figures emerged. "Quickly! Get in! We'll settle who you are later!"

Mervyn, coughing and wheezing, was assisted to the small opening and through it, followed by Ivan and the two priestesses. The slab closed again, but there was much foulness from the gas still in the air.

Almost immediately they heard a powerful explosion that vibrated through the tunnel and dimmed and shook the lights for a moment. They hadn't been fooling back there.

"Now—who are you?" one of the priestesses asked suspiciously, studying both men in the enemy's garb.

"I am Mervyn. Her Holiness was expecting me, although probably not this way. This is a—fellow wizard— who saved me from the enemy. In spite of my shave and haircut, I can prove who I am to her, and I'll vouch for my friend. I know you can keep us under arms until it's proven, so let's go. They'll try blasting through that wall any moment now."

It took two interminable hours and much pain on Mervyn's part before they could reach the right people and he could prove his identity. He knew he'd refractured the leg, but it didn't matter. In Flux, he could even restore the beard.

He introduced Ivan as a Fluxlord from up north named Hadley, and it was sufficient. The High Priestess, though, was both relieved to see him and highly agitated.

"There are rumors that the hostages have been betrayed and transformed," she told them.

"I'm afraid it's true," Mervyn replied. "I have some information sources available to me and they have pretty much confirmed it."

"Hadley" nodded solemnly. "I, too, have confirmation of this. Who would have thought it possible? Over eight hundred thousand people transformed in a matter of days? An effective Fluxland covering thousands of square kilometers! It is staggering!"

"Yes, and without cost," Mervyn responded bitterly. "The fools just wouldn't listen! The worst part is, if we could undo it and give them a vote, a fighting death or that, the vast majority would vote to return to their New Eden state!"

"I fear so," the High Priestess sighed. "I fear for poor World. Why is the Goddess suddenly so cruel?"

"Perhaps," said Ivan slyly, "because you have been looking for Hell in the wrong places. Hell is not at the Hellgates. Hell is New Eden transforming World into its own dark vision."

She looked at the strange man and frowned, but did not reply.

"At any rate, I need to get passed through into Flux as quickly as possible," Mervyn told her. "I'm afraid I might have some internal bleeding and possibly infection. We must move, anyway. At nightfall their newly transformed population will stream through the gates led by top officers. They will drive the remaining defenders here like a moving wall, or pull their men back and set up progressive death rays near all opposition.''

''At least they will have some problems starting up again,'' the High Priestess noted. ''By what they did to the women they've closed off half the skilled work force.''

''The other half will train the new. Don't get your hopes up. We managed some minor damage to a number of installations, but nothing that can't be fixed in a few weeks or months,'' the old wizard told her. ''No, Tilghman's won and we've lost. Best cut and run while we can. Please—I am in terrible pain. Get me to Flux!''

A number of hefty temple wardens who'd fashioned a litter for him carried him down to the basement to where Flux fed Anchor. One spot, round and about three meters across, was the invisible connector, then one spot of Flux, the only point at which Flux intersected Anchor internally. It was from that area that power was drawn for the capital's and temple's needs.

It took only a minute for Mervyn to heal himself as he stood there, and appear again as he was, robes and all. Ivan tensed, knowing that, at this moment, Mervyn could sign his death warrant and it would be instantly carried out.

But Mervyn, as he had counted on, was not one to do such a thing, and reached out his hand. Together they traced the mental pattern that was etched somewhere on the old floor below them, and found themselves in a moment transported to the mouth of the Hellgate itself.

Zelligman Ivan looked around at the round tube-like tunnel which terminated at a great machine with a vast number of controls on it, and beyond that to the source of Flux itself, a swirling mass of pure energy.

''Don't get the urge to punch in the combination now,'' Mervyn said lightly. ''I have no wish to survive what we just did only to be instantly vaporized.''

Zelligman Ivan laughed. ''Don't worry! I have no desire for that either! Not now. But consider, my old foe—consider what we barely survived by luck and guts today. New

Eden is going to win. They will be so strong that nothing in the end will stop them. Tilghman will never civilize them. World will fall into a dark age from which it may never emerge. The animals are overrunning the light, Mervyn! Sooner or later the few of us who are left with our own minds may turn those seven locks in desperation alone, aided and abetted by all that is sane.''

Mervyn sighed. ''I pray you are wrong, but at least things have now forced themselves into clearcut positions. I prefer to always deal with the devil I know; you are so repulsed by that devil that you prefer the devil you do not know and possibly cannot comprehend. I may fail, but I would rather fight something I can at least comprehend than something I may be powerless against.''

''Well, perhaps. But you created the system that created these men, and then you disrupted that system and taught them war, revolution, and empire. Now you reap your own havoc. Now you see the basic difference between us, and why we feel we are right. You have sown this horror, and yet you feel you can reverse it. You must understand that the difference between us is fundamental. The Nine are incurable optimists!''

Mervyn looked at the other wizard. ''You realize, of course, that after this we are even once more?''

''That, sir, goes without saying,'' replied Zelligman Ivan.

It took a bit over ten days to secure the Anchor, although there was scattered resistance going on for quite some time afterwards. It was still extremely easy to subdue, for it was simple to determine the ''loyal'' from the ''disloyal'' population by appearance and attitude alone.

Sorting out, classifying, and assigning the population their roles was far more complex, but it was something New Eden had had a good deal of practice doing, and they did it very efficiently. Turning the mighty industries back on would take far more time, but it could be done. New Eden had done what it had to do.

The bulk of the army, strengthened by a hundred thousand of Anchor Nantzee's men whom initial interviews had determined to be "nonessential," moved immediately south to Anchor Mareh. They hoped that word of what they had done to the Nantzee population had not yet reached the lone remaining independent in the cluster, but knew it probably had, and that, in the end, it made no difference. Mareh was not an Anchor whose population had essential and irreplaceable skills. They would submit, or New Eden's forces would kill every human being they encountered. General Champion had a dislike for long campaigns.

Adam Tilghman remained behind, mostly because Cassie was due at any time. He was determined to get back to his own home as quickly as possible, but he wanted no chances, even in Flux. He killed the little time remaining by tending to routine duties, one of which proved a bit more than that.

He had presided over a thousand court-martials and civil trials, but this one was unusual in that he knew the defendant and had placed him in command. He felt personally betrayed, and somewhat humiliated, and was determined to handle this one forcefully himself.

The members of Colonel Weiz's command testified one by one to his hesitancy, incompetency, and cowardice under fire. The story was repeated again and again, and the facts were not in doubt.

Weiz, nervous and unhappy, told his own version. "In my judgment there was no purpose to wasting men on what seemed to be a futile mission. We had an effective fighting force in position numerically and materially too weak to accomplish our goals. I felt we were better as a mobile force, taking the pressure off anyone coming through until reinforcements arrived, rather than as a totally defeated force."

"But they took the position," Tilghman pointed out. "Took it and held it and used the two positions to control and neutralize the town until reinforcements arrived. Had they not done so, those reinforcements would have ridden into a massacre."

"Perhaps, but with all due respect, sir, that is hindsight. There is a certain amount of luck in combat, and that luck turned with the company, but I could not count on luck. Had their attack failed, the worst of all possible alternatives from a military standpoint would have occurred."

"Indeed?" said the prosecuting officer. "Colonel, we have testimony that you were under heavy and destructive fire and that you ordered a full retreat knowing that the enemy was not only in his fixed positions but below and all around you. Sheer numbers indicated you could not retreat in that manner, for there was really no place to retreat to. Your original battle was long enough to give that enemy plenty of time to block your escape. Your only alternatives were to stand where you were, which was untenable, carry out the attack anyway, which was done successfully, or surrender. I submit that testimony and your own statements show you to be a bright man and knowledgeable in military tactics and procedure. You were either too blinded by cowardice to realize this, or you were ordering a surrender without actually saying the words. The facts allow for no other alternative. I must ultimately point out to the court that, when command was assumed by Lieutenant Taglia and the operation proceeded, Colonel Weiz removed himself to a former enemy emplacement out of rocket range and remained there. He did not accept and lead the mission, nor remain with the support troops, woefully shorthanded, on the hilltop. I believe the case is proven."

The Judge, a colonel, and a major who made up the Board did not even have to retire to reach a unanimous verdict. When the terrible word "Guilty" was pronounced, Weiz seemed to sag and shrivel.

"Colonel Weiz," Tilghman said solemnly, "do you have anything to say to this court before sentence is passed?"

"Sir, I will *never* believe that I was a coward! But, as you have judged me, I plead for mercy. I have served New Eden long and well from the beginning. Its very system I made possible. I have a wife with child, and six out of ten children still at home. The most I will admit to is that I was not qualified for command, but I do not believe that is a mortal sin. I beg the court's mercy."

Tilghman sat back and sighed. Finally he said, "This court agrees that death is not appropriate in this case, but it rarely is in cases of cowardice. We are not unmindful of your long service, but we are also not unmindful that you played every political trick known to gain this command, and you accepted it when offered. A man who will be directly responsible for the lives of other men does not have the luxury of taking on the task without accepting the responsibilities. Yours was a key action, and a great many lives could have been lost had you had your way. The fact that you have induced, at the Brotherhood's behest, a program of conditioning and drug control is irrelevant to this discussion, except that it raises the question of by what moral authority do you alter others' lives when you are unwilling to risk your own?

"No, Colonel, it won't do. Certainly a man who distinguishes himself repeatedly by his courage is entitled to wave his record before the court for one instance of failure. We're human, and our laws recognize this. But you have no such record, except getting rich and fat on the blood and sacrifice of others; and the one time you were called upon to repay that debt you refused. However, as a personal favor to you in recognition for whatever length of service you've provided, this record will remained sealed. You will be listed and reported as killed in action in the line of duty, and will receive a medal for valor. I will personally see to the welfare of your wife and family, and guarantee it. But the sentence of this court must be the one proscribed under these conditions, and it is singularly appropriate in your case."

Weiz jumped up and shouted "No!" but was restrained by the marshalls.

Tilghman made a gesture, then whispered to the two other judges for a moment and received nods. A young man in wizard's robes stepped forward.

"Does the defendant possess Flux power?" Tilghman asked for the record, knowing the reply.

"Negligible, your honor," the wizard replied. "With training he might develop as a minor false wizard, but no more."

"Very well. Colonel Weiz, it is the judgment of this court that you have shown yourself lacking in those qualities which we deem 'manly' and 'masculine.' It is one of the duties of a man to fight bravely in the service of his land. We therefore empower this wizard in the court's employ to render you as you have shown your inner nature to be."

Weiz struggled to free himself, but the wizard was already at work, the spell prepared beforehand and used more than once in this campaign. Weiz was enveloped in an eerie glow, which froze him and then began to quickly change him. In a matter of moments his physical form had been changed, and now the one who stood there was not a man at all, but a Fluxgirl—and quite a different sort. Only art, not nature, could create such a voluptuous, sexually-exaggerated form. Of course, that was not the end of it.

"The second spell removes your volition," Tilghman told him. "You will be subject to the extremes of animal urges, insatiable but totally obedient. You shall be barren, and the property of First Company, Twentieth Calvary. Your name shall be 'Whore' and you shall forever be the total and obedient slave of the Company and any of its members. You will be unable to act or speak in any other way but in this nature, and you shall crave their bondage. But, unlike the others, you will *know* and you will *remember*."

As Tilghman said, an appropriate punishment indeed, and

one that he didn't feel very bad in rendering. Conditioning was one thing, but he had never liked the easy tool the drugs had been for the Champions of New Eden.

That evening, Cassie gave birth to identical twin girls. That last was a shock to him, for somehow he had never considered the idea that his first child might not be a son, and now—*two* daughters! Perhaps, he thought, reforms are due earlier than I had intended.

Cassie was very happy. Unlike Spirit's, the delivery had been quick and efficient and only mildly painful. So well prepared was her body for it that it seemed simply a wonderful thing, and required very little aid from the doctor. Within two hours she was up and around and feeling just *wonderful*. She had already tried breast feeding, and discovered that her swollen breasts had enlarged to accommodate the twins just fine. She seemed to have an ample supply of milk, at any rate.

Adam Tilghman sat beside her, and hugged her, but she could tell he was either hesitant or slightly depressed. "You seem less than joyous, my husband. Is it because they are girls?"

"No, not really. I think it just may be a sign to me of things that have to be done. I'm happy for you, for them, for us. No, I'm just trying to think of a way to break some bad news."

She looked suddenly concerned. "What? I had heard things went well."

"Oh, they did—but there were casualties." He took a deep breath. "I'm afraid your friend Suzl's husband is one of them. He won't be coming back."

She felt shock, but mostly sorrow for Suzl. "This will hit her hard, and the children, too."

He nodded. "That's what I've been thinking about. It's partly my fault he went out there, and I feel a little guilty. I've been trying to think of what I can do to help, and I've come up with a possibility, although I won't do it without your approval as well."

She frowned. "What do you need *my* consent for, my love?"

"What if I were to—marry Suzl as well? It would put you two together, and would give the kids the best care and attention."

She was delighted. "Oh, Adam, that is the most kind and generous thing I could think of! Of *course* I approve! Oh, you'll love her!"

"I was hoping you'd say that. I don't want it to be—awkward."

"Oh, no! She'll be devastated, of course, for a while, but she'll come around. She was always strong."

"I know that very well. All right, then. The doctor says we can head home tomorrow, and I think we should. No stops. Uh—have you thought of names for the girls yet? As girls, the mother by tradition names them."

She nodded. "I know. I wished to keep their names somewhat similar, and I have been trying to think of two that sound nice and aren't overused in our circle. I stare at them and I think how *sweet* and *delicate* they seem, and two names came to me—Candy and Crystal. Sweet and delicate."

"I like it. So be it, then. We'll register them as soon as we return." He paused for a moment. "We'll tell Suzl together."

She nodded. "I'd like that. Adam—sit close to me. Put your arm around me, please."

He did so, and said softly, "I know this has been hard on you. The trip, I mean. I know you've been crying and keeping it from me."

She nodded and sighed. "I—I just can't help it. I thought I was ready and could handle this, but I can't. The questions about my past all the time, the soldiers, the war, deaths and dying, meeting Mervyn—it brought it all back. I've done enough, Adam. I can't handle that sort of thing anymore."

He looked at her. "What do you want, Cassie?" he asked gently.

"I want to forget. I want to be your wife, a good wife, and a good mother to my children. I don't want to know about wars and politics, and I don't want to spend the rest of my life defending or attacking what I was before. I want a family and a future, not a past. I want love, and security. Every time I was asked about my past on this trip I wanted to deny it, and *mean* it. No, I'm not the same Cassie. That was somebody else who died years ago."

He sighed. "Poor Cassie! I've been selfish in the extreme, I think. I shouldn't have put you through this no matter what. I wish I *could* exorcise those demons within you."

"There *is* a way, perhaps the only way to permanent peace for me, but it's rather final in itself. There's an old spell the Fluxlords use when they get new people to fit into their lands. An adjustment spell, they call it. It's somewhat like being hypnotized, but it really does what it says, and not just make it seem so like Suzl's relatively crude power. I *used* to know it—before."

"I'm familiar with it," he told her. "Just what would you have it do?"

"Build me a false past to replace my real one. In my case, it would be a memory of being born and raised in New Eden, and taking everything for granted. I would still be as I am now, but it would replace those memories with a logical past that would make me this. All of my past would be erased, beyond recall. I was often tempted these past years to do it to myself, but I could never feel that it was the right time or situation. Now I do. I know that it will harm your politics, and if you refuse permission I will forget the idea, but the only time I've been happy, really happy, in a very long time were those few months under Suzl's power."

He thought it over. "Is it what you *truly* want? You're really sure?"

She nodded. "I am certain. Suzl said it best, back at the farm. I am what I am, and I'll never be any different. That's all right—I like myself more now than I ever have before. But I saw it in Suzl, too. The agony, the memories, the hopeless struggle inside. She coped with an add-on spell, but deep down there's a sickness in her that's kept her from happiness. I think she's craved what I'm asking for years, but she never had a way to do it.''

He felt her pain and understood her problem. For others it was not so much to bear, but she had shouldered a load far too heavy for anyone to bear and stay completely sane. ''If that's what you truly wish, it can be done. And for Suzl as well.''

Tears came to her eyes. ''You would do this for us?'' She knew how he hated magic, and even when he used it it was always through others.

''I would. Any time you wish. I really do love you, Cassie.'' He kissed her gently.

She thought a moment, deeply touched. ''Do it now, Adam. Let it start here.''

''You're sure?''

She nodded. ''Now I am.''

He placed a hand on either side of her head and turned her face to his. ''All right, then. Here it is. All you have to do is let it in and take it. If you don't, that's all right, too.''

It was a probability spell, as they were called. The formula basically postulated an existing end product and then created what was necessary to reach it by moving backwards along the probability path the wizard selected. He himself had no idea from where the new past would come or its details—although he could establish certain basic elements that had to be present in it—but she would still be as smart and loving and supportive as now. It was, in fact, one of the most common spells on World.

So depressed was she that she simply let it flow into her and relaxed almost totally, so much so that he had to support her body.

Her name was Cassie; she had been born sixteen years ago to parents who ran a large farm just outside the capital of New Eden. Her father had later died in battle, her mother a year later in an accident. She had not been attractive as a child, but her father was influential enough to have her made into a Fluxgirl shortly after puberty, guaranteeing a good marriage. They were social equals of the ruling class and had known Judge Tilghman socially, so when her mother died he had shocked and delighted her by making her his wife. She knew it was partly out of pity and partly out of respect for her father, but she had grown to love and respect her husband and believed she had the best life possible to have.

The details were exacting. Memories of growing up, of playing games, neighborhood girlfriends and secrets—all of it. New Eden was the only culture she had ever known, and she had no concept of any other existence than that in New Eden. She did not know that World was round, or even that it was a world. She knew Adam had taken her with him on this trip because she looked like somebody famous who used to be important and because he wanted to be there when his kids were born. Flux and magic mystified and scared her, but she knew she was safe under Adam's protection.

She neither imagined nor desired any other life. Adam gave her love and protection, and provided all a girl could ever want. She'd never want for *nothin'*, and that was all any girl could really ask for.

10

TRANSITIONS AND LEGENDS

The rider was expected; even so, his arrival was the cause of great excitement and anticipation as he rode up to and through the gates of Mervyn's Fluxland of Pericles. Sondra, looking as striking as ever, accompanied him; Jeff, with Spirit, had preceded them using wizard's power.

Having little such power himself, the tall rider in black disdained using it even though, through Sondra, it was easily at his disposal. He was always a firm believer that use bred dependence upon it, and while most of World lived in respect and fear of Flux power he had only respect for it, as one would respect a potentially threatening fire or a loaded pistol. He was a survivor in a world where only those with the power were survivors.

In only one respect had he allowed his daughter, who possessed Flux power and was closest to him, to use her power to his advantage. His hair was thick but gray, as was his drooping moustache, and his face was worn and weathered by both age and experience, yet his internal health was as good as that of a man of twenty, and he could still take on youths less than half his age. He didn't like Flux power, but as a man well over seventy years of age in various lines of work where the life expectancy, even for wizards, was under forty, he was not a fanatic about it. He was, instead, the quintessential survivor.

Jeff watched him ride in, relaxed and confident, and immediately felt the man's power. He had heard stories about this man since he'd been a baby, and there were legends galore about him in every corner of World, and Jeff had always wondered if anyone could live up to that sort of reputation. One look at Matson, however, and he knew that there had been little exaggeration. It was a hard thing to put your finger on, but the tall, dark figure drew the attention of all around even without saying or doing a thing, and everyone who looked upon him felt a slight chill and sense of awe. This was the man who'd stalked and killed the most powerful wizard World had ever known and killed him in Flux. To see him was to hope that he was always on your side.

He pulled up to Jeff and dismounted. "So you're Spirit's boy," he said in a deep, authoritative voice. He put out his hand. "Glad to meet you, son. Go ahead—I don't bite my grandsons unless they bite me first."

Jeff trembled a bit but took the hand. The shake was hard and firm.

"Sorry we didn't get to meet before this," Matson continued. "It wasn't for lack of wantin'. It's just that I don't tend to go around like I used to, and a visit would've been kind of awkward."

Jeff warmed a little, although there was only so far you could go with this man. "I understood, sir. In fact, until Sondra showed up most folks thought you were dead."

"Still do. I like it better that way. I'm not immortal, son. There's a ton of little cowards waiting to backshoot me at the first opportunity just to make themselves a footnote. I hear you got more of me in you than is good for your health. Sondra tells me you're gunning for both

Zelligman Ivan and Adam Tilghman. That's a tall order, son.''

"If there's one thing I've learned from you, it's that nothing's impossible if you're smart enough and patient enough to wait for the right time and place. I'll get them, sooner or later. You understand why.''

The big man nodded. "Yeah, I do, son. It's true that if you're willing to wait for the time and place it'll come to you, but you better be sure of yourself and sure you can take your mark before you do it. You're too young to get your fool head blown off.''

"I almost had Ivan in Anchor up north a couple years back," Jeff told him. "I was *this* close, but I finally couldn't take him out without taking out a bunch of innocent folks, too. I'll get him, though. Tilghman, now—he only comes out from his Anchor when he's surrounded by both amplifiers and an army, but he'll slip, sooner or later.''

"Maybe. You watch out for Tilghman, boy. He's smarter than any of them others, even Ivan, and don't count on him in Flux. He's a little nuts, but he's one world-class wizard if he has to be and the kind of man who, if he knows he's going, will make sure you go with him.''

Jeff's eyebrows rose in surprise. "You *know* him?''

"Knew him, long time ago. I doubt if he remembers, but we'll see." He sighed. "I guess I'd better track down Spirit and say my hellos, then get down to business. Then I got to sit down with the old man for a spell.''

Jeff told him where Spirit might be found, and Matson went off, leaving Sondra behind with Jeff. She dismounted and let her horse graze for a bit.

"So," she said, "what do you think of the great man?''

"I'm impressed.''

"You *do* look a lot like him, or like him when he was younger. I can see it in you, and I think he could, too. He likes you.''

"Well, I'm glad to hear that. I wouldn't have guessed from his manner."

"Oh, that's as nice as he ever gets. You don't want to see him when he's in a bad mood. Still, I think he's having the time of his life getting back out and into action again."

"Your mom didn't object?"

"Mom and he split years ago. I don't think they were ever really in love. They just got married when both needed somebody and stayed together just for us until my brother and I were grown."

"Sondra—what's this business about? I mean, it's been all this time and nothing, and suddenly, now, here he is."

"I don't think I can tell you that right now, Jeff. It's the Guild that asked him, and he's operating as their representative. Still, he's seen Spirit off and on with me the past few years and I think he's always felt a little guilty about not seeing you. He's just never been all that good one on one with other people, and unless it's something like this he'll never make the first move."

"Well, I can understand him staying away from Grandma, but it's been more than eight years since she got swallowed up in New Eden."

"He's been busy lately with the Guild, training new stringers and holding down some important Guild posts. That's the way it is in the Guild—anybody who lives through all he has gets the power and the position. He's the only false wizard to make it this far in anybody's memory." There was more than a little pride in her voice.

They paused for a moment, and then Sondra asked, "What do you think of your mother?"

"Huh? Oh, yeah, I know what you mean. I'm getting used to it now, but I wish I understood it better."

"I wish any of us understood it at all."

What they both referred to was the change in Spirit the past few years. She had the most restrictive spells in the history of World upon her, and even Jeff tended to think of her as a wild thing, a child of nature not truly human. No speech, no understanding, no use of clothing, tools, buildings, or other artifacts—just her, wearing her emotions and nothing else and taking a tender if childlike delight in things. She'd been that way for his whole growing up, but eight years ago, during the turbulent time when her world had come apart, she'd changed. It was not that she could do or use anything more, but it was more in the way she moved, the way she looked at things, and the way she reacted to those around her.

One could almost swear, for example, that Spirit was totally aware of what was going on around her and perfectly understood everything and everyone with whom she came in contact. She examined everything in the most minute detail, including things that the spell prevented her from ever comprehending, and you swore that she could almost peer inside a person's soul and know its innermost thoughts and feelings. There was something in her eyes and her manner that was at once reassuring and alien, unknown and unknowable.

The truth was, Jeff had gotten used to that by now, but could never really get used to his mother becoming rather heavily sexually active again. Intellectually he knew that it was perhaps the only pleasure she could really have in common with the rest of the human race, but it's pretty tough to think of your mother doing that, and with total strangers both male and female. He was too embarrassed to raise the subject, though, particularly when he already knew the response—but she wasn't anyone else's mother, after all.

It had been more than eight years since New Eden had taken Nantzee and failed at Mareh, and many things had changed other than just Spirit.

Jeff had studied long and hard with Mervyn and with others of great power, and was a formidable wizard. He was the kid just hanging around only when with Sondra or

Mervyn; otherwise, he was a strong and powerful figure who was getting a measure of fear and respect in his own right. He traveled widely throughout World, and was as good with a gun as he was with a complex spell. He still tended to be far too emotional in crisis situations for his own good, but he could be cold and deliberate as well. Still, while he was known as an adept of Mervyn's, he kept his lineage concealed from others and his objectives as well. Ivan, for example, knew of him of course, but thought of him as one of Mervyn's employees detailed to keep track of the current leader of the Seven. The wizard had no idea that Jeff tracked him for his own purposes, and to a more dangerous end.

Sondra had retired from riding the string, and hadn't been seen much in the past couple of years. There was word that she'd had a child of her own and was working in the mysterious place where stringers trained and raised their children and coordinated the commerce of World, but she was closed-mouthed about it and Jeff knew better than to ask. And now, suddenly, both she and Matson had come out of hiding on some mysterious business. Jeff didn't know what it was, although he was dying of curiosity, but he knew that this wasn't just a family gathering and social call. Certainly it had something to do with the fall of Mareh just two months before, not by outside attack but by a clever and nasty New Eden-inspired revolution from within backed by black-clad troops. With total surprise and treason from within on very high levels, the Anchor that had fought New Eden to a draw eight years ago was now in its enemy's hands, and even now the population was being systematically rounded up and "processed" in Flux as Nantzee's had been. New Eden now held an entire cluster of four Anchors around a Hellgate and essentially controlled the Flux in between as well.

Although now surrounded by his enemy, Mervyn had been preoccupied for years with the location of Toby Haller's journal, convinced somehow that it existed. With

New Eden's threat waning after the initial defeat at Mareh, and with the Seven going their separate ways and involving themselves in individual mischief rather than collective action towards their ultimate goal, the threat that had seemed so imminent eight years earlier now was long forgotten. Mareh's fall now might awaken it, but it would take more than that action to create a feeling of crisis on the rest of the planet.

Jeff hadn't seen Mervyn much since Mareh's fall, and hadn't wanted to. That development had totally depressed the old wizard, and he was something of a holy horror. He hoped that Matson would at least cheer him up.

Matson had been warned of Mervyn's mental state, but found the old wizard as cordial and active as always, which was something of a relief. He took the offered plush padded chair and took a swig of excellent beer. Knowing that the old man didn't mind, he took out a cigar and lit it and looked very much the Matson of old.

"I'll come directly to the point," the legendary stringer began after the niceties were done with. "The Guild has recently uncovered something that is of equal concern to it and to the Nine. They've asked me to go and investigate it, and I've already done so, and there's real reason for concern."

"I knew it would take something disastrous to bring you out in the open again. Go ahead. When the sky has fallen on your head and you've been knocked helpless and senseless by it there's no room for anything but more bad news."

"New Eden has a way of communicating through Flux."

Mervyn's heart seemed to stop for a moment, and he knew instantly that he'd been wrong. The moment you truly believe things can't get any worse there is a fickle law of chance that says it must. "Communicating? Through Flux?"

Matson nodded. "I know they can do it. I've spent the

last two weeks monitoring their calls. It's a fairly crude system using an on-off binary code, and they can only send one message at a time through a given string, but it's real enough. The theory's always been known to the Guild, and we've kept it a tight secret. We never were able to use it ourselves, first because we didn't have the amplifiers needed to make it practical and second because even a limited use would show to everybody that it was possible.''

"You have crystallized all of my nightmares in one comment. You say you knew this was possible all along?''

He nodded again. "You must know that the Guild grew out of an ancient military order. We have most of the ancient manuals and the like from those days, and we've always kept ourselves as a military group. Right now I'm a full colonel, for example, although we never use those ranks outside our own.''

Mervyn knew the military organization and structure well, but he had no idea that so much of the ancient writings had also survived.

"This knowledge is only known to field grade officers and above,'' the stringer told him. "I didn't know it until just a few years ago myself, although I always wondered why it wasn't possible. After all, a string's only energy in a fixed form. If you can send signals over wires in Anchor like they discovered during the Empire's time, there's no real reason you can't use the strings for that as well. The only reason I figure it took 'em so long to figure this out for themselves was that we had all the books on the subject and they had more immediate things to think about. They got it now, though. They're using a relay network of their own strings off the beaten paths, but they're in constant two-way communication with Bakha and Nantzee and probably Mareh too by now. They had to rig their own to keep it secret from the stringers on the main routes, but one of our people got off the beaten track on a tip from a Fluxlord and found it anyway.''

Mervyn was silent for a moment, although his mind

seemed totally incapacitated for a brief period. Finally he said, "You realize what this means? If the Seven can learn how to do it, and they will, it's touch-and-go if we could stop them from opening the Hellgates."

"Yeah. Well, don't think we haven't thought of that. Luckily it's not that simple. You need a *lot* of amplifiers to link up the whole of World in even the most basic communications net. They need twenty just to establish and maintain the network they currently have for this cluster, so you can see what it would take to connect all seven Gates."

"The operative thing is that it can be done," the wizard noted. "What can be done eventually will be. What is primitive now will become sophisticated fast. It's been that way since we opened the magic box of ancient writings and began to compile and study them."

"Well, it's possible to run thousands of messages—even voice messages—over the strings at the same time, I'll tell you that much. But in all those years they've never built a bigger and better amplifier, and the signals you send tend to fade out as they go. They have to be received by another amplifier and returned to full strength and then transmitted again down the line. Of course, it's done at the speed of light, but so long as they can't get more power they can't use fewer amplifiers than they do now. My best guess is they don't know how those amplifiers work any more than you or I do. They don't understand half of what they're using now. They just find the instructions, build 'em, and use 'em. The machines they use aren't any different than the ones Coydt used almost thirty years ago. If they don't understand how they work, they can't build 'em better."

Mervyn sighed. "I wish I could be optimistic even about that. If what you say is true, and remains true, it becomes something of an advantage for us. It reduces the problem to purely military terms—disrupt only one transmitter and you destroy their whole plan, and the locations of those transmitters would have to be known and tested.

Considering what Coydt alone was able to accomplish, and given the principles of it, they may find a way.''

"Well, I don't want to panic you, but there's always been communication through Flux, you know.''

"*What?*"

Matson shrugged. "It's like a web, sort of. Every single temple is in contact with every other temple through that top center spire of theirs, sending out a continuous signal. The four Anchors in a cluster intersect through the Gates, and there's an identical signal running from Gate to Gate through the whole thing. We've always known there's something funny about those temples. You know that.''

"Soul Riders,'' Mervyn mumbled.

"Huh? What?''

"Soul Riders. That's where they get their orders from. That temple network or grid. You know, a very long time ago, when you infiltrated Coydt's takeover of Anchor Logh, Suzl met up with the Guardian. The way she told it was too confusing to make any sense, but you remember, don't you?''

He nodded. "Sure. It actually turned Temple Square into Flux for a very short time to get us out of there. But that was the Guardian of the Gate.''

"I wonder. Do we really know just what the Guardian is? Or even if it's anything like what it calls itself? Suzl said that the power coming into the temples went not only to the power transformers but *down*, down into the ground below the temple. We tried and tried to repeat that sense she had, but to no avail, and, of course, she was no longer available for it. But what if she was right? What if the temple is only a building *over* what's really there? I've occasionally intercepted signals coming from some source to the Soul Rider within Spirit. I got an undefined sense of it, once or twice, as the sort of speech machines might use to talk to one another. I don't know why—it was far too fast and too complex for any human mind to more than sense. Still, I've always wondered. Under each temple, say, a machine. A great amplifier, as it were, setting up the rules for World, keeping Anchors stable. A great machine beyond our imagining that not only governs, it *thinks.*''

Matson chuckled. ''A thinking machine? Thinking like a man?''

''No, not like a man, I'd wager, but thinking all the same. You've seen Spirit?''

''Yeah.''

''You wouldn't notice as much of a change in her as I would. I'd almost swear, though, that she and the Soul Rider had somehow come together as one individual. You know—it all fits. If I were a big machine that thought, but was stuck far underground in one location, I'd have a way to find out what's going on beyond my own immediate area. The Soul Rider would be its eyes and ears.''

The stringer thought it over. ''Well, maybe, but if so why would Spirit still have that damned spell? Seems to me that any machine that smart could break it. Even Suzl managed to do it, if I recall.''

Mervyn sighed. ''That's true, but how would we know how a machine thought, or what its motives and purposes might be? Still, it's a fascinating idea.''

''And another thing—why would it use so few eyes and ears? I mean, the Soul Riders can only see and hear so much. Most of what's going on would pass 'em by.''

''One piece of the puzzle at a time,'' Mervyn told him. ''Every answer gives a hundred questions, but that's still a step forward. If I only had Toby Haller's journal, *that* might supply the missing pieces.''

''Sondra told me about that. We always put that down to a fairy tale.''

''So did I—but I know where a copy is now. It's exactly where I thought it was all along, but I could never be sure. I think I'd die happy if I could but read it.''

''Huh. So why haven't you gotten it by now?''

''Because it's in Adam Tilghman's personal library in

his house just off Temple Square in New Eden. That's pretty damned hard to break into, for one thing. Oh, I have agents in New Eden—lots of Fluxgirls there since the start whom I was able to cover with dual personalities—but they're all under a lot of restrictions and spells. None of 'em could read and tell which one it was, and it's not in printed form but contained in a module with a lot of other junk, probably not labeled as such but prominent enough to be missed. The fact that it's known and yet unattainable has come close to driving me mad for years now!''

Matson put out the stub of his cigar and scratched his chin a moment. ''You think it's that important?''

''I don't know, but I know it must have something. Tilghman captured the High Priestess of Mareh, you know. He knew he couldn't break her spells, but he brought her, stripped naked, back to New Eden just two weeks ago and displayed her in Temple Square. When they were through torturing and debasing her and realized they could never get her to recant, he had her brought to the house in chains and forced to read the journal. My associates and I use the Holy Mother Church, but we are not compelled to actually believe in it like she was. She was faced with truths she couldn't deny yet the spells would not allow her to accept. It drove her completely stark raving mad. She's a lunatic with no reason at all now, held like an animal in a cage on public display in their zoo.''

''So the legend of the thing is borne out. You *sure* you want to read this thing?''

''As I said, I don't have the problem she was confronted with. But even if it had the same result, I would gladly do it. It won't, though. Coydt read it, and he was just as insane before as after. Tilghman read it, and perhaps many others. If our enemies have read it, I think it is vital that we do as well. Now more than ever, with the real threat that this communication system presents. We're pretty sure there's something terrible beyond those Gates, but we don't know what. We *do* know that our ancestors were so frightened of whatever it was that they sealed them off and then systematically reduced human civilization to a state of ignorance of its own technology, even its origins, just to keep those seals secure. They did a very thorough job, but not thorough enough. We're now beginning to relearn vital parts of what was lost, destroyed, or suppressed. There is a very real danger of those Gates reopening, and we don't have the skill to suppress civilization again, even if we wished to. It becomes vital, then, that we know what we might be facing.''

"I know enough," Matson told him. "It could be nasty, but it sure isn't hopeless.''

Mervyn stared at him. "What could we do, in our primitive ignorance, that our ancestors with all their machines and technology could not?''

"Seems to me it's the old story of World and nothing more. Look at World. The stronger and more powerful a wizard is, the more he thinks he's some kind of god and the less he thinks or knows about things that aren't wizardly, you might say. When you can zap somebody with your little finger you never bother to learn how to shoot a rifle, or win a bareknuckle fight. They couldn't milk a cow, or grow a flower in Anchor. Nope, it's all magic, magic, magic—but what do you really know about your magic? Can you actually invent a spell, or do you just know the *procedure* to follow so that the spell flows into and out of your head? I don't mean the simple stuff, I mean like Pericles. Could you write down the formula for it on paper? Sure, you know how to command a flower to grow or appear, but do you really think about how that flower's made? All the biochemistry that goes into that flower? Do you understand it?''

"You know I don't.'' Mervyn replied. "No human mind is capable of such complexity.''

"So what you are, as a powerful wizard, is a guy who knows how to push just the right buttons—just like those guys in New Eden know how to read the manual on how to work their machines, and how to make 'em, but they don't really understand them. Same difference."

"But if you can *use* that power, what's the difference in practical terms?"

"A big one. Like I said, you get to be a wizard, you forget or never learn the practical stuff. I think it's the same with machines. In fact, I'm *sure* it is. You get born into a society that is completely run by machines. You take those machines for granted. You pick up some little communicator and you talk into it and the exact person you wanted to talk to picks up his and talks back. Neither of 'em know how it works. It's always been there, and if it breaks they get a new one. They don't even *think* of how it works. They take it for granted, just like wizards take their powers for granted. Now let's take those Gates. Whatever's been kept out, if it's still there and still alive after all these centuries, is from the same kind of machine culture as our ancestors. Otherwise, they wouldn't have made the Gates at all. They'd have used something else."

"I'll grant you a point for argument's sake. That's assuming they're keeping out somebody rather than something—a weapon, perhaps, or Flux flowing unrestrained or uncontrolled. It could be a natural calamity."

"Not likely. If it was something like that, you might seal 'em off, all right, but you wouldn't keep what's there a secret, and you sure wouldn't go to all this trouble to keep humanity down. You'd want *everybody* to know just what the disaster was. Up north in Anchor Jamzh they got a big lake. You ever see it?"

The wizard nodded. "Long ago, but I remember. It's quite impressive."

"I learned to swim in that thing. But it's not a natural thing, it's something left over. There's a real thick dam across the valley there made of the same stuff as the temples, although it's layered over with rock and dirt. Everybody knows what would happen if that dam ever broke. All that water would tumble out at once, instead of over the falls, and take out half the Anchor. Not even the craziest nut has ever thought about blowing up that dam. Looking after it is a sacred duty. Same thing with the Gates. If it was some kind of natural thing, they'd have dammed it up for sure, but they'd take pains to make sure that everybody knew what it was from the moment they got out of diapers. Uh uh. Instead we get demons from Hell. So I figure that's pretty much our way of looking at just what they were keeping out. The savages, the monsters, whatever were at the door and they knew they were outnumbered or outgunned or whatever. So they barred the doors, told us there were evil demons there, and took away all we knew to keep somebody from waving a white flag and surrendering or making a deal with the enemy.''

Mervyn was fascinated. "Go on."

''Well, let's assume that the enemy's still there. Hard to believe after a few thousand years, but who knows? Maybe nobody's home. Maybe they gave up and forgot us a long time ago. Maybe it was even us—some early New Eden revolution or something. With their machines and total control of Flux they could probably come up with a nightmare we couldn't even *have* now. But maybe they're so complete that they've been there for all these centuries and are just waiting for one of *their* machines on the other side to say the door's unlocked. Well, if it is, I'd say we probably have a better crack at them than our ancestors did.''

''Indeed?''

''They're gonna have to come through the Gates. We know where they're coming. They'll be real confident, more than any Fluxlord you've ever met. They'll *have* the power of gods, thanks to their machines. All their defenses, all their tactics, will be geared to fighting somebody just like them. They'll face millions of flies who can sting and bite and the only thing they'll have against those flies are twenty ton sledgehammers. Cannon don't do much good against a mass attack by cockroaches.''

"I wish I had your confidence. More, I wish I had that journal. It would tell me what I had to know! I'm sure of it!"

Matson sat back and lit another cigar. "I'll see what I can do."

Mervyn suddenly felt excited again. "You mean that? You're going there?"

"I have an audience with His Nibs the Judge himself. That's why they sent me. I'm the only man who's an outsider that they respect enough to talk with as an equal. The guy who killed Coydt van Haas and, of course, the guy who came up with the plan to let them live and keep their spoils of war. Give me the layout of the house, if you've got it, and anything else I'll need. Maybe I can't, but if the thing's as important as you say I might be able to manage it."

Mervyn felt real hope for the first time, but he managed to control himself as another thought came to him. "Uh— you know that Cassie and Suzl are his wives."

"Yeah. I know. I hear tell they don't remember anything about you or me or anything else, though."

"That's true. I suspect for their own sanity both took spells on themselves for transformation into what they appeared to be. The ones we knew have been erased. They think they were born and raised in that culture and for all intents and purposes they might as well have been. It's sad."

Matson shrugged. "Well, yeah, it's a waste, but I got to thinking on it and, you know, under the same circumstances I might've done the same thing. They were stuck in their own way the same as Spirit's stuck in hers. Don't worry about me—I can handle it. If she don't remember, it'll be easier. I've had to live with the sight of her face when I walked out on her thirty years ago."

The Central Committee of New Eden did not meet very often of late, and only when planning major moves or finding ways out of deep trouble. The Committee consisted of the nine Judges, the original leaders of the takeover of Anchor Logh and the administrators of its system, Champion representing the military staff, and Onregon Sligh representing Research and Development. Clearly the balance had been intended to keep both science and the military subordinate to the central government.

It met now in a period of near absolute triumph, not to consider what had to be done to make it complete—for that had long been determined—but to chart the next steps. Adam Tilghman, as Chief Judge and Chairman, presided, although it was he who'd called the meeting.

"Gentlemen," he began, "I think it is time we considered again the final aims of this movement. We are a conquering army and victors with spoils, but in that we're no better than the Empire that preceded us and which we all abhorred. In spite of our high-sounding principles and moral platitudes, nothing really has changed, which is why the rest of the world is essentially keeping its distance from us rather than making a concerted all-out attack. They know what we are. We are Fluxlords—yes, we are, you and I, no matter how you deny it. Oh, we are lords of Anchor, but we are absolute in four Anchors—many times the size of the largest Fluxland—by our technology, and by that technology we hold or control the Flux between. We the leadership and those we hold dear are as powerful as any Fluxlord, and as immortal and unchanging. You have put me off for over eight years because of our failure to secure the cluster, but that is now done. It is time to decide what we are and what we wish to become."

"Is it necessary to do that?" Champion asked. "We have a system of beliefs and a culture that works. We are strong enough to defend it if we have to, and to spread it when we feel able to do so. The Chairman calls us Fluxlords, as if the term itself were not simply a product of the inherent imperfect nature of mankind. We are lords of

Flux and Anchor, and we are *right*. Why is that such a dirty thing?''

There was numerous nods of agreement among the others listening, but Tilghman was unimpressed.

''The general asks why it's a bad thing. I think I can explain it. I must, or from my standpoint this has all been for nothing. All of us—every one of us—came from Fluxlands. In point of fact, no matter how high our station in those Fluxlands, we were slaves. Some of us were slaves because our lords were simply too powerful for us to defy; others were enslaved by spells that made us satisfied to be slaves; but even the latter had the full force of hatred and contempt when taken from their Fluxlords and allowed perspective and alternatives with the spells removed. Beyond this, we have one more thing in common—all of our former Fluxlords were female.''

''This isn't going to be another plea to ease up on the girls, is it, Adam?'' Henri Rhoten, one of the younger Judges, interjected. ''I think we've gone as far as we like in that direction.''

''No, it's nothing in that direction, Henri,'' Tilghman responded, ''and I am deeply appreciative of the moves the Committee has made in the past few years.'' Girls, in fact, were no longer subject to mind-killing drugs; they were allowed to make and wear any clothes that complimented the female form and did not resemble men's clothing; and, thanks in part to the wars that made them outnumber men, they were allowed some basic employment—under male supervision, of course, and in mostly menial and ''girl's areas'' such as clothing, decorating, beauty, and children's things. There were a few other liberalizations, but this was partly due to a program of applying Flux conversions on all the females not previously converted. ''My only concern is our over-reliance on Flux even in that area. We are as dependent on it as any Fluxlord.''

''What's the point?'' growled Laroche impatiently.

''The point, gentlemen, is simply that after attaining

power we simply reversed what we had experienced and made that our sole objective no matter what we mouthed. In so doing, we said that our own past slavery was not wrong or evil, only to be reversed. We agreed with our former mistresses that might was the only thing that mattered, and that we had no moral objections to the system, that the only thing that was wrong was that we were on the bottom and they were on the top.''

''A generally unnatural position,'' Champion cracked. ''Again I ask, 'so what?' It is the way of things.''

''It is the way of things because we were raised to believe it was!'' Tilghman almost shouted. ''If we are nothing more than a bunch of petty Fluxlords then I have wasted much of my life here. The general wants another Empire. I want a revolution. I want a world where somebody draws a line and says it's wrong. I want to establish the concept of nation, of culture, as it is in the ancient writings. I want a *country*—that's the ancient term for it. A country in which people live and work according to a set of fixed laws, not somebody's unrestrained fantasies. A country that eliminates magic as its basis, so that the *best* may move to the top, not those with some inborn power. We have the means, do we not, Doctor Sligh? Haven't we, in fact, had the means for better than eight years?''

The big, dark man nodded. ''We do. Or, at least, we believe we do.''

''I tried to establish this quickly, when Nantzee was overrun, but was argued out of it by the doctor. Wait for Mareh, he said, and I agreed. But we took a very long time to take Mareh, and in the meantime my proposals were always shoved back by this Committee. I've heard all the reasons and rationalizations, but they really disguise the true problem. It's fear. Fear of reprisal from the other Anchors and Fluxlords, fear of whether or not our system can really stand without the crutch of Flux, fear, really, of the very concept of revolution itself. Well, we now can manufacture anything we need without a Fluxlord to duplicate it. We are far more vulnerable to a mass attack now than if we take my path. We know how to feed, clothe, house, and administer society in large groups. Now it all boils down to the basics—which shall we choose for our people's future? Mind—or magic? Empresses and goddesses with a sex change—or men with guts and vision?''

That stung them all, but eventually touched off a long and searing debate. Champion, the least visionary of the ruling group, was always the most opposed to any change, even the slight ones they had allowed. He had not come by his god-like looks and magnetic attraction naturally; he had been one of a host of ''pretty boys'' who were consorts to the Divine Empress, the male counterparts to the most glamorous Fluxgirls and possessing the same overendowments and insatiable appetites, who existed to service and carry out every whim of their Fluxlord. When the Divine Empress had refused to make an accommodation with the Empire, she had fallen, as had so many Fluxlords, and Coydt van Haas had been there to pick up the pieces most useful to him. Champion's long pent-up frustration and rage was ready made for the master wizard's plans, and that hatred translated into tremendous aggressiveness, a cold and callous ruthlessness that had matched Coydt's own, and a burning urge to get even with everyone female.

He was quite dangerous, although useful and politically naive. Much of the old officer corps had come from origins similar to his and he retained its loyalty. He was content to run the army while others ran the day-to-day affairs of New Eden, but he could be pushed just so far. In the end, however, even he had to concede that Tilghman's plans would make defense far easier in military terms, and many of the others agreed in the end that it would also make administration and government far easier and more efficient.

Sligh had never been one to really like the plan, but he tried to keep as politically neutral as possible, and after clinically and professionally explaining the plan he couched his own objections in scientific terms.

"We don't know what the ultimate effects are," he told them. "I expect some cooling, perhaps greater seasonal variances. From a climatological point of view, I can predict changes but not what changes, for so much depends on what comes out, as it were. It was intended to be part of a mosaic—a puzzle—and not a whole in and of itself. Its effect on the rest of World will be significant, but again there's no way to say just how. Certainly, while it will be irreversible here, it will not produce a chain reaction, although if all clusters were so treated it certainly would."

"But will you ever know for certain, speaking as a scientist, without doing it?" Tilghman asked him pointedly.

"No. The machinery and its instructional sets are far too complex for any human mind. They are the products of generations of evolutionary research under conditions we could not hope to match. These are machines and instructions and languages designed by machines which were also designed by machines—how far back I cannot say. We have the end product but not what designed and produced them."

"So you see, gentlemen—it's what we have, permanently and forever, or this last gamble on something dramatically different but something which will secure New Eden forever. I call for a vote." Tilghman sat back and breathed a sigh. He wouldn't have called the meeting if he hadn't thought he had the votes, but some of the questioners in the debate had sounded less firm than he'd thought and now he wasn't so certain.

The vote, however, was seven to three in his favor, with Sligh abstaining as usual. Champion was not happy, but this was not the time, place, or issue on which to stake his future.

"Very well," said Adam Tilghman, satisfied and a little

excited by this now that it was imminent. "Doctor, when can you be ready?"

Sligh shrugged. "I can set it up in a matter of weeks. That's no problem, if we have the people to trigger the machines, and I now believe we have men with sufficient power to do that among our own local ranks. It doesn't take much of the power, just enough to issue a single command to execute. We could, in fact, use just half the amplifiers we're now using in the communications net without moving them very far."

The Chief Judge nodded. "That's fine. I will ask the army to notify those Fluxlords who might give us some problems and give them time to vacate. We'll call it a potentially dangerous testing of a new system that could cause some temporary disruptions in Flux. We want none of them to believe it is permanent, however. General, we must be prepared to ruthlessly move on those who ignore us and remain. We want no hostile populations in our midst."

Champion nodded. "I don't think it'll be much of a problem." The best and most powerful Fluxlords had been vanquished in the days of the Empire in the southern cluster, and most of those who remained were small ones with relatively limited powers or populations. There were a few, including Pericles, not under their control, but these were not considered much of a threat. "I might ask Doctor Sligh, though, a question," the general added.

"Yes?"

"Would it be possible, considering the number of amplifiers out there now for the communications network, to program and create a grid ahead of your main wave that would impose the basic master spells we used on the populations of Nantzee and Mareh on those caught in the middle of all this?"

Sligh thought about it. "The answer is basically no, because we lack the power to cover such an area, and while we can increase the number of amplifiers, we are working with a finite and regulated amount of power. The losses we incur now are negligible, but measurable. To do what you suggest would dilute everything, and call the entire project into question.''

Tilghman, anxious to mollify Champion, thought about it. "But do we have to do it to tens of thousands of square kilometers of void in any event?" he asked them rhetorically. "We know the cluster. We know where the people are, where the Fluxlands are. None are so large as to require more than three amplifiers, most one or two. Timing is crucial, of course, but our communications system is functioning. If the attacks could be made a matter of seconds before the main project was engaged, or time-linked so that they traveled just a moment ahead of the main wave in each case, it would give us what we needed. The few thousand in the void would be minor irritants, easily expelled, captured, or integrated into the system afterwards.''

The scientist shrugged. "I haven't the faintest idea if it'll work in whole or in part, but I see nothing particularly against it if you wish it except that I'll need a few more weeks of preparation and a few more operators. The worst I can see happening is that we wind up with the same result we'd have by not trying it.''

"But if it does work," Champion said, "we'll convert our enemies on the spot and by the time the rest of the world reacts we will be the dominant force in it for all time.''

Matson was loading up his packs when Jeff and Sondra came over to him. He glanced up, but continued his work. Unlike a wizard, he had to take a certain amount of supplies with him on long journeys in Flux, although he could supplement by using the caches in stringer pockets.

"I understand you're going to New Eden," Jeff said casually.

The old stringer nodded. "That's about it. Got business there I can't avoid."

"I *still* don't like you going in there alone," Sondra told him. "There's no telling what they might do once they have you."

"Try and convert me, most likely, but nothin' more. They're just people like any others around this world. As long as I'm representing the Guild and not goin' in as an individual they'll behave themselves. They got to live on the same planet we do, and there's no percentages to pissing off the Guild. Still, if you're that worried, you can always come along."

"Sure. If I make myself into one of their Fluxgirls and act the proper slave."

"Or make yourself into a man. Wouldn't be the first time."

Jeff stared at Sondra. "You've changed into a man?"

She laughed. "Sure. Didn't you try it as a woman during your early lessons?"

"Well, we did the spells, sure, but just as an exercise."

"I did it for two whole years including riding string. You can never really understand men unless you live as one. You ought to try it the other way around. You guys don't know what you're missing."

"Don't embarrass him, daughter," Matson chided. "Any wizard who likes himself as he is has a point in his favor. You're still beggin' the question, though. Go or stay?"

"It really *doesn't* make any difference to you, does it?" she asked him, a little angry.

"A little time as one of those Fluxgirls might give you a whole new perspective on what the common folks' lives are like," he responded calmly. "Still, I'd spend half my time worrying about you and not get a full mind to the business at hand. The freer I am to move the safer I'll be. You know that."

She nodded, came to him, and kissed him. "I know.

But you take some of your own advice. Don't go believing your own legend.''

He stopped what he was doing, turned, and faced her, a dead serious look on his face. "Ain't nothin' in my legend that's not fact. I always expected to be bumped off sooner or later, but it won't be in New Eden. I understand them and they understand me. You just watch yourself here. They're up to something over there in New Eden. Lots of troops running around in Flux of late, or so I hear, and lots of warnings to Fluxlords to get out or get hurt when they test something big. They got word to Mervyn just this morning, which is why I think it's time I got along.''

Sondra looked over at Jeff. "You know about this?''

He nodded. "I got the original message. We've got two weeks to clear out temporarily or suffer the consequences, whatever they are. Mervyn thinks it's a test of some new kind of super amplifier.''

"Is Mervyn going?'' Sondra asked.

"He's taking the precaution of moving his most valuable records and research and most of his people to a temporary pocket outside the cluster, but that's all,'' Jeff replied. "I think he's more curious than afraid and wouldn't want to miss what they're trying.''

Matson nodded. "Still, a super amplifier would drain a lot of Flux energy. You've already seen what just one regular amplifier could do in the hands of a man who knew how to use it. Pericles might collapse like a house of cards and sweep the bunch of you with it.''

Jeff was unmoved. "Still, sir, I'd like to come with you.''

"To New Eden?''

"Yes. It's the first time I've had a way in.''

Matson shook his head from side to side. "No, son. Same thing applies to you as to her, and if you think you're a better shot or bareknuckle fighter than she is, forget it. Besides, all she wants is to keep an eye on the old man. I'd lose the whole show and any chance of success now or in the future if my associate made an attempt on Judge Tilghman's life. Uh, uh, son. Sorry. No, you, Mervyn, Sondra, and Spirit and that Soul Rider of hers should be strong enough together to get out in one piece. I'm not so sure if you break up and scatter.''

"What about you?" Jeff asked him. "What's *your* protection?"

"Me? I'm gonna be guest of honor in their own Anchor. I'm gonna be the safest outsider in the whole damned cluster.''

11

SOME COMMUNICATIONS DIFFICULTIES

It had been more than half his lifetime since Matson had ridden this particular string to this particular location, and almost that since he'd been in or near the place at all. It wasn't as easy as the old days even to get here; armed patrols backed by amplifiers checked every bit of all strings leading to or from this point, and he'd already had to pass several dozen checkpoints. As a stringer this offended him greatly; the void was a place without governments and rulers, where a man was free and independent and the only authority his quick mind and reflexes and maybe a good gun. The stringers had owned and controlled the void since the beginning, and finding it in the hands of others, even in this relatively small area, made him feel as if his house had been robbed.

Still, they had been expecting him, and hadn't impeded his progress. They had been, in fact, quite kind and helpful, and he hated their lousy guts for it.

There was a sudden brightening of the void just ahead, and in a few moments he rode through it as if through a curtain of fog and into a warm, bright day. The Anchor apron was another armed camp, this one bristling with well-disciplined troops, but he'd expected that. In their own land they could play at anything they wanted; they just shouldn't be in his.

The old stone wall still rose up in front of him and went off in both directions as far as the eye could see. Both men and machines manned the top of it for that distance and probably completely around the Anchor, and he knew that the trick that had taken them into Anchor wouldn't work twice. The old, thick Gate, with its ancient booby traps, was still there as well, but they had rigged it so that both great doors were open at the same time. He had no doubt that they had defenses that made the double doors unnecessary in this day and age.

He rode straight to the guard post at the Gate and pulled up, ignoring the others, reached into his saddlebag and pulled out a large envelope and handed it to one of the sentries. The soldier opened it, then gave him the once-over with his eyes. Finally he turned to another sentry and said, "This is the one they told us to expect. Notify Major Taglia." He handed the papers back to Matson, who put them back in his saddlebag. "Go on through and hold up on the other side," the sentry instructed him. "You'll be met in a couple of minutes."

Matson nodded, tapped his hat brim with his finger, and rode on through. Then he stopped, dismounted, lit a cigar, and settled back to wait for his escort.

Major Taglia proved to be a short, stocky man with bushy black hair and an olive complexion. Matson got up and shook hands as they exchanged introductions.

"Mr. Matson, it's an honor to meet you. They still drill your theory and tactics in school here."

"Didn't know I had those things," the stringer responded. "I wonder if I wrote the textbook?"

Taglia looked blank, and Matson rescued him.

"We've got a ways to go, if I remember rightly, Major,"

he said calmly. "You want me to just follow the road or do I get company?"

"I'll accompany you, sir," the major responded. "We're something of a closed society, as you may know, and it'll be a lot easier if you have someone in authority along."

Matson nodded. "Might as well get started, then. I assume it's still a good two-day trip to the big city."

Taglia seemed awed and uncomfortable with the old stringer, and it was easy to see his problem. On the one hand, Matson was something of a hero and legend in New Eden, the man who'd shown that you didn't need Flux power to survive or even triumph, and who had worked out the deal for New Eden's independence to save the lives of the population. Still, legends are awesome things, particularly when real life actually does measure up to the mental image, and Taglia was acutely aware that this man was both extremely dangerous and an outsider not likely to be too keen on the ways of the land he'd helped bring into being.

Taglia joined him on a sleek, black military horse, and the two set off down the broad highway to the capital. "You want my weapons, Major?" Matson asked him.

"No, that won't be necessary, sir. We're honored to have you visit, even in an official capacity. I mean, sir, well, uh, they taught us in school that you were dead."

"Son, I die every once in a while, but I always come back when things are important. What you mean about the weapons is that my popgun and my whip aren't much of a threat against your whole society no matter what I did. The real question is how you know I'm really Matson and not some Flux creature made up to look and sound like him?"

Taglia grinned. "You know the answer to that, sir. Your credentials are spell-encoded and were checked time and time again as you rode in."

They took it nice and easy, and it gave Matson a chance to get a feel for this land and its changes with the aid of a native guide. He was pleased to see that there were still trees and broad farms and that this new machine society hadn't paved it all over like they had the central part of the road, leaving only a dirt strip down each side for the horses. The central road as it was, though, provided a smooth ride for wagons and coaches.

Along the roadway spaced every forty meters or so were barren tall poles set deep in the ground, with crossbars at the tops carrying wires and containing funny-looking shaped things as well. Taglia explained that this was actual voice communication by wire, as well as steady electrical power gained not just from the old temple—he called it the Scientific Center—but from other sources as well, including wind and running water. Every once in a while, high up on a pole, there'd be a lineman checking or repairing the wires, perhaps with a whole support crew.

The economic pattern of New Eden soon became clear to him. The fact was, no matter what the ideal, women were required to do far more work than just that in the home. Their illiteracy and mathematical limitations limited the types of jobs they could perform, but there were far more women than men and a lot of necessary work had to get done. He saw large numbers of women in the fields planting or picking crops—he couldn't tell which—and grooming animals. Wherever their physical limitations did not interfere with their capabilities, women were working and working hard.

After the twentieth time they'd had to identify themselves, Matson had a whole new definition for the term "regimented society." You couldn't buy or sell or use anything without identification. Even the public johns had a sign-in sheet. Finally he had to ask Taglia, who took it all for granted, how the powers that be kept from drowning in all the paperwork.

"Oh, it's not that bad," the major replied. "They have recording machines that they just feed the information into on a district by district basis. It all goes over the wires to the bigger machines in the capital, and they spot anything odd and notify the local authorities. Those machines have everybody's numbers and descriptions on them. New Eden is crime-free and peaceful, thanks to the system. Everyone knows his place and does his duty.'' He said that like it was something to be very proud of.

Machines, Matson thought sourly. That's what the place was—one big machine. Everybody was cared for, absolutely, cradle to grave, and protected from all harm, so long as they did everything exactly the way it was ordered. Individuality was frowned upon, and creativity might rock the boat, but if you conformed and did your duty you'd have everything you needed. If you didn't like it, well, the government had ways of making you love it, too. To Matson, it made people of equal importance to the electric poles and other gadgets: all were just cogs and gears in a larger machine.

They spent the night in a small town that had once been much larger, but wasn't as necessary now to supply the surrounding farms and provide a rural cultural and service center. Still, in the town he saw his first Fluxgirls at close range, and realized how different they were. Nature could never make such exaggerated beauty and sexuality, yet in their own way they were as dull and docile as the female workers. The only difference was, the Fluxgirls had more fun, and mooney-eyed men made fools of themselves around them. Yet in the dining room he saw men making it with other men while Fluxgirls served them dinner and drinks and always with a smile. Fortunately, Taglia seemed to be the kind that doted on the Fluxgirls—fortunately for Taglia, Matson thought sourly.

He had expected not to like New Eden, and he hadn't been disappointed, but he certainly hadn't expected the men to be as oppressed as the women. The Fluxgirls probably had the best of the bargain, he decided. They didn't know any better, and he bet they enjoyed what they were designed for more than any man or normal woman.

He couldn't help wondering if those fools of the old

Anchor Logh would have fought against liberation at the cost of mass death if they could see what their society had turned into. Hell, probably some of them were still around, turned into what he saw. It was one thing to be at the mercy of a wizard in Flux, unable to do or even be anything that wizard didn't wish, but it was quite another to have a choice, even this or death, and see how somebody could choose this.

It took another day and a half to reach the city, but once there he was quickly quartered and his horse bedded down in government stables. The city was so radically changed he could hardly recognize it, with its tall buildings and stately mansions and mass apartment blocks stretching out in all directions. Still, it was a very big city with all the basics needed to support a large population, including various shops and markets, and it seemed to have the kind of life of its own cities seemed always to take on. General use of horses was banned in the center city, but the masses of people seemed to get along well on foot and using various kinds of bicycles, tricycles, pedicars, and even pedal-powered wagons.

Here the Fluxgirls roamed freely, in various states of dress and undress, and it seemed like every other one was pregnant and carrying at least one small infant in a carrier on her back as well. This was the home of the key bureaucracy of an expansionist empire, and it looked and felt it, even if the place and most of the buildings were pretty dull and drab. Still, the people seemed generally happy, not the dull-eyed creatures he'd so often seen populating Fluxlands.

He had a special visitor's card and they'd not given him any restrictions on where he could go, but he didn't feel like walking around much. It seemed like there was a cop on every street corner and while they didn't spend all their time asking for I.D.s—the paperwork would have killed them young—he was a marked man if only because he stood out.

From the officer's quarters where he'd been housed he could look out the window and see Temple Square, about a block away, and he felt a little of the history of the building and the place itself. From there, many long years ago, he'd hauled Cassie and Suzl and a lot of others, most dead now, into Flux for the first time and had somehow started the chain of events which had now come to this. He didn't feel particularly guilty—he knew that everything he did from then on he'd do the same way over again—but he did feel a sense of the stream of events that had so radically altered World, as a key participant in that history.

He thought of all those people down there, trapped by this crazy culture, and then wondered if he should be all that smug. He'd taken Cass on the trail because she'd wanted it, and he'd been down about Arden's death and wanted some, too. He still might have taken up with her, if he hadn't gotten shot down in the fight over Persellus and if she hadn't decided to become a saintly priestess before he woke up, but he knew he'd never have married her. He was a stringer, and stringers married stringers. Everybody knew that. He'd been trapped by his own culture just as sure as they'd been trapped down there.

And he'd married a good stringer woman, finally, and they'd had kids and a new and more settled life up north in the Fluxland hideaway for those who were running from World and those who had done things preventing them from ever going back into it. He and his wife had each needed somebody right then, and that had been the basis of it. They liked and respected each other, but mostly stayed together out of habit and for the sake of the kids. He wondered if he ever really loved anybody, and wondered, too, for the millionth time, whether it was in him to love. Loving was being out of control, and stringers could never be out of control. It was a condition of the job and the life. Stringers had duties and responsibilities, that was all, and it was supposed to be enough.

He looked down again at the people going back and

forth in the street below. Duties and responsibilities. Was it possible to be poles apart from another society and culture and yet pay the same price? Stringers were individualists because the job required a high degree of independence, intelligence, and stubborn, confident egomania. But they were so because as cogs in the Guild's machine they needed it to work effectively. Kill a stringer, though, and ten would avenge him while another out of more or less the same mold took his place on the job. And when you got to the top, if you did, you wound up like him, protecting and refining the machine.

Like those men in those big mansions off Temple Square or whatever they were calling it these days. The top men, they weren't dull-eyed or ignorant; their minds were creative, individualistic, strong, and ambitious. Yet what were they doing at the top but protecting and refining their own machine and making it grow bigger? Perhaps the basic difference between the Guild and New Eden, in the final analysis, was that the Guild could not grow any bigger, and spent its whole time preserving the status quo. *"We are a military organization,"* he'd told Mervyn, and that was quite true. Why did he feel uncomfortable in this one?

Adam Tilghman lived in one of those houses down there, as did Cass and Suzl and probably a mess of their kids by now. Not the Cass and Suzl he'd known, but the products of all this. Looking down at the city with its criss-crossing maze of communication and electrical wires he was struck by just how similar those things looked to the strings he followed and used in Flux. Just blot out the city and color code the wires as to function and it would be very, very familiar. . . .

He lay down on the comfortable bed and relaxed for a while, but the depression would not go away.

Maybe we just ought to let them open those Hellgates, he thought sourly. *What the hell are we protecting now, anyway?*

*   *   *

When they had returned from the war and Suzl had been informed of Weiz's "heroic" death, she'd taken it so calmly that it was clear that any love that might have been there once was long gone. She'd been mostly concerned about her fate and that of her younger children, and when Adam Tilghman talked to her and made her his offer she jumped at it. Even more, she jumped at the idea of a binding spell such as the one Cassie and had taken, and it was easily done.

The "new" Suzl, complete with a new tattoo and number, knew that she had been born in pre-New Eden times, but didn't really remember any of it. She had just remembered being a farm girl, sort of, who'd been claimed and married to Weiz in the early days, and had met and became best friends with Cassie only when both were married and living in the capital. Like Cassie, she neither remembered nor had any concept of another life or culture. The memories had not been merely suppressed, but erased and supplanted by the spell's details.

Once the marriage to Tilghman had taken place, things seemed to sort themselves out very well in the household. Suzl had been used to handling a large brood; the kitchen was her domain, and she seemed to remember every recipe she'd ever devised and was a whiz as a cook and kitchen manager, and with the easing of the clothing restrictions she also proved skilled at sewing, clothes design, even the making of drapes and curtains. Cassie made up the beds, did the basic washing, and kept the house clean and spotless. Both virtually worshipped Adam, but they also loved each other, and although Cassie was nominally chief wife it was Suzl who was dominant by sheer personality. Each felt that she was at the top, as far as any girl could hope to be, and they were more than content to stay there. Neither felt any sense of ambition, curiosity, nor saw any sense in competition.

Suzl's oldest daughters still at home, ages twelve and

fifteen, were heading the household staff; she also had two sons by Tilghman, both now in the hands of the state, and a daughter barely two. Cassie's twins still had a ways to go to puberty, but had already developed into the absolute image of their mother as she was now. They were absolutely identical and real charmers; only their tattooed names allowed even their mother to tell them apart. She'd also had two other daughters—Cori, six, and Cissy, three—but no sons. A staff of ranking daughters of other officials was still retained which helped to take care of the younger children and helped manage the housework.

Today was particularly busy, since Adam had told them that there would be a guest for dinner, an outsider from beyond New Eden—a realm they thought of only occasionally and always with a mixture of fear and distaste. But this man, called Matson, was a very important man out there, or so Adam had told them. Their husband had, in fact, seemed somewhat nervous and ill at ease when telling them the man's name, but it meant nothing to either one of them and he'd relaxed. They had spent the day shopping and then cleaning and preparing for the meal, which was far less of a task than the parties and state dinners they had hosted so many times in the past, and now were fixing each other's hair and adjusting one another's makeup and outfits.

Adam had been clear about what they should look like. Although there was a loosening of all codes and they had formal dresses for many occasions, Adam had specifically asked them to look as they had at their weddings, wearing the coarse netting at the hips which hid nothing at all—silver for Cassie's bronze complexion, gold for Suzl's lighter shade—and matching jeweled belt and the highest heeled matching shoes it was possible to wear, with heavy makeup, lashes, and jewelry.

Adam Tilghman never missed an opportunity to make a point.

The man who arrived, right on time, was a different sort

than either of them had ever seen before, despite his dull black clothing. His broad-brimmed hat, creased in the middle, the left brim fastened to the crown, his shiny, thick belt with the genuine silver trim, and his lack of any insignia, rank, or ribbons, marked him as someone apart. It was his look, though, that indicated something odd and frightening about him. The thick, neatly trimmed gray hair and drooping gray moustache only served to set off his ruddy, worn complexion, and his reddish-brown eyes seemed cold, almost artificial, hiding everything about the man within. He was ruggedly handsome and looked about Adam's age, although they knew that looks could be and usually were deceiving. He looked in his fifties, but the eyes seemed hundreds of years old.

Matson hadn't looked forward to this, and he'd wondered much of the day how he'd feel, how he'd react, when he first saw the two women. The one reaction he didn't expect was to feel cynical, but that was exactly how he felt when he saw them, Flux-modified, made up like bar girls and mostly naked to boot. He would not have recognized Suzl at all under any circumstances; Cassie bore a resemblance to her former self, but had he not known the truth he would have dismissed it as merely that—a resemblance. He knew it wasn't going to be very hard for him, anyway. The two people he'd known may once have been this pair, but they were dead as far as he was concerned.

"Our husband'll be down in a li'l while," Cassie told him. "Meantimes, you kin sit'n 'lax in the li-bry. There's brandy'n good cigars in there always. Adam don't 'low no smokin' in the house 'cept in there." Her voice, he noted, was still unnaturally deep for a woman's, but the spell had given it a sexy, throaty quality while taking away her pronunciation and grammar. As a "girl" who'd grown up uneducated and ignorant as the law demanded, this was to be expected, but it was the final break with the past for him. She had lost far more than her memories.

He nodded. "Thank you, ladies," he responded, in a voice that was melodious but one of the deepest they'd ever heard. "Show me the way, and tell him not to hurry."

Once the awkwardness was over, Matson's mind went right to work. He went into the library, which was a large room with several comfortable chairs, a single oversized ash tray, two walls lined with printed books and a third with modules—small square objects that would fit in one's palm easily and weighed only a few grams, but which, he knew, contained more information each than a hundred walls of printed books. He helped himself to a cigar but not the brandy, a drink he'd never much cared for, lit the cigar and studied the printed titles on the spines of the bound books. He was relieved to see that neither of the wives nor any of the staff had stayed around, particularly after he'd lit the cigar, and he idly looked at the titles. Most, he saw, were of relatively recent origin—books on New Eden's laws, religion, and the like, some histories both of New Eden and of other areas including a standard huge book on the old Church and its doctrines, some on math and wizardry, some on geography, but nothing odd. The old stuff, and the interesting stuff, was on the modules.

Each little cube was in its own short binding, attached to a page in a pocket, with a typed index that often ran a hundred pages of single-spaced type included. The spines were number-coded and gave little indication of what the contents were, although he noticed that a dozen or so were in older, worn bindings of a distinctive purple shade. He took one out and saw embossed on the front in gold the initials "CvH"—just like that. Idly he wondered how much time he had, but he picked one at random and thumbed through its yellowed index, mostly in longhand. The first had nothing unusual from a quick scan, nor did the second or third, but the fourth had, in the middle of the index, an entry circled in red with a red exclamation point attached. The entry merely said, "Misc. longhand ramblings,'' but he took a guess that was it. Glancing out the doors to see if anyone was coming, he removed a small cube that looked identical to the one in the front from a small concealed pocket in his pants, slipped the cube in the binder out and slipped his own in. He reshelved the binder, but still had his finger on the pocket when Adam Tilghman suddenly entered.

Slickly, Matson turned, prayed that the cube was secure, smiled, stubbed out his cigar, and extended his hand. ''Matson, Stringer's Guild,'' he said pleasantly. He hoped he hadn't been observed for some time before the old man revealed himself. It would be very much in character with the man and the place.

''Adam Tilghman,'' the other responded, taking the stringer's hand and shaking with a strong, firm grip. ''I see you've been looking at my private collection.''

''Just browsing out of curiosity. The old ones with the purple bindings—they were Coydt's?''

Tilghman nodded. ''Indeed, they were the ones he kept to himself pretty much. There's a lot of crap in them, mostly stuff we'll never understand, but some very interesting things that it would be best not to reveal at large are in there as well.''

''Oh? What sort of things would be so dangerous they shouldn't be read?''

''Well, the legendary journal of Toby Haller is up there, for example.''

Matson tensed a bit. Was the old boy having fun with him? Still, he kept it cool and casual. ''I've heard of it, of course. I guess everybody has who's been around a while. I don't say I disbelieve you, but I have a pretty hard time believing in any book whose printed words can drive folks nuts.''

''*Some* folks,'' Tilghman responded with a slight smile. ''Actually, it *will* be common knowledge someday, even required reading, but the world isn't ready for it yet. You, for instance, would find it instructive and revealing, even shocking, but while it would change your world view forever it would simply cause you to get yourself in hot water with most of the population, perhaps tried and executed for blasphemy by the old Church." He went over, took out the volume that Matson had pulled the switch on, and held it up. "Here it is. Want to read it? I have a machine in my office, if you want to spoil your dinner and a lot of dinners afterwards."

Although still inwardly tense and poised for some sort of emergency action, Matson thought that there was real humor in the situation if Tilghman *didn't* know of the switch. "It's tempting, but not tonight, thanks, unless you want to do a print-out and let me take it with me. We have more immediate matters to discuss."

Tilghman shrugged and put the binder back. "As you wish—but I can think of no one more than yourself who's entitled to read all this." He changed the subject, and Matson relaxed a bit. "I see that you have met my wives."

"I met 'em. Two extremely attractive and sexy young ladies, if I can take the liberty."

Tilghman smiled and nodded. "You can. You know, of course, who they are?"

"I know who they *were*, and I know who they are now, and who they are now is all that counts with me."

The Chief Judge seemed slightly disappointed by the visitor's pragmatism. Although not a petty man, he allowed himself the pleasure of rubbing noses in his triumphs when he got the chance, and Matson's calm was something of a letdown.

They went in to dinner, Matson sitting on one side of the table, while Tilghman, flanked by his two stunning wives, sat on the other. The meal was served by the twins, whose resemblance not only to each other but to their mother was startling, and by Suzl's two oldest, and was passed mostly with small-talk or no talking at all.

For his part, Tilghman's playful time had passed, and his mind was all on his visitor now. Matson was not a man to be trifled with, even here and now. He tended to imagine figures in history as being disappointingly ordinary if one were to meet them; Matson really was larger than life and every inch the legend, animated and sitting in his dining room. There was tremendous power and confidence there, at least equal to Tilghman's own presence and possibly greater, and something else, too, that neither he nor even Champion had—a sense of chilling moral ambivalence, of a man who could play cards and trade jokes with Coydt van Haas as an equal, then kill him without fear or regret because his personal code demanded it. Sheer brilliance totally devoid of passion or conscience. Even Coydt had had passion, although of a destructive sort. Tilghman knew from Taglia's reports that Matson considered New Eden a human machine. Well, he thought, it takes one to know one.

Suzl served dessert and Cassie poured after-dinner drinks for the two men, as they talked vaguely of conditions on World and swapped general information that went over the heads of the two wives. Matson, however, seemed a bit irritable, and finally betrayed a measure of human weakness. "If you don't mind the smoke, can we discuss these things further in the library?" he asked Tilghman. "I always like a cigar after a fine meal. I don't get too many of them in my line of work."

Tilghman nodded, and the two men got up and walked out and over to the library area. Cassie and Suzl started to clean up the table, and Suzl whispered, "Ain't that the *creepiest* man you ever seen?"

Cassie nodded. "He's handsome 'nuff, but I can't 'magine no girl ever takin' up with him. A girl'd freeze t'death with what he'd put inside her."

"Yeah, but I can't 'magine no girl or no man neither turnin' him down."

"If that's what them outside men're like, I'm glad to be here in New Eden," Cassie said firmly.

*   *   *

"The Guild asked me to come down for several reasons," Matson told Tilghman when both were settled in the library. "I haven't been too keen to get back into action of late, but I thought it had to be done, so here I am."

"It was a big shock to a lot of men here when we received word that you wished to come. Our own people and even our contacts outside indicated that you had died several years ago."

"Not hardly. I tried dying once, and I'm not too anxious to repeat the experience. I'd just as soon stay officially dead, though, as much as I can. I got sick and tired of killing young wizards who wanted to make a reputation by nailin' Coydt's killer or young punks in Anchor who wanted to show me how tough they are or how perfect some spell's made 'em. I'm a pretty good false wizard, but I don't put much stock in the power, real or false. Somehow you lose all the ability to do things the hard way, and sometimes that's the only way. I got a daughter with all the power you want and I can't knock a lick of practical sense in her head. Never could."

Tilghman didn't want to press that, wondering if the daughter he meant were Spirit or someone less awkward to talk about. "I think we agree on that, although I have to admit Flux made all this possible. I understand you don't like what we've done here."

Matson shrugged. "Don't mean nothin' to me one way or the other, to be frank. I've seen better and I've seen worse. I got to talking about that with some people a few weeks back, in fact. New Eden may be Anchor, but it's really just the biggest Fluxland, and the system's no less total than the one the Church ran here and runs in most of the others. Sorry if that offends you, but I think you're the kind who wants the truth."

"I do, I do. Would it surprise you to know that I'm in agreement on that as well? No matter how convenient Flux and magic spells and the very long lives that go with them are, they're the ultimate crutches. I wonder if we could survive *without* the set of crutches? I have pretty good evidence that our ancestors once did, long ago.''

"I might accept that, but I don't see that it matters. I think we forgot how to live without it. Oh, it might have been different fifty years ago, although I doubt it, but not now. Maybe not for the past couple of thousand. This place, for instance, is going to be strained when that work force starts growing old and having all sorts of old-people illnesses, and when most of the people here who run things but aren't high enough to have been treated to these eternal youth spells start aging and even dying.''

Tilghman was interested. "You really think so? That we can't have a generational changeover? The old teaching the young and then retiring?''

"Never happen. You and your leadership and even your wives are protected, pretty much. You're never going to surrender that power to a younger generation that might get it in its head that it'd be cheaper and easier, not to mention safer, to just bump you all off.''

"You may be right, but I hope not. At least as we develop more and more machines we'll be less dependent on this slave labor concept. I dream of a time when machines do all the labor, freeing both men and women for creative work of a higher order, wanting for nothing. There's no medical reason why human beings can't live a hundred, maybe two hundred years or more without any Flux magic. The brain is the only organ, they tell me, whose cells die and are not replaced, and we use only a small fraction of it. Yet some of the really old wizards seem to live beyond half a millennium without losing their mental faculties.''

"Maybe, but I think there's a trick to it. I think they cheat and generate new brain parts by magic, then still forget most of their early lives. Me, I'm eighty-three and I find real holes in my memory now. I remember the *important* stuff—or at least I think I do—but most of the rest just isn't there any more. I may not be making any new brain cells, but the brain's always housecleaning and throwing out all the stuff it decides I don't need any more. I suspect it's the same with you.''

Tilghman thought about it. ''I suppose you're right, but it doesn't alter my own vision. It's *possible*, and if it's possible and worthwhile it's worth attempting.''

''Maybe. That's really your affair, none of mine. My business is more here and now. First off, we know you've set up a communications network along strings. This disturbs us for two reasons.''

Tilghman grew suddenly cold and deliberative. He hadn't known that the network had become such common knowledge so quickly. ''Go on.''

''First, the Guild doesn't like Anchors or even wizards making their own strings. You know that. Let one group do it, and soon every Fluxlord and half-baked wizard on World will be doing it. The void'll get so crowded with 'em that it'll become cluttered and confusing, and the overlapping networks won't be good for anything. You have all them communication and electrical wires strung out there and it looks like a mess as it is. Now set up a hundred, or even a thousand, *competing* networks of poles and wires, each belonging to somebody else, and you get a real mess. Now wipe out all your roads and all your road signs and just follow the wires. That's the kind of thing the void can become and real quick.''

''I suppose the Guild's monopoly on the existing network isn't a factor,'' Tilghman responded slyly. ''This is all in the name of altruism and a safer, saner World.''

''The two things are the same thing, and it doesn't matter if the safe and sane coincides with our own business. The Guild has always run the strings, and maintained them, and not only turned a good profit but also provided a steady, dependable service. We believe in it, and we enforce it as well as protect and service it.''

''And what, might I ask, could you do about it if I weren't in the mood to accommodate your demands?''

Matson sighed. "Judge, you *never* wondered why we keep such control, and have held it all these centuries? I mean, there have been some really powerful wizards out there, and at times some pretty big armies, yet we're still here and still in control."

Tilghman said nothing, but, in fact, he *had* wondered about it when they first began their own network. At the time he'd dismissed it as an idea whose time had come.

"You see us in our black outfits moving trains and hauling passengers and cargo from one place to the other," Matson continued, "but you only see the bottom of the Guild. You never see the linesmen who service it, and you never even think about the organization behind it, but it's a big and powerful one. It's a skilled trade guild run like a big corporation, Judge, and it's a corporation run like a tight military organization. We have specialized units that are like nothing you've ever seen. You got all your knowledge out of the ancient books, Judge, ones like those on the wall over there that got scattered around all over creation. We never lost ours. There were stringers here from the start, and we know our business. We use very different and very specialized equipment, including amplifiers of a type you've never seen or heard of. Judge, just one of those units, if activated, could disrupt your communications, overload your amplifiers and cripple or kill your linesmen just like that." He snapped his fingers. "You'd never see or hear them, either, even with your whole army and a wizard's convention."

Tilghman was at one and the same time fascinated and uneasy. Such information explained a lot about the stringers and their grip, but it was not easy to hear. Still, it couldn't go unchallenged. "If the Guild is really that powerful, why don't *you* use the strings for communication?"

"Well, first of all that requires a lot of power and amplifiers of a type big enough to be visible and obvious—and easy targets. Ones like yours. Second, and

most important, we don't think it's in the best long-term
interest of World to have a mass worldwide communications network. About ten days after you set it up somebody
would figure a way to tap into it and all seven Hellgates
would fly open just like that.''

"Do you really believe that?''

"Yes, *I* believe it would happen, and the Guild board
believes it, too. We could secure *conversations* along the
network, but there would be no way to secure the entire
system from illegal extra use. Guild men and women have
died to prevent the establishment of such a network. I'm
not as afraid of the Hellgates opening as most of World is,
but I never saw a reason for fighting a war, with all its cost
in lives, if you can avoid it.''

"And you think that's what we'd get from the Hellgates?
A war? I'm fascinated by this, Matson, I must admit. I
have strong documentary evidence that war is exactly what
we face if they are ever opened, but a war with an enemy
that even our ancestors feared to face. You seem to think
we could where they could not.''

Matson restated his arguments with Mervyn. "There are
ways to make the odds even better for our side, if we
wanted to, but most folks don't want to even think of the
possibility. Every time I've brought up such plans any
place here they always bring up the cost and the point that
nothing has happened for over two thousand years so it'd
be a waste of time and resources. Me, I think you people
have opened the magic box with all the tricks and parapher-
nalia to make it happen, and I think the Seven will get
their hands on it and use it, maybe not soon, maybe
tomorrow. But I'm getting off the subject.''

"No, no! I'm very interested in this," Tilghman insisted.
"That won't be Coydt van Haas coming through there,
you know. It'll be something totally inhuman, totally different than anything we know or can imagine, but it'll
have all of the ancients' science and technology as well as,
most likely, total control of Flux.''

"They'll probably breathe what we do. Otherwise, why be interested in this place? It's no threat, particularly as we are now, so they either want our world to use for themselves, which is why they're attacking, or they're missionaries willing to kill us if they can't convert us. You seem sure they're not people."

"I'm sure."

"Then I doubt if they're missionaries. So they want this place, either to live on or because we're blocking traffic, I don't know, but it's a good bet that they're air breathers. If they're not they'll have to carry their air with them or make it from Flux, and that gives them a real weakness. If they are, then anything that breathes can be stopped by making it stop breathing. There's a thousand ways to do that. I don't know about the rest, but enough to do any harm will probably have to fill up the big hole, not that puny little inside Gate. You pile those tunnels with several tons of high explosive and a detonator triggered through the passageway or whatever it is to the temples. The explosion won't hurt those walls—we haven't been able to carve so much as an initial in whatever those temples are made of. So what you get is the biggest damned cannon in the history of World, and if we figure that the Gate end is damped—otherwise all that stuff would just keep shooting into World and do nobody any good—you ran it all right up the ass of anybody sitting in that big hole in the ground. Then you attack them from outside and pick up the pieces."

"You make it sound so easy."

"No, it'd be a hell of a dirty, messy war," countered Matson. "They'd still have their weapons and all that knowledge like you said, and we would have cut off their retreat. They'd have to win or die. I'm betting on sheer numbers. Way long ago, when they sealed up the Gates, there were probably not many people here on the whole planet. If there were, we'd be up to our armpits in people now, I figure. Now there are maybe forty, fifty million people in Flux and Anchor, and all of them have the same problem as the enemy. Backs to the wall and no place to run. There are only seven Gates and those holes are only so big. So you take forty million against maybe a few thousand very well-armed, well-trained combat troops with nothing to lose. They might take out half the population, but we'd get them."

"What a fascinating concept. Matson, I wouldn't have believed that you of all people would be such an optimist."

"I'm no optimist. I may be way off the mark in my ignorance of the enemy and the Gates. All I can do is look at what we do know and what I can see and create the best possible military scenario. If you want the truth, what I just said might work, but it won't. All seven tunnels aren't packed with high explosive ready to go off. None of them are, or are likely to be. If you don't get their bases or whatever they are and knock 'em out early, they'll have defenses set up and be well deployed before anything can be brought to bear against them. If they control intact Gates, they can be reinforced. Or they just set up there with all the Flux power in the world at their disposal and a base that's the biggest amplifier we can ever imagine and ignore our attacks, then just increase their perimeter as they can while feeding in reinforcements and material until they all meet up. That's what's *going* to happen someday, because everybody's so bent on keeping the Gates closed they're not willing to accept the idea that we can still win even with them open. You let an enemy confuse ignorance with stupidity and you just have another fat, powerful wizard begging for a shotgun blast in the back. You be stupid *and* ignorant, and they got you where they want you."

Tilghman nodded, taking it all in. Finally he said, "I'm ready to discuss our problem with the Guild now. If anything, you make things easier, not harder, for me."

"Yes?"

"I hope you can remain here another six days. In fact, I would advise it anyway. Flux in this cluster could become very dangerous at that time. It'd be two days, maybe three to the wall anyway. Stay around three days and we'll go down to the wall together. I promise you that what we're going to do will end the Guild's primary objections. Seven days from now the network will be dismantled, and you can be on hand to assure yourself of that. We will also cease at that time making the full-scale amplifiers for outside markets, and repairing or renewing the ones now in the field. We have no more interest in opening those Gates than you, and every stake in keeping them closed and secure. All research and attempts at Flux communication will cease as of now. Will that satisfy you?''

Matson didn't like the sound of that, and he hadn't expected such a cave-in without a demonstration of power. It was too easy. The man was up to something, that was for sure, but he wasn't going to say what. ''Well, I'm sure it'll be fine with the Guild. Me, I'm a little tired of being Exhibit A every time I walk down a street, like I got two heads and four arms or something, but I guess I can stand three days of it. I have to admit I'm a little curious as to what you got in mind anyway, and the closer I am to you the less likely it is to hurt me. Still, it bothers me personally. I got two daughters and a grandson out in Flux in this cluster.''

That was news to him. ''Didn't they get the warnings?''

''Oh, yeah, they got them. One of 'em you can't get much through to, and the other two are determined to ride it out.''

''Well, if they're not in a known Fluxland they'll probably be safe. If they are, well, it's too late to warn them and talk them out of it anyway now. I'm sorry, but we did all we could to warn people. You yourself have noted just how hard it is to convince a wizard of anything.''

Matson sighed. ''Well, you're right, there. I can't say I'm gonna feel good until I know they're safe, though.''

''Understandable. As for remaining here, I can't do much about people's stares but I can order that you be unmolested by the authorities. I can assign an officer or even a Fluxgirl to you, if you like.''

"I'm not too keen about any more junior or middle officers, and I might have some reservations about a girl.''

"Oh, don't worry about that. There are several unattached ones around who know the city as well as anyone and will cook, clean, or do anything else you want—or not, if you don't want it.''

He protested, mostly because he didn't want somebody going through his things, and he thought he'd settled it when he'd left for the evening, but when he returned to his apartment he'd barely begun washing up when there was a knock on the door. He opened it, and found a Fluxgirl there. She was perhaps a hundred and fifty centimeters tall in high heels, with curly, sandy-colored hair tumbling over her shoulders, and deep, huge green eyes, and was at least 115-50-95, which seemed even when looking at it to be anatomically impossible. She wore a backless, shiny satin slit dress of a green that matched her eyes and clung like a second skin, leaving nothing to the imagination.

"Hi, I'm Sindi,'' she said in a soft, sexy voice. "I'm to be your companion.''

He was, in fact, more human than they thought. "Come on in,'' he managed.

12

ON LANDSCAPE ARCHITECTURE

Matson found himself fascinated by Sindi, the spelling of which he only found out by reading it off her, in spite of himself. He suspected full well that she would be required at some point to search just about everything he had, and to report on his conversation and activities, but he also knew that this was why he now had a certain measure of freedom in the city. Sindi was not a gift—she was the requirement.

Her life story was interesting, although possibly as authentic as the life stories Cassie or Suzl would now tell with full conviction. She had been born and raised in the city, and really hadn't been more than a few kilometers outside it. She had an immediate, but no long-term, time sense. She could tell if it was late, or early, and roughly what time of day it was, but she had no idea how old she was or how long ago some past events were—and, more important, she didn't care. She was a Fluxgirl but not a Flux*wife*, an important distinction that had up to this point eluded him. She could not have children, about the only thing that bothered her even a little but something she accepted as part of life, and she was more or less married to a place, not a person.

She was, she said, "a part of" the bachelor officer's quarters in which he now resided. She was basically a porter and maid for the place, although she also, in the evenings, provided company and whatever for visiting young officers from elsewhere in Anchor or from other parts of Tilghman's empire. She was actually quite happy about being able to provide for such a variety of nice young men, and the variety couldn't be beat. She lived out of a service closet on the second floor; she always spent the night with someone there, or in rare cases in an empty room. She thought that was kind of neat, too, and in a way she considered herself freer than any of the Fluxwives, who were limited to one man and didn't have the fun on the town she had. When asked where she got the clothing and jewelry, she responded quite matter-of-factly, that "the men like to buy me things."

Like all the Fluxgirls, she was totally sexually uninhibited. She seemed to need and crave sex for her own sake, and not just because it was part of her function in life. She appeared an avid listener, but it was soon clear that anything she didn't understand or didn't need to understand went in one ear and out the other with no stops in between. Part of her function was to listen if somebody wanted to talk; comprehension wasn't required. She had no concept of, nor interest in, anything beyond her narrow life and what she had to know. She took her society totally for granted and had no real interest in it. Her concept of government was that it was "something that ran things, I guess" and an army was "a bunch of guys who go off someplace and beat up on a bunch of other guys 'cause that's one of the things you men do." No, she didn't ever want to be a man because she couldn't think of a single thing men did that girls didn't that she wanted to do.

Girls were the opposites of men. They did the things

men couldn't do either physically or by their natures, or that men didn't have the time to do. No, she didn't want to be a man—she'd seen 'em come in here all banged up and depressed and nervous wrecks, and she'd never been any of those things. He found, somewhat to his amusement, that she actually felt *sorry* for men, who paid a big price for all that responsibility and for all that power and playing those silly power games. They kept everything bottled up inside them, while girls let it all out. In that one area, he wasn't really sure that she wasn't right, and he had both the scars and the latent ulcers to prove it.

He liked her, partly because he thought he understood her, but he still took the opportunity later on to remove the small cube from its hiding place in his pants and push it down into the bottom of the small jar of skin cream in his travel kit that he carried for use against burns and minor wounds and bites. He hoped that would be sufficient to avoid any nastiness during the next couple of days. He wouldn't like to harm her, and he preferred to worry only about whether Adam Tilghman might get the urge to look at Toby Haller's journal while he was still here.

Sure enough, late into the night, after they had both supposedly fallen asleep, she slid professionally out of the bed and began a very silent but very methodical search of every inch of his possessions. As an old stringer and true survivor, he'd awakened the moment she'd moved, but pretended to sleep on. Confronting her was meaningless—she'd only say she was going to the bathroom or something like that—and it would be far better to get a clean bill of health than to thwart a search and imply there was something to hide.

She *did* check the travel kit, and even took the lid off the cream jar, but the odor was unpleasant and the stuff had the consistency of axle grease, and she didn't even think of swirling her finger around in it. He had carried that cream, or one just like it, for all these years, and never once used it. He had no idea if it really worked or not, but it definitely had always done the job in concealing small objects.

Matson idly wondered just what criteria she'd been given concerning what to look for, and how she could possibly recognize anything suspicious for what it was with her world view. She could come across a detailed written plan on how to assassinate New Eden's leaders and the mathematical combination to open the Hellgate and wouldn't have any way to tell them from a book of the latest dirty jokes and a record of his gin rummy scores, and since half his possessions would be unfamiliar to her simply because they were from another culture she might well have dismissed the cube in any event as a good luck charm or something while reporting on the sinister substances like the cream and the jar of wax for the bullwhip.

It was, of course, simply a case of the root nature of this society—and that made it easier than usual to beat if you really wanted to. He relaxed and went back to sleep.

Sindi took him on a tour of the city over the next three days, and he had to admit some interest in it purely on comparative grounds. It certainly *was* true that the thing worked economically—there was food in abundance in almost infinite varieties, including fine cuts of meat both fresh and preserved by a process known as "freezing," rather than by magic. The pedaled vehicle was everywhere and in constant use, sometimes hauling surprising tonnage, and there were not only regular garbage collections but a block-by-clock campaign in which the women living or working on a particular street got together at the end of each day and almost scrubbed the exteriors clean right down to the streets themselves. Littering was a social crime that provoked instant stern lectures, and there were plenty of public waste baskets about covered with slogans about pride and cleanliness.

All transactions were now through credit accounts at the central bank. To buy something, you handed in your identification card and the vendor punched in your number and that was it. His "visitor's" card seemed to have ample credit; nobody ever called him on it, but he resisted the temptation to abuse it. Not one single cop or authority figure challenged him, though—quite a change from when he'd arrived. When the Judge gave an order it was instantly received and obeyed to the letter. The stares he could put up with; stringers were used to being stared at out of fear or suspicion by Anchorfolk.

The old temple looked pretty much the same, and pretty much as all the temples looked, although, of course, it wasn't a temple any more. Sindi called it the "Bigbrain place" although she had no idea what went on in there and no interest in it, either. In any case, it was off limits, not only to him but to anybody without specific business there. Matson suspected that he could get in if he really wanted to, although he wasn't so sure about getting out again. He'd once held that temple against the entire New Eden army and he knew how tough it would be to move around in there undetected.

There was nightlife in the city as well, something that surprised him. There were limited gambling parlors and private clubs, some bars—but for men only—and some entertainment establishments, including a couple of places with small bands and dancing. He wasn't much of a dancer, but he liked to sit and watch the others, particularly the nude and nearly nude Fluxgirls, gyrate all their ample body parts into erotic frenzies. Even there, though, it was the cleanest, most antiseptic public area he'd ever seen, with the girls who worked there practically catching spills and scooping up trash and even buffing scuff marks off the polished floors by hand before you could even blink.

He could see the Judge's vision, but he wasn't sure about it. Certainly this was a society that worked; there was no crime, no poverty, no apparent disease, no dirt or filth, plenty of all the necessities and more of the luxuries than had been available to the general population in the Church-run Anchor Logh days, full employment, and apparently ample leisure time. The price, of course, was a different matter, but there was always a price. For the men it was regimentation, which also meant that you did what your superiors wanted the way they wanted it done no matter what *you* might want; for the women it was a dual reduction to menial laborer and/or sex object. The society was directed from the cradle so tightly and efficiently that each sex believed it had the better part of the deal; that was the trick and quite an accomplishment.

The population, all of it, he realized, would be terrified if they one day awoke free to do whatever they wanted—and free to do or get nothing as well. Theirs was a society in which you did what you were told and in exchange were provided with everything society could give you, including cradle-to-grave security and the basics of life.

After three days he'd decided that Tilghman was right in one thing at least, that if the Judges and the Central Committee suddenly all died, but the system and bureaucracy remained untouched, this society could and would by this point go on indefinitely. Still, that was where Tilghman the idealist and dreamer and Matson the sour pragmatist and cynic parted company, for the Judge really *believed* that such a state would come to pass, where Matson knew with conviction that any gaps in the top leadership would be instantly filled from just below. The state would never fade away or retire because human nature loved power most of all, and there would never be a group tough enough and ruthless enough to get to the top who wouldn't hold on to that power and use it themselves. The Fluxlord never surrendered; he or she clung to power until deposed by an even stronger and more powerful Fluxlord.

The only free people he knew or knew of were those so powerful they could not be challenged, yet also smart enough to be bored playing tinpot dictator or god. Even he was not really free, or he wouldn't be in New Eden now or anywhere near the place. He'd retired and gone to work for a powerful Fluxlord who'd also been a pretty nice guy—but he was still the Fluxlord's man, dependent on him for everything. Then he'd gone back to the Guild, and there he was a colonel, which always seemed to him when he was young a high and mighty rank and position. But the first thing a colonel learns is that there are five ranks above him, all able to give colonels orders, and there were an awful lot of colonels.

He spent one last night with Sindi, then rose early in the morning on the fourth day and started packing up. She seemed genuinely sorry to see him go and her affection seemed quite genuine and touching, but the cynic in him wondered how many times a year she played out the same scene with equal sincerity.

His clothes had all been neatly cleaned and pressed, and when he walked over to Temple Square in the predawn chill he found they'd taken very good care of his horse and apparently had cleaned and waxed his saddle. Even the old shotgun looked brand new. He hoped it still shot.

Tilghman was there in full uniform, as was a whole troop of spit-and-polish cavalrymen. It was really impressive when you stopped to look at it. He was escorted over to the high-ranking group and Tilghman spotted him and greeted him warmly. The old guy seemed in exceptionally high spirits, and was quick to introduce him around. He met too many men to keep track of them, but he knew that there were three other Judges here, just slightly less powerful than Tilghman, and Gunderson Champion was impossible to miss. Only the general seemed less than overjoyed to be there on what Tilghman kept referring to as a "historic occasion," but he was a good soldier. Champion knew of Matson but did not remember him, but the old stringer remembered the general well. He'd been Coydt's chief henchman, lieutenant, and troubleshooter, the only man as psychotic as Coydt himself and, therefore, the only one Coydt trusted to run his operations and affairs while the chief was away. Elsewhere around had to be the man who was Coydt's ''left hand'' as much as Champion had been his right, but there was no trace of Onregon Sligh this morning.

The main road led to the east and west Gates, always the only real entrances and exits from Anchor Logh, but the great banded multicolored orb that the Church called the Holy Mother was barely a third of the way to mid-Heaven before they turned and took a side road through the rolling farms almost due south. Even at the slow pace such a huge group had to take on these roads and under these conditions, they would arrive at the wall fully a day ahead of deadline if they continued in this direction.

Matson tended to be quiet and rarely initiated a conversation. He was a guest of the big shots, but he wasn't privy to their councils or secrets and he really didn't like Gunderson Champion in the least, so he stayed with the men of the headquarters company on the frequent breaks. He learned very little, except the fact that not one of them, including their top sergeant and their commander, knew what the hell all this was about, either.

When they arrived at the wall he found that it had actually been breached in this location, and professionally, too. A new, if primitive, gate had been cut in it with a steel mesh bridge carrying patrols over the rectangular opening. Sturdy temporary wooden stairs had been built on both sides of the opening, and up top he saw where a section of wall had been widened into a platform a good thirty meters long by twenty wide. The timber was fresh and untreated, but the thing was sturdy as a rock. He saw grooves and holes in and around it, indicating that something was to be put on it, but what that something was turned out to be platform walls, or shields, perhaps three meters high, also of wood but with metal sheets nailed firmly to their outsides. There appeared to be only three walls. There was a fourth stacked up against the wall below, but it seemed the wrong size and shape to fit anyplace up top.

Below, a tent city had already been established, and now the various parts of the VIP detail found their temporary homes and stables and proceeded to move in. There was no specific place for him, and he was told pretty much to pick his own spot and just stay out of the way. He found an empty spot in the tent with the detail who'd been here setting all this up for weeks, apparently. They knew who he was, and seemed amiable enough to talk about their work. After several hours he had a very good idea of their orders and the layout of the place, and found out that none of them really knew what was going on, either.

He had to admit, though, that he was increasingly worried, not for himself but for Sondra, Jeff, and Spirit. In Flux they felt that they were in their element and that nothing except an attack by a stronger wizard was to be feared. Of course, he knew that you could blow a wizard's head off with a shotgun just as easily in Flux as in Anchor, but he also hoped that Sondra remembered her own experience in the attack on Spirit's refuge. One strong wizard—Zelligman Ivan—and one New Eden amplifier had collapsed a Fluxland maintained by both Cass and Mervyn—two of the strongest—sent Sondra in flight and knocked Cass cold for maybe days. Mervyn was hooked to the old, pre-amplifier days and the pre-amplifier reflexes. Could he and the other two wizards withstand a power that might be three, or even thirty, or perhaps even three hundred times the power of one amplifier? New Eden had warned the *entire cluster*. Clusters were 3017.5 kilometers across, no matter which way you sliced them. Let's see, that would be that number times itself—nine *million* square kilometers! Could that be right? Or was he rusty on his math somewhere?

At any rate, it was one hell of an area. What could they possibly do to it to affect it all?

It was to be another day and a half of waiting and worrying before he found out.

The platform atop the wall resembled a cross between a war bunker, a command post, and a parade reviewing stand. It was all decked out with chairs, table, lectern, and some sort of powered sound system. In the center, however, was a motorized winch to which were attached a series of cables along carefully delineated aisles. The three metal-covered walls were attached to the main platform on great hinges, and by cable to the master winch—or winches, really, although one motor served them all. He had watched them test it out several times in the past day.

Apparently they had been told no rear wall, facing Anchor, was needed. The fourth section was to block the passage blasted or dug out of the old wall itself. Matson, smelling something lethal for those still in the void, mounted the wall nervously and took a seat well away from those cables, which he didn't trust, and about halfway back in the grouping of chairs. He began to wish that he'd relented and allowed Sondra and Jeff to accompany him here. They would have presented a sticky situation and a potential danger to him and to themselves, but now it seemed they would have been safer in the hands of the enemy.

Just inside the void he could barely make out the hulking shape of one of the amplification machines, with a lot of wires leading back to a small temporary building on the Anchor apron. Some wires then ran from the building to the wall and entered the platform through the floor where it jutted out from the wall and over the apron, and where the hinged section would not interfere with them.

There had been some delay, and it was well past the appointed time; the assembled big shots of New Eden and their one lone visitor began to get the fidgets. Matson regretted his seating choice now that it was too late. He had to go to the bathroom and was afraid he'd never get out, get down to the outdoor privy, and back up in time. The old law applied—if he didn't go, they'd sit for hours; if he did, it would start when he started his business down there. He decided he would hold it until he blew up or until they were told to take a break.

Finally, though, Adam Tilghman emerged from the old stone guard house near the platform flanked by two white-uniformed men. He looked annoyed and kept saying things no one could catch and nodding occasionally to the two in white, but he continued on to the platform and up to the podium.

I bet he went to the john just before coming here, Matson thought grumpily. There was no greater personal demonstration of power to him than this. Tilghman's utopian dream would never come about because no man in his position would pass up being the lone individual able to hold up the proceedings while he took a piss. *Sit here with a full bladder, Judge, and see what equality really means.*

The sound system came alive with a screech, and a couple of technicians leaped to adjust it. The screech stopped, and there was only a buzzing noise and the vague sound of some nasty-toned conversation in the air. Tilghman turned to the crowd and began, his voice surprisingly easy to hear.

"Gentlemen, we are here, finally, to witness a true revolution, an act that is irrevocable and which will change our world forever. Some of you know what we are about to do, but most of you do not, for security was essential to this entire operation.

"I have now been informed that, after some technical problems, all is now in readiness for the act. We are doing nothing here, today, that our ancestors did not plan and design. For various reasons they were unable to carry out the full operation, but we will do our part today."

He paused a moment, mostly for dramatic effect, and then continued. His audience was all ears.

"We have used the amplifiers whose plans and designs we discovered in the ancient papers mostly as weapons to this point, but they were not designed as weapons. It was never the intent of our ancestors to promote the conditions under which we've lived for twenty-six hundred years. Flux is a tool, not an end; a tool to be used by these machines to accomplish a specific task. For various reasons, some of which we do not fully understand, that task was not carried out—until now.

"Nine years ago, a research project of ours discovered, quite accidently, a series of modules designed to instruct and operate the amplifiers. We'd not known what they were for, as they were classified under the general term 'Landscape Architecture,' with their use guide making reference to various machines we didn't until now understand. For unknown reasons, we found that these and many other modules were called 'programs' by the ancients, which means that they are incredibly complex sets of instructions intended to be fed automatically to the amplifiers and which the amplifiers will then carry out."

Again he paused, and except for the buzzing in the public address system there didn't even seem to be the sound of breathing.

"Now, then," he went on, "these modules, or programs, were originally given to the botanical group because of the name, and it was a young, bright botanist named Kerr Endina who finally put it all together, mostly in his spare time and at the cost of some ridicule from his colleagues."

Matson wondered what remote outpost those colleagues were now staffing, and what Endina would be doing if this, whatever it was, didn't work or didn't work like he said it should.

"We have deployed one hundred and twelve amplifiers in the cluster," Tilghman told them. There was a collective gasp at this. "This number, or so the scientists tell me, is the largest number that can be used within a cluster, since all of them use and modify Flux and there is only so much Flux. We actually don't need but a fraction of these for what we will do, but the rest are deployed with a different purpose. Once the signal is given, every Fluxlord and every Fluxland population that remains in the cluster despite our warnings, and this is a very large number, would be against us. General Champion was brilliant enough to come up with what we think will be a solution which involves the other amplifiers."

Matson glanced over at Champion and saw the general smile and nod. No matter what you could say against Tilghman, he was one *Hell* of a politician.

"The great work that we do today," Tilghman told them, "is nothing less than the conversion of an entire cluster from four Anchors and Flux to solid Anchor!"

Suddenly everyone was talking at once, and it took a while for Tilghman to calm them down. When he did, he continued.

"Think of it! An Anchor the size of a cluster, stretching from where we stand to the southern tip of Mareh and to the westernmost point in Nantzee and all the way to the easternmost point in the former Anchor Bakha. Those names in a moment will have no meaning. There will be only one—New Eden, largest and dominant Anchor on this planet!"

That set them off again. Matson, like many, was stunned. No wonder the wily old bastard was so agreeable to dismantling the communications network! If this crazy, impossible scheme actually worked, the Guild was out of business in the south.

"We have among our ranks many with substantial Flux power, and we have used them in our secondary move—which actually comes first, by a few precious minutes, thanks to General Champion's foresight. Every known substantive Fluxland is now covered by mass amplifers. When the signal is given, they will begin to direct on those Fluxlands the massed power of the amplifiers and our own adaptation spells that worked so well at Nantzee and Mareh.

Those spells will roll like a great wind into all the lands, immediately followed by the activation of the ancient program. As Flux is transformed to Anchor, the wizards so attacked will find themselves powerless to react or to undo what we have done. Those who survive the onslaught will become as ordinary as you or I, and as mortal. All of this is coordinated by our own Dr. Sligh, whose own communications breakthroughs make it possible for us to time this down to the last tenth of a second throughout the entire cluster. Just one signal will trigger the adaptation and a few seconds later the ancient programs. Our troops have withdrawn into Anchor or outside the cluster. The individual volunteers on the amplifiers are there merely as safety checks and observers. Everything is being handled by what Dr. Sligh calls 'preprogrammed remote control.' "

Preprogrammed remote control, Matson thought, his heart sinking. *Could the Hellgates, too, be opened this way?* Now, at least, he understood why Tilghman had insisted on this specific timing for his visit and had been anxious to keep him here. The Judge wasn't as naive about the Guild as he'd let on. He wasn't about to let Matson go when an order from the stringer might disrupt the vital communications needed to pull this off. After it was over, the mere elimination of this much Flux would be New Eden's answer to the Guild. He wondered if they really knew all the consequences of what they were doing, and doubted it.

"I will now give the order to commence the operation," Tilghman told them. "As soon as it is completed, our troops are ready to spread out and assess the total effect and, hopefully, contact and establish control over the populations affected. Detailed mapping and exploration will come later. I must tell you, though, that we have to trust our ancestors on these programs. Except for the fact that they will not alter existing Anchor, we have no idea what sort of world we now will create, and I find that more exciting than frightening. The protective walls will go up for a brief period here only because there is some indication of a backlash in the air from the change in power. Records state that a very thin lead sheeting will be more than sufficient protection for the less than three minutes required, so have no fear. This is it, gentlemen—the dawn of the new age that will permanently revolutionize World and create a single New Eden so large and so secure that it shall *never* fall!'' He reached down and threw a switch in front of him.

Bells and sirens went off all around them, up and down the wall and behind, as well as on the apron. The winch motor came to life, coughing and chugging and giving off a somewhat foul smoke, but the walls came up dramatically and were soon locked in place. Although the back and top were open, they all felt cut off from reality. Now a second section of the front wall was pulled up creating a roof about two-thirds complete, cloaking them in semi-darkness. Matson felt simultaneous urges to make a run for it or to somehow attack and kill this assembly and break that communications link. He did neither, both because there was really no place to run and because the signal had already been given and there was no chance of stopping it now.

There was a sudden series of loud, terrible explosions that shook them almost off their chairs and rattled the temporary walls. Then there was a great rush of air, a terrible windstorm that swept into Anchor. Below, men and animals shouted and screamed and panicked and the wind picked up every loose particle and whipped it around. Trees and tents toppled, and it grew suddenly very dark, and the temperature seemed to drop several degrees in a minute. The sound of fierce thunder and the echoes of lightning continued.

Below the wall, those with a view of Flux who were not propelled into emergency action by the terrible windstorm could look out and see startling changes take place. The fixed, familiar curtain of reddish-gold with its sparkles stretching up to the heavens as far as the eye could see was no more; there was now a reddish-brown swirling fog. Observers in the blockhouse on the apron watched as much as they dared in awe as the mass reached the ground, and there was a sudden line of electrical fire moving from the very lip of the apron inward into Flux. As it did so, with increasing speed, the far observers could see the mass of swirling clouds withdraw with the line of energy, as if the whole were some living, alien force.

By the end of three minutes, the entire mass had receded from view of anyone in Anchor, and beyond the apron and above them was no longer void but open sky, mostly gray in color and obscuring the great orb the old Church worshipped as the source of World's light. It was a turbulent, storm-tossed sky, but it was not such a sky as had never been seen in Anchor.

They all waited anxiously as the shielding walls were carefully lowered, revealing what now lay beyond. All on the platform had been pretty badly shaken up, but aside from a few minor cuts and bruises there was no other damage apparent.

Everyone stood and then rushed forward to get a view, and even Tilghman was forgotten in the crush of the excitement.

There was no more Flux, but there was a true landscape now. The apron, for all intents and purposes, no longer existed, but merely extended into the new land. To the right stretched a vast, unbroken plain covered with tall yellowish grass whipping about in the still strong wind and looking like great waves upon an alien sea. To the left was a far more breathtaking sight: a vast expanse of deep blue water whose great waves washed up on a large but gentle black sand beach. It seemed to stretch out to the southeast as far as the eye could see, and there was a strong and alien salty smell to the air and the roar of crashing waves hitting upon the beach. It was more water than any of them had ever seen in their entire lives, and it frightened and disoriented them.

Huge thunderstorms seemed to be all around, both out over the water and over the great grassy plains, with dramatic lightning that shot from dark clouds and grounded itself on whatever surface was beneath.

Tilghman had been almost bowled over by the rush to the front, but now pushed his way before the awe-stricken crowd. He saw the scene in front of him and froze, jaw dropping, all the color seeming to drain from his face. The plains were familiar enough, and the only surprise was that the program came complete with its vegetation. He had expected to have to plant it or to wait perhaps years for it to grow out. But it was the huge expanse of blue water with its waves foaming and crashing into the shore that truly shocked him. He had never imagined that such an expanse of water could exist. Broad rivers and great lakes, yes, but nothing like *this*. They should have known, he realized. They should have guessed, at least, that all that water, deprived of conversion back into Flux at the boundaries, would have to collect somewhere—but this much water was beyond comprehension.

Sitting incongruously a few hundred meters beyond the edge of the sea was the master control amplifier that had created this, now clearly visible, its rectangular form having sunk a bit in the soft, moist earth, now a useless relic, the agent of its own obsolescence. The door to the lead-lined operator's cage opened, and a shaken figure eased himself out and dropped down to the ground, then stopped, struck as senseless as the rest of them by the sight he'd helped create.

The temperature of the air at this time of year was generally twenty-one or twenty-two degrees centigrade; now they began to shiver a bit, for the temperature had dropped fully five or six degrees in the operation and continued to do so. By early the next morning it had dropped all the way down to seven, but it would take weeks before it was determined that the temperature range had altered to a spread of about sixteen for a high to five for a low. They were heading into the warmest season under the old conditions, and hoped that it would hold true now, but no one wanted to think right away about what the cold season's temperatures might be.

Communications had been severed the moment that the program had been activated, but troops from all four Anchors and from positions outside the cluster now proceeded in to check out the new land and pick up the pieces. Without strings or familiar landmarks, however, it would be slow going, and many would be dispersed or lost. The only thing that allowed them to negotiate the new land was the instant discovery that magnetic compasses, used for generations by stringers as a supplementary aid and known to all, were still apparently drawn to the Hellgate; but with only that one reference point and the known point of departure, it was going to be tough going.

More difficult was the discovery of just how much of the new area was water—and not fresh water, but contaminated with salt to such a degree that it could not be used for agriculture. Estimates ranged between a third to more than half of the former void now being covered by water, which greatly raised the humidity of the entire region. Clearly the new climate was not only going to be far chillier, but also much wetter.

No one would ever be able to know how many thousands, or perhaps tens of thousands, of innocent people and their arrogant Fluxlords, not to mention stringers, duggers, and travelers of all sorts, were drowned in the massive transformation of Flux energy to water, but bodies washed up on shorelines after every storm for months.

After the terrible shock of the sight had lessened and the men on the platform had regained enough composure to leave, either to investigate this new place or to organize their commands for the aftermath, Adam Tilghman and four bodyguards remained, gazing out on the strange and terrifying landscape.

Matson, too, remained. He would have to travel that landscape soon enough, if he could. He took out a cigar and lit it, then approached Tilghman. The Judge didn't turn his gaze from the new scene to see who it was, although from the whiffs of cigar smoke he certainly could surmise it.

"Well, Judge, that's a right pretty trick," the old stringer said. "Looks like everybody in New Eden's gonna have to learn how to swim, and it's gonna be another neat trick to string wires across *that*."

"It's so—*huge*," Tilghman breathed. "It must be what the ancient writings call a 'sea.' I—I never thought of a sea as anything more than a lake. Nothing like—*this*."

"You had all those nice programs and instruction manuals to do all this, but did anybody give you an instruction manual for how to live with it? Those ancient boys, they were smart ones, with smarter machines and a whole lot of experience, I bet. You got the basics all right, but I bet you don't have any idea what's supposed to be done next. What kind of fish could live in that stuff." He sniffed the strong salt air. "You can tell it's all contaminated water from here. Best that you can do with it is try to corner the salt market. Hell, Judge, didn't you ever wonder, if they know how to do all this, why they didn't?"

Tilghman could not turn away, but the question stung him. "What?"

"You know what we talked about. They came here to live, somebody got to chasing them, and they locked the doors—but they kept all their machines and the power to do this. Why didn't they? Why'd they leave it as Flux?"

"I—I thought the powers of Flux corrupted those who could use it. I—we, all of us, the scientists as well—thought that the first wizards moved to prevent it. It's the only explanation of why it wasn't done, and why the records, manuals, and programs were dispersed. They took them into Flux so that no one could enact them.''

Matson puffed away on his cigar. "Uh uh. That's as good a theory as any, but it might have been different. I don't have the old history that you have, Judge, but if you look at all this you can see that this sort of thing isn't a simple kind of spell, it's the most complicated thing in the universe, maybe. Somebody planned this all out as part of a whole, part of what World was supposed to look like, but then the enemy came knocking at the door. You don't create a world like you create a Fluxland, Judge. A world's a zillion zillion elements, all of 'em in some kind of balance and working this way or that together. You got the landscaping for this section right, but not the fine tuning, the finishing touches, the things that make it real nice and homey. You got the land, and the water, and the plants, and maybe the basic animals—judging from Anchor, there'll probably be insects and that sort of thing. But no big animals, no water creatures any more complicated than those insects or grasses, none of that. I don't think they had all the programs, as you call 'em, yet. Or maybe it takes a hundred years or so of real careful planning. Maybe they didn't do it because it wouldn't work right, and with the door locked they couldn't go get the rest. Maybe they dispersed all that for the same reason they made it so hard to unlock the Hellgates—so nobody would get tempted to do what you just did.''

Tilghman suddenly turned and stood up, facing Matson. "No! Even if you're right, it doesn't matter. What's done is done, for one thing. For another, there's every sort of plant and animal, bird and insect, in the Anchors. They'll spread out there now, and in time, the land will teem with life in abundance. We have the plans for great farm machinery and we have a large population that knows farming, cultivation, and land management. No matter how big and how deep that sea out there is, we'll learn how to use it and how to cross it or at least how to live with it. There's still land out there enough for all who want it. The army can police it, but will never be large enough to control it, and the chance for one's own land will increase pressure for orderly exploration and settlement. You said it, too, Matson. We are not our ancestors. We're a rougher, cruder, more primitive breed who can learn to build and use ancient technology without being totally dependent on it. The army will be the police, and the stringers, of this new land. We'll win, Matson. We'll win, over time.''

''Maybe,'' Matson replied dryly. ''Seems to me you've just proved how easy it is now for anybody to open the Hellgates. The only thing I can say in your favor is that you've got a hell of a defensive position now. They can't use Flux against you so they'll have to cross overland by land and sea. I hope you have the time to prepare for it. Me, I've got to survive without getting lost, starving or freezing to death, and see what happened to my kin in all this. At least they were on the land side near as I can tell, if this big water doesn't curve around just out of view.''

Tilghman was relieved to hear that at least they probably hadn't drowned. ''Uh—Matson, I don't know what effect Champion's business had on them if they *did* survive. I think we were fair, though. Gave them every warning, every cut.''

The stringer nodded. ''Don't worry, Judge. I'm not coming back gunnin' for you and New Eden no matter what. As you say, it was their choice, and no malicious intent towards 'em on your part. That don't mean a lot of others won't be out to get all of you pretty quick, though. You know that. And it still means I got to find 'em, if I can, and if they're alive.''

''Just tell the quartermaster below what you think you'll need and you'll have it. You'll make it. You always make it. And, when it's all over and you've reported back, you're welcome back here any time. It'll be decades even at our birth rate before there's enough population to really explore all the possibilities out there. There's almost anything you could want for a man in on the ground floor.''

"I'm not sure at all that you got decades, Judge, or even years. You just better pray that after twenty-six hundred years that damned war our forefathers shut their door on is long over.''

13

THE NEW LAND

Although its location was kept secret for centuries, Pericles was in a very logical spot for Mervyn, due south of Anchor Logh and exactly halfway from Anchor Logh to the Hellgate. Nothing, however, could be kept a secret indefinitely when determined groups wished to know that secret, and for decades Mervyn had suffered and tolerated a crew of watchers from many groups, including the Seven and New Eden, simply because it was far too much trouble to move and because they still couldn't get in without his permission and he had not been worried about an attack since. When his forces crumbled the Anchor Logh defense years before, he'd actually gone one-on-one with a very good wizard wielding an amplifier, and fought it to a draw without using one himself. It had been the toughest challenge of his long life and career, but his shield and his sanity had held, and with Jeff or some other adept of great power always around for reinforcement he had dismissed any threat.

The tale of Mervyn against an amplifier was well known,

so New Eden had taken no chances with the mysterious Pericles, whose contents they could not know. While the sixty or more Fluxlands had rated only a single amplifier, with a few exceptions where two was thought to be needed, Pericles rated four linked in tandem to a single master program and assaulting from all sides. Those inside would not be fighting an amplified wizard so much as a program, one drawn up by the same machine that Coydt van Haas had first used and developed to create the intricate spells for Spirit, Suzl, and many others, and which New Eden had used for its conversion programs in Nantzee and Mareh. The spell was a twofold affair, beginning with a sudden and simultaneous attack by sheer brute force, all power at maximum, followed immediately by a coercive command spell set at the least common denominator possible. In theory, the shock of the permanent shield being crushed would be followed immediately by the command spell, before a wizard could recover and realize he was under attack and reinforce that shield. The landscape program, following immediately behind, would freeze them in the spell before they could shake it, and they would be set that way with no Flux to call upon to change it.

Most of Pericles had been evacuated as a precaution, along with the most important books, papers, and art, to a temporary location just outside the cluster in Flux, so it was a pretty deserted place now, reminding Jeff, at least, of living in a house where all the furniture had been removed as the owners were moving out. They had tried every way to get Spirit to go, but she was adamant about staying, even though they could hardly explain to her the reasons why. Mervyn finally deduced that it was the Soul Rider, not Spirit, that was adamant, and he gave up. Soul Riders had an insatiable curiosity that often led them to place themselves and their hosts in jeopardy simply to see how it worked and how to get out of it. They, after all, seemed to be immortal, although hosts were not.

So it was that Jeff was lazing in the warmth near one of

the ponds while Spirit took a swim, Sondra was tending to the horses in the stable, and Mervyn was going over some new reports from his agents when Tilghman's signal was broadcast.

Ironically, it was Spirit who received the first, and only, advance warning. The message came in from that mysterious far-off place as it always did, too fast and too complex for her to understand, but now she had a translator. The Soul Rider had made a bigger difference in her life than anything since she'd been trapped by Coydt's spell. For the first time she had someone she could talk to, even if only in her own head, and it had brought her alive again.

Spirit, you must get out of the pool immediately.

She was puzzled, but she went to the side and hauled herself up and out onto the grass. She thought of the Soul Rider less as a boss than a friend, and she was not compelled to take such advice; but when it came it usually meant trouble and was to be ignored at her own peril.

"What's the matter?"

The fools in New Eden have activated the landscape program for the cluster. An attack of overwhelming force will be mounted any second now on Pericles, followed by the direct transformation of Flux to Anchor.

She grew suddenly afraid, the memory of the collapse of her own little Fluxland still a nightmare in her mind even after all this time. *"Can we warn the others?"*

No. The nature of the attack, the landscape program, and the relative powers here present too many variables to be restructured in the time remaining. We can only attempt to repair some of the human damage once it has been done and its strength can be assessed. Brace yourself.

She looked over at her son, half asleep propped up against a tree. *Jeff!* she practically screamed with her mind.

Incredibly, he stirred, looked suddenly up and around, a confused expression on his face. "Huh? What?"

The blow struck Pericles with a force that was beyond

any experience, beyond any level that even allowed for rational thought. The great shield crumbled, and the full force of the master program drove in upon it.

Mervyn was thrown backwards as if tossed by an invisible, giant hand, but prepared and instinctive survival spells came into play before he had recovered even a small part of his wits. The Pericles shield could not be rebuilt and strengthened in the few seconds the attack allowed him, but his personal shield came up immediately, dulling the force to a still terrible yet manageable attack.

The line of electrical fire snaking across Flux crossed the boundary of the four attacking amplifiers and shut them down, but as their attack spell was written, in the same basic machine language as the master landscape program, it was incorporated into the master program itself. Throughout the cluster, the full force of Flux energy existent inside the cluster now included the New Eden spell, and it was not one to be denied by any wizard.

Pericles did not melt and collapse; instead, it simply winked out, leaving a very brief moment of pure Flux containing only the human and animal forms there, and some trinkets with a lead base or alloy. Other than that, everything created by the handiwork or mind of man was reconverted Flux energy and then used again in the master program.

There were, in fact, two writhing, snake-like lines of fire a thousand meters apart, the front line doing the erasing and reconverting and the rear enacting the program itself, but so swiftly did the lines move that no human eye could have seen that.

All humans and animals were stripped bare and frozen as the first wave rolled over them; then the second wave hit, and behind it winked in an entire landscape. In and around Pericles hills and thick green forests winked in at the blinking of an eye, and water rushed through new stream and river beds that looked natural and well-entrenched.

Sondra felt dizzy, weak, and helpless, and slid to what was suddenly a grassy forest floor.

Mervyn summoned all the protection he had to his mind, and when the second line struck he felt horrible, searing pain throughout his entire body. The pain was beyond standing, but the line was past before it could completely break him down. Still, he collapsed on the ground, breathing hard and waiting for the pain and shock to subside.

Like the other two wizards, Jeff's defenses snapped on automatically, but like Sondra he felt himself consumed by the force and sank down to the ground.

Spirit alone was able to watch it come, although she was powerless to stop it. To her, what was nearly instantaneous seemed to happen in slow motion, and she watched the snaking fire approach and cancel, then roll through and past her. As she could wear no clothing or other artifacts, there was absolutely no effect. The second line approached like the leading edge of a gigantic, invisible artist's brush that with one stroke painted an elaborate and complex scene as it came toward her. Her own formidable defenses were already on, and were now tremendously reinforced by the complex mathematics of the Soul Rider. The line hit, then passed, and she fell forward as if she'd been standing on a rug that had been suddenly jerked out from under her. Yet the program had somehow ignored her, and she remained unaffected.

Spirit was, perhaps, the only human being not changed or affected by the master and subordinate programs in the entirety of the affected Flux. All others not drowned in the formation of the great sea and lesser bodies of water were left naked, transformed, and bewildered, whether they had been wizards or common people, inhabitants, travelers, or guests.

Mervyn did not understand what had happened or why, but as soon as the shock had faded sufficiently for movement he managed first to sit up, then bring himself to a standing position. Physically he could see and feel that he had changed; his body, even the color of his hair, beard, and body hair, was that of a much younger man, a man in superior shape with bulging muscles and even a rather large and prominent male sexual organ. This hardly fazed him; he had always been able to become whatever he wanted, male or female, young or old, human or creature, and this wasn't as bad as many of the alternatives, even with the bad headache. More important to him was that he still seemed to be himself; there appeared no discontinuity in his personality, memories, or knowledge—except that he knew such changes would be undetectable, and he also knew he couldn't count on knowing either way.

He looked around and saw the hilly landscape and forest, and for the first time felt the chill that had settled in. The air was quite damp, beading water on his body if he moved, and there were clouds lower than some of the treetops and wisps of gray fog reaching down here and there to the forest floor. In the distance, he heard the rumbling of thunder.

He heard a woman scream, and instantly shook off his confusion and as much of the headache as he could and made off in the direction of the sounds. About a hundred and fifty meters through the forest and downhill he came upon a confused and frightened young woman he'd never seen before. She was stunningly beautiful, with rich orange-brown skin contrasting with shoulder-length hair, brows, and even pubic hair of pure golden blond. She was quite small and delicate-looking, yet she had enormous breasts and the thinnest waist he'd seen on a woman. When she saw him she rushed to him and clung to him, sobbing. She was fully a head and neck shorter than he, but he had no idea how tall he was so that fact was meaningless. He did, however, find himself feeling a bit embarrassed by it all.

He tried to calm her, then stopped a bit to bring himself face to face with her and took her by the shoulders.

"Easy, child," he said soothingly. "Now tell me who you are."

"S-Sondra, sir," she sniffed. "I—I'm so scared and confused!"

You aren't the only one, he thought sourly, but aloud he said, "You're the same Sondra that was here with Mervyn?"

She looked blank for a moment, then seemed to decide and tentatively shook her head yes. "I—I think so. It's kinda hard to remember."

He frowned. At least there no longer was any doubt about which bastards were responsible for all this. They had managed to reduce a brilliant, highly competent stringer wizard to just another common Fluxgirl. Well, he told himself, it wasn't a binding spell, being involuntarily applied. All he had to do was get her into Flux to reverse all this, particularly since she still had the memory information. He looked around at the nearly silent forest. But which way was Flux? Did it even *exist* anymore?

He thanked whatever fates there were that he had evacuated his staff and precious library and artworks during the grace period, and only hoped that New Eden was as good as its word and that this—effect—was limited strictly to the internal cluster area. But where were Jeff and Spirit and what had happened to them in all this?

"Hello!" he shouted as loud as he could, his strong voice echoing among the trees. "Jeff! Spirit! Is anybody still here?"

At that moment he heard a rustling sound that made Sondra jump. Whirling around, he saw two of the horses idly grazing just a dozen meters away. He sighed. Well, that was *something,* anyway.

He turned back to Sondra. "Tell me—how do you feel? What are you thinking of?" He wanted to get a general idea of what he was dealing with.

She looked at him in some distress. "It is easier *not* to think, sir. Thinking—*hurts.*" It was obviously difficult for her to even force through this much of a conversation.

The spell, however, was a basic one, and he had it now. Quite clever, really, since they had to deal with a massive population whose numbers and character were unknown. Physically, the basics were given—not above a certain height, build between certain predetermined exaggerated parameters, hormonal levels pushed to unnatural highs, and then a random choice of specific characteristics. No two would be identical, but all would be basically the same. He was quite familiar with the psychological conditioning ideas New Eden had developed—they really weren't that new—and he saw a variation of that in the spell that was diabolical. It didn't matter how bright or capable you were, or what your background was, it *hurt* to *think*. The more you fought it, the more it hurt. The only way to feel all right was to try to make your mind a blank. Just do exactly what you're told. He tried to imagine the huge mass of women in the cluster all this way. Those who were with smart, capable men would survive—until discovered and picked up by a New Eden patrol, which would have a huge number of submissive and totally compliant women on their hands.

Sligh was getting even more diabolical in his old age. But there had obviously also been a rider spell for those with a male orientation, as witness his own physical transformation. Clearly that spell provided for those qualities New Eden valued as "male"—largeness, strength, bravery, dominance—things like that. But if the object was to keep women from thinking very much, then men had to have all their knowledge, skills, and experience, and many, if not most, wouldn't think kindly of New Eden's presumptions. Great power, fixed protective spells, and over seven centuries of experience had obviously shielded him from the more subtle mental orientation, but that left him ignorant of what they did.

"Come on," he told her, taking her by the hand. "Let's find the others."

They walked back up the hill and over to the left, where

he thought Jeff and Spirit had been, and he called out their names. Spirit might not be able to respond to her name but she'd recognize voices.

A man stepped out in front of him, as naked and as big and well-built as he now was. There had been a little fine tuning, but it was recognizably Jeff. ''Who the hell are you?'' Jeff asked. It sounded like his voice had dropped an octave.

''It's Mervyn, Jeff.''

Jeff frowned. ''Mervyn? But he was *old*.''

''He still is, and getting older by the minute, I'm afraid.''

''Who's *she*?''

''It's what they did to Sondra.''

He grinned wolfishly. ''Well, now, that's a big improvement. She'll make the trip a lot easier to take.''

It was Mervyn's turn to frown, and he tensed. ''Trip? What trip?''

''It's our duty to locate and report to any New Eden authority. You know that. We should leave as soon as we can.''

So *that* was it: a compelling command to check in. Perhaps other minor adjustments as well—a heightened aggressiveness, certainly, and perhaps a suppression of conscience? The way Jeff was looking at Sondra and getting very obviously turned on indicated the latter.

''Jeff—where's your mother? What happened to her?''

For a moment that threw him, and he looked suddenly confused. Suddenly he brightened, then replied, ''Oh, her. Nothing changed on her. Nothing *ever* changes with her. She's over there someplace.'' He gestured in the direction from which he'd just come.

Mervyn left Sondra and walked into the woods, looking around. He spotted her in a few moments, lying there against a tree, and rushed to her. She looked unsteady and confused, and he saw as he knelt down that she had a nasty-looking gash on her forehead. She started, frightened, when she saw him, but the Soul Rider reassured her.

Do not fear. It is Mervyn. The process changed him physically but not mentally. Trust him.

She relaxed, and he sensed it, understanding somehow that she had recognized him in spite of his physical change. Using what sign language he could come up with, he tried to find out what happened, and gradually pieced together the story. She had rushed to Jeff, and he had come to, and he'd been like an animal. He had angrily resisted her attempts at communication and finally had shoved her hard against the tree, which she'd hit, knocking her out for a while.

Mervyn felt sudden rage, not only for New Eden but for Jeff. It took a lot of willpower for him to calm himself down, and it was only then that he realized that his own hormones were heightened as well. Signing for her to wait, he walked back to where he'd left Jeff and Sondra, and came upon the appalling sight of the two of them together in the grass. Jeff was raping Sondra—no, that wasn't the right word, exactly, for she certainly seemed to be enjoying herself. New Eden, in fact, was raping Sondra and all like her.

"Jeff! That's your *aunt!*" he managed to say, trying to keep himself under control.

"So we'll keep it in the family," Jeff shot back, then continued with what he'd been doing.

Mervyn returned to Spirit, unable to resist the urge to kill her son and his adept if he'd remained one more minute. He had to decide, and quickly, what to do next. Short of killing him, there was no way to control Jeff, who was firmly in the grip of the spell. Because he intellectually couldn't blame Jeff any more than he could blame Cassie or Suzl he knew that killing was not the tack to take, and he also knew it would be unavoidable if they remained together. Or Jeff, discovering that Mervyn was not in New Eden's grip, would kill him. There was Sondra to think of, of course, but at this point he couldn't see any way of getting her away from Jeff—and if he did, Jeff would simply follow them and kill him and take both women back.

His first duty was to regain his power. Without that, no operation against New Eden, which was now a point of honor and necessity, was possible. To do that, he had to make it to Flux, praying that Flux was still where he'd left it when he'd moved the staff and contents of Pericles.

He helped Spirit to her feet and they made their way cautiously down and around, the sounds from nearby clearly indicating what was happening between the two others. The two horses were still there, although there was no sign of the two spares who might be around and might have panicked and be kilometers away by now. He thought he could still tell direction from this point, although it would get difficult later, and he'd never had to ride a horse bareback, let alone bare and with this amount of genital equipment. Spirit tended to be afraid of animals, but the urgency of the situation overcame the fear for at least the moment. The Soul Rider could not affect her spell-created aversion, but could dampen the fear areas and heighten confidence. With Mervyn's help she actually was persuaded to mount one of the horses, and with considerable difficulty he mounted the other. He started off slowly, then checked and saw that she was holding onto the mane for dear life but maintaining her balance, and her horse was following the leader. Due to the forest and the terrain he couldn't go fast, anyway, but he prayed he could go faster than a man on foot if need be.

Several minutes later it started to rain; a cold, uncomfortable rain that beat among the treetops and then filtered down onto them, thoroughly soaking them both. At least twice, partly due to the rain, both he and Spirit slipped off the horses, but managed to break their falls and recover. It did, however, become increasingly difficult to remount, and he was just about to give it up and wait for a clearing when they came out of the forest and onto the shore of a large freshwater lake. The trees thinned noticeably along the shoreline to the right, and became tall grass and bushes. He headed for it, and they stopped and dismounted just barely concealed by the trees. They would have to rest here, and while it was as wet and chilly as everyplace else it offered concealment and a wide view of the opposing shoreline, which might give him some edge should Jeff be following.

He knew, though, that their main problem wouldn't be exposure or capture but hunger. Even if they surmounted all the other obstacles that seemed impossible, there was no getting around the fact that only the horses were provided for in this new land. There was nothing to do now, though, but pick out a spot of wet grass and try and get a little rest.

Mervyn hadn't believed it possible to sleep under those conditions, but he did. When he awoke, he saw with a start that Spirit was nowhere to be seen. He jumped up and checked the shoreline, but saw nothing threatening, and the two horses were grazing nearby. The rain had stopped, and a slight wind had come up which dried him off a bit but did nothing to help the chill. They needed food and warmth, in that order, and there was no way to find either.

He was afraid that Spirit had returned for Jeff, but shortly he saw her return, with a small armload of berries and some greenish-looking fruit. He couldn't ask her where it had come from, but seeing that she'd obviously already eaten he wasted no time. The fruit was bitter and the berries not quite ripe, but the idea that they were poisonous he simply dismissed from his mind. If they were, then that was that. He had little choice.

They were filling, and the only result seemed to be a case of acid indigestion that passed after a while. For the first time he felt some confidence, even optimism, in the affair. There *was* food in this place for people, even if not just right. He prayed that there was sufficient food near the major population centers. Otherwise, cannibalism would quickly rear its ugly and repulsive head, and he knew who the victims would be. He only hoped that New Eden realized it, too, and was rushing first to those areas.

Still, he now realized that Spirit's spell included one for survival under almost any conditions. If there was food, she would find it along the trail.

She did not wish to ride again, but at the speed he could go on horseback in this condition it was just as well. The other horse, although not tied to them, seemed anxious not to be lost and followed calmly along, which was a relief.

There were many breaks in the clouds now, and the sky was filled with the wonder of what the old Church called the Holy Mother in all Her glory. Except for the wilderness aspect and the extra chill in the air it might have been any Anchor. Spirit, on foot, took the lead and often ranged far ahead of him. Although he had a general sense of direction from the way the Holy Mother came in on the east and went out in the west, she seemed to know where she was going and what she was doing and he decided to let her take the lead. At this speed, he knew, it would take a month to get out.

They huddled together at night to share what body heat they could, and he was quite surprised to find her coming on to him rather strongly and suggestively. He fought it for a while, but it was difficult to contain his own urges and impossible to conceal them. He had suppressed such urges with a flick of his mind for centuries, but now he was no longer a wizard, no longer was his humanity protected by the cloak of an ancient body and wizard's powers, and he ultimately gave in to her.

To Spirit, it was a simple act of warmth and companionship. As Mervyn himself had explained, it was the one way she could truly interact with other human beings as an equal, and, because it *was* the only way, she was better at it than almost anyone else.

It became evident to him after not too many days in the new wilderness that his entire situation had been reversed.

Matson was right—a wizard simply forgot how to do the most basic things because he never had to. He could just wish for them. Now he had been shorn of his power, and he was dependent on Spirit for food, for direction, and even, possibly, for protection. The spell and the Soul Rider gave her maximum survival potential—not a guarantee, of course, but as good as one could get—and he was merely hitching a ride. He had never felt dependent before, not even with his shattered leg back in Mantzee. Helpless then, yes, but not dependent on another. Ivan had finally rescued him, but not out of altruism or the goodness of his heart.

For decades he'd been trying to understand what went on behind those big, brown eyes and he'd gotten nowhere to speak of. Still, like everyone, he'd tended to think of her as a child, a permanent innocent, not as a human being with a handicap. Now, it seemed, she was truly in her element. Because she could use no artifacts, she neither looked for them or depended upon them. She found food where he saw nothing, or would be afraid to try, and she found shelter where he'd never think to look.

Sign language was only one form of communication. Touching, stroking, and intimacy were also forms of communication, very different and more basic things but still very important. Perhaps, he began to think, I have denied my humanity too long. To have power alone, to deny the basic relationships and feelings of all humans, was not enough, he decided. One could not aspire to a higher state and level of humanity by denying the basics of that humanity.

That was where New Eden was really wrong, too. Like the spell that had consumed Jeff and Sondra, New Eden was a least-common-denominater society. Its values for *both* sexes were incomplete. Love was equated with sex, intimacy with coupling. Even their predetermined social roles were biology-linked, as if humanity were merely any other animal, easily quantifiable, with any elements common to both sexes clinically filtered out. Women bore and nurtured children; therefore, they were to stay home and keep house and have a lot of sex when the man wanted it and, because this was rather boring and limiting, they should also be limited in their intelligence. Men were on the whole bigger, stronger, and one man could sexually service quite a large group of women. That made them the workers, the managers, the providers, the warriors—and also, of course, expendable.

But love wasn't sex; sex *could*, however, be an act of love. It was sharing, trust, friendship, commitment—all those things. He had always downgraded sex because it seemed a simple animalistic urge, available to anyone who really wanted it and wasn't picky about who it was done with. Now *he* was the weaker and the dependent, and he was learning quite a lot about himself and about the human condition generally. He was very much falling in love with Spirit, almost to the point of it coloring everything else.

For Spirit, it was just as personal but not magnanimous. She was well aware of the fact that fate had cast her, after so many years the outsider and alien, in a leading position, and she was particularly grateful that Mervyn not only understood this but accepted it. She reciprocated in the only two ways she could—by doing the job and by giving of herself to him, although she had no idea the profound effect that was having on the old wizard. She could lead because the Soul Rider was always in at least passive communication with its unknown master which it knew or took to be in Anchor. The Anchors were connected overland and through the Hellgate, which always gave the Soul Rider specific position within a cluster. The overland link weakened the further it was from Anchor, although it was a very slight difference, and from the strength of the broadcast signal it could compute how far away that signal's source was. That more than anything was how it knew that its unknown master was in the center of Anchor Logh.

As for the food supply, the master program had been instructed to construct a mature and balanced ecosystem, not a virgin land ready for planting. The higher animals were not included, nor were they intended to be, but wild fruits, vegetables, nuts, berries, and more were there if you knew where to look, and it knew where to look simply because it had read the program as it was enacted and had a perfect map of the new land in its memory.

Despite the Fluxlands, most of the void had been void, unformed Flux, and thus it was not unusual that many days out they had still not met another living soul. That changed on what Mervyn guessed was the tenth day—he had not thought to count at the start. Spirit had spotted them across a rise and then ran back with her tireless stride to stop him and sign a warning. He approached on foot, and cautiously looked down on a lush river valley lined with a large variety of fruit trees. There was a sizeable population down there, and it had not been idle. Someone had found a way to cut and shape branches, and there was apparently some sort of large-leafed palm in the neighborhood which had served as walls against the branch frames, creating crude but efficient conical huts. Either through a natural lightning-caused fire from the first day or by friction, they had also gotten fires going and obviously had them constantly tended to keep them from going out. Cows, horses, chickens and pigs, all obviously survivors like themselves, roamed the place. That, at least, eased Mervyn's mind somewhat—he should have remembered that almost all Fluxlands had had fairly large animal herds and the like. It was hard to tell from a distance, but the bulk of the population appeared to be Fluxgirls.

He would have loved to have gone down there and seen what sort of primitive New Eden these people had created, but not only would Spirit stick out with her spell restrictions and her hundred and eighty centimeter height, nearly thirty above the Fluxgirl average, but he would have a very hard time getting out of there again—and the last thing he wanted was to be there when the army found them.

They skirted the settlement and the valley, although it added a half a day to their journey. Further on they encountered a few others, always with time for Spirit to warn him and for them to conceal themselves or avoid contact. Many were small groups on the move who hadn't yet encountered a part of civilization, such as back in the valley where common sense said to remain where you were until discovered.

Finally, they encountered the army. The troops were obviously having to go very slowly in their marches, since they continually picked up numbers of people and had to detail some of their own to take them off to what had to be pre-established processing stations. Although it was a very large army for a very small civilization, they had a vast area to cover and had to map and mark it as they went.

Finally, Mervyn had to reluctantly free the horses and proceed on foot, although he could never keep up with Spirit and only held her back. It was becoming downright populated and more and more difficult to remain inconspicuous. They took to going by night, and without food or water for long periods when necessary. There were quite a number of close calls and many times when they simply had to freeze and wait, but since the soldiers weren't prepared for an enemy or stealth, fully expecting anyone to simply turn themselves in, it wasn't as hard as he feared it would be.

They passed near large camps where great numbers of Fluxgirls milled and waited, lit by electric floodlights from lines that stretched off into the distance on temporary poles. They had devices there that were basically the tattoo devices used by the old Church before the Empire to tattoo those chosen in the Paring Rite, branding each new Fluxgirl with a name and number and then having that information put into New Eden's files. The men, of course, would be classified, entered, given a uniform and impressed into the search for more victims.

He couldn't help but wonder what had happened to Jeff and Sondra; whether they were still out there somewhere, or had not survived; if Jeff now wore the lightning and black and Sondra was another dull-eyed beauty in one of these camps. How many of those minds, some of them excellent ones, had already cracked and crumbled inside those beautiful bodies? With a little extra conditioning they all would, in time, just as he would under similar conditions.

"It hurts to think. . . ."

What a terribly dehumanizing, damning statement that was!

Spirit, too, was able to figure out basically what was going on and she, too, felt depressed. She had not seen Sondra, but she had not liked leaving Jeff, knowing that it was a spell and not he who had struck her, but she'd seen little she could do for him there and she had decided that if Mervyn felt helpless, she certainly was. The first step in undoing this terrible wrong was to get the wizard back into Flux.

That proved difficult even when the familiar reddish fog curtain was in front of them, for the area was strung with barbed wire and patrolled on foot and horseback. It was a two days' walk skulking about in the dark and without food before there was any kind of a gap, and it wasn't much of one. This was a point, though, where there was only a token fence and for half of the time a lone sentry patrolled. Spirit, too, understood the chance and knew they couldn't walk much more in this area before either collapsing from hunger or being discovered, and she tried hard to get an idea across to him. It took him a very long time, but he finally got it.

There were two sentries, but they came from opposite directions. It was supposed that they were to meet each other at this point, then pivot and meet another at the other, but the fact was that those chosen for this dull duty were neither the best nor the brightest of the troops, and first one would make the point, turn, and march back, then the other would come. At a point most of the way to the turn, Mervyn clutched Spirit's hand, then got up and walked boldly up to the sentry. He was filthy, still stark naked, and smelled. The sentry spotted him, stopped, but so did he. Finally the soldier broke from his line and came over to him.

"I am commanded to report in, sir," he croaked, standing as straight as possible.

"How the *hell* did you get all this way without . . . ?" the sentry started, but then he saw movement out of the corner of his eye and turned quickly, rifle coming down. It was not quick enough. Spirit leaped and kicked him as hard as her powerful leg could right in the balls. He went down with a scream of horrible pain, and they wasted no time in running for the void, Spirit actually grabbing his hand and pulling him to run faster than he believed he could. There were shouts and curses behind them, a random couple of shots were fired, but suddenly they were enveloped in the wonderful silence and monotony of the void.

Instantly, it was like having been struck blind, deaf, and dumb and having your sight, hearing, and speech come back in a rush. He was in his element once more, and he had power again. Behind him, a small company of soldiers on horseback came into Flux, obviously in pursuit. The five men were suddenly struck by a blinding beam and toppled from their horses, but the unconscious forms hitting the ground were all those of naked Fluxgirls.

Spirit laughed, and hugged and kissed him. She could not be transformed, but he would not be stopped. Instantly he was a centaur with full saddle and even safety rails, and he lowered his hindquarters so she could mount and ride. She didn't like the idea, but as she had at the start, she forced herself to do it.

Inside the basket-like saddle appeared a great variety of

wonderful and familiar fresh fruit, which she tried simply to settle herself. She was feeling a little dizzy and sick from the ride, though, and would wait before the feast. Mervyn no longer required such things; he drew what he required from Flux, as always, and continued onward with a speed that was even more inhuman than his form. He had a string in moments and from its color and shape and texture read exactly where he was. He was forty kilometers northeast of Anchor Logh, and less than twenty from his temporary hideaway. Spirit's navigation had been on the mark indeed.

Still, he scouted and checked when he reached the Fluxland shield to make certain that it was as he'd left it and designed it. Only certain people could make it in, and he knew that he'd have to take two of them off the list as soon as possible.

Satisfied that at least he could fight any potential enemy within, he entered. It was small and crude by Pericles' standards, but it was all he had right now—a few small stone buildings, some grass and fruit trees and a little water. It was enough—for the present—although most of his records and artwork would have to be unpacked and probably recataloged.

He let Spirit down, then changed back, not to his old man form but to the form of the younger, virile man he'd become, now neat, clean, well-groomed, and wearing the purple and gold of a master sorcerer. Spirit smiled and nodded approvingly, then looked past him, gasped, and ran behind him. Mervyn turned and saw a familiar figure now being smothered with kisses and hugs. Finally the man was able to free himself and look over at Mervyn.

"You look pretty good for an old man," said Matson. "What took you so long?"

"And so," Matson concluded, "I suddenly figured I'd be a fool to go in there looking for what used to be Pericles, without maps, landmarks, or anything except a gate compass, particularly when I couldn't be sure what anybody even looked or thought like anymore. There I was in Anchor Logh, and to the north was still Flux, so I figured I'd just find a stringer lineman, send off my report as best I could, then come and wait for you here."

"I'm very sorry about Jeff and Sondra, but, damn it, *I* wouldn't have made it without Spirit, and there was simply nothing else I could do at the time."

"Not your fault. I can't do much about Jeff, I'm afraid, but I think I can pull Sondra out of there given enough time. The old man likes me a lot, I think, and from now on he'll need every outsider he knows to stay friendly, if you know what I mean."

Mervyn nodded. "I've already sent out messengers. I expect we're going to have the first true summit meeting of Flux and Anchor since the Concordat was signed years ago, and with nothing predetermined. Those *fools!* I warned them about New Eden, but they wouldn't listen. Now our worst fears are realized."

"Worse than you thought, I bet—and worse than you think."

"How's that?"

"I think Dr. Sligh's discovered wireless transmission. He's got enough potential power there just from water to give a broadcast station the capacity to blanket the whole damned planet, and enough Anchor area now to get a real firm signal that'll punch through Flux like a knife through butter. I don't know if the Seven know it yet, but there's no way of keeping it from 'em and Sligh'll build that thing simply to give instant transmission throughout his whole cluster. I'll try to talk Tilghman out of it, but the fact is he's so blinded by his visions he can't see the enemy at his throat. I think we better load up and get set, Mervyn. I think there's no way now to prevent those Gates from being triggered—by wireless remote control. Maybe not this year, or next, but you and me and a lot of other folks are gonna find out who's right about what's on the other side."

"Then it is even more imperative that New Eden, all of it, must fall."

"If it's possible. This isn't any big Fluxlord, remember—it's all Anchor now, and these boys are the world's greatest experts at Anchor fighting and they have the weapons that took three other Anchors and secured a cluster. If you don't think Tilghman and Champion aren't ready for it, you're still underestimating them."

"And you're still going back?"

Matson sighed. "I have to, if only to try to save Sondra's neck. Also, this place has possibilities. I think it's gonna be the easiest area to defend when the Gates come open, and I think Tilghman's ready to listen on that score. Also, bet on them pretty well evacuating the Anchors as much as possible and moving their main centers inland fast. It's their best defense. With their limited manpower, the Guild's in the best position to contract to service the new areas they're gonna build." He shrugged. "Don't look so shocked. We do business with just as bad, always have. And maybe we can dampen down that broadcast scheme a little. Gates open, Gates not open—somebody from the Guild's got to be there to represent our point of view and our interests."

He got up to leave, then stopped, turned, and reached into his pocket, removing a small cube which he bounced like a die on the table. Mervyn just stared at it.

"I hope you can duplicate that *exactly*," Matson said. "That there's your precious Toby Haller journal, and I think I can sneak it back into the old boy's library if you can."

Mervyn stood up and stared at the cube in wonder. "Toby Haller's journal. . . . You're sure?"

"I'm sure."

He picked it up and looked as it as if it were some magical jewel. "This is a service I can never repay. Perhaps it will have the answers. Perhaps it will make the difference."

"You can make a copy?"

"Easily, although by more conventional means than magic. You're leaving right away?"

"Tomorrow. No sense wasting time with a daughter at stake."

"It will be read, printed out, and duplicated tonight, I swear."

Matson nodded. "Much obliged. Make two printouts and I can read it before I leave if it's not too long. I'm kind of curious myself." He paused a moment. "Uh, Mervyn?"

"Yes?"

"Thanks for saving Spirit."

The wizard shook his head and sighed. "No, that's not necessary. In more ways than one, it was Spirit who saved me."

14

TOBY HALLER'S JOURNAL

The device produced a book of several hundred very large pages. What was surprising about it was that the thing was handwritten, in very small, close script that was not very easy to read. Apparently it had been kept entirely in longhand, and then simply photographed onto the recording slate to preserve it.

Much of it was illegible, and there were large gaps, and often great events took only a line or so, while he went on and on about mundane matters that were of no consequence to anyone alive these past twenty-five hundred or so years. But when fitted in with what Mervyn already knew, it painted a stunning picture.

March 28, 2117: Talley ho! We're finally on our way! Four bloody years shot to hell on Titan, which once bore a strong resemblance to our little project but now is less akin than Spitzbergen is to Nassau, but now it's going to pay off. At .8 light speed it takes almost no time to get to the Borelli Point, even though it's halfway to the stars.

April 2. All sealed up in this damned shell, can't even see the Borelli Point. They have photos of it, looking something like an eclipsed sun, but I sure wish I could have seen it. (Unintelligible) . . . Heigh ho! Wonder what it feels like once you're strapped in that tube and turned into a lot of particles? Find out tomorrow, and so will you, old record book!

April 3 (I think). Well, they took us down and strapped us in just fine. First of a whole bunch of people, but the forward party's been there for four years already. The thing looked like the biggest room you've ever seen, going on for kilometers in all directions, all with very narrow aisles. Place looked like a breeding ground for giant test tubes, only we poor humans were the stuff what's in 'em. No clothes, no nothing. You get taken there in the buff, and some tech boy barely out of college pushes a button that raises the tube and you get on the little platform. Then down it comes, and you stand there for what seems hours waiting, while a bunch of women techs walk through and make lewd gestures. They pipe in music, but it's a bore. Finally, they break in, tell you to relax, the lights dim, and you just go off to beddy by standing up. Damn Einstein for being so right! So instead of a nice faster-than-light drive, we get turned into atoms, shot through a well-regulated hole punched into another universe, and squirted along highways of energy there where energy is solid and the lightspeed thousands of times faster than in this universe. I keep telling these young people that it's nonsense to shoot a whole gaggle of people, cows, chickens, even pigeons, God help us, and a thousand million tonnes of seed to a place they don't even know where it's at!

Gravity pulls between the universes dictates the bends and swirls of the energy strings, but most times we never know where exactly we are. The Old Man agreed it was a hell of a way to run a railroad. . . .

April 10. Busy, busy, busy! Don't know how long I was out or how long it took for them to get to me, but aside from the gravity it all felt the same. I'm just dating this on guesses, but it'll show how much time passes for me. Exit in the middle through a hole in the floor, and down the egress tube. You can actually see the stuff pouring out of that stupid universe next door and the Borelli Lock that keeps it nice and regulated. Wonder what would have happened if Borelli had lived to see corporations like ours using it to build worlds? Probably shit ten bricks. He was an Italian who did most of his work in America, but he was a good old commie. Of course the Russkies are doing as well as we, and the Chinese are out populating half the universe, but we're good old Westrex Ltd., a nice, cozy, unified culture, all American, Canadian, Australian, British, Nigerian, Indian, Japanese, and a few more. At least with the corporate headquarters currently in Aukland they all have to speak English on this job.

Another short electric squirt and I'm in Anchor. Doesn't look like much, yet. We've got the masts up but no building yet—took ten full shiploads just to get the bloody computer through and a crew of machines weeks to burn out the basement, pour the foundation, and set the machine in it. Control room and engineering modules came next, and then the towers. Now we've got an Anchor—twenty-eight, in fact—and they all look like Hell. Burnt out wasteland, mostly hot. Well, we've got a heat source, and that mother of a gas giant just fills the sky all day, making it bright and a rainbow of colors. The brown landscape just ripples all the time. Fantastic effect, good selling point.

May 11. Getting sick of living in tents, but, oh, my! Is it ever intimate! More all-around nudity here than in Cannes, but without the privacy, damn it. We must get some modular housing up. Not that I really mind, but it's that damned priest and his corps of nuns tramping about. I still wouldn't mind, since the Vatican's paying for this and the Board's half Catholic anyway, but why should a good Presbyterian boy from jolly old Wellington have to endure it, too?

June 16. Maybe the Russians have the right idea. Multinational corporations wind up infested with culture shock. I can take the idea that India has Hindus and Nigeria is infested with Moslems and Methodists, and they all have their rights, but when they're all dumped and squeezed into a little place barely the size of Belgium it's bedlam. Some fun, though. The Moslems had a big to-do about which direction faced Mecca and decided to pray heavenwards, to the sky. Well, at least it's finally gotten the Catholics and the Moslems to pray in the same direction, but I wonder in a couple of generations if their kids will think they're praying to that planet up there?

June 29. Hurrah! Finally enough energy Flux has bled out from the Anchors and the Gates to create a minimum field. Now maybe we can do something with this cursed place.

July 19. Bingo! Do I know how to write a program or do I know how to write a program? We've got grass now, and even some trees. But today was our first real gully-washing rainstorm, and we celebrated so much we all went out in the mud and acted like kids and got ourselves filthy. Did you know you can't tell an Ibo from a Yorkshireman or a nun from an Imam when all have been covered in ten centimeters of the best mud you've ever seen?

August 12. What a transformation in so short a time! Our little world is coming into being. I know how it works, and it still looks like a miracle every time we use the energy converters to duplicate trees and shrubs and the like. Landscaping has already started work on drains and laying out stream courses. No oceans yet, but I hope to live to see the day when this merry little land doesn't end in a drab void.

October 9. Army signal corps rode in today, all the way from Engineering on horseback, in their shiny black uniforms and silly cowboy hats. We're connected now. Sufficient Flux has built up and settled uniformly around our little world that they can now run energy strings between the Anchors. Seems some folks can see 'em without the glasses and some folks can't, but for me I'll stay close to home for now. The thought of getting lost out there in that nothingness scares me to death, and horses scare me worse. Here we are, 22nd Century Homo Saps, riding horses like the wild west! But Flux plays hob with conventional power supplies, and causes all sorts of nasty reverberations to the programs, so back to pioneer days it is. Give me an Anchor and a good Indian racing bike any day!

December 17. Temperature has been stabilized and smoothed out. We're too far from the star to get anything but gravity, but our old planetary friend gives us plenty of glorious light. The heat we must supply using Flux, but that's an advantage. It means no polar caps here. We've left the equatorial Anchors permanently warm, but introduced some mild sea-

sonal variations in the two northern and one southern cluster, just for variety. Since Flux within the cluster zone stabilized at 33.333etc. degrees centigrade, just where it should be, we get enough radiated heat to keep our own needs small in any case. Since we're losing only a half a degree per degree of latitude, the whole place should be quite comfortable.

December 25. First Christmas. With the Operations Building newly poured and settled, it's the dominant thing in the Anchor. Somebody said the seven broadcast antennas looked like steeples, so Engineering managed somehow to come up with some brightly colored lights and festoon them top to bottom. I wonder what the preachers in Dickens' time would think of their descendants squirting through space and creating worlds out of nothing? Blasphemy, I suspect. As for me, if God hadn't wanted us to fashion pretty worlds out of rockpiles He would have made only Einstein and struck the relativists and high energy particle physicists to dust with lightning bolts. Or at least made only one universe. I always wonder if we were the main one or were we just practice?

I take it back, all my comments about the polyglot here. The sight of those sari-clad Hindu women and turbaned Moslem holy men sitting there listening to a bunch of nuns in workboots and jeans singing O Little Town of Bethlehem *is worth all the rest of this nonsense!*

There was much more of it, including a detailed account of how Toby met and let himself get trapped and tied down by a "tiny, beautiful-looking mathematician named Mioki Kubioshi—Mickey for short," and tales of wedded bliss.

What he'd said, even up to that point, would, if known,

shake World to its very foundations. Mervyn tried to imagine a civilization that could punch holes in space-time and ride great strings through to another universe and other worlds, yet still produce so ordinary and likable a fellow as Toby Haller. The names and faiths of that ancient civilization meant nothing now—how was a Japanese, for example, different from a Nigerian? It was impossible to say. But for all his cynical good humor, Toby Haller had hit the nail on the head when he wondered whether people praying to an indistinct Heaven might wind up praying to the most dominant and spectacular object in their skies.

Mervyn understood enough of gravity to at least get a general concept of the process. Haller seemed to say that in the universe of men nothing could go faster than light, which seemed logical, or you'd get someplace before you started. The same was true of this other universe, but light traveled so much faster there that distances that would take perhaps centuries to cross. This was evident from just looking at the astronomical distances Haller casually noted for the distance to the big planet, and to the solar system's sun—so dim it seemed just another star from here yet dense enough to hold a world as big as the Holy Mother in tight orbit. Somehow they had managed to punch a hole between the universes and control the very different energy that was there as wizards on World controlled the Flux.

He tried to imagine it—an entire universe filled only with the densest Flux energy. They took some sort of machine, threw it into that universe, and it just kept going, but deviated due to pulls of some sort between our universe and that one, telling scientists where things were.

How would they start it? Punch back out with their machines, probably, and record what they saw. Follow it up with more specific machines that could see and measure and find worlds, worlds that had the elements, even if in the wrong order or mix, to be turned into places for human beings to live using the same energy flowing from that other universe, but harnessed and under control. All of

World, all of the Flux, was that energy, coming out in a regulated stream from the Hellgate.

So they punched seven tiny holes to get at this limitless source of power and energy, and then they used it to transform a world. But not all worlds would work. There were more failures, it seemed, than successes, for technical reasons Mervyn, and perhaps no one, would ever understand. To find out if it would work, you had to experiment.

To this end, engineers and masters of the machines and of the greater Flux came in and built a variety of little worldlets out of Flux, and stabilized them and introduced a variety of plants, animals, whatever, from their home world. And people, too, who would make it all work and build the place into something livable, then try to survive there.

Clearly, in Toby Haller's time, it was still very new and they were still learning. There seemed no indication in the early years of the journal that he knew what power some humans could command over Flux without his machines, and he never seemed to make the jump from creating trees and flowers from Flux to creating Fluxlands and remaking people. To him, Flux was merely a tool to do a job.

His employer was a private company of some sort, that was clear, yet the army—the army from his old world— was there, had been there, apparently, first. Mervyn thought of the Signal Corpsmen creating the network to travel between Anchors and all he could see was the Stringer Guild. It was a total vision both grand and glorious—and something of a comedown. The fact was, these people really had the technology to do miracles on a scale that would put the most powerful wizard to shame, yet they were oblivious to their greatness, took it for granted, and were, in the end, pretty much the same as people today. How many worlds had they tried this on? How many had succeeded? One could infer four or five from the journal, but it could just as likely be fifty, or five hundred, or fifty thousand.

Toby Haller chronicled the development of World, which he generally called the project. When the first children were born, he rejoiced that they were "completely normal—crying, helpless brats that made life miserable." Yet when his own first born came along, the child was "absolutely beautiful, perfect in every way. She has her father's brains and big mouth and her mother's beauty. What a terror she's going to be!"

But the project was never completed. Man, it seemed, wasn't the only one riding the strings of that other universe, and it had the tremendous bad luck to run into another quite quickly. Nobody knew their name, and they were just called "the Enemy" most of the time, although quite often terms like "demons" and "devils" came into it. It was only certain that if they somehow found your string, and rode it to you, you were never heard from again.

There was no way to guard against them, for to do so you'd have to shut off the flow of energy from the Gates, and that would kill World. The military assumed general control of the planet and redirected much of its efforts for defense. There was some talk of pulling out, abandoning the project, evacuating for home, but not a lot. It had been thirty years now since Haller had come to World, and he was a man who helped create and shape it. His children had been born here. More, most of the population had nothing to return to. This was the new frontier, the outlet for the dispossessed who were perfectly willing to be guinea pigs in an experiment for a chance to be the first families of their own world. What exactly made it profitable for a company wasn't clear, for it certainly was long-term in the extreme and had to cost a fortune, but profit there was. It just wasn't in any of the surviving records.

And then Earth, as they called their home, had sent a delegation with an ultimatum. Losses were running high. They could not protect the colonists until they knew much more, and could take the battle to the Enemy. In the interest of Earth's own security, the master terminal—the

Borelli Point as Haller had called it—would be sealed. The project families had just one month to evacuate or they were on their own.

They didn't have a month, even though many, if not most, would have stayed anyway. There was nothing to return to. Military monitors on the Gates revealed a sudden, massive surge along the string, which when converted to matter using their formula would be a very large mass, and headed for them with only a few days remaining. The nature and size of the energy indicated it was nothing Earth had generated.

The army moved quickly. Its engineers worked feverishly to seal all seven of the Gates, and, effectively, to seal off the humans of World from the rest of their kind. By this time there were over fifty thousand people on World, and all of them were stuck.

Because leakage had to be allowed to maintain World, the mysterious Enemy knew that they were here and now had it on their maps. But because most of the energy was blocked, they could not flow from the Gate into the large dish-like area where buried machines would reconvert them into matter once more. There were fears that the Enemy, knowing the location, would punch through elsewhere and invade, but something made that impossible. Scientists ran it through their machines and decided that the most likely explanation was that the Enemy invasion force itself was present to arrive on World and was now in Flux form against the Gate but unable to crash through. Powerful automated amplifiers held them back.

The Enemy was trapped in energy form in the other universe, unable to even know it had been stopped, let alone back up and return. And because it was there, nothing else could punch through without punching through that invasion force first. By attacking at all Gates simultaneously, the Enemy had trapped itself and blockaded the string for the defenders.

With time to breathe, the defenders of World worked

long and hard to create better, more powerful self-repairing mechanisms. Nothing would come through those Gates except the specific amount of Flux necessary to maintain World. But that limited the available power, and made it very unlikely that the "terraforming," as Haller called it, could be extended much beyond the Anchors, "or at least not much more than the clusters around the old Gates." And because they hadn't received the "shiploads of semen and eggs and all that", they considered population expansion too long-term a project to really consider. With their relatively small population in Anchor, any population problem seemed centuries down the road anyway. None of them, Haller included, seemed to think that this would last forever, or, in their situation, none could think much beyond the immediate moment and crisis.

There was always the fear, though, that some madman might loose a seal, and there was a reluctance to make it forever impossible to gain access. What if Earth sent a force to them, and it was behind the Enemy? What if the Enemy dissipated over time? Might they not be able to reopen contact with their universe, then? So the Gates could be opened, but only by a complex mechanism. The seven cluster commanders each had a combination, one they alone knew. Using the psycho-conditioners, the combination would be impossible to pry out of them. Their juniors were each given a small part of the combination and also conditioned.

The center tower of each Anchor headquarters linked with and coordinated with the other Anchors of the cluster. A combined signal, an automatic check, could be bounced off the upper atmosphere to the other clusters. Those thinking machines, which Haller called "computers" but were apparently much, much more than mere adding machines, would require the seven locks to be keyed to open within one minute or they would run a charge through all seven tunnels electrocuting everything inside. To insure extra security, just in case one day one of the invaders would punch through anyway, the tunnels would fry anyone entering from the dish side. The headquarters side remained relatively unguarded, since it would be necessary sometimes to check them and perhaps check the Flux transformers, but this was considered relatively safe. Any enemy that got through would now have to attack overland, over hundreds of kilometers of void, opening them up to attack without cover. They would have to take the headquarters to gain control, and the computers were reprogrammed as tremendous defensive weapons of death, which could be activated only when the Gates were opened.

Mervyn sighed and rubbed his eyes. So much. Too much. Yet, these people had a world, and a strong measure of security, and all that knowledge and power. How had they fallen to their present state? The seeds of World's culture were certainly there, and told much. An intermarriage of cultures would eventually produce one. Religions might get all mixed up, and new ones grow out of the old in subsequent generations. They had agreed on a common language, implying that there were several, but that language would change over the years. But how had we lost, or forgotten, so much? And why did Seven otherwise sane individuals work like mad to let the Enemy in?

There weren't many more pages in Toby Haller's journal, but, as tired as he was, he knew he had to find out. The script was changed quite a bit from the last entries, indicating that Haller had changed a great deal, and there was no pretense at a diary any more, just a narrative even harder to read as it got squeezed down to fit into the remains of the book.

Hunting through some very old stuff when I found this book. Actually, Christine, my oldest, found it while rummaging around. No sense in rummaging around for the dates; the old ones were probably off anyway. Well, no matter. There are official histories and such in the Anchor libraries that will be of import;

this was mostly a lark although, looking back through it, I recaptured, at least for a little, the joys of my youth.

There are only a few pages left in the old thing to tell a lot, if it's worth anything at all. Perhaps, at least, my children will read this one day and know from whence they came and maybe hoist a beer to the old man. I could start another, of course, but after all this time it hardly seems worth the effort.

Well, where to begin? The Anchors were never intended as fully self-supporting enterprises, just as test zones and bases for experimenting with Flux transmutation. The latter, I fear, works all too well.

We needed the transmutation, of course, for that which we had to have but couldn't possibly make for ourselves. The population is booming and we had to provide for the future. For all we know, we're the last humans left. Probably not, but we have to act as if we are at all times.

A small percentage of the children born here seem to have an inordinate sensitivity to the Flux. We're studying this, but don't quite understand it. From the start some folks were able to see the strings— which is why they were in the Signal Corps to begin with—and see, or sense, energy flow and changes. We engineers could do it through the amplifiers, of course, but we found that the more we used the machines by direct input—brain to computer to Flux—the more we managed to see it without needing the machines. It's a fascinating and somewhat terrifying sensation which I, of course, also have, since I've spent half my life on those damned machines.

The military has developed into a supra-government of its own, using its exclusive knowledge of string maps to regulate commerce and travel between the Anchors. There's a District Commander for each cluster, plus General Yoshida's Headquarters com-

mand and General Coydt's Engineering command, and they're a closely knit group. By controlling and regulating commerce in Flux they have us by the short hairs, but since they also are responsible for guarding the Gate locks they get away with it.

But all this leaves our destinies in others' hands. There was a message received by the military just before the big energy power surge, one that was suppressed for some time but which was recently revealed and admitted to. I'd hate to be the soldier chap who shot his mouth off, but the thing apparently said, "Do not worry, we are friends, and together our two races will become gods. We are coming, wait for us," or words to that effect.

This caused quite a split in the civil ranks. The Anchors have developed steadily enough, but our standard of living has become quite basic due to the limitations on the amount of power required. The company field directors, which constitute the Anchor's civil authority, are being pressed by many of the scientists and engineers to, would you believe, open the Gates. They argue that the best we can hope for is a stabilization of clusters which might unfavorably alter the ecological balance of existing Anchors, but that Anchors can't support their populations at their rate of growth. Better to gamble on the message's validity than to starve and sink into savagery. I personally see it as just another engineering problem, but the pressure on the directors is enormous. The military, of course, opposes taking any chances on the Enemy, and is fighting like hell to sway people to their side.

I, for one, have been experimenting with this odd Flux power. A number of us have achieved amazing results on a small scale, although stability is poor. Basically, you just stand there in the nothingness and concentrate on something real hard, and you watch and there it is. Somehow our minds have gotten boosted, or linked, by those amplifiers after years of use so that the amplifiers, on a small scale, aren't really necessary. Too bad we can't get the amps to work much away from Anchors or Gates—they require a very hard and direct access to Flux before it's been dissipated—or it would make life easy. All of my children seem to have the power to some degree, leading either to the conclusion that use of Flux has changed us, somehow, or that they have the power simply because I want them to have it. That last, I fear, may be closer to the truth.

Apparently it works like the amplifiers, to a degree. One thinks of what one wishes, this is somehow transmitted along lines of force to the terraforming sectors of the nearest Anchor computer, and almost instantly back come the mathematical strings needed to do the job. This is an almost godlike power we don't quite understand, and since it's mainly limited to those with massive overexposure to the amplifiers and their offspring, it's created a sticky situation. The civil groups are scared to death of men and women with such powers, and I've actually heard the terms "witches" and "warlocks" and even "wizards" used, all with more fear than awe. The military also seems to fear it for more pragmatic reasons, since it threatens their power and control. They would prefer the civil population to remain in Anchor, fearful of Flux, where it can be ignorant and controlled. Most religious groups denounce us, and there have been some incidents of violence, and there's a new and bizarre religious movement growing up that seems to advocate the military's ideal. I saw the same movement, which seems all-women, when up in Engineering, and I'm suspicious. Coydt, after all, is a tough old woman, very creative but with a ruthless military mind.

There was then a break, since the final entry was in a different pen and was obviously written rather hurriedly, spilling over into the margin of the last page.

What we've feared has come! With the failure of the Company to oust the military and open the Gates, the army's taken over with a vengeance. Coydt's made that idiot cult the only permitted religion and is ruthlessly stamping out opposition. Power was cut beyond the capitals in a well-coordinated move. There are executions galore, and (unintelligible) must flee into Flux and depend on our powers there to provide. They might as well open the Gates, for Hell is already here. Remember, my children! Remember. . . .

"Oh, my God!" said Mervyn Haller.

15

THREE BLIND CONFERENCES

The Seven who Come Before, also known as the Seven Who Wait, did not meet very often. All were extremely powerful wizards, masters of their craft, and each had large staffs to handle their worldwide enterprises. The current Chairman, by majority approval, was Zelligman Ivan, and he looked his colleagues over with a serious eye and grave expression.

"There is no need to tell you that this is the most important meeting in the history of this association," Ivan began. "Until now, we were more or less playing the game, mouthing our ideals and our goals and using our own and each other's power and wit to comfortably strengthen our position. And we *are* powerful—we truly control, through well-concealed webs, much of World, with such finesse they don't even know it. Discord among us is minimal; none of us has been fatter, richer, more powerful or more content than now. Our enemies delude themselves that things are as they were, but we know differently. And for what? Allegedly for our ultimate goal of opening the Gates and attaining more than human beings could imagine.''

''That's all true,'' Rosa Haldayne put in, ''but so what? I admit I'm kind of bored with it all, but considering the alternatives boredom is not too high a price to pay.''

Ivan nodded. ''Now, however, my dear Rosa and you others, we face a dilemma, a crisis, a decision point that all of us have paid lip service to throughout our long lives but never really felt we'd reach or have to deal with it. The time is close at hand. The technology exists and has been checked out. We are facing a bald fact: within this decade, and perhaps within the next couple of years, we can open the Hellgates. There is no doubt of that fact, and I have checked and rechecked my computations. Oh, events might delay it, or hasten it, but the decade figure is a worst-case one. I don't mean it will be easy to accomplish, but if we are to do it we must lay the groundwork for it now. If we do, success is inevitable within that decade. And that, of course, brings up the ultimate question—do we really *want* to?''

Chua Gabaye, a stunning woman dressed in silver and black silks, stood up and pointed a finger at Ivan. ''What do you mean by that crack?'' she demanded. ''Is this some sort of silly test?''

''No, my lovely Chua, it's no test at all. It is instead an honest question. You all know that I met and talked at some length with Mervyn of the Nine, and during that time he asked me why in the world I wished to open the Gates. I gave him our pat answer, but, of course, it was just that—the pat answer, ready when needed even among ourselves and used to justify all our actions to ourselves and to any others we felt compelled to answer at all. It got me to wondering just how much of our ritualistic dedication was simply self-justification, and whether we really *would* open the Gates if the opportunity arose. I finally, after much agonizing, concluded that I would, but I have been a part of this group for centuries and I must honestly say that

I only really decided a few years ago. There can be no deviation. If six act properly and one hesitates, even at the last moment, those six, at least, are dead. I want each of you to address that question and answer it, because if all of you really want it, I can tell you how it will be done.''

"And what if somebody balks, or doesn't want to give the right answer?'' Gifford Haldayne asked him. "We lie a lot anyway, you know. It's part of doing business. Why should we be expected not to lie now when we sometimes even lie to ourselves?''

"I'll tell you why,'' Ivan responded. "Although I have decided that I want the Gates opened, it is not something that I feel any imminent compulsion to do. If *any* of you vote against, then I, too, will vote against. The technology that is now there will continue to be there, and it will get better as time goes on. That's tempting. I will not support any move to oust anyone who votes against, and I will be on their side if any move or attack is made upon them. The reason is simple: I wish an honest answer.''

For a while they were silent, pondering his statement, but finally Ming Tokiabi spoke. "Zelligman, I must admit the truth of what you say. The game has been amusing, the rewards great, but faced with actual checkmate, a total victory—I don't know. Perhaps it would help if you explained why *you* wish to have the Gates opened.''

"Fair enough,'' Ivan agreed. "I have multiple reasons, and they're compelling to me. First, as Chua said, I am bored. I have attained as much power and wealth as I believe it is possible for one individual to hold on World. The game is amusing only so long as there is a chance for one to lose. When, over eight years ago, I placed myself in Anchor Nantzee during the New Eden attack, I had what I thought were good reasons, but after I almost lost my life there I can tell you that those reasons were false. The fact was, I had every reason to know I was at great risk, and I *allowed* myself to be trapped there. I got out with Mervyn's help by a matter of seconds—and I had the best damned time I have had in two centuries! The thrill was incredible, but it was also a telltale sign. We always wondered why Coydt spent so much time in Anchor, and now I know why. He was vulnerable there, and he walked with danger every moment. He was compelled to do it. That disease is now striking me, and, I know, sooner or later, just like Coydt, I'll lose. Someone will kill me, and I will cease to exist. The more you tempt it, the more inevitable it becomes.''

He paused a moment, looking at their faces, and saw in at least a couple of expressions glimmerings of comprehension of what he was talking about.

"Second," he continued, "is the reason I was bored and regressing to a thrill-seeking idiot. All of us, when we start out in life, have lofty goals we aspire to, and very few of us attain all of them. I have. The only thing left for me is to perhaps take you all on and see if I can control the whole of human civilization on World. But don't worry—I can see nothing in it. I would inherit a larger slice of what I now have, and I have exhausted all my possibilities with that. Nor is there any long-range goal, ideal, or vision within me. I would probably lose and be killed, but even if I won—*even if I won*—I wouldn't know what the hell to do next. I have no goal but the playing of the game itself, and that is truly a terrible thing to admit.''

He sighed. "And so, still I look at the alternatives," he went on. "I do nothing, and, inevitably, the cancer of New Eden spreads. I would not like to live in a world without Flux, and New Eden's mix of animalistic humanity and ancient technology is *worse* than evil—it is incredibly *boring*. Their society is boring, their culture and values are simplistic and boring, and once they achieve that system throughout World they will become a static society, without imagination or creativity, in which everyone will be perfectly happy, essentially identical—well, they might as well all be dead.''

"Do you actually believe they will do that?" Gabaye asked, appalled at the thought.

"As our newest member can assure you, they can and they will. Oh, because it is so spiritless and mechanistic we can take it over in time, but what do we do with it then? Do any of you have a vision for humanity? What fun is there in being the one who orders the animals to jump through hoops? We can be worshipped by masses made in our images *now*. Would it mean any more if those masses were larger? I can only see to the horizon; the number of multitudes beyond that horizon are irrelevant. It has become a simple decision for me. Eternal boredom, death, or—take a chance. Open the Gates. They know Flux—they *must* know it far better than we, for they are coming from the source of all Flux. They promised to make us gods, and we are already gods as far as World is concerned. What do *they* mean by the term? What kind of beings are they? What kind of place do they come from? These are the only questions left for me, the only challenge, the only game. With that much power *they* certainly did not grow bored. It is a chance, one I am willing to take."

"And if the other side is right, and they are here to kill or enslave us all?" Varishnikar Stomsk asked worriedly. "What then? With their knowledge and power we could hardly stop them."

"True. It might be some monstrous version of us out there, more powerful than we could ever know. So then my choices are death or death. So, of the possibilities, two are death and one is godhood. Two to one odds against are not the best, but they are the best I have. And if you have not reached my point—where I would *grab* those odds and *embrace* them with all my heart and soul—you will one day, and the votes might not be there to save you, either. Discussion?"

There was a telling deadly silence, with each of them looking not at Ivan or each other but within themselves. For many, being so brutally honest with themselves was a new and revealing experience. Finally it was Gifford Haldayne who said, quietly, "Let's take a vote."

Ivan nodded and looked at them all, his expression still grim. "Rosa Haldayne?"

"I'm getting a little sick of it myself. You're right, Zell—it's all or nothing. Open them."

"Gifford Haldayne?"

"Why not? All the interesting enemies are dead."

"I take that as a yes. Chua Gabaye?"

"I never would have considered anything *but* a yes vote. All or nothing, darling—always."

"Ming Tokiabi?"

She hesitated a moment, as if still undecided. Finally she said, "Yes," without elaboration.

"Varishnikar Stomsk?"

"Our ancestors sealed the Gates almost twenty-seven hundred years ago now, and World as we know it and see it today is the end result. Had they been able to see what we've become, they would never have closed those Gates— *never!* Better the end, better slavery, better *anything* than *this!* Hell, yes!"

All eyes now turned to the seventh and newest member, Coydt van Haas' replacement. He alone would now decide, and he alone had the most stake in keeping things as they were.

"I know what you all are thinking," he said. "With burgeoning power and new discoveries being made almost daily, and with me ranking high on the side that will win, why should I? It might interest you to know what I am really like, inside. I want a different thing than the rest of you; I want the ultimate power. I want to know *everything*. It is not enough to know that something works, or how it works—I must know *why* it works, what forces and principles guide it. I want to know *everything*. That is power to me, and that is my dream. Godhood is not being worshipped by slaves, nor is it creating a little world of your own design by sheer force of will, as if you just told a machine to do it and then it read your mind and did exactly what you desired. Godhood is knowing how to *build* that machine, how it works, how it does what it does. Wizards aren't gods, they are machine operators—lowly operators; button-pushers and switch-throwers—and they're too ignorant to even realize that fact. I want to understand why and how it works.

"And I cannot know," he sighed. "We have sunk too far. We hold the end product of thousands of years of accumulated knowledge in our hands, but that chain of accumulated knowledge is denied us. It was cut off when the Gates were closed. In thousands of years we might be able to reinvent it, but as friend Zelligman points out, we are mortal gods, liable to be victims ourselves eventually or victims of our own minds. Human culture is not going in the direction of rediscovery, either, but into a permanent dark age of the mind. I am pessimistic, and I am impatient. That chain of knowledge exists, somewhere—on the other side of those Gates.

"There is a fellow in New Eden right now, the very same Matson who killed Coydt van Haas. He suggests a fourth alternative, Zelligman, one that may be far-fetched but which nonetheless tips the odds a bit more in our favor. He suggests that it might be possible to defeat them if they *are* an enemy. If we defeated them, we would be capable again with an irresistible lure to discover and link up once more with our relatives who created this world. Not two to one, but perhaps three to two—still against, but I am willing. No. I am *compelled* to vote yes."

Zelligman Ivan sighed and sank back in his chair. "The resolution is adopted unanimously with the chair, obviously, voting yes. Now I'm going to tell you exactly how we are going to do it."

Neither Mervyn nor anyone else had ever seen pain and anguish on Matson's face before, but it was certainly there now and he couldn't conceal it. It had taken almost five months to find Sondra in the still rampant confusion of the enlarged New Eden, and Matson still could hardly believe that the one he had was his daughter. She neither looked nor acted in any way like her, and only the tattooed name on her rump indicated any connection with the woman he'd raised.

After months of relative inactivity while he got the lay of the land and determined his next movies, Mervyn was suddenly in a hurry. Still he would not, could not, desert Matson and Sondra at this time.

The wizard identified her at once, and took her inside his small office in his new and increasingly permanent Flux haven, but before he went to work he talked with Matson.

"This won't be easy," he warned the stringer. "Even with all my power and experience, the fact is I revert to that New Eden body I have every time I sleep or relax for a while. I've found, too, like many other wizards caught in it who got out, my power is diminished. It's part of a worldwide situation—that much Flux removed has caused perhaps a fifteen percent overall decline in everyone's powers and abilities. Those caught inside when it blew lost additional power, since whatever power was needed to stave off complete domination by that damnable program was quite literally lost."

"What's that mean in layman's terms?"

"It means, first of all, that their attack and assimilation spell, being written in the same language as the landscape spell, got appended to it. Everyone caught in it was essentially made a part of the new reality, so that my default body, my genetic makeup, is not my old self but this new one. That's why I've kept it—it takes a lot of will to keep any other form."

"You mean that what's in there now may be a spell creation, but it's replaced her real self? There's nothing of me or her mother in her?"

Mervyn nodded. "I'm afraid so. Second, my powers are

still considerable, but they are perhaps sixty percent of what they were. That's still better than almost everybody else's eighty-five percent, but it's a major decrease. As strong as I was, look at how much damage it did to *me*. Sondra had great power, but we never knew how great because she never developed it fully. Her own protective spells and reaction time were a hair too slow, as was Jeff's, and he had far more training than she. What I'm saying is, I'll do what I can, but I don't know how much that will be, particularly after nearly six months and some preliminary conditioning. The mental spell is far easier to work with, since it wasn't complex or in what I call machine language, but as I'm finding out myself, behavior has far more physiological causes than I would have believed. Uh—she has a husband, children?"

"No. She spread that rumor herself to get folks off her back. After she quit the trail she tried retirement, went nuts after a few months, and was back out as a linesman for the Guild."

"What about her mother?"

"I've sent word. They weren't particularly close after Sondra joined the Guild, and her brother's her mother's boy all the way. You know her mother and I split years ago. The kids were grown, and I decided to go full time into the Guild officer corps."

"No, I didn't know, but it explains why you've been down here so long with no rush to get home. All right— I'll see what can be done."

The vacant, servile girl who was there showed no trace of anything going on in back of those beautiful but empty eyes. Only a dozen or so wizards had managed to stave off complete domination by the program; for the others, it seemed the harder you resisted the more extreme the result. Mervyn placed one hand on each side of her head and probed.

Eliminating the mental block that caused a sensation of pain when any but the most basic thoughts were formed was easily dissolved—it apparently was set to slowly dissolve over a year's time anyway. But six months of that might shatter anyone's ego, no matter how strong. He had to try to rebuild it. He probed and poked and stimulated memories, and was not surprised to see her fight against his efforts. The amount of fear and conditioning was enormous, but so was her subconscious, madly fighting to keep from facing those last six months. It was long, difficult, careful work, and he was soaked with perspiration at the effort that still was, basically, mental, but in four and a half hours he achieved a breakthrough.

Sondra began screaming hysterically, and Matson rushed in to see her pressed up against a wall, looking wild and terrified. He started to move towards her, but Mervyn put out a shaky hand and prevented him. It went on interminably, until both men thought they could bear no more, but finally she collapsed into a sobbing heap. Then Mervyn allowed Matson to go to her. But it was another day before she came around enough to even recognize him.

"They took me and they made me into cattle," she managed to utter at last. "They took from me all that was human and made me an *animal*!" She sat there on the bed, legs up, arms clasped around them, as if trying to shrink into a tiny ball. "I was raped, even gang raped, so many times I can't count. Raped and beaten, too. I hated it. I felt *filthy*, *degraded*—but I couldn't resist them," she said, with a faraway look in her eyes and a flatness in her tone. "After a while, all that's left of your mind just surrenders. You just don't care anymore. Your mind stops working, and only your senses are left." She paused for a moment, then added, "You wind up doing any disgusting thing they want—and they want a lot. We ate human flesh near the start to stay alive. They killed her and we ate it *raw*."

Mervyn looked over at Matson. "Some friends you got. Some real high ideals there."

Matson just shook his head sadly. "It only hurts real bad 'cause it's kin. I have to be honest about that. You and me and even her spent a lot of our lives going to and even working with places just as depraved. It just wasn't us, or our people, and when we got sick of it we could quit or go into Anchor and drink some sanity. Now it's come to Anchor. Seems to me it was inevitable.'' Sondra didn't even hear him.

"You're still going back there?'' the wizard asked.

He nodded. ''When it's necessary. There's a big Central Committee meeting next week to address the problems that'll develop when the main Anchor populations are moved inland. They're talking about defense and an early warning and navigational system using wireless transmission. You be sure and tell them that where *you're* going. You tell 'em, too, that if they want to crack New Eden they better do it quickly. In another year it's going to be as permanent as that new land out there.''

Mervyn nodded. ''Remember, it's taken six months just to assemble this conference at all, and it would never have happened even now if they hadn't all received detailed reports of the truth. They're suspicious of and frightened to death of New Eden, but they're also scared and suspicious of each other. We're talking a coalition of twenty-four Anchors and all the Fluxlands in between. It's unheard-of.'' He sighed. ''I wish you were coming with me.''

"My place is here. Sondra's gonna need me for a while, and I'm better off in New Eden, where I can give them the shakes and they don't even realize it.''

Mervyn left the next day, since he had many stops to make before reaching the conference, which by default was being held in the only Anchor with no army—Holy Anchor itself. It was a long trip for a weary and weakened wizard who could only stand there and scream, ''I told you so!''

Sondra improved daily, although it was when she saw Spirit that things seemed to get much better. Spirit was shocked at what had been done to her half-sister, and she felt the pain and humiliation. She pleaded with the Soul

Rider for some help, but the Rider could do little. Only a master computer could undo the matrix, as it called the spell, and master computers could not alter such a prime matrix without specific instructions from a human commander. And there hadn't been a human commander for almost twenty-seven hundred years.

For Sondra, it was difficult to look at the future at all. She could not change the way she looked, or the powerful urges of her body. She had been physically strong, and now she was weak. She had been a powerful wizard, and now she found it impossible to create the simplest spell. She had hardly ever cried, but she cried a lot now, and had trouble sleeping. It was the inability to fathom the printed word, though, that was most troubling to her. Not only did the scratches mean nothing to her, but she found she couldn't even *comprehend* how they worked. She felt, somehow, less than human. Finally, Matson sat down with her.

"Look, honey, you're gonna have to decide things now, whether you want to or not. I'm not gonna be a Mervyn and say 'I told you so,' because that don't mean shit anymore. What's done is done. Your first big decision is just who the hell you are."

She looked puzzled. "What do you mean?"

"Are you my daughter, Sondra, who got wounded in a fracas and maybe isn't what she was but she's still daughter of Matson? Or are you Sondra the Fluxgirl, totally surrendering to what happened and giving up doing anything except being somebody's slave?"

She felt like crying again, and fought back tears. "You don't know what it was like. What it's *still* like. Half of me wants to get up, find the biggest gun I can lift with these arms, go back in there and blast away at every man I see until they cut me down. The other half"—she did sob at this—"keeps saying, well, maybe I ought to just do what they say Cass and Suzl did. I think I can understand them now. The only thing I'm good for is a good screw, but that life would drive me up the wall."

"Well, maybe that's where you're different from them. They gave up, but they were *inside*. You're not."

"You heard what Mervyn said. I'm going to be like—this—forever. My Flux power's shot to hell, and those six months and this body are with me, too. O.K., I'm outside—but what's that get me? This Fluxgirl thing isn't just vacant eyes and saying 'yes, sir' to everybody. My mind always ran my body, but no more. The body—this body—runs the mind. It's like a drug you have to have all the time, one that you'll do anything for. I'm still an animal—I'm just one who *knows*."

"There are still possibilities. You could stay here with Spirit and the staff. No matter what I think you're still better off than she is. You could go home, or take refuge with the Guild."

"I—I *couldn't* go back, not to where people knew me. I couldn't *stand* it. The Guild would just be a constant reminder of what I've lost. Anyplace else and I'd be a traveling whore or a captive of some Fluxlord in no time. And staying here wouldn't give me what I have to have. So I kill myself, or I go back. That's not much of a choice."

He thought about it. "What about being a spy and a hostage?"

"What?"

"The big shots of New Eden know who you are, and they'd like very much to trust me but they just can't—quite. They need something to hold over me, and I need something for them to hold over me so I can crack their inner council. That's the hostage part."

She was suddenly very interested, and he could see a little of the old fire coming back into her eyes. "Go on."

"You think you could act the part? I can't know what you've gone through, or how you feel—how can anybody who didn't go through it? But I get the feeling that you're looking for any excuse not to stick a gun in your mouth. Could you be a good little Fluxgirl among the upper crust?

Good enough to not only fool the men but the other Fluxgirls, too?''

''What are you getting at?''

''Fluxgirls can go places men can't. They're safe. They're servile, obedient, fearful, and, besides, they can't read or write or understand complicated machinery. They service and clean the science building, and they also clean the offices of the important. Nobody cares if a Fluxgirl's around when they're discussing plans, politics, and projects. That's the way Mervyn and the others have gotten their information from the start, but nobody has ever had direct access to the top. But that's just where they'd want you, so you were always around my haunts. It'll be rough. They'll re-run you through a conditioning program that'll make the other one seem tame, just to be on the safe side. You might have to marry a big shot, and if you survive all that and get caught, well, they'll give you one of the dumb drugs and don't even think of what'll happen to me.''

''But one reason it's so safe around Fluxgirls is they can't even read. Some spy I'd make.''

''You still got your brain, and it always was a pretty good one. You're still tough as nails—and anybody but you would be broken and hopelessly insane from what you went through. You got eyes to see pictures and maps and diagrams; you got ears to overhear all sorts of chatter. You can get lots of stuff from sheer girl's gossip—who's come to town, who's leaving town, all that. Only you can decide if your wounds are fatal.''

She smiled, then hugged and kissed him. ''I'm your daughter, remember! I won't get caught!''

The Central Committee meeting had gone on for days. The large-scale building projects were going well, and thanks to the Glider Corps and the science team's use of the new field of photography they had a pretty good, if somewhat rough, idea of what the New Land was like.

The Great Sea, as they were calling it, was enormous—it

cut an irregular shape from the former Anchors Logh, Mantzee, and Mareh, and seemed to cover about sixty percent of the old void. It also appeared quite deep, although nobody knew how deep, but while much of it was still unmapped they had the outlines and the positions of some major islands.

The Hellgate remained intact, although all the amplifiers the Nine had established to seal it had been destroyed in the program. The sea came almost to the Gate, but stopped short by a kilometer or two. The Gate itself retained a flat, greenish apron not heretofore visible stretching about three hundred kilometers around the saucer-like depression. While some Flux power was possible there, it was quite weak and limited; only in the rear part of the tunnel nearest the swirling Gate itself was the old magic possible. Since it was so limited in area but accessible from all four former temples this was considered quite handy. The link between the four temple basements also still worked, which simplified communication and interaction between commands enormously, but since traffic could enter only from and between the temples, and not from the Hellgate due to the defense mechanisms, it would not be as useful if the centralized capital were moved near it, as they had planned.

Although they were still finding small knots of people, they basically knew what they had to deal with now, and even Champion was pleased and impressed by the thoroughness of the transformation program. The prior population of all four Anchors had been 1.4 million males and 1.9 million females. They had thought they'd known their own Flux neighborhood well, and after the Great Sea they had dramatically reduced their expectations, and they were pleased, if a bit shocked, to now count over seven hundred thousand new men and almost nine hundred and fifty thousand new Fluxgirls. While there had apparently been some period of infertility after the transformation, it appeared that almost half being processed now were pregnant. It was a sizeable population, but one that they felt they could feed and clothe. The problem was adequate housing. Most were now living in makeshift camps with primitive shelter and facilities, doing extensive cultivation and planting, while several battalions of men were erecting temporary and prefabricated housing units far inland. It was hoped that they would be ready for occupancy, if not exactly cozy and comfortable, by the time cold weather set in, which would not be too long from now.

These things were proceeding well, but basic communications between the outposts and settlements was still dependent on hastily strung wires that often as not didn't work, and hardly covered more than a fraction of the distance. Matson had ingratiated himself with them for suggesting that while one couldn't walk *into* a Hellgate one could most certainly walk *out*, and they'd strung wires from all four temples into the tunnel and back up, giving them all communication with the still-primitive new capital, between the Hellgate and the Great Sea.

Their mind-set was such that they had accepted Sondra back without even being surprised. They *had* insisted on a thorough reconditioning by their top experts, and he sympathized with what she had to be going through but knew that it couldn't come close to what she'd already survived. If that old spark could be rekindled after her first horrible experience, it was not likely to be extinguished by the usual methods; but the further conditioning would serve to make her instinctively act as this society thought she should. That was good for the safety of them both.

Finally, the Committee got around to the nub of the problem.

"Gentlemen, this new land is so vast—we *must* have near-instant communications. We must know when we're being invaded, not three weeks after the fact. We must be able to coordinate schedules, goods, food. We need faster means of transportation and we need instant communications. Dr. Sligh?"

"I have put our best minds on these projects," the

scientist replied, "and we have solutions, but they are not immediate ones, I fear. Communications is easier. You can imagine our chagrin when we discovered, after working there for over twenty-five years, that the intercom system in the old temples is wireless! A signal is broadcast and it travels by the easiest and best route to the assigned destination. A large system could broadcast through the air to every corner of the land from its center—and vice-versa. It is a matter of power. We have the diagrams and small systems with which to build it, but we have no sufficient power source as yet. The ancients depended far too much on Flux, but they knew exactly how to use it. We do not, and unless someone wants to suggest opening the Hellgate we can't get to it anyway."

There were chuckles all around at that.

"However, in the historical library in Holy Anchor, of all places, are many books with basic principles apparently dating back far before Flux. They are elementary physics books, possibly teaching aids for the young, but they are most fascinating. We know the principle of the storage battery— even the city's Flux-gained electricity comes from there. We know that steam under pressure will generate great force, and from those books we have the principle of what they call the turbine. They will be tricky to build and trickier, and very dangerous, to test."

"Where are you going to get the steam—boil the Great Sea?" one Judge cracked. "It must be there for *some* reason." They all roared.

"No, although perhaps someday you'll eat your laughter. But we *do* know how hot peat and coal can get. Many Anchors have it—Mareh is full of the stuff. There is a *lot* of it as well in the new areas. We will dig it out with machines now being manufactured in our western factories."

"That'll take *tons*," another Judge pointed out. "How will you get it to your turbine or whatever the hell you called it?"

"The very same principle. In the van Haas collection is

a toy that is quite clever. It's a small vehicle that runs on steam directly turning the gears that turn the drive wheels. It chugs around on tracks, and it can pull quite a toy load. It was either a toy or another instructional model, but there seems no reason why that scale has to be the limit. Again, tricky and dangerous testing, and a fairly long time to lay tracks, but we first have to lay them only two hundred and twenty kilometers from the main source of peat and coal to the capital. There it feeds our generator, powers our city, and eventually powers our broadcast and receiving tower as well."

"Incredible," one of the Judges said. "I thought the ancients just relied on Flux like super wizards, but this is *really* advanced!"

"The coal and peat will eventually be limited, but by then we should have many other ways to get our power. And these steam cars will run on wood as well as coal, I feel certain."

Tilghman was fascinated. "How long would something of this magnitude take with what we have now?"

"Mining could begin as early as three months from now. We have the equipment, and the new men can be put to work there. A working turbine and generator system is far more complex. We have the theory and the plans, but it might be three to five years to get a basic system up, seven to ten to produce really adequate power for both the new city and the broadcast system. The same thing goes for the steam vehicles—three years to build, test, and produce, another two for laying down the track and that's not going to be easy. Much as I hate to do it, we can still use amplified Flux west of Nantzee to duplicate rails and cross-beams that require precise size standards, as we are now doing with the housing kits. Still, I feel that within a decade we can criss-cross the new land with at least two rail lines and have full, steady broadcast communication."

Tilghman and the others nodded, impressed. The Chief Judge looked over at Matson. Many still had strong reservations about him, but as he himself had predicted they needed every outsider they could get who was not automatically against them. "Mr. Matson, you had some objections to this in your status of observer?"

"Just one. The rail thing I don't know much about but I can't see any but good from it, but the broadcast system tells me that ten years from today the Gates of Hell will be opened, and without even a risk to the Seven. You just take the remote control devices, or improvements on them, that you used for the big project, set them to trigger at a specific signal, and that's that. They all key in the combinations at once, and there we are."

"Impossible!" Sligh retorted. "The broadcast system does not go far in Flux. The amount of power required for a worldwide broadcast is beyond any hope of generation even if it did. There is no danger. We have already tested and retested this."

Tilghman looked at Matson. "Do you know something we don't?"

"I will tell you that it's possible, that's all. And what's possible *will* be done. In ten years, I tell you, whatever is on the other side of those Gates will be here."

"Over my dead body!" Champion snapped.

"Very likely," Matson agreed.

The conference in Holy Anchor did not go well. The Fluxlords, fearful of their loss of power and control, were determined to attack New Eden, but they hadn't a prayer without the combined support of the Church and the Anchors, who were used to dealing in an Anchor environment. The Church, too, was upset, but the scars from the old Empire ran deep, and memories of the massive losses and inconclusive ending to the struggle produced a great deal of reluctance to commit themselves again to a massive military campaign estimated to cost up to a million lives. They'd have to go entirely in Anchor against a foe whose approaches could be guarded by amplifiers and whose terrible weapons had been so well demonstrated at Bakha.

The greatest shock was from the Anchors themselves, many of whom found the weakening of Flux an excellent idea and some of whom, although a minority, were tempted by the landscaping program themselves. There was never any love lost between Flux and Anchor, and old hatreds and suspicions ran deep.

Mervyn had expected far more, particularly from the female leaders, almost all of whom found New Eden extremely repulsive, but he received backing from only a small fanatical handful within the large groups. Like the others, they were fearful that they could not succeed in an attack on an area as vast as New Eden now was, and they seemed far more concerned with protecting what they had than in stamping out what they had not.

The most damaging argument was that New Eden was not any longer, or in the foreseeable future, a threat to the rest of World. It was still only six percent of the inhabitable area, only a seventh of the Anchors, and, after a strong expansionist period, it by necessity had to turn inward to build and develop what it had. It was also forcefully argued that their technology and development would be entirely Anchor-oriented, and that they would be even less a threat to Flux in the future. New Eden itself sent a message saying as much, and also stating categorically that the landscape program could not be implemented much beyond its present extent without serious risk to World's overall climate and perhaps other conditions as well.

Mervyn and many others argued with equal force that, while New Eden was in fact opposed to the opening of the Gates, its research into communications and alternate power sources would bring the means of such an opening within reach of the Seven within a few years. Flux was inadequate as a power source or transfer medium, but the New Eden scientists were learning—or re-learning—fast, and while refusing to go into details the stringers affirmed that such a communications system was not only possible but probable.

This was countered by the bulk of leaders who, it was found, didn't really believe in the existence of the Seven, considering it an old tale designed to reinforce control by the Church in its areas. When named as one of the Seven, Zelligman Ivan himself appeared and did a virtuoso performance mocking the very concept.

All of this was most disturbing to the Nine, who saw and felt the hidden strings of the Seven in much of the attitudes and fears reflected in the group. Clearly the Seven and the Nine agreed on New Eden's potential, but the Seven wished that potential fully realized.

In the end, what they decided upon was not war but a policy of containment and watchfulness. New Eden could survive and prosper, but it must not expand its borders. An attack on any remaining Anchor was to be considered an attack on all remaining Flux and Anchor and would automatically trigger war. Otherwise New Eden could continue, and even export its technology. While uniformly deploring the theology and morality of the place, a pragmatic approach was prudent to keep it from spreading.

Mervyn gave a stirring speech before the final adoption of the agreements, reminding them of his prior warnings and stating flatly that if New Eden were given the time it would become invulnerable. He pointed to the large Church leadership and the female wizards and warned them that it was their future they were seeing in New Eden. He made them uncomfortable, but the issue had already been decided.

About the only accomplishment he made was in getting copies of the Haller journal to Ivan and to Gabaye and Stomsk as well, both of whom were also present and active behind the scenes. As Haller's great-great grandson, he thought he had the right and the duty to show them what had happened. They were fascinated, but undeterred. They were completely amoral and egocentric. To them, only what they did or what happened to them was important or even relevant. They were willing to open the Gates no matter what the consequences because they were bored or wanted something different. Absolute power had so jaded them that they were willing to risk their own lives and the possible annihilation of humanity just to see what happened.

The Nine could do nothing now on their own against New Eden, although they now granted Mervyn's point, previously rejected, that it was the real threat. Their power was in Flux, not Anchor, and New Eden had effectively placed itself outside their control. They would guard the Gates they could. As for Mervyn, he was beginning to come around to Matson's point of view. As hopeless as it sounded, they had better prepare to defend World from invasion from an enemy they didn't know, couldn't understand, and which was as technologically far ahead of them as man was from the horse.

16

MAJOR STORM WARNINGS

New Eden had changed a lot in the six and a half years since Matson had moved there. Anchor Logh, called simply North Borough, was still agricultural, but it was now a backwater save the science and technical research complex in the old temple, and even that was mostly a library and university-style facility, as were the other three. The population had shrunk from more than a million to now just under a hundred and eighty thousand, and that counted the soldiers on permanent duty there. It was amazing now quickly the old capital had become a provincial backwater, and how quickly it had gone to seed.

As he'd predicted, it had taken Sligh's group almost three years to perfect the steam boiler and generators, but once that had been done production proved easy, particularly when the shortcut of Flux was used for mass production. Determining a proper weight-size ratio for the steam vehicles before producing one had permitted the production of and laying of track almost from the time of the decision, and in fact a rail line was already in full operation using horse-drawn cars and spring-assisted hand-cars long before the first steam engine was placed on line. The new capital city of New Canaan rose from the plains between the Hellgate and the Great Sea in record time, using timber from the virgin forests and rock quarried from the canyons and fissures to the northeast. By the end of five years there was a single-track rail line from New Canaan to West Borough, the former Anchor Nantzee, and they were hard at work on the northern line, first to North Borough and then to the former Anchor Bakha. The Great Sea blocked direct access to Nantzee, but eventually a rail line down the shoreline was in the plans, and a study group was looking at the feasibility of large ships, possibly wind-powered, that would be even cheaper and more efficient in that direction.

The bulk of the men with nonessential skills were put into mining and construction; the women's role was broadened again so that they did almost all of the agricultural work, and a clear division of labor was developing.

New Canaan still wasn't luxurious, but it was serviceable. Long lines of poles connected it through telegraphy with many of the centers of civilization, and while the streets were still mostly dirt and the buildings more utilitarian than homey, it was taking on the look of a growing and bustling boom town.

During this period Matson had arranged for stringer aid in the telegraphy system and had established a network of trails and regular trade and supply routes which were handled by New Eden locals but under stringer supervision. Matson had to admit to himself that as much as he had doubts about the people and the system, he found this new land an invigorating challenge and was somewhat caught up in the excitement of the pioneer experiment. The fact that they had cut the stringers in, in exchange for exclusivity on some technology, seemed to satisfy all and was a very smart move on New Eden's part.

Matson himself had chosen to live in a log cabin about

five kilometers north of the town itself. It was a spacious but single-room affair with fireplace, hand-hewn furniture, and, incongruously, an electric line going in, a telegraph line spliced in, but with no indoor plumbing. He did have a well, with a creaky hand pump in the front yard, and that was all he needed.

After all his services and all this time, no one in any way questioned him. He was quite well known, and enjoyed official protection. Even Cassie and Suzl had warmed to him to a great degree, which he found gratifying although he couldn't explain to himself why. Cassie's twins, Candy and Crystal, were well past puberty now and they were startling in that both differed from each other only in their tattoos and their fingerprints, which were direct opposites. Both also were almost physical carbon copies of their ageless mother except for higher-pitched voices and thicker lips. The pair were very close, often seeming to be thinking the same thoughts, and one often completed the other's sentences.

They had been raised as upper class Fluxgirls, so they had no education to speak of and had learned how to behave and how to sew, cook, clean, host functions, and that sort of thing. They were, however, far brighter than Fluxgirls were supposed to be, and experts at concealing it except around the home. They did, however, have the Fluxgirl's curse, as Matson thought of it, in that no matter how smart they were their bodies increasingly ruled their minds. In the end it was that, and not any fancy conditioning or machines or spells, differentiating the sexes and their roles in the present and developing New Eden.

Cassie and Tilghman had "loaned" him the twins when they were fourteen to come out every once in a while and straighten up his place and do housekeeping chores. He liked them a lot, and they began to let down the guard on their intelligence around him and ply him with questions to which there were no answers in New Eden—except from him—and he discovered their innermost fear. So far, they shamelessly admitted, they had been able to satisfy themselves on each other, since each knew *exactly* what the other liked, but the tension and pressure was still building, and they knew they would soon have to be married off. They feared being married off to different men and separated.

Still, he was surprised when he was asked to dinner one evening and found himself the only guest; not even the children were at the table, although both Cassie and Suzl were with Tilghman. After dinner, when everything had been cleared, and the Tilghmans all remained, and Adam startled Matson by saying, "If you'd like to smoke, use the saucer there as an ash tray. You have my permission to do so here."

He took advantage of the offer, but wondered what bomb was about to be dropped on him. He looked at the three of them and had to marvel at them all. None had changed one bit since he'd first met them, and he no longer had any real feeling that the two women were in any way the same people he had once known. They were now friends, but they had been strangers.

"Matson," Tilghman began, "you've pretty well settled down here now. I know you don't go along with everything we do, but you're still an accepted part of the community."

Yeah, he thought, amused. *I'm the one group eccentric.*

"I know that none of us can know the future, but you seem pretty well settled and content," the Judge continued. "Our daughters think highly of you, you know. In fact, I suspect they have a very strong crush on you."

It must be in the genes, he thought, but aloud he said, "Yes, I'm very fond of them myself."

Tilghman smiled. "As you know, they pose a problem of sorts. They are more like one person in two bodies than two individuals, unusual even for twins. They're also a bit too bright and curious to fit into the usual social scene around here, and because of who their parents are there is a lot of contention over who will marry them, something that can't really be avoided. The other kids pose less of a problem, but I'd rather they didn't become the wives of one of my colleagues on the Central Committee or of one of the top army officers, if you understand what I mean.''

He did. Once married, they could by their very intelligence be a gun at Tilghman's head, since their husbands could literally do anything with them, including arrange for mind-dulling injections, and they were clearly his favorites. Rather quickly, Matson guessed where this was leading.

''Adam, I'm as old or older than you are, and I have kids three times their ages.''

Tilghman looked at Cassie and Suzl. ''It didn't stop me, and it did me a world of good. You're the only one I'd trust them with, truthfully. We've all three discussed this, and we all agree it's the best solution.''

He sighed. ''Look, all of you. I've never been the family type. The only time I was a husband I was a poor one. I think of them like I think of my own kids, not any other way. I've got a one-room shack and I'm on the move a lot.''

Cassie looked him straight in the eyes. ''Please,'' she said softly. ''For *my* sake.''

He cursed her silently, even though she didn't understand the meaning or the import of what she'd just said. Finally, he sighed. ''Let me sleep on it. Let me think about it a bit, will you?'' He hesitated. ''Uh—have *they* been told about this?''

''No,'' Cassie replied. ''Anyone who tells 'em will be punished bad. Only if you say yes will they know.''

He got up from the table. ''As I say, let me think on it a little bit. How old are they now?''

''They've just turned fifteen,'' Tilghman told him.

''Let me wrestle with it a bit, and I'll let you know.''

He left the house, but he didn't immediately go home. He had gotten a signal earlier in the day and now rode just a few blocks to another house as spartan as Tilghman's currently was, and just as drab.

Sondra was glad to see him. They had married her off to General Levett, now Chief of Security forces for New Caanan, which had pleased Matson from an information point of view and apparently had pleased Sondra as well. The general was hardly known as a wonderful fellow—he was, perhaps, the most feared of all men in New Eden because of his job—but he was ruggedly handsome, very much a lover of beautiful women, and he'd wanted children. He must have—he was away quite a lot, yet Sondra already had two sons and a daughter by him and was noticeably pregnant now. The number of youngsters afoot kept her constantly very busy and she assured him she was never bored for lack of work.

When he'd first met her after her reconditioning he feared that all of the old Sondra had been vanquished forever, but much of it was still there, under the surface. She had thrown herself into her new role of mother and housewife as intensively as she had ridden strings in Flux. To her surprise and satisfaction she found that the iron man of security wanted a wife who really *ran* the home, and, in fact, was bright and somewhat forward with him. She found it easy; she said she just let the conditioning take automatic control and stopped fighting the body and let it run. In six years the feared and efficient security chief, secure in the knowledge that his wife was permanently deep-programmed and could not read or write, never dreamed that she was still interested in far more than her family and concerned with issues far beyond his own welfare and hers. When she cleaned in his study, she observed. While it was frustrating not to be able to read the documents, it was less so to look at drawings and photographs, and with her father supplying an incredibly small and simple camera, even the documents could be passed along.

And nobody was going to be mean, nasty, or in any way

question the Chief of Security's wife, particularly when that Chief was almost always the guard's boss. And could anyone question the occasional visits of a father to see his daughter and grandchildren?

"What's new with you?" she asked him, while rocking the youngest in a rocking chair. The boy was nodding off, more interested in his thumb than her breast at this point.

"Would you believe the old man wants me to marry *both* his twins?"

Sondra giggled. "Now *that's* something! You've needed a woman's touch for some time. Are you gonna do it?"

He sighed. "I'm being engineered into it. Damn it, when *Cassie* looks into my eyes and says, 'Do it for my sake,' I feel a cannon at my head. If I just didn't *feel* my age. . . ."

"The spell's not holding?"

"Oh, it's not the body, it's up here," he told her, tapping his head.

"If you *act* old, you *feel* old," she chided him. "Maybe this is what you need to get young again. Me, I feel like I been reborn. Oh, I still wouldn't like to be out there pickin' tomatoes or whatever it is, and I feel sorry for most of the girls, but for me it's O.K. I don't have the dreams so much any more, and I keep thinking of all the Fluxlands I knew. Maybe one in ten was better than this, and things keep getting better around here."

He nodded. "It's too big for them. They can't keep tight control and they don't have enough of a labor pool to manage it the old way. They made you girls so you can't handle a pick or a sledgehammer or do that kind of heavy work, so the men are doing their share and marrying the farm girls. This place has long-term possibilities, I'll now admit, if we live long enough to see them."

Her expression darkened. "That's what I wanted to see you about. There's some very secret project going on just east of the Hellgate. Lev had to send about a third of his force up there to seal it off from the public. I don't know exactly what it is—I'm not sure *he* does—but it has something to do with welding a lot of steel girders, and using a lot of very heavy cable. They've had to secure shipments of those from the west.''

He sighed. "The broadcast tower. They've gotten to it at last.'' He got up, then bent down and kissed her on the forehead. "Good work, honey. You keep your eyes and ears open for anything else on that, but don't take any chances. Now that I know it's on, and where, I have other means of following up. You take care—you hear?''

She nodded. "You, too, Daddy. And you might as well marry them. If all hell's gonna break loose they deserve at least a little fun.''

Spirit had remained in New Pericles with Mervyn. It seemed to make him happy, and he was otherwise in a state seesawing between depression and despair. She herself was quite depressed at times, thinking of all the people close to her who were now changed and gone. Although Matson visited her when he could, the move to the center of New Eden had made it a major expedition and thus cut down the frequency. He had, through signing, managed to convey to her that Sondra was doing as well as could be expected under the circumstances, and that her mother was well and seemed happy, but there had been, according to him, no real sign of Jeff.

And that was almost literally true. Sondra had, of course, accompanied him until they met up with a larger band of men and women, but by that point she'd no longer been able to distinguish individuals, particularly men. A records check had indicated that he had indeed checked in, and had been assigned to duty somewhere in the west, but records now went with the individual—they could no longer be centralized—and Matson had not pursued him after hearing Sondra's story. He was afraid he'd kill him, and he didn't want *that* on his conscience.

When the Soul Rider had wanted to get a sense of the

country, she'd ridden with Sondra and the train. Now it seemed only to want to be as close as possible to New Eden, although it wasn't sure why. Orders. It *did*, however, in due course, admit to a few things that shocked Spirit, and showed why Soul Riders had never before been allowed to communicate with people directly.

Soul Riders had the ability to influence others with Flux power without their knowledge, a fact that was well known, but the extent of such meddling was shocking, particularly when it was merely following orders and did not fully understand the reasons for its actions.

The Soul Rider had subtly convinced Matson to remain in New Eden.

The Soul Rider had reinforced Sondra and Jeff's resolve to remain in old Pericles despite New Eden's warnings, even though it knew at that point what would happen. And when Spirit had been comforting the "new" Sondra, it had blotted out much of the horror of her immediate past and had muddled her Flux power so that it was useless— although it was actually still there. It had also changed her mind from a determination on suicide to a willing acceptance of being a Fluxgirl, and had suggested to Matson the espionage role. It, or its master, had *wanted* Matson, Sondra, and Jeff in New Eden on a permanent basis. It was routine, it said lamely, and those weren't the first. There were many others.

"Others! What others? My mother, for instance?"

Your mother and I go back a long way, it responded uncomfortably. *I was her before I was you. Do not be so shocked. You, yourself, are the result of one of my actions.*

"Don't evade the question! Is my mother the way she is now because you caused her to be depressed and be so vulnerable?"

I did not cause the depression. But your mother is no longer a prime component in the ongoing master plan. Because of her previous disgust at the war of the Empire, she is considered less certain to be objective when the time comes. She remains, however, a backup.

"What do you mean, 'prime component'? What master plan?"

I don't know. When the time comes to implement it, only then will I be told.

"Who are the other 'prime components,' then?"

Mervyn is important, of course, but I would have thought you would understand. It is why I am here, inside you. You are my prime component. Your son, and then your mother, are backups.

That both startled and frightened her too much to press on for now. Instead, she changed the subject.

"I have been thinking of having another child." She had near total control of her body, and could choose it or not as she wished.

I know. I wish you would reconsider. The time for action is drawing near, I fear. You are letting your emotions over Jeff's loss cloud your thinking. Pregnant, you might not be as free to move as you might need to be. With a baby, even less so. Wait. There is time.

"All I've got are my feelings and you," she retorted, "and I'm not so sure about you anymore. Will you stop me if I do it?"

In the absence of orders, no. I can only recommend against it. There is a good possibility that none of us will survive through the next year or two. Not even I.

That sobered her, but it didn't change her feelings. What would be would be. You could never assume you were going to die, you always had to act like you're going to live forever. You just might.

Sondra had been both right and wrong about the twins. He *did* feel great relief as the loneliness he'd borne all those years was lifted from him, and he greatly delighted in having two wide-eyed wonders under his wing, but having two fifteen-year-old virgins around whose genetic and hormonal makeup was designed to give and receive every sensual pleasure made him feel old and inadequate in many ways. It wasn't *quite* like marrying two women, though; more like marrying one with double everything. Their Flux origins, however unintended, showed in a number of ways. They tended most of the time to talk in unison when together. If he told something to one of them inside while the other was outside, the other one seemed to know it anyway. This wasn't the fooling around of many identical twins; he discovered that they actually thought of themselves as a single individual. When one hit her knee, the other's knee bruised, too, in an identical pattern. And even when one was well away from the other, which was rare, each seemed to know exactly what the other was doing.

He did not have to teach them about sex. They seemed to know instinctively just what to do and they did it like seasoned veterans. The fact that he seemed to satisfy both of them made him feel young and vigorous; the fact that he was able to made him generally very tired.

He got them their own horses and saddles, and while they knew how to ride in a general sense he taught them how to do it effortlessly—and skillfully. They took to it quite well, although it was a problem getting them riding gear that was useful and yet didn't violate even the relaxed dress codes. Pants were generally forbidden Fluxgirls, but the pairs they made out of some tough but flashy silver glitter material and the other pair out of orange fur passed muster, because while they served their purpose he had known few men in or out of New Eden who would be willing to be found dead in them. Together with their silver high-heeled boots and fur jackets—or nothing, if the weather permitted—they were certainly attention-getters on horseback.

Like their mother, they preferred generally to wear as little as possible, and nothing around home, unless they needed it for warmth or protection. Although pampered all their lives, they considered the rough life an adventure, even to going out and pumping the water, then heating it on the stove, then carrying it over to the tub to take a bath. They did not mind getting dirty in the least, but it seemed that that was because it gave them an excuse to take another bath, trouble or not.

They were curious about the outside world and the past, and he was free and honest with them, within reason. There were, however, disconcerting cultural problems, such as when he described independent women who led independent lives and did many of the same jobs men did either as well or better.

"Why would they want to?" they asked him. Try as he might, and he tried mightily, he could not convince them that the role of women in New Eden was limiting, or unfair, or even undesirable. For a woman not to want a husband and family and to prefer to work at whatever career she wanted they considered sick, a mental illness. Like Sindi, long ago, they actually *pitied* men the roles they had to play. Men's lives were all work and worry and pressure, and society gave them generally uninteresting bodies. Even their dress and manner was dull and boring. Girls, they told him, were far more free in society than men were. "Let's see you kiss a man in public and not have everybody drawing all the wrong conclusions about you," they taunted.

He told them, with some hesitancy, about their own origins. He felt he had to, when he figured out the right way to do it. He told them about Cassie's origins and her legendary rise and fall, and he even eventually told them about Spirit and who her parents were, and why they hadn't married. "When your mom came here, she fell in love with your dad, but she had too much of a burden on her mind, too many memories, and, I guess, me, too." And that was why, he concluded, both their moms had chosen to have their memories just wiped away. He emphasized that they chose to do so, and did not describe the coercive nature of both their arrivals in New Eden.

They were fascinated by the romance of the adventures but unable to reconcile the two women who'd raised them as having done all that in the past, and they ultimately rationalized it as two girls who'd been raised in a sick society who'd been forced by accidents into roles girls shouldn't ever have to play, who'd eventually found true peace and contentment here.

Sondra found the twins fascinating and delightful, but she also continued to play *her* other role. "There are very strange things going on," she told him. "Lev's been meeting with Champion and a bunch of other old officers from the early days. Secret meetings, mostly at night and away from the city. Some of the names are commanders of places that are very far from here. None of the Judges know, I'm sure, but I've heard Sligh's name and somebody named Conrad."

"Sligh's chief administrative officer," he told her. "That fits."

"But the craziest thing is that in Lev's study I saw some pictures taken by balloon, I think, showing what they're doing at the Gate. It looks like a tower all right, but there's no power lines anywhere. Not even poles. Just a big, ugly black line like a snake going right down into the Gate!"

With that, he went to Tilghman, making certain that there was no one who could overhear. "My stringers have been taking a good look at the broadcast tower at the Gate," he told the Chief Judge.

Tilghman frowned. "How could you do that? That's off limits to everybody."

"We have our methods in the Guild. You should know that."

"Or expected it. What of it? You knew the plans."

"But your power cable doesn't run south to the city or to any generating plant we can see. It runs into the Gate. That's how they're going to tap the required power. They've found out how to patch into the step-down transformer that feeds Flux to the temples. It'll black out everything left that runs on Flux, including the west's factories, but it'll send one *hell* of a signal. It'll send a signal straight out of New Eden and straight through Flux in all directions all the way to the poles. It'll trigger remote control devices on the other Gates that I'll bet are either already in place and booby trapped like mad or soon will be. I warned you, Adam!''

He shook his head in wonder. ''But how is it possible? I mean, any downward shift on a cable that size, and even gravity will cause some of that, would activate the defenses and vaporize the cable.''

''There's some kind of signal you can send to turn it off. Coydt knew it, so I assume that it's somewhere in those records of his and the Seven finally discovered it. I know that signal exists because I've walked in a Gate just that way myself.''

''My God!'' Tilghman breathed. ''I'll get the army on this right away.''

''No. That's why I made such a search of this place. I'm using a gadget now that scrambles our conversation beyond a few feet and plays hell with all listening devices. There are a half dozen in this room. The major army commanders are all in on it. Sligh, too. He'd have to be, as well as all the old Coydt loyalists except you politicians who would oppose it.''

Tilghman looked suddenly very old and very weak. ''Champion, too?''

''And Levett, I'm very sorry to say, and most of the district commanders.''

''Not all,'' the Judge said, suddenly growing firm and angry. ''I made certain of that early on. Few know I'm much of a wizard at all, and only a very few know just how powerful I am. I can count on at least ten thousand good men from West Borough—if I can sneak them through." He paused a moment. "You're *certain* about this?"

"I wish I wasn't."

"How long do you estimate until they're ready to go?"

Matson shrugged. "I didn't see the place myself, after all. When did they tell you the master tower would be completed?"

"In ninety days."

"Count on that, then. Right now they're probably planning a whole charade, with you and the others lined up to cut the ribbon and make the first broadcast. They'll probably put up four walls and string some meaningless wires that'll look convincing. But that broadcast will be heard 'round the world, and you'll still be standing there when whoever or whatever shows up in that big hole out there."

Tilghman was all thought now. "What will you do?"

"I'm overdue to visit Spirit, and the twins have been anxious to meet her and also see what Flux looks like. I'd like to use that as an excuse to coordinate with Mervyn and see what steps can be taken to dismantle those remotes on the other Gates or, failing that, to prepare for invasion. They'll think it's normal and be glad to be rid of me. Stringers might also try, if we have the time, to jam or disperse that signal. But I'll be back here in plenty of time for the deadline, no matter what."

"I'll start things in motion as soon as I can devise a safe way to do it. If it's this pervasive, though, I don't know if anything will work short of bombing the thing from spring-launched gliders."

"That's a chance. As a last-ditch attempt. I doubt if the big boys have told the ones in on the plot that the opening of the Hellgate is the plan. They must think they're going to overthrow you for some reason—old grudges, going too fast, whatever. I can't imagine why Lev would make four babies and then go open the Gate."

"Matson—take care of my daughters. Leave them with Spirit for the duration if you can."

"No, Judge. For one thing, I can't hide anything from them. You must know that. For another, they're very loyal Fluxwives. Where I go, they go—remember? Besides, if these idiots actually open those fucking Hellgates what difference will it make where *any* of us are?"

17

TWISTS AND TURNS

For one with rank and position, getting to the border was not the ordeal it had been only a few years earlier. Matson didn't really trust the steam trains, as they were being called after the stringer trains of Flux, but he had to admit they were faster.

The driver car in front didn't look like much; a giant steam boiler on wheels with a large stack a little more to the front than center of the boiler. In the rear was a platform for the driver and the fueler, whose job it was to haul wood from the platform on the next car back and get it into the boiler furnace at a steady rate while keeping from knocking the driver off the platform and controls. In the rear, held to the engine by heavy steel pivot bolts, were a half-dozen cars each the size of the engine, one of which was for carrying horses and other livestock, one for passengers which was basically four thin wooden walls and a wooden roof atop a flatcar base to which ten benches that must have come from some Anchor park were bolted, and a series of wooden cars with low or no sides to which was lashed cargo.

The first line had been from the coal fields and peat bogs of the northeast to New Canaan, passing through much virgin forest which provided a lot of wood for fuel and construction. The second line had been to West Borough, so that the industrial products there could be easily shipped to the center of the country. They had not yet gone all the way to North Borough, the former Anchor Logh, but the land was flat, track-laying had been easy, and they were only thirty kilometers south of the old wall now, close enough to cut the time north for passengers from twenty days' hard horseback riding to just about thirty hours at the engine's average speed of fifty kilometers per hour. That meant New Canaan to Anchor Logh in just about two days even with the ride at the end, and that was blinding speed to any of them, although many of the strongest men quaked with terror at the thought of going fifty kilometers per hour.

It was still a very uncomfortable ride, being shaken and tossed all over by the minimal springs on the car. It was nearing the end of the hottest season, which meant that the car soon became stifling if you kept the windows shut, but filled with foul-smelling smoke and occasional cinders if you dared leave them open for the breeze. If you had to go to the bathroom you had to wait for one of the fortunately frequent stops for the engine to take on more boiler water and use the open pit toilets usually found there, or, considering their smell and condition, bushes or fields. You ate and drank what you brought with you, although there were usually water towers supplied from rivers and streams available to fill up canteens.

What had started out as an exciting adventure for the twins quickly turned into the grueling ordeal Matson expected. There was no privacy, and there were always members of railroad building crews, army men, and the like jumping on and off at the water stops and forcing the girls to act the expected ways and not kill the time with Matson's stories and general conversation as they did at home.

An extra ten hours were added as well because the trainmen still weren't confident enough to run at night except in emergencies. The schedule was set so that they arrived just after nightfall at a small complex of shacks that was a now-abandoned former rail gang camp. Since the buildings were run-down and jammed with sweaty, tired men, once Matson and the girls had seen to their horses they elected to sleep outside under the stars.

Ever since reading Haller's journal, Matson had been unable to look at the night sky without wondering what great strings between those points of light his forefathers had ridden. One intangible string at least reached from them down the years to him. The Signal Corps still existed, and still functioned as a service *and* fighting unit.

Although it was almost dark at the end of the second day and they all felt like they'd been shaken, battered, and bruised enough, they agreed to ride well away from the forward rail camp, with its rough, hard-drinking men and its "service girls." He had no intention of being killed in a fight with some drunken railsmith over the twins.

Although it would have been a simple day's ride to their old home, he elected almost immediately to head west. Once out and away from the sights and sounds of the new technology he felt very comfortable, and the twins were able to relax and treat it as an adventure once more. He wasn't sure if they were just playing up to him or not, but they seemed to have a genuine liking for the quiet and emptiness of the bush and they certainly had taken to long rides as if born to it.

Six days after setting out from New Canaan, they reached the Flux wall, looking as solid and imposing as ever. Incredibly, neither of the girls had ever seen it before. They had spent their whole lives in the capital of New Eden, then rode south in wagons to New Canaan. They were awe-struck and a little afraid, as he'd expected they would be. To one who'd never seen it before, it looked as if the very planet stopped there. Looking at their faces, with so much of their mother in them, his mind flashed back to those earlier, simpler times. Then he said, "Come on. After that damned steam train this will be nothing, and it'll be warm and quiet in there." He went on, and they followed, but reluctantly.

The void embraced him and felt like an old friend. He saw the girls tense, then relax as they felt the peace and quiet without threat that was there. It was still about the same temperature here as in New Eden, about twenty degrees centigrade, but as they pushed in it began to rise as the conduction was lessened. Overall, New Eden's creation had caused Flux to drop about half a degree.

They came to a blue string wound with great complexity, and from it he read its code which told where it went and where on it they were.

"What's *that*?" the girls asked.

He was surprised. "You can see it?"

"Sure. A funny blue line of fuzzy light. A bunch of them, sort of all twisted together."

"Most people can't see it. It means you have the power."

That excited them. "You mean we can do magic like you said?"

"Maybe. It depends on how much of it you have. When we get to New Pericles we'll have Mervyn take a look at you, if he's there."

Mervyn *was* there, and he was fascinated by the twins. "Just as a guess, they're each at least at their mother's potential, but the fact that they're so closely linked mentally gives an enhancement possibility that staggers even me," the wizard told Matson. "They have a Flux bond so strong that they are essentially one individual."

He nodded. "Yeah. Sometimes even *they* forget which one they are."

"With the proper training and education, it's my guess

that either one could summon the power of both, and this is magnified, not diminished, by their uninhibited, irrational emotionalism. Even now, if they were really angry at somebody or something, and had a specific goal and target in mind, they could probably defeat an amplifier. Unfortunately, they will remain untrained and untrainable. Coydt's spell was based upon the math of the master program. It's fixed, even in Flux. You can add to it but not subtract from it. Their inability to read and write and do more than a toddler's counting is physical, not psychological. It gets scrambled in the brain somehow, and won't process. Still, if they were emotional enough and really *wanted* something, they could still level a Fluxland. Remember Cassie back in Persellus? You don't need training and math ability if you're powerful and charged-up enough.''

That was sobering news.

Spirit was rather startled by the twins. Just as Jeff had never reconciled himself to his mother's sexual activity, she had never thought of Matson in that way. Still, she could understand why he'd bent in this regard. Although they looked quite different, very attractive—hell, they were *gorgeous*—they still had a strong dose of Cassie inside, particularly in the face and eyes and the various small gestures they affected as well. More than even Mervyn, she could also see the enormous power potential in them.

"That's who your prime components should be," she told the Soul Rider.

For sheer power I would have to agree. Together those two could potentially break and defeat almost any wizard on World. They are unsuitable, however, for other reasons. They are far too young and inexperienced to make hard decisions, for one thing. For another, although they are quite intelligent, they are products of their culture and believe in its basics, quarrelling only with some specifics. This is not by coercion or spell, as with Cass, Suzl, and Sondra, but something they take utterly for granted. It

*would be fascinating to see just what sort of Fluxland they
would create, but I assure you that you wouldn't like it.*

She let it drop. More and more she was becoming aware
that events were closing in on them, and that time was
running out. She had never been that much aware of time
before, but now she simply had the sense, through the
Soul Rider, that things were soon to change forever, and
that a crisis was imminent that even the Soul Rider was
powerless to influence. She knew, however, what the Soul
Rider's overriding mission was, and its justification for all
that it had done, because the Soul Rider itself was receiving more and more information daily from its controller.

The Soul Riders were part of the defense of World, and
that cause was so absolute that the rights and lives of
individuals were of no consequence. For twenty-six hundred years they had managed to foil, confuse, or stave off
any real attempts at opening the Hellgates, but now it was
beyond their individual control. Individuals, and sometimes events, could be manipulated, but World was now
too complex, too populated, and too diverse for the Soul
Rider and its controller to deal with. They could only warn
and, as always, prepare for the worst.

Mervyn, for his part, was doing much the same. He had
already seen the information Matson had gained through
Sondra, and, in fact, had done an overflight himself in bird
form. His sources were better than Matson's.

"There's no question that Sligh is the newest member of
the Seven, something I pretty well guessed long ago.
Tilghman was too dedicated to his great vision, and Champion has limited Flux power—enough to form a pocket
temporarily, or enslave an individual—but not enough to
really matter. He has the right attitude, but not the inborn
abilities the position requires. No, it had to be Sligh. I
suspected that when I saw how much he was pouring into
power studies and broadcast communications, and how he
fought against and delayed for many years the implementa-
tion of the landscaping program, which made things a bit

more difficult for him. He was with Coydt almost from the beginning, though, and well known to the others."

"I just don't see how he could have gotten this far, though," Matson said. "I mean, he's *still* suckering everybody and he's on top."

"The key was Champion, I suspect. The man's brilliant, but he's also ruthless, vicious, and petty. I think he has his own, far uglier vision for New Eden, and I think Sligh played on his ego. He's never forgiven or forgotten his slave-boy origins, and he's driven by blind hatred. Sligh has played on that, and on Champion's feelings that Tilghman's devolved into a silly dreamer and is of no more practical use to them. They needed the old boy's organizational mastery to set it all up, but they don't want what he wants for the new land. The only chance we may have is that Tilghman's now tipped off to the plot and they will almost certainly have to rush their *coup*. That will mean civil war, and we have to pray that Tilghman can reach that tower before it is completed and blow it up."

"No chance of anything from the air, then? Cass and I, years ago, did a nice bombing job as big birds."

"With Flux right next to you, and with a small blockhouse as an objective. Consider how many you'd have to get in, and how far they have to fly—and do you think that the amount of explosives a large bird could carry could knock down that thing, solid steel anchored in tons of concrete? Not to mention the fact that when Tilghman moves, or even before, they'll have all sorts of defenses set up in no time. Those ray projectors of theirs could knock everything living from the sky for ten kilometers."

"Anything on the other Gates?"

"Plenty. In separate but well-timed incidents, Krupe, MacDonna, and Hjistoliran have all been assassinated in Anchor, all by people they believed friends, allies, or loyal priestesses. Various attempts have been made on others of the Nine in Flux by members of the Seven and affiliated wizards, many using amplifiers. The devices Sligh created are heavily booby-trapped and tied directly into the regulator circuitry. Our experts have said that without the circuit diagrams and top engineers and a lot of time we couldn't hope to deactivate and disconnect any of them, and if they blow they'll take the regulator with them. Our experts claim that this would cause an unrestrained release of massive quantities of raw, uncontrolled Flux that would make at least that cluster a horrible wasteland in which nothing could live.''

''After so long they make it look so effortless, so *easy*.''

''No, it's complex. Not only did they have to gain hidden political control of the clusters and maintain it indefinitely, they had to wait for the mechanisms to be developed. That was Coydt's job. It took him a century to break through anything at all—the amplifiers, and the codes for access to the Hellgates, for starters—and to be confident enough to test and use them. That's why he needed Anchor Logh to get any further. He needed a large area where scientific testing and research could be undertaken under constant physical laws. To do that he needed to totally control an Anchor, and that was the source of the New Eden movement. Sligh continued the work, but found he hadn't the resources or industrial capacity to properly develop and test what he discovered, which was why he fed the weapons research and the expansionist aims of Tilghman. Now Tilghman's in the way of the last great experiment and must be disposed of.''

Matson sat back in his chair and shook his head sadly. ''How could we have let this happen? How could we have sat back so complacently and let them do it?''

''We *did* try it another way. When it was clear how pervasive the Seven's influence was growing, we created the Reformed Church movement and the Empire. However, speed was essential before they could regroup, and that meant we had to have a physical center to unite the peoples of Flux and Anchor for war. She was their motive force.''

"Cassie."

"Exactly. And we were winning! They were beaten back, unable to cope with such devotion and fanaticism. That's why Coydt kidnapped Spirit, then chose Anchor Logh particularly for his new research laboratory. He had to hurt Cassie, divert her, and draw her in where he was certain he could finish her off. And, even in death, he did just that. He removed the Empire's heart, and its momentum collapsed. Because of that disarray, we of the Nine actually accelerated the Seven's takeover process. The half of World still under their influence easily picked up the shattered pieces of the Empire in disarray. It's all over, Matson. Everyone on World is now waking up to that fact, with the discovery of the timing mechanisms, but it's too late. They've won. Our only hope, and this is the irony of ironies, rests with Adam Tilghman."

"I wouldn't underestimate the old boy, but I wouldn't sit here and sulk, either. Get out the word. Fly around World as you never have before. The stringers will help you, too. Mass every damned army you can muster. Keep a well-armed and fortified twenty percent in Anchor and block those temple accesses. Through everything else, everything and everybody, to the Hellgates. Put a million damned troops in the field! Let the invaders shoot their cannon into a horde of a million fanatical cockroaches who must either win or die! *Give it to 'em!* It'll cost ten, maybe even a hundred, for every one of them, but *we can take them!* Believe it!"

"I don't know if I can," Mervyn sighed. "I'm suddenly feeling very old and very stupid. But I'll do it. If it can be done, we'll do it."

They both stood up, and shook hands. "Where do you go now?" the wizard asked the stringer.

"Back. If I can expose Sligh, I can turn the army. If I can't, and get away, I can still organize my own band of cockroaches."

The two men looked straight into each other's eyes, and

in them was the understanding that they would probably not meet again. Finally Mervyn asked, "If they want to surrender? Make a deal?"

Matson smiled. "Tell 'em—tell 'em to remember Anchor Logh."

Sondra took the small key from the parlor dresser and crept into her husband's study. The previous evening she had seen him going over a whole new batch of aerial photographs, and she was determined to have a look at them. The house was pretty well deserted today. She'd sent the older kids to a sitter's and the youngest was asleep in his crib. Lev had been awakened in the wee hours of the morning and had rushed out without an explanation. She didn't know when he'd be back, but she suspected it might not be for days.

She turned the key and slid open the drawer, then removed the photos. They were worse then she'd dreamed. The tower was nearly completed, and lacked only a preassembled top section that was clearly on the ground nearby. Judging from the tiny size of the people, buildings, and equipment below it was obvious that the height of the thing was enormous, taller than anything ever seen before on World. She'd been a stringer and she'd had the full range of Signal Corps training. There was no question in her mind as to what the tower was for, and it was obvious that the thing could be topped off in a day or two. That would leave only the power and electrical connections and some guidewire support to go. If these pictures were recent, it was a matter of days. If older, it could be any moment.

"I knew it was you," said a man's voice behind her. "It had to be."

She whirled and found herself facing Gunderson Champion himself. She mustered up all her courage. "*What are you doing in my house?*" she asked him, giving up all pretense at servility.

"Catching a spy. I don't know for who—Mervyn, your

father, or old man Tilghman—but I don't really care. I just led a high-level group to Tilghman's house to place him under protective arrest, and you know what I found? *Nothing!* But I suspect you already *do* know that, don't you? No Judge, no wives, no brats. I suspected something about you from the moment the old man married you off to Lev, but he was so certain and you were so good you even convinced *me*—for a while.''

"How long have you been here?"

"Not very long. I didn't really expect to catch you in the act." He reached out for her, and she resisted, pounding on him, but all he did was laugh and tighten his grip. "You want to see the project? Come on—I'll *take* you to the project."

She stopped fighting, realizing it was no use. Even if she got by him, somehow, there'd be others. "The baby—my children. . . .''

"They'll be well taken care of, as long as you behave yourself and don't try anything funny. *Anything*, even the slightest resistance or disagreement, and your daughter dies. Anything beyond that, and we'll start work on the others.''

"Lev would *kill* you if you did that!"

"Lev isn't in any position to do that. Right now he's out chasing down our missing ex-leader. If he succeeds, he may be lucky enough to be only a sergeant bossing a mining detail somewhere when this is over. If he fails, he'll die.''

"You seem to have it all figured out, except for one thing. Your precious project is really to open the Hellgates. Once they're open, nothing after will mean a thing.''

They went outside and she allowed herself to be assisted onto a horse. They rode along in a procession of troopers, Champion at her side. He had her, and she knew it. Her usefulness was over now in any event, and the only thing left of importance was saving the children.

"You know, you and your group may be wrong about

this Gate business," Champion said to her. "They might not be enemies at all. Or there might be nothing there after all these years. Sligh doesn't think there will be. He just thinks we'll have them open, so our relatives can visit and give him all the power he needs to do things no wizard ever dreamed of doing. Me, I don't care. If they're there and friends, I win. If they're not there, then we will have such power as none have dreamed of. If they're there and the Enemy, whatever they are, it'll be an interesting challenge to see if your papa's right. If we can beat 'em, we'll have the means to go back along those big strings ourselves."

"And if you can't?"

"It is a soldier's duty to fight and die if necessary," he responded calmly, and she felt a chill as she realized he meant absolutely every word of it.

Matson and the twins were gone, much to Spirit's dismay. She felt, rather than having to have the Soul Rider tell her, that her father was saying farewell to her, and perhaps to life. She wished she understood exactly what was going on.

Mervyn, too, had gone, with that same feeling in his eyes and manner. She felt alone, helpless, frightened, and confused.

Spirit—it is time.

"Huh? What? Time for what?"

I have received key elements of the master defense program. It is now more than certain that the Hellgates will open. The probability is better than eighty percent, which triggers a sequence of moves.

She knew she should have felt great fear, but instead the news calmed her, yet excited her as well. It had been her mother's time, and her father's time, and Suzl's time, and Mervyn's time.

Now it was *her* time.

"What do you want me to do?"

First, call Jeff.

"*Jeff! But—*"

Call him. Call him with all your will and all your might. Call him with your mind. Summon him to you, through Flux. Do it, and he will come.

She wanted to see him, no matter what he'd turned into. She very much did, and now she gathered up all her will, all her concentration, and called to him.

"*JEFF! COME TO ME! COME TO ME IN FLUX!*"

She could visibly see a string shoot from her, so quickly that no eye could follow it, going out and curving off to the southeast.

"*Now what?*"

We wait. It will not be long. One of my own kind has arranged to keep him very near Flux. He will come almost at the speed of light once he reaches Flux.

"*But—why? Why now?*"

For six years he has been in the New Eden army. He has become a weapons and ordinance specialist. It was thought this would be—useful.

With forty minutes he was there. She *felt* him come before he arrived, and watched as the great string reversed itself, and burst in front of her, reforming into the shape of a man.

He had changed, even from the last time they'd seen each other. He had a full, thick beard, which partially masked an ugly facial scar. His skin was hard, rough, and weather-beaten, and his hair was actually going gray. He looked, for the moment, totally confused. Then he spotted her, frowned, then brightened for a moment, and that insane look came into his eyes and expression once more. He advanced towards her confidently, menacingly.

She was pissed off. When he got close enough, she threw the meanest and most powerful uppercut she'd ever managed and connected with his jaw. It snapped shut and he fell backwards onto the ground, face up. He picked himself up slowly, and felt his jaw in wonder, but before he could get up again the Soul Rider had taken control of her.

She leaped upon him, her unnaturally powerful body pinning him down and holding him. He was confused and frightened by this turn, but found he couldn't struggle, couldn't, in fact, move a muscle. She reached into him through her mind and contacted his Flux power.

They were suddenly bathed in an eerie glow and for a moment their physical forms seemed to fade into a great single burning mass. Then it died out, and they were solid once more. She got off him, bounded to her feet, and looked down at him, then smiled and offered him her hand.

"My God, Mom! *What have I done?*" He took her hand, and got shakily to his feet. "If only I could talk to you," he said sorrowfully. "If only I could tell you. . . ."

"Cut the bullshit and pity, Jeff," said Spirit, in perfectly clear speech. "We haven't time. You and I have work to do. First I'm going to conjure up some clothes. After all these years I hate the idea, but I'll be *damned* if I'll give New Eden the satisfaction!"

Matson had crossed from Flux back into Anchor just west of Anchor Logh, with the intent of reversing his route on the train and getting back to New Caanan. The army had pretty well guessed his probable route, and had been waiting for him.

They were *very* polite, even apologetic. They didn't really know what was going on, but they had received clear and confirmed orders to intersect and detain him and his wives.

They were taken into Anchor Logh by the familiar old west Gate, but they were not to take the usual time riding to the old capital. Sligh had taken advantage of the ability to experiment, and had constructed a scale model of the steam line down the main road all the way in to the capitol itself. Flanked by a stern-looking and uncommunicative security patrol who refused to take his word as an officer that he would give them no trouble, all three of them were stripped to nothing. Conditioning collars were snapped around their necks, and were demonstrated. Now they were unceremoniously shoved into the tiny car behind the engine and, with security men sitting all around, any one of whom could trigger the collars, they were off.

Matson understood the futility of resistance at this point. His only hope was that he would eventually be taken before some higher ranking officer or authority whom he might have a slim chance of convincing that the thing was not a *coup* but the first step to opening the Hellgates.

The twins had never felt so helpless in their lives, and they were clearly frightened to death. The implications of all this also started to sink in, and they wondered if their parents were dead or alive. No communication of any sort was tolerated, although Matson was permitted at the start of the trip to tell them to relax and take it easy and not do anything foolish. His one plea, for his cigars, was answered with stony silence.

The train stopped for nothing but water, and used some sort of floodlight with a wick and mirror system mounted forward of the boiler to keep on through the night. They were fed basic soldier's field rations, which tasted like centuries-old library paste, given one cup of water to wash it down with, and were allowed bathroom privileges only at water stops and only one at a time.

Matson knew he should have expected it, but he'd hoped they wouldn't have moved quite so fast. He wasn't really worried for himself or even the girls, since when that Hellgate opened he knew his status would change fast. What frustrated him was to be kept nearly a thousand kilometers from where the action was until it was too late for him to participate.

With a change of security and train crews, they reached the old capital in ten and a half hours and chugged right down to Temple Square. He didn't approve of what they'd done to the nice old park—it was now all dug up and changed into a turntable and service center for the train. They were met by an officious security lieutenant who had his orders and was all arrogance.

"To restore stability and reason to New Eden and foil a plot to kill several senior officers and seize complete control of the nation, it was necessary for the army to take charge," he told them, offering no introductions. "Our orders were that if any of you crossed our boundaries again you were to be held and interned. When the crisis has been resolved and order has been restored, you will be brought before a military commission at which time you may make any pleas or statements you wish and at which your ultimate disposition will be determined. Until that time you are to be interned here. Follow me."

Matson shrugged, giving up any hope of an early chance to plead his case, and they followed the lieutenant and his squad. To their very great surprise, he led them to the old Tilghman house and up the steps. Armed guards were stationed front and rear, and there was a heavy lock on the door and all the windows, first and second floor, had been barred.

The place still looked nice from the outside, but inside it was completed barren of furniture, the paint and wallpaper were peeling, and the now-exposed wooden floor had splinters. The lieutenant's voice echoed ghost-like through the place.

"All electricity to the house has been cut. Sufficient food for cold meals has been provided, and will be restocked as necessary. The plumbing still works, but all doors have been removed throughout the interior. The upper floor is off limits, and a small transmitter is positioned there which will activate your collars if you get halfway up. You have the run of the first floor during the day, but after nightfall you will be confined to the front room. A number of army mattresses have been placed there so arranged that they cover the floor. You will sleep there. No conversation with the guards is permitted, and you must obey any order they give without question. Any infraction by anyone in the house will result in all of you getting a jolt. If you cause trouble, the guards will condition you out of it. That is all." And, with that, the security men turned and left, and slammed the door behind them. They heard the lock turn.

Matson sighed. "Well, it's not much, but I guess it's home."

"Uh—do you think they . . . killed. . . ."

He put on a false smile and kissed them. "I wouldn't count your old man out yet. He's pretty—*listen!* Did you hear something?"

They went down the hall and peered into the old library, then went through the former dining room to the living room and stopped.

"Candy? Crystal? Matson? So they got you, too. . . ." said Suzl sadly.

18

THE WORMS TURN

It was well past daylight when Sondra, Champion, and the security party reached the Hellgate. Although she'd seen the pictures, she still gasped at its sheer height and the massive size of its base and foundation. Above, far into the sky, she saw two huge balloons tethered with what seemed to be a kilometer or more of strong cable. They didn't seem to be of the hot air type, but she now at least understood where the photos had come from. What was far more sobering was that the tower had been topped off, guy ropes were in place and a horde of tiny figures far up were working and welding.

"Not a word about the Gate opening to anyone," Champion warned her. "You may not care about your own life, but you hold the life of your children in your hands."

The general kept her waiting while he went inside a small administration building and checked with his communications people. The news was not good. Communication lines to the west had been cut, a vital bridge had been blown on the rail line, making it useless. Several messengers sent through the Hellgate passage to West Borough had not returned, indicating either that General Borodin, the west's military commander, had been taken out, or that he had lost his nerve and double-crossed the plotters. That meant that Tilghman's loyal forces could be reinforced by train from the west, stopping just short of the blown bridge. They, however, controlled the capital and all sectors to the north and east. Champion knew that Tilghman would regroup his forces and with whatever reinforcements he got would move on their position as soon as he felt able.

He had established defensive perimeters in concentric rings around the position and the Hellgate, with his major force concentrated just out of heat ray and rocket range of the tower. He had almost twenty thousand men in the field, but it was a large area to cover, and Tilghman could pick the direction of attack. He had concentrated his main strength where it was the most mobile. More, he didn't really need to win; all he needed was to buy enough time. He called Sligh on the local wire system. The science chief was at the base of the tower, personally supervising the work.

"How long until the big broadcast?" the general asked.

"We can't work up high at night, but we'll finish by midday tomorrow for certain. After that I have to run some checks in the tunnel to make sure we don't just fry ourselves, and then it's any time we want."

"Call it thirty hours, then. I can hold *anything* for thirty hours with this force. Are you sure, though, that that thing will withstand suicide attacks by gliders?"

"Who can be certain? I know that our ray defense can blow them up before they reach the tower, at least. About the only other holdup could be the weather. A major line of thunderstorms is moving in ahead of a cold wave. I wouldn't want to work around this kind of juice, let alone broadcast, in *that*. But I wouldn't want to have to attack this place in it, either."

"Very well. Get back to work. I have to attend to a little personal business here, then I'll be in the situation shack."

They broke communications, and he went back outside to Sondra. "Get down!" he ordered, and she obeyed. "What do you think of our little project?"

"I think you're all insane," she told him.

He laughed. "Insane is the label they pin on great men with big ambitions who gamble big and lose. The winners are called great and genius and they build monuments to them. Follow me."

She had no choice but to obey him, already having decided that her life was forfeit. She had no doubt that with his peculiar sense of soldier's honor he would spare the children if she caused no trouble, and kill them without losing a wink of sleep if she did not.

He led her to the edge of the Hellgate. She'd seen it, or ones just like it, many times before. She stood there on the apron while he undressed her. Now naked, she was led to the ladder and told to go down into the depression, which was shaped like a deep saucer. He followed, and they walked to the small central hole, the "tunnel" back to the true Gate itself. There was another ladder, and then a smooth floor that gently sloped down. She had never been this far before; it was well known that automatic defenses disintegrated anyone trying it, but Champion seemed unconcerned. The long, extremely thick power cable had traced their route, and continued on down.

They reached the Gate itself, and she saw the large machine with its dials and gauges to one side. Only now an access panel had been opened on its side, and the fat cable went right into it.

Beyond was a short space and then the Hellgate itself, a swirling mass of multicolored Flux denser than she had ever imagined. She could feel its massive, pent-up power. She felt too, that she could draw upon it, and reached out to take it.

Champion grabbed her, turned her around, and squeezed her bare shoulders hard, nails biting into her flesh. It hurt, and for a moment she let go of the Flux. He took the opening and drew upon it himself. As Mervyn had said, the general had very limited power, but when that power was amplified by the Gate itself and directed with emotional fury at a single individual, it was powerful indeed. The shock of his turning her and digging into her flesh had distracted her, as he'd intended, and he used it to draw full on his own hatred and fury and drive it all right at her mind.

Her mind burned, and she was powerless to do anything. The commands and the spell could not be resisted.

You are a girl, it said, *and girls are animals, like horses and chickens and pigs. You do not speak, but you hear and obey. Your sole purpose in life is to make men happy. There is nothing else. You are . . .*

The power was suddenly broken, and she fought for what she could retain. Champion suddenly straightened up and looked very confused. "What the hell . . .?" he muttered, and his hand went to his holster as he turned.

Facing him were two figures, a large, muscular, bearded man in a New Eden soldier's uniform and a strikingly beautiful but extremely tall woman in the black uniform and boots of a stringer. The pistol came out and pointed itself at the strange pair. "Who the hell are you and what do you mean by this?"

The bearded man looked at the woman, who with her boots was almost the same height as he was. "He wants to know who we are."

She smiled. "We are the spirits of Flux and Anchor," she told him.

"You have five seconds to turn around and march back out!" the general barked, forgetting all about Sondra who slumped unconscious to the floor of the tunnel. "I mean it! I'll shoot!"

"I'm sure you will, General," the woman responded. "But this is *my* domain."

"I warned you, bitch!" Champion snarled, and fired three shots point blank into her. She smiled back at him and put out her hand in front of her. The boiling Flux suddenly reached out a finger of living fire and wrapped itself around his mid-section. Champion screamed and struggled, and the more he struggled the deeper it burned into him.

"Why not just change him into one of the Fluxgirls? Poetic justice," Jeff suggested.

Spirit shook her head. "No, there's been too much of that. Besides, he's already had it the other way." She looked down at Champion, who had dropped to his knees, face contorted in pain. "No one can free you from that, General," she told him. "It'll bite into you, burning away bit by bit, until finally it meets in your mid-section somewhere. You won't be alive by then, General, but it works *very* slowly if you don't struggle."

They stepped by him and Jeff gave him a kick away from the machine. He screamed. Spirit examined the machine and the cable connection in detail while Jeff looked over the still form of the woman just beyond. "Hey! Damned if it isn't Sondra!" he cried.

Spirit continued her examination of the removed panel and its connections. "Is she still alive?"

"Yeah, but I don't know if there's anything left inside her head but mush."

"That's all right. We'll take her with us. If she's still alive we can tap into records and get her back. Ugh!" She pulled at something.

"Can you disable it?"

"Oh, sure, but all he has to do is slap on a new connector. It's no good, anyway. He's damned clever. They know a *lot* more than anybody was ever supposed to. But it was real confused at the time they did this, and I guess they had enough warning to smuggle out copies of all the corporate files and as much engineering as they could manage. He's got a constant current running through directly to the Gate lock, removing and replacing one of the boards. Interrupt that current and the whole cluster goes up in a rush. They want to make very sure that anybody who got this far couldn't afford to meddle, or even switch the defensive screen back on." She got back up and joined him. "I've done a few little dirty tricks in there that'll give them fits and maybe fry one of the Seven if we're lucky, but it won't stop them. You pick her up and step back beyond the machine for a few moments. Right now this timing is all second-hand, and the clock is running."

She walked almost up to the swirling Flux itself, taking it in, becoming almost one with it. Jeff, a little worried, could only hold Sondra's limp form and watch.

"Farewell, Soul Rider."

Oh, no, Spirit. Not ever. You and I are one.

She took a deep breath. *Activate. Merge shell with station commander "L" for Luck. Operational request.*

There was nothing visible but the dark form of his mother against the hypnotic swirl of the pure Flux, but he sensed an immediate and incredibly powerful burst of Flux energy reaching to the point just before the great machine. So powerful was it that it felt burning hot, like pure fire.

Small jets of a different, more familiar form of Flux came from both walls, the floor, and the ceiling of the tunnel and seemed to intersect her body. Jeff could only stare and frown as he thought he heard strange voices stating things in eerie, machine-like tones.

"ANCHOR LUCK VERIFIED. COMMANDER ON STATION."

And then it was gone. No, not quite, for although she turned and faced him he saw that all of that concentrated power seemed concentrated within her. He stood there, frozen in mixed awe and fear, wondering what strange creature his mother had now become.

And then she winked at him.

He blinked, and she laughed. "Come on!" she called. "Let's go on through to good old Anchor Logh—Anchor Luck, ironically enough—and get to work!"

He started breathing again. "There's going to be a nasty welcoming committee at the other end, you know."

"Not where *we're* going," she responded, and stepped through. In another moment, he mentally traced the same pattern she'd just shown him and stepped through himself. All that he'd been taught told him that he'd come out in the basement of the temple at Anchor Logh.

But he didn't. There were other patterns, and other destinations, that only Soul Riders knew.

It was dark before Suzl could fully tell them her story, and they were confined now to the living room.

Adam Tilghman had come home early a few days before and talked to them in a more somber mood than he'd ever taken on in the house before. He'd told Cassie and Suzl that very bad men were about to take control, and if he didn't stop them, both he and they would be killed. Suzl told Matson and the twins how they had discussed what to do, and he had insisted that the two women take the younger children and go north. He had good excuses all worked out, and a few men loyal to him would accompany them and see that they were safe.

They'd argued against it, since they didn't want to leave him, but they had finally realized that the children were in danger. Cassie was adamant about not leaving herself; she insisted that her place was with Adam no matter what. Suzl, with the help of the loyalists, would be able to handle the children. She had gone along with it that way only because she realized that she, Suzl, had the difficult job, and the most important one.

They had boarded the train, with a special escort and special crew, and gone north. Shortly after, the telegraph wires were to be cut in two places to prevent any fast inquiries, and they were to be met by other loyalists at the end of the line and taken to a place of safety.

New Eden's women were generally weak and fearful, but in the matter of protecting their children they were fierce and willing to give their own lives for the children's safety.

Tilghman, in his haste, had forgotten about the two-way nature of the Hellgate. Officers, when finding the lines out, had simply used it to personally go to the temple at Anchor Logh and raise the alarm from that direction. When they reached the end of the line all looked fine and even the proper code words were given, but once away from the camp her loyal escorts were disarmed and made prisoners and she found she could do nothing. The rest of the story was much like their own. She didn't know what happened to the loyalist soldiers, but she'd been brought here with the children and imprisoned. When it was clear that the kids could not be adequately cared for under these conditions, though, they were given over to some local Fluxwives. Suzl had been allowed to see them for a short period once a day, both for her sake and to calm the kids, but otherwise it was just dreary waiting.

"Do you know what they plan on doing with us?" the twins asked her.

"Right now we're all bein' kept as holds over Adam if they find him," she told them. "Later, if they win, they're gonna give all the girls what don't already have it the stuff that burns out your brain. Turn us all into pet animals or som'thin'." She shivered.

"I wouldn't worry about that," Matson consoled her. "They may have more than they bargain for if they win."

Suzl looked at him, obviously confused and frightened. "Do ya think—" she began, then stopped.

"*Before we can do anything more we need the operations officer.*"

Suzl looked around. "Did you just hear somebody talkin'?"

Matson looked at the twins, and they shrugged and shook their heads.

"We're going to have to read in—oh, my god! It's Suzl!"

"There it was again!" Suzl exclaimed, and saw in the others' faces that they still heard nothing at all.

"Who's Suzl?" a man's voice asked.

"They never told you about her? I—I thought she was long dead. Well, let's get to it."

"Two people, a guy and a girl, are talkin' about me in my head!"

RESTORATION PROGRAM SUBJECT SUZLETTE ANN LAMARTAINE AO544M36287L14K1478.

The twins jumped. "What was *that*?" Even Matson heard it. He didn't know what it was, but he felt a rising excitement in him anyway.

"Something's going to happen," he told them.

Suzl suddenly stood up, eyes wide, her expression vacant. She stayed that way for perhaps a minute, then her mouth dropped open, she swayed, and fell to the floor. Matson caught her and gently laid her down on the mattresses.

Suddenly her eyes opened, and she sat up with a quick motion, staring not at them but off into space somewhere. *"Ho-ly shit!"* she said at last, in a tone of voice only one other in the room had ever heard her use before.

She jumped up to a standing position. "Matson! Kids! Get over there and get hidden! Something's coming that's gonna bring them in here fast!"

From the depths far beneath the old temple it came, riding the electrical lines. As it passed, going much slower than the electricity, the lights and other electrically powered devices slowed, skewed, or dimmed.

Now it was free of the temple and riding the underground lines beneath Temple Square. It emerged at the new substations, dimming almost all the lights in a full city quadrant, then came along the overhead poles and over to the old house itself. Power to the house had been cut at the pole, but the wire was still there, and through that wire it ran into the house. The outlets in the living room sputtered, and suddenly the entire room was bathed in an eerie, unnatural glow.

Matson watched from the hallway, fascinated. The twins were concerned, but he held them back.

Now all of the glow seemed to coalesce around Suzl, and she seemed to absorb it into her. The glow faded, and while they heard some yelling outside Suzl stood for a moment, motionless, almost a living statute from Mervyn's lost Pericles.

OPERATIONAL SHELL VERIFIED INSTALLED.

From the hushed stillness, Suzl was suddenly a blur of motion. The twins watched in awe, having grown up with this woman as one of their mothers and never before seeing her like this.

She reached up, grabbed the collar, and there were sparks where she touched it. She pulled it off and threw it against the wall. "Quickly! Let me get those damned things off you!"

Matson looked worriedly at the door, but bent down. The removal stung for a moment, but the sense of freedom it brought him more than compensated for that. She had barely gotten the twins' collars off when the bolt slid back. "Matson!" Suzl called. "Back me up. I'll handle this!"

A black-clad trooper entered. Suzl leaped and kicked with her left foot, hitting the man in the crotch. He screamed in pain, and fell back from the force of the small woman's blow. A second man rushed in, and she scrambled under him and tripped him. He went sprawling towards Matson, but quickly regained his feet. Matson damned near broke his knuckles with the force of three quick punches, then as the man doubled over he brought linked arms down on the back of the trooper's neck. The other one continued to writhe in pain near the door, and it was clear that Suzl had broken something far more terrible in the man than bones.

She didn't have much arm strength, but did she have a kick!

Suzl was up and giggling. "God! That was fun!"

"If you've got an idea for us going anywhere, we'd better move it!" Matson said sharply.

"In a minute." She fumbled through the unconscious trooper's pockets, then came up with a pack of cigars. "*Now* we go!"

"Which way?"

"To the temple," she told them. "Fast as we can."

"But they're gonna be swarming all over the place! We'll never make it across the square!"

"Oh, yes we will. *This* was just to get it out of my system. I don't worry about anyone in Anchor. It's *my* element."

The twins seemed undecided between horror and excitement at Suzl's performance, but they were clearly shocked in any case, and Matson had to pull them out of the house.

As soon as Suzl reached the porch, all the power went out in Temple Square and the immediate vicinity. None of the others could see much, but Suzl seemed to have the same vision as if it were bright daylight. She actually stopped on the porch and handed Matson a cigar, putting another in her own mouth.

"Are you still our Momma?" the twins asked in a hushed whisper.

"You bet I am! There's just more of me, that's all. Can't have enough of a good thing," she responded lightly. "Look, don't worry about this part. This is the *easy* part. Tomorrow it gets hairy."

Matson was more used to strange changes and transformations than the twins. Like most people of Flux, he simply accepted them when they came and adjusted his situation accordingly. "It doesn't sound like anybody's out there," he noted. "I'd have expected a near riot by now."

"They're all knocked cold," she replied. "And they'll

stay juiced until I decide otherwise. Come on—let's get over to the temple.''

"You forgot his matches!" Matson grumbled.

She laughed, and pointed a finger at the end of his cigar. A spark leaped and it was lit. "Cute trick," she said admiringly to herself, and lit her own. She coughed once. "Damn. I'm out of practice!" And they were off across the street and by the small rail yard, its floodlights now out, towards the looming hulk of the temple.

"How the hell are you *doing* all this?" Matson asked her as they walked briskly towards their goal. "I thought your old self was erased!"

"It was. But nothing is permanent if you have Flux power here," she told him. "Nothing but death. First they read my memories back in, so I have the whole record. That also negated Coydt's spell."

"I notice you kept your Fluxgirl body."

"Honey, if you had *this* body would you go back to being a fat, dumpy broad with stringy hair?"

The twins were recovering from their shock in the excitement of freedom, and joined in. "So you've got Flux power. But, Matson, you said it don't work in this place."

They were going up the vast, high stone steps now, Suzl slowing only to make allowances for the others' vision. Their eyes had somewhat adjusted now, but it was a dark and cloudy night.

"It works when I want it to work," Suzl told them. "Like when this square was turned to Flux once."

She was at the door now, and waited for them to reach the same place. "The Guardian did that," Matson pointed out, feeling a little out of shape. He was breathing hard from just that climb.

"Matson, darling, haven't you figured it out yet? *I* am the Guardian!"

The technician was a blubbering, quivering mass of terror. Onregon Sligh looked at him in complete disgust.

"Get hold of yourself, man! What the hell is wrong with you?"

Finally, the technician collected himself enough to speak. He was terrified out of his wits, but he was at least as terrified of Onregon Sligh.

"I—I monitored a surge in the line. I went down to check on it, and I s-saw—*him*."

"Who?"

"G-General Champion! God! It was horrible! He'd been cut completely in two, his guts and blood are all over the place. . . ."

Sligh frowned. He didn't like losing Champion at this stage of things. Still, there were others. "You've seen dead men before."

"Not like *that*. *Burned through*, he was! And the look frozen on his face—I'll never be able to get that face out of my mind!"

Sligh turned away and summoned some of Champion's aides. They told him what Champion was doing down there. He took out his big cigar and spat on the ground. "Stupid hung-up psychopathic son of a bitch! He just loved torturing the girls so much that he couldn't resist it even now. Well, it's clear what happened. She was a wizard, and he took her down where there was maximum power. She was stronger than he was, and absolutely terrified, and that terror pulled so much force out of the Gate it killed him. Serves him right, risking his life and command in a crisis." He sighed. "Well, you were his aides. Take some men, get down there, and clean up the mess. I don't want it fouling the cable. When you're done I'll send some of my boys down to check and see if any damage was done."

He walked back over to the communications shack. He'd have to call up von Heilman and Narjawal and tell them that their precious general had cut his throat and that they would be expected to shoulder the load now. He didn't care which one of them took over here. They were good military men, but otherwise both were just as batty as their fallen commander.

General Borodin jumped off the platform to the first car before the train had come to a complete stop and ran over and saluted Adam Tilghman. The Judge returned it, then shook hands warmly. Borodin had been thought by Champion and Sligh to be on their side, and, in fact, he had been—for a limited *coup*. He had never felt right about it, though, smelling something odd, and when news came of the Hellgate plot it all fell into place for him. Tilghman knew that Borodin had been ready to stab him in the back before, and Borodin knew he knew it, but neither let it influence their actions now. Any ideological differences could be settled later—if there *was* a later.

"I had to sacrifice men for ordnance," the general said apologetically. "How many have you got?"

"Almost two thousand," Tilghman replied. "We've picked up a very large number from nervous junior officers and sergeants who have little stomach for revolution if it means civil war. I'm hoping that more of them won't fight when we move."

Borodin nodded. "We'd better. With only two trains on this damned single track I was lucky to pack in another three hundred, and half of those are ordnance experts. Still, we've alerted a lot of commands along the way, and we might get substantial reinforcements overland if we can hold that long. I wouldn't count on them, though. There's one *hell* of a storm front between there and here. We almost didn't make it through!"

There were rumblings in the west, and the occasional glow of far-off lightning flashes to emphasize his point. Tilghman was delighted with the ordnance, particularly the heavy ray projection equipment and the rocket launchers, but he was under no illusions as to their chances. Even though the enemy force was currently spread out in all directions, once either their scouts located him or he struck they would all move to close in. If they couldn't punch through quickly and in total secrecy until the actual point of engagement, there was no chance at all of reaching the transmitter. It sounded simple, but even with an all-night trek it would be midmorning before they could be in any kind of position for a solid attack.

Tilghman walked back to the small, fast carriage he was using. Cassie had used a small portable stove and offered him hot coffee and a two-day-old sandwich. "Them san'wiches don't look like much, but they're better'n nothin'," she told him, forcing him to eat and drink something.

Not for the first time did he wish for the "old" Cassie back, the veteran warrior queen who'd conquered half of World. Still, he understood that that woman had hated war, and had hated being forced to wage it. Even this one had guts, though. She could have been safe but chose to be here, knowing she might die or watch him die—or both. She'd kept him going out here, forcing him to rest, to eat, to catch a little sleep. "I ain't much good for fightin' an' wars," she'd told him, "but you take care of the war and I'll take care of you."

Soon they were breaking camp. The trains had been unloaded, everything was hitched up, and he and Borodin and the brigade commanders had agreed on routes, strategy, and tactics. There was nothing left to do but to fight.

He had driven himself like a wild man, without rest or comfort, for many days, and he'd driven all those on his side the same way. The word was spread through Flux and Anchor, by wizard, by messenger, by stringer, that it could not be stopped. The Gates of Hell were opening, and the final battle and final test for humanity was at hand. They would be a massive force in each cluster, but a disorganized one. The stringers tried to help with that as much as possible, as each assumed an area command and switched roles. For more than twenty-six centuries the men and women of the Guild had studied and trained for just this sort of conflict, but this was the first time they, as a group, were called upon to put theory into practice. Still, they formed a ready-made senior officer corps as trained as any could be for an unprecendented situation. For the first time, Mervyn began to believe that, while World might well lose, it was not as unprepared as it seemed.

He had stuck to Flux, not wanting to be caught in Anchor as had Krupe and the others, and now he circled in the form of a great bird around the Northeast Gate. It was the least defended, since Fluxlands tended by chance to be closer to the cluster rims there, and entry from the temples had been somehow jammed. He circled, saw nothing out of the ordinary, and then landed and changed back into his human form almost at the lip of the dish-like depression.

All seemed deathly still, and he climbed down the ancient ladder to the dish floor and walked over to the tunnel entrance. Suddenly a head poked out, so abruptly that it startled him. The man in the tunnel grinned, then quickly hauled himself up to the surface of the dish.

"Hello, Mervyn," said Zelligman Ivan. "Well, it's just as I planned it. I waited until I heard you were in the region, then made more of a ruckus here than I had to in hopes it would bring you to me."

"Zelligman—there's still time to stop this."

"Had a last-minute glitch in the remote receiver," the Chairman of the Seven continued, ignoring the old wizard's plea. "It wouldn't do to have a mechanical failure undo all these carefully laid plans."

"Zelligman—how are you going to do it? You have no receiving antenna."

"Very astute. It's because you can't really ever be sure about broadcasting through Flux, old boy. So the signal will be beamed down, full strength, and concentrated on the tunnel in the south. There's a carrier signal of some sort connecting all the Gates, you know. Our signal will piggyback onto that carrier, and they'll all open—not within a minute, but within a second or less.''

"So the tower is only so that the real transmitter is high enough to beam directly down into the tunnel."

Ivan nodded. "I know what you're thinking, and, yes. Knock off a bit of the top and it's no go. But they'll never get that close, you know. And even if they did, and stopped it, they couldn't disconnect what we've put in. It's inevitable, Mervyn. If not now, then next week, next month, or next year. It might as well be tomorrow.''

"There might still be ways."

"And if there are, I'm sure you can think of them, but it's rather obvious that you and I are going to sit up there and be the welcoming committee. It should be instructive to one of us."

Mervyn looked at him. "You mean to take me on, then?''

"You're done, old man. Your cause is lost, your power is half what it was. Why fight me at all?"

"My cause is lost when it is lost, Zelligman, not before. My power may have diminished, but I need no machine to amplify it, so great is my hate and disgust of you and your works, when pitted against your cold and soulless rationality. You are dead inside, Zelligman. And if your cause is inevitable I can still hurt you, for I can cheat you out of ever knowing for certain."

Zelligman Ivan smiled. "This was ordained from our births, Mervyn. This is the moment for which we were born.'' He rose into the air and there was a sudden, blinding sheet of fire. The match was on.

They went down stairways and walked dark halls, the only sound in the the temple complex the noise of their bare feet on the cold floor. Finally, they reached their destination, and the emergency lighting came on to aid them. About twenty meters from the small area which was the switching center from temple to Gate had been sheathed in bright metal; floors, ceiling, and walls were all covered.

"They rigged it as an electrocution zone," Suzl told them. "Anything coming out or going in without somebody on a remote switch upstairs holding down a button was zapped. In a way, it was their version of the tunnel defense system, and it's been pretty effective. Don't worry about it now, though. There's no power to the mains."
She stepped onto the metal, and, after a nervous moment, Matson and the twins followed. It was always chilly in the basement area, but the metal made it more so. Still, they made it to the spot, now clearly marked on the floor, where the transfer could take place. "Huddle in close together," Suzl told them. "We all want to go at the same time."

"Go where?" the twins asked nervously.

"Down. Down to where the others are, in the master control room."

"What others?" Matson asked. "Who else is involved in this?"

"I haven't the faintest idea right now, but we'll find out in a second. Ready? Here goes!"

Suddenly all reality seemed to wink out, and they felt as if each of them were floating in a black void, without bodies or any sensations. Then, just as abruptly, they were themselves again and it was light.

They were in a circular room perhaps twenty meters across. There were banks of alien-looking equipment lining the walls, and above them screens on which, at the moment, nothing showed. The entire ceiling was a source of soft but adequate light, and somewhere there was a soft rumbling of air being recirculated. Spaced evenly around the room, racing the equipment, were large padded chairs, at least two dozen of them.

"*Daddy!*" a woman screamed joyously, and before he knew it Matson was being hugged by a familiar figure. Sondra still looked like a Fluxgirl, and had a singular lack of self-control. The twins just gaped in amazement at the place, while Suzl walked forward and across the room to where a tall figure turned in one of the chairs and got up.

"Spirit!" she breathed, awed and suddenly hesitant.

Spirit looked at the other woman and shook her head in wonder. "You've sure changed a lot, Suzl." Then they hugged and kissed and cried a little. Suzl's small form was almost smothered by Spirit, yet she was the first to recover. "Damn!" she said, voice cracking. "You made me break my two remaining cigars."

Spirit sighed and smiled and looked down at her, wiping away the tears. "Well, finally it all makes sense, doesn't it?"

Suzl nodded. "Yeah. Personally, I think our ever-loving ancestors were a bunch of paranoids." She stopped, spotting another figure behind them. "Who's he?"

"That's Jeffron."

Suzl almost choked. "*That* is little Jeff? Holy shit!" Jeff looked somewhat bewildered, and Suzl immediately realized that he had no idea who she was. How do you explain to a big, strapping guy like that that the voluptuous little Fluxgirl with the foul mouth and cocky expression is his *father*? She decided that Spirit was right to leave it for another time, if there *was* another time.

Matson, who understood the situation, stepped in. "Well, I'm glad it all makes sense to *somebody*," he growled. "Now will you make sense of it all to *me*?"

And as they all began to check out their systems, they told him.

The sealing of the Gates had been an army decision, as he knew, supported by the non-Company authorities and the fearful general population. Once sealed, this had given the military authorities time to set up defensive actions.

Each Anchor was established and held firm by a master computer so huge and complex it was larger than the temple above it and went down several hundred meters below the foundation. These computers were the products of two hundred years of development since the first crude computers had been developed; they were self-repairing and self-aware, and each in its memory sections could contain much of the sum total of humanity's knowledge.

There was another universe outside their own, a universe as different from theirs as a flower was from fire. At certain points, apparently because of the interplay of gravity and other forces not fully understood, the two adjoined, creating at once a weak spot and, if need be, a way to punch through from one to the other. How scientists had determined this and how they had managed to punch through without intermingling the two was in the computer but really beyond any of their abilities to understand. One such spot was in the region of space near humanity's birthplace; another was right here, on World.

Humans had built gates and controls for these points, much like the Hellgates and the Gate locks and transformers. The other universe did not have stars and planets, but was filled with a massive yet plastic energy which was popularly called the Flux. They learned how to convert that energy into other, usable forms, assuring limitless power resources. They learned, too, that under the right circumstances and controlled by a computer complex enough to hold in its memory every single detail of a thing down to its atomic structure and beyond, Flux could be converted from energy to matter. Computers were developed with chambers that could take something, break it down into its smallest components and store it as infinitely complex mathematical formulae, then restore it—while keeping the formulae on file.

And, eventually, they learned that this method could be used to transmit almost anything, even human beings, through the Flux universe, whose speed of light was almost a million times greater than in their own universe. Probes could be broken down, cast into Flux, then trailed by an energy "string," where they came under the complex and not understood forces of that universe. They would eventually be attracted to the next weak point, where they could be reconverted to matter and survey what they saw. Time and distance seemed to have different meanings there, not understood and perhaps not understandable by any from their own universe. The star patterns might be unfamiliar for the first dozen or so "stops" the probes made, then be recognizable on the next. In many cases, such as World, they had no idea where exactly they were.

Some were nowhere useful; only a very tiny number were in solar systems—another concept all in the room had problems with. None of the solar systems contained planets suitable for human beings, but experiments with planets in the home system had shown how Flux could be used and shaped to artificially create what was called a "life zone," with sufficient heat and the proper mix of air and water for humans, plants, and animals. World was one of these.

These were, in essence, Flux factories, in which experiments could be conducted and new discoveries for all humanity made and transmitted to all the human race. Some were established by private companies; others were established by governments of the individual nations that still existed and competed on the home world. Because these nations were not always friendly, and were historically highly competitive, even the private companies had to work first through the military commands of their own nations. Eleven nations that were friendly with one another and allowed multinational companies were involved in World's project; a combined military force, headed by two branches, a Space Defense Command and a Signal Corps, went first and established the basics. Defense handled basic security, prepared mostly for enmity from the projects of other, unfriendly nations; Signal used Flux to establish communications and routes, since maps were useless in a Flux void.

It was also the first opening in centuries of a new frontier, for once the system was built it was labor-intensive for the first few years, after which a stable population was desirable from the company or government's stand point: farmers could make the projects self-sufficient; limited trade and manufacturing, particularly skilled trades, would also serve the project and the people, so that things would not have to be imported and an overall level of self-sufficiency could be sustained.

For the first time, space was a frontier where the poor, the destitute, and the desperate could go—and were welcomed, even needed.

But it was not without risk. Building worlds to order was a very inexact science, and one slip in controlling the massive Flux power could vaporize everything. For that reason, the home system, which wanted the benefits of Flux, didn't dare play around much with it in its own back yard.

Humanity, however, was not the only race riding Flux between the stars. There was clearly one other, one which, against all odds, had intersected one of humanity's strings and wound up at the same point. The Gates had been closed against this race, for none who encountered it were ever heard from again, nor did any emissaries or military forces return. One by one, the bright colonies of humanity were winking out, and as the Enemy's home was linked through only one already-lost colony, there was no way to carry the fight to the Enemy or even find out who or what the Enemy was. But that Enemy was also a captive of natural forces; it traveled the Flux universe in converted form, as energy and equations, and depended upon its own or human's bases for reconversion to matter. It could not get through, nor take any action, while in converted form.

Once the Gates were closed, the army ousted the company leaders who had decided that dealing with the unknown was preferable to a life trapped on World, and set about a two-pronged program for security. It took an odd locally grown cult religion and made it the centerpiece of its Anchor policy. It attempted to sequester or destroy all documentation, all history, advanced science, and Flux knowledge, knowing that the army monopoly on the computers would give it a monopoly on that knowledge. The Church began a pogrom wherever it seized control against those scientists and engineers who knew how to build and work the machines.

The system might have been complete, but for a totally unexpected and previously unknown phenomenon that might well have been unique to World's experimental programming. Those who used the Flux devices, the heavy amplifiers linked to the main computers, had themselves been placed somehow in the chain from Flux manipulation to computer program. The master computers seemed unable to distinguish between these people as human beings and the amplifiers themselves. Thus were the wizards born. In the void, within the influence of the Hellgates and their Anchor-based computer complexes, those with strong wills, some mathematical ability, and the ability to concentrate almost to the point of excluding all else, were able to send commands to the nearest computer in much the same way as their programs, and the computer had responded. Whatever genetic changes had occurred to cause this seemed due to overexposure to amplified Flux on World. In other experiments, people had died or been twisted or deformed, but not here.

Matter and energy, machine and operator, were one to the computers, and they did not have access to the scientific heart of mankind back home to solve the problem. The military had always feared the computers even as they used them, and had always insisted on a "human link" between any self-aware computer and major actions. They could not "fix the bug," as they called it, but they could render the computer useless to the company men by fragmenting its consciousness. They placed a human link requirement between the computer and its defensive systems, which were considerable but still had obviously failed elsewhere; they placed another human link between the master programs that maintained World and any attempt to change that program.

Thus, the computers were split; the massive part they could not touch, but they could limit access to the "wizard" structure. They elected to not cut it entirely, not quite seeing all the implications, because the Signal Corps insisted on maintaining the strings and its monopoly on commerce and communication as an additional safeguard—and a way to survive under these new conditions. To permit the strings was to permit "wizards" to exist. But these could tap specific mechanical data; the programs themselves could not be altered, nor was there sufficient Flux allowed through the Gate to keep World warm and habitable, as it was a huge moon of a gas giant so far from its sun as to make that sun just another star. Once the locks were off, however, sufficient Flux *would* be available. Someone would have to decide the manner and level of its use.

In case the Gates *were* opened, it was necessary to keep all defensive systems at the ready, but again those in the hands of the company or madmen could make World a hell of its own. And, of course, there was always the chance that the invasion would be terminated, or home would get through, or even that the invaders could eventually be dealt with through friendly or hostile means. Again, a human being would be required as a link in the chain, to decide if those systems should be unleashed.

By splitting the self-maintenance program from the master computer, they thought they had it contained. By feeding specific criteria into the defense systems that had to be met before activation, and by giving that system remote capability to monitor World and decide whether or not to call in its human link, they thought they were safe.

But the master maintenance system and the remote sensors of defense somehow developed their own self-awareness. Unable to tap into the main computer directly, they did their jobs as they were programmed to do, but changed and evolved as they did so. Clearly the engineers and scientists were not the only ones altered by the balance of Flux on World; the army also hadn't reckoned with the possibility that communication between wizards and the computer could go both ways.

Thus the "maintenance shells" became the Guardians, and the remote sensing programs became Soul Riders. Originally just complex programs in Flux, they took on a logical reality of their own as symbiotic creatures, attaching themselves to and living within the bodies of those with strong Flux power. As information evaluators, they fed the master program data it had no other way of acquiring. As information gatherers they were unneeded; every single human being with Flux power beyond a certain level broadcast as well as received from the data banks.

That was how Jeff, Suzl, and Sondra had been restored. They still had their peculiar physical limitations, but the computers did not.

The Soul Rider's primary mission was always to provide a human link with sufficient Flux power to interface directly between it and the master computers. It knew it had to have such a person, and backups easily accessible if need be, but aside from a sense that it was a defender of World against enemies beyond the Hellgates it did not understand why, nor could the computers with which it was linked tell it—except through a human interface, and then only when certain criteria were met. The Guardians, too, needed a proper human interface on hand, but as their jobs limited them to Anchor and the Hellgate machinery, they required the Soul Riders to bring them suitable receptacles.

Nobody, but nobody, thought it would go on for two thousand six hundred and eighty-two years. The Church was supposed to provide the interfaces. The nine district commanders would work hand-in-glove with the Church to insure that suitable personnel, including a powerful wizard, were always on hand. That was why the Nine trained and selected the High Priestesses. And nobody, but nobody, realized that the Soul Riders and Guardians would develop personalities of their own.

Thus it was that when the previous "interface" the Anchor Luck Soul Rider had selected met an untimely end, it followed the route back to its computer source until it found, in Anchor, one with the proper power potential and mind-set, even though it didn't know that that was what it was looking for. It had selected Cassie, and then manipulated her to get her into Flux, where her power could be trained and developed.

Cassie had not worked out in the end. Its own internal programming told it that, if it came to the choice between surrender or the destruction of humanity on World, she might well surrender to save it. So this time it had taken a different tack. This time it would create its own human interface from conception on. And so Spirit had been born, and bred, and molded for just this job, and had been effectively removed from human affairs so that what happened to her mother would probably not happen to her.

Then Suzl and Spirit had come to the Hellgate, and the Guardian saw in Suzl the power and personality it decided was correct for its own interface. It, however, was limited to Anchor, and required that she remain there, so it had arranged for Coydt van Haas to be fed the spell that would keep her close at hand. When the opportunity came for Cassie to be likewise held, it took it, considering her a more than adequate backup. The Soul Rider, by that time, had shifted its primary backup status to Jeff.

As both Soul Riders and Guardians had sensed from their master computers that the time of danger was drawing increasingly near, they both took every opportunity to increase their backups just in case. Sondra was one such case that could serve for either. She could be chained to Anchor but had experience in Flux. There were others, including many they didn't even know about and might never know, and there were four Soul Riders and four

Guardians per cluster, one per Anchor, and twenty-eight of each in all.

And now that the vast amount of information had been computed and the master program had determined that all the criteria were met and that the danger was real, the Soul Rider, the shell, had merged with Spirit, with Spirit in control. She now had access to the whole of the computer, and she did not have to understand it to maintain constant two-way communication with it. She had then evaluated the danger as real and ordered the Guardian to merge with its primary, which was Suzl. It was only chance that Suzl had been in Anchor Logh, and it wouldn't have mattered where in the great Anchor she had been. Like Spirit, she would have gone to and through the Hellgate, and nothing could have stopped her, for she controlled the master program that made Anchor real.

Because all that happened to those with Flux power was recorded, it had been a simple matter to restore the minds and repair the physical damage to Sondra and Suzl. They could do it to anyone. It frightened Suzl a bit to realize that if Spirit wished to form the likeness of one who was dead out of Flux, she, Suzl, could probably provide the life record.

They were more powerful than any two human beings had ever been in human history—but two of fifty-six equally powerful humans now on World. Suzl could do literally anything with Anchor and pure data files; Spirit could command Flux within her quadrant to the exclusion of all else. Together, *they* were the Holy Mother incarnate— for at least one more day. After the Gates opened, nobody knew what would happen.

"If you're so damned powerful, why can't you just vaporize that tower of theirs and put an end to this?" Matson asked them.

"We could," Suzl responded, "but that's where it's tricky. I'm not *the* power in New Eden; I'm one of four. Originally it was just supposed to be Anchor Logh, but now we somewhat control all of New Eden—by unanimous vote. Those ancient soldiers believed that with the kind of power we had at our disposal, we ought to be able to meet and beat any threat like this. But the Seven have had twenty-six hundred and eighty-two years to figure ways around it, and they have. If I break the power connection to either the timer or the tower, it'll cause a massive short. They've reversed the polarity of the Gate lock. Pure Flux power will come pouring out of that hole, and it'll devour the entire cluster and us with it at the very least, maybe destroy all of World in one big overload. Right now the computers all say there's only one way to get it back to normal. See, it's like a spring-loaded switch. It has to be reset, and the only way to reset it is to open the damned Gate and close it again. We have power over Flux and Anchor, but the Hellgate's neither. It's our connection with the other universe and with our relatives out *there* someplace. It's out of our jurisdiction. I can *repair* it—but to do that I have to open the Gate, so what's the difference?''

''Some goddesses!''

''Look!'' Spirit snapped. ''It wasn't meant to be us! I was supposed to be a general or something, and Suzl was supposed to be a scientist or engineer. Things went all wrong with their plans no matter how smart they were, or how advanced they were, but their biggest mistake was in not being able to imagine that it would hold for so long. They figured years, maybe decades or even centuries, but not this! It's amazing so much of their organization has survived. The concentration of power in the hands of a few and the near-immortality the most powerful achieved did it, at the cost of never growing, never learning, never experimenting.''

''So they *were* planning to open up themselves some day! How were they supposed to know it was safe?''

''The Gates were made back in the home system and shipped and assembled here by machines. Obviously, the lock codes were set there as well. When Earth, as it called itself, won, it would show up with the codes from the other side.''

Matson clapped his hands. ''That's the best news I've had in years!''

Everyone turned to stare at him.

''Don't you see? If this Enemy took everybody else, it would have captured the codes and unlocked us! That means there are other human worlds out there!''

''It also means the war might still be going on,'' Suzl noted. ''They never came back to reclaim their long-lost children, either.''

''Well, we've got our war here and now. If you can't mess with the Gate or fix it, can you help out Tilghman?''

Suzl seemed to freeze, as if thinking of something far away, then snapped out of it. ''He's moving on the position right now, but he's outnumbered four to one. He'll be able to break through initially, but they'll be able to push him up against the Hellgate with no place to run. He can get in range, but he can't get that heavy stuff he'll need close enough before they're on him.'' She shrugged. ''You're the fighter. I've seen you in action years ago, remember? Relative to a wizard our powers are enormous, because we can tap directly into the big computers. But my power comes from the power connection between here and the Hellgate; Spirit's come from the remaining Flux, and there ain't much of that between us and the Gate. I'm geared to defend an Anchor; Spirit was supposed to try and keep me from ever being used. Nobody counted on a landscape program being activated—they ruled that out. That's real stuff out there. If we make any changes in it it'll kill a hell of a lot of people, us and them.''

Matson thought a moment. ''What *can* you control?''

''There's a cold front moving down on them. Nasty thunderstorms, lots of hail and mud. I could stall it out between Tilghman and the encircling forces, maybe buy him half a day or more, but weather's kind of funny. It might bog him down, too, at least his heavy stuff. It's not easy, but weather is one thing that can be directed, to a degree.''

"Pour it on!'' he told her. "Make it miserable!''

"Yeah!'' Jeff added. "They're pros—they'll make it, but the encircling forces have farther to come, and they'll drop their heavy stuff just to increase speed. That gives 'em a slight edge. And the storm'll make the defensive ray setup useless. They might overrun the fixed positions.''

"What about a lightning strike that'd knock the top off that tower?'' Matson asked, thinking furiously.

"I can't make weather all that specific,'' Suzl replied. "Besides, it could cause a surge through the whole line that'd break the connection and cause the regulator to crumble. In fact, Tilghman's boys have to disconnect that cable, not cut it. Disconnect and ground it. *Then* we can deal with it.''

"Excuse us,'' the twins put in. They had kept very silent through this, but they were paying close attention. "But shouldn't somebody have told Daddy that?''

The others all stared at each other. Then Suzl exclaimed, "Holy cats! We forgot Cassie! She's out in that mess!'' She looked at Spirit, and Spirit looked at Suzl, and then they both looked at Matson, who nodded, a disgusted expression on his face.

Spirit simply gave the order. "Activate restoration program,'' she ordered, and the computer acknowledged the individual she wanted and found the proper file.

"Can we get a direct link with Cassie or Tilghman in the field?'' the stringer asked.

"Not through the computer, no. We could do it, but she wouldn't recognize it for what it was,'' Suzl responded. "If this was Flux it'd be easy, but not in Anchor. To do it here and now we'd need somebody with even more power than I have and a genetic link to Cassie so close the computer might not be able to tell the difference.''

Matson looked over at Candy and Crystal. "Girls,'' he said, "get ready to go to work!''

19

THE HELLGATES OPEN

Cassie was bouncing along in the carriage, her head against Adam's shoulder, and in spite of the speed and bumps she managed to nod out. She generally dreamed basic, erotic dreams or dreams about the children, but now the dream she was having seemed to fade, and she heard a strange voice talk about a "restoration program" or something. . . .

Slowly, strange thoughts and memories began to fill her mind, and in a matter of moments she was not one person but *two*, only one, she knew, was false. It was a horrible dream, and she fought it, fought back that other person, refused to face her, refused to—

She awoke with a panicked scream that jolted Tilghman, then sat up and looked around, eyes fearful. She knew who, and what, and where she was, and she hated it.

"What's the matter, love?" Adam asked her, concerned that the experience was finally getting too much for her.

She shivered and let him hold her close. How was it possible? It was a binding spell and the old had been *erased*.

"*Momma! Momma!*" Now it was echoing voices in her mind. Had she died, she wondered? Was it all over, and were she and Adam on the road to eternity?

"*Momma! Momma! You must listen to us! You must!*"

She knew those voices now, knew that tone and inflection. But how could it be Candy and Crystal? What was happening to her?

"*Momma, momma! You must tell Daddy not to knock down the tower! It'll do something awful to all of us!*"

What the hell? She concentrated hard on those voices. "*Is that really you, children?*"

"*Yes! Yes! You got to listen! This is kinda hard! It hurts in the head!*"

In point of fact, it was hurting her, too. "*Who's doing this? Mervyn?*"

"*No, no! It's Momma Suzl and Spirit and Jeff and Matson and Sondra and all! Just tell Daddy he's gotta—what's the word? Dis-kenit the big wire from the tower and put it on the ground or something like that!*"

"*You mean to disconnect the cable and ground it?*"

"*Yes, yes!*" they responded happily, and faded out, leaving her only with a headache and even more frightened than ever.

"Adam?"

"Yes, my love?"

"Adam—I—I don't know how to say this, but I'm back. The old me."

He stared at her. "Are you sure you're all right?"

"No, I've never been more miserable in my whole life. Something reached into my mind and gave it all back. All of it. Without taking anything away. I couldn't fight it, I had no choice."

He could tell simply by her speech pattern and accent that it was the truth, but he found it confusing and ominous. This sort of thing was unprecedented anywhere, to his knowledge. "You want me to let you out?"

She clung to him. "Adam, I've been married to you for

sixteen years. I've borne your children, and raised them well, and I have another within me that I pray will live to be born. But I love you, Adam. We live or die together in this.''

He hugged and then kissed her. ''Then maybe it's a good omen! Maybe we're going to make it!''

''Uh—Adam. There was something else.'' She told him about the eerie message from the twins.

He thought it over. ''Wasn't Spirit the one with the Soul Rider?''

''Yes, but she is mute and cut off from society.''

''Maybe not any more. Maybe the Soul Rider's joined our fight. I wish it was easier, though. They're saying we can't *use* the big stuff. We have to overrun it.''

There were thick clouds obscuring the sky, but it was still clear that day was approaching, and the engagement must begin at that point. Suddenly there was the sound of rumblings, and thunder and lightning blanketed the sky just behind them. It began to rain, hard, cold, large drops of it.

Tilghman signalled for a halt and called in Borodin and his commanders. ''Never mind how, I've learned we can't knock it out. The whole thing will blow and take New Eden with it. We're going to have to take it and get that cable off that tower.''

The general whistled. ''That's a tall order.''

Tilghman turned and looked into the dark, fierce storm whose fringes were just reaching them. ''Drop everything we can't use or carry easily in bad weather. We'll slow to a march and let the storm catch up to us. The way it's coming, it'll be smack on top of us in a matter of minutes. We'll move in under its cover.''

They had fought for fourteen straight hours, and in that time some forces of Flux had reached the Hellgate. They could do little, though, to interfere. Both Mervyn and Zelligman Ivan were exhausted and weak from their ordeal, having thrown at each other enough horrors and pure Flux power to crush half a cluster. And now they stood and faced each other, neither recognizable to anyone, including themselves. They were deformed, bloated creatures with burns, scars, and dangling limbs, as horrible as any two of the worst duggers lost in Flux.

They were nothing now but two snarling, monstrous animals, motivated only by their mutual hatred, and determination to survive.

They leaped on each other, all their power now reduced to sheer physical force, and they clawed and bit and chewed and rolled back and forth, ever closer to the great saucer-shaped depression. One opened gaping, bleeding wounds in the other's stomach, and entrails dangled out, but that only enraged the other, who leaned forward and bit into his opponent's neck, removing a large chunk of flesh.

The Fluxlord commanders knew that they were watching the end of a horrible battle between two of the greatest and most determined powers ever in World, and they debated stepping in. "But on whose side?" they asked each other, and shook their heads.

Now the one with the neck wound fell, and the other was upon him, snarling and tearing and slashing far beyond the moment when the one on the ground had stopped resisting. Finally, the victorious creature stood up and screamed, "I've won!" in a deep, guttural voice.

Then he collapsed on the body of the other.

"Two goddesses with the power to bring back the dead can't help a man win a fair fight," Matson grumbled.

"The Seven knew too much. Far more than anyone guessed back when they closed them down," Spirit told him. "Look, we have power over Flux and Anchor but they had the code that shut off the defense systems—and shut down maintenance as well. When that happened, they had just the right boards and knew just exactly the right things to do to jump the circuit, replace the board, then reverse the polarity. As for Tilghman, Cassie gave him his storm cover, then the thick fog, then caused that fissure to appear that delayed all the troops closing in on him. There's just too many, Dad! We can't raise him an army unless it's in Flux, and that evil old man made sure there *was* no Flux there!''

''Adam is *not* evil!'' Suzl practically shouted at her. ''He's a product of the worst kind of culture this world can produce, and he came out of it with a determination to found a perfect society here no matter how long it took and no matter what it cost. His dream might not be your dream, but it isn't Coydt's or Champion's, either, which is pretty much what New Eden is now.''

''But he didn't care if he had to get in bed with the devil himself,'' Spirit snapped back. ''The end justifies any means—war, torture, the reduction of women to inferiors . . . .''

''Yeah, that's true, but he didn't see it that way. He thought conditions for the masses of World were so wretched as it was that any cost was worth changing it if their children or grandchildren could live his dream. The only alternative he had was to do nothing, so even the grandchildren stayed slaves. When even the so-called good guys of this world worked like hell to make sure nothing changed it, he had no choice but to choose the devil. Check the records here. In twenty-six hundred years humans went from primitive empires built with stone and bronze-tipped spears and arrows to being able to do *this*. Look at what we are after the same period!'' She stopped a moment, choked with emotion. ''No, Adam is a great man,'' she added quietly. ''All the dreamers were great men. But he's lost.''

Matson looked around. ''Can one of you all-powerful beings whip me up a pair of pants and a shotgun?''

''What's the matter, Daddy?'' Sondra asked, sounding a

little sour. "Does you good to learn how the other half lives."

"*Touche!* But I'm serious. They're up against the Gate, and the only cover they have is the fog. Kids, tell your Mom and Dad to head for the tunnel with everyone else they can. Tell 'em somebody will be waiting for them."

They all stared at him. Finally, Jeff said, "I'm coming with you."

"Me, too!" added Sondra, but he stopped her with a look. "Like that? With your Flux power shot to hell? No. It'll be crowded as it is."

She started to argue, but knew it would be futile.

"You watch us on one of those screens up there," he told her. "If you see we're down, you come get us—hear?"

She smiled and nodded.

"Hey, Goddess of Anchor, get me a decent pair of pants, a good gun and some ammo, and a good cigar! And the same for my friend here, minus the pants."

There was the sound of cannon fire all around, and automatic weapons seemed almost constant. Cassie moved now as if in a dream, a slight wound on her thigh. She didn't feel it, or anything, really, but she knew it was the end. Only the thickness of the fog had prevented the enemy from knowing that there were less than a hundred of them remaining, huddled around dead bodies of men and horses and firing in all directions at a foe none could see. They couldn't even tell that they had been stopped less than three hundred meters from the goal, but it didn't matter. They had been stopped, and the area in between was thick with traps and defenders.

Suddenly there were bugle calls all around, and Tilghman accepted them. "*Cease firing! Cease firing!*" he ordered. Slowly, through the fog, an ominous silence fell.

"Judge Tilghman! Are you still alive?" came a shout from the curtain that reminded Cassie of the void.

"Yes!" he called back. "I'm here! Who's that?"

"My name is Gifford Haldayne," came the voice. "You don't know me but I'm now in overall command here. Champion is dead."

Cassie's head snapped up at the mention of that name. She had been unable to manage a submachine gun but she fingered the automatic pistol in her hand. If she could die accomplishing one straight shot she would be happy. . . .

"I assume this is where I request terms!" Tilghman shouted. He guessed that Haldayne, whom he didn't know, knew that they were beaten beyond a doubt but could not determine the size of the force as yet. Tilghman was literally right on the edge of the Gate; they had almost fallen in when they reached it. His remaining troops flanked him and Cassie in a semicircular formation.

"We can take you out, with total loss of life, as you know, but you can still do some harm to us. If you surrender now, and all of your men come forward unarmed and hands in the air, I swear to you nothing will happen to them. They fought with uncommon honor and bravery and will be treated as such."

"Not very generous when you open the Hellgate. Afraid you don't have enough soldiers for that? But, very well. They have earned the right to see the end of it. What of me and my wife?"

"Throw down your weapons, and you and your wife walk along the bowl until you reach a ladder. Proceed down the ladder to the central tunnel and enter it. You will be met there, and taken to the old capital to be interned with the rest of your family for the duration. I think that's more than generous."

"Don't trust him!" Cassie hissed. "He's one of the Seven. One of the worst! He makes Champion seem like a saint in comparison!"

Tilghman sighed. "What choice do we have, Cassie? He's right—we've lost. And because we've lost, I'd at least like to know the answer. If we're going to die anyway, I'd like to know what's beyond that Gate."

She seemed to wilt a bit, and gave a sad smile. She tossed her pistol into the bowl and heard it clatter and slide. "I'll do whatever you say, Adam."

"All right! We accept! My troopers are hereby ordered to lay down their arms and advance forward, hands raised."

There were scattered shouts of protest, but they did as ordered. Then he got up, helped Cassie to her feet, and together they walked cautiously along the edge to the ladder, which was surprisingly close. Still fearing she might do something rash, he made her go first, then followed her.

The fog was thin down towards the tunnel, and they saw it and the huge, thick cable going into it, and for the first time realized just how close they had come. Tilghman was bare-chested and had kicked off his boots before climbing down. The driving rain had soaked them all, and he didn't want the muddy boots to slip on the smooth floor. Cassie had long ago discarded all clothing.

Again she preceded him down the tunnel ladder, and he found her standing there, looking at the cable.

"Forget it," he told her. "You and I together couldn't move it down here, and you couldn't ground anything in the Gate itself. We'll need whoever's left to fight whatever comes."

A lone man in familiar black uniform approached from the direction of the Gate. He went past, pistol drawn, then turned. "Sir, if you and your wife will continue."

They continued down until they came to the regulator. There they found another black-clad and well-armed trooper, and, getting up from the machine, Onregon Sligh.

"One of your friends had a great deal of fun with us in there, Adam," the scientist said. "I lost two good technicians." He walked past them and behind the rear trooper. "You may proceed," he told them.

"My God, Adam! They're going to shoot us!" Cassie shouted, and leaped on the gunman in front. He went down with her, and his pistol fired, sending a deadly ricochet pinging through the tunnel.

Tilghman had turned at almost the same moment and grabbed the gun arm of the man behind. It was an effective move, and they both tumbled to the floor, wrestling for the gun. Sligh had disappeared in the tunnel, and probably had taken the first shot as the first execution. Tilghman and the man fought furiously for the pistol, and finally the old man managed to turn it down, down.

The pistol fired, the trooper jerked once, and then was still. Winded, Tilghman picked himself and the pistol up and then froze.

The other trooper, a good hundred and eighty centimeters tall and a hundred kilograms of mostly muscle, could be knocked down by the thin, very light woman, but he could hardly be overpowered. He held her with one arm, and he had a pistol pointed at her head.

He grinned, the pistol came away from her head, and he fired twice at Tilghman. The Chief Judge grunted, went back two steps from the recoil, but did not fall.

"No!" Cassie screamed, and struggled to bite the gunman.

But Tilghman wasn't finished. Incredibly, blood streaming from two gaping wounds in his chest, he came on. Startled, the trooper fired twice more, and this time the old man sank to his knees.

The soldier grinned. "O.K., girlie, don't get upset. You can join him in a minute."

Suddenly he felt something coil around his neck, and he dropped both Cassie and the pistol and screamed. He found himself being pulled around and looking into the most horrifying face he'd ever seen. Matson shoved him against the wall and held the big man with one hand while he slowly twisted the rope he'd placed around the killer's neck. The man's arms came up, but there was no fighting that cold fury. His eyes bulged, and his tongue hung out, and then there was a sharp but not very loud *crack*. The trooper slid slowly to the floor with open eyes that would never see again.

Jeff rushed to Cassie, who had gone to Tilghman and was now cradling his head in her lap and sobbing uncontrollably. She was smeared with his blood. Incredibly, Tilghman still lived, and he opened his eyes, saw her, and smiled. "Cassie," he managed to say, coughing up blood after he called her name. "I'm dead. Swear to me that you won't let the dream die with me."

She fought back sobs. "You're *not* dead!"

"Swear—to—me."

"I—I swear, Adam."

The Chief Judge of New Eden seemed to smile, but then the smile was frozen and the eyes remained open, staring at her no longer.

Jeff knelt down. "Grandma. He's gone."

She looked up at him and recognized him, despite her extensive change. *"No!"*

Matson came over to her. "Come on, Cassie. Me and Jeff will bring him with us."

She looked up at him, her expression one of hurt, shock, and incomprehension. "Will he rise from the dead like you?"

"That depends on how well you can sweet-talk our daughter," he replied. "It's pretty much the same method, anyway."

Suzl administered a sedative effect on Cassie, and she slept for quite a while after that. Only the fact that Suzl and the twins were there and assurances that the other kids were all right had given her any lift at all, or any thoughts beyond what had just happened in the tunnel.

Matson and the others could only marvel on the singular *lack* of activity on the part of Suzl and Spirit in their roles as interfaces and authority figures for the computer systems. Clearly the "shell programs" that were now a part of them gave them almost a dual mind, able to tend to all of the necessary things automatically while still retaining their identities. Spirit shrugged at his comment to this effect, and said, "Would you like a playback of the activation? It happened in a few trillionths of a second, but here's what it sounded like."

Sound filled the room, with strange voices only slightly distorted by electronics uttering foreign words.

"Headquarters checking in. All battle positions report in sequence."

"Station Abel activated!"

"Station Baker activated!"

"Station Charlie activated!"

They went on and on, mostly women's voices, he noted, but with a few men's tones in there as well. The litany of Anchor positions had names that were very strange, yet bore an uncanny resemblance to names he knew well.

Delta . . . Edward . . . Frank . . . George . . . Henry . . . Ida . . . James . . . King . . . Luck . . . Mary . . . Nancy . . . Oscar . . . Peter . . . Queen . . . Roger . . . Steven . . . Thomas . . . Uncle . . . Victor . . . Walter . . . X-Ray . . . Yankee . . . Zebra . . . Technical Services Group. . . . Spirit told him that the last one was also often referred to as "Engineering" in the old days, which is why it was usually abbreviated "NG" on maps. The code names were those in use by the Signal Corps at the time the Anchors were established; the language itself was basically a corruption of English, although it included Company and majority of the early settlers knew or had in common, and was called English. Their language today was basically a corrupton of English, although it included much of the noncommon languages of the early settlers, including Hindi, Urdu, Ibo, Arabic, Amharic, Bantu, and Flemish, to name some of them.

They all agreed that the idea of even two languages for a world was horrifying. None had ever even imagined the idea, except as codes.

But the final statement from headquarters stunned them all.

"All being in agreement, *Forward Fire Base Fourteen is operational!*"

"So that's the sacred holy name of World," Suzl remarked. "All this time the Church has been reverently invoking the name of an army base." She giggled, then suddenly grew serious. "All those years I grew up praying to a big ball of gas and feeling holy at the sacred name Forfirbasforten. And we thought we knew it all."

"Now I know a lot more than I did," Matson responded. "We know that there are, or were, at least thirteen more colonies like this one somewhere, so there's hope on that score, and we know by the name alone the precedence of the military in its planning and construction. Who drew the command job at headquarters?"

"I'll check," Spirit told him, then almost immediately said. "She says her name is Angela Robey, and she was a coordinator on the Codex Project."

"Not a priestess, though. They'd go nuts with the truth like that one did here."

"No, not a priestess. She was, in fact, a senior librarian in Anchor Yonkeh. Cassie herself tapped her for the Codex more than thirty years ago in Hope. She remained in charge after the Concordat. She's got enormous power but is only partially trained in it."

"A librarian! Does she know anything about military strategy and tactics?"

"The computer in Holy Anchor has everything there ever was on that. She knows how to organize people and she has on tap every single potential of the firebase defense system."

Matson thought a moment. "That's not the same as being under fire. Besides, all that strategy and tactics didn't help the other worlds that were invaded. Can you patch me in to her or something?"

"Not directly, no. I'm afraid you're just a false wizard,

Matson. You can't directly access the computers and they won't recognize you as an output device. That's why all you can conjure up are illusions."

"How about voice?"

"O.K., but you don't realize the speed at which these things, and we, operate. Both Suzl and I are sitting here talking to you, and doing literally millions of things, passing thousands of communications along, all in the pauses between sentences and our exchanges. It's fascinating, but it's also why I can't explain to you just exactly what's going on."

"But you can contact any damned wizard in Flux and Anchor?"

She nodded. "Ones powerful enough to make a dent, yes."

"Well, if you'll make room in those thousands of messages to give the commander some thoughts given you in normal speech, and if you'll cue me in on just what defenses we've *got*, maybe I'll have a few suggestions on how we can beat the bastards."

"That's why the computers arranged for you to be here, Dad."

He was struck by the irony of the comment, and very pleased at what it did for his ego. *Here I am*, he thought, *in some sort of fantastic contraption I'll never understand, surrounded by two daughters, a grandson, an ex-lover and two wives who happen to be that ex-lover's kids, and even the damned computer is asking me for advice! Demons of Hell, what a family!*

As the day progressed, the fog lifted until there were only tiny wisps of it left. Gifford Haldayne drank a cup of stale coffee and looked down into the huge crater.

"I don't like it," he said to Sligh. "Something's not right. I can feel it in my bones. First Champion's cut in two, then those two crack soldier boys are found, one shot with his own gun, the other strangled, with no sign of the old man *or* his girl. Just some blood."

"Have a little confidence!" Sligh admonished the other. "You were never one to fail under pressure before. What if they did escape to Nantzee or Mareh? Here we stand on the verge of reuniting World with the universe, and you worry about a couple of mere humans."

"Not mere," Haldayne pointed out. "The old boy's one smart, tough cookie, and I once went head-to-head with that broad of his in Flux and damn near didn't escape with my life. Uh-uh. Too much funny business. She was once crazy over that stringer Matson, and he's here, too, and now we found out that the girl that got Champion was his daughter. Matson nailed Coydt and wound up with Tilghman's daughters. You tell me it isn't all connected."

Sligh shrugged. "What if it is? We will be all-powerful if the ancient message is fulfilled. We will be in control of New Eden, its army, and an unlimited supply of Flux if nobody arrives. If some of our own kind show up, we'll be here with our story first and we'll be the ones they trust."

"And if it's the Enemy after all?" Haldayne asked nervously.

"Getting cold feet at a time like this? If it's the Enemy, then we'll need our army *and* the Tilghmans, Cassies, Matsons, and the rest, won't we? You can't back out now, anyway. That's why we all agreed that once our remotes were installed and tested we'd all be here, in New Caanan, so we couldn't go back at the last minute."

"All but Ivan. I wonder what happened to him, too?"

"There was a faulty signal from one of the northern remotes. He went up there to fix it. There is no more faulty signal, so he evidently did. Time works against his being back, and I'm not going to hold everything up until he gets here. Wherever he is, I'm positive he's no threat to us right now."

Haldayne shrugged off his unease and reported, "The Judges that wouldn't go along are taken care of, and the army's been pretty well pulled back to defensive positions. I've notified all commands that we have discovered a plot to open the Hellgates and that it might not be stopped. They're going to bring every available man and every piece of heavy equipment we've got, and we're organizing in five battle groups. I'm going to miss that bridge Tilghman blew, though. It could make us short some heavy guns we might wish we had. I assume Ivan's notified all those that the remains of the Nine couldn't and our people didn't. As we figured, the stringers have taken over operational command of the combined armies, so I think we can feel reasonably safe that nobody's going to be too trigger-happy.''

The Seven were no fools. They understood that they were taking a gamble; a gamble they might well lose. They had as much percentage in a strong military force at each Hellgate as did the rest of World, if only for insurance.

Sligh chuckled, and Haldayne looked quizzically at him. ''What's the joke? I'd swear you aren't any more human than those damned computers of yours.''

''I was just thinking. Here we finally have a way to open the Gates, and insure our own survival against a double-cross. Yet six of us stand here at this one Gate for that very reason. Suppose they only sent one ship? Or two? Suppose they don't land at this Gate?''

''Now's a fine time to think about *that*!''

''Oh, don't worry. When the Gates open, all access to the Gates from Anchor will be shut down. Then there will be a purging but very controlled rush of Flux from the other side. This will destroy our cables and receivers, by the way, but don't worry. Once open, all they'll do is reset the regulators, not blow them up. Then whatever is out there can come in—apparently into this depression, and the others. Then the Gates will close once more, and they will once again be locked, to prevent two objects from occupying the same space. Whatever comes in must either move out or leave the same way it came before something else can come in. All our forefathers did was essentially tie in a bomb with a numerical code to the regulator and then reset the Gate for outgoing, as if something were here. We will key in the code to deactivate the bombs and then throw the switch, as it were, from outgoing to incoming. If nothing comes in this Gate, there is no purge, and we are still in communication from this end. But I think something will come, if they're still out there. This was one of the three Gates in which the message was received.''

Haldayne looked at his watch. ''It's eleven forty now. When will you throw the switch?''

''I think we want a look at this in daylight, but I want to give the forces as much time as possible. Four hours of light should be sufficient, I would think. Fourteen hundred on the nose, then.''

''Fair enough. I'll notify the others and the commands. I still feel something's not quite right, though.''

''After all these centuries, it is as right as it will ever be.''

''The computer's been tuned in to Haldayne and Sligh,'' Suzl told them. ''We've got a little more than two hours. Fourteen hundred, they said. They also said that the Gates will be purged, then whatever comes comes, then it all locks and switches back to normal.''

Matson nodded. ''Then that's when we have to move. Fast. Notify all commanders, and get the word to whatever wizards with forces are at the Anchor capitals. As soon as they get word that something's in the dish, get in there and pack it solid.''

Sondra shook her head. ''You really think it'll work? I mean, nobody's been able to dent the walls of *this* place with anything we've got. If something's built to travel in Flux that thick. . . .''

''We don't need to dent it, if I've guessed right. Look, you and Jeff are both strong wizards. You've had military training and can tie into the communications system like I can't.'' He turned to Candy and Crystal. ''Girls, neither of you have had any military training in your lives, but you sure as hell can tie in like those two and send what I tell you. Are you willing?''

''We'd like to have sons and daughters and grandchildren, too,'' they responded. ''We said we'd love, honor, and obey. Just tell us what to do.''

He kissed each of them and said, ''This time don't get mixed up as to which one you are, huh?'' He looked around. ''As big as this family is, I still should'a had either two more daughters or two more wives. We can only cover four Gates with direct broadcasts to the wizards.''

''Don't worry so much,'' Spirit responded. ''There are very good people at all the sites and they know what you're up to. The orbital scanning satellites all decayed and burned fifteen hundred years ago, but through the transmissions I think I can get a general picture of each Hellgate on the screens. I—''

She stopped as she saw Cassie come out of the doorway between two screens. It led to a bathroom they still hadn't completely figured out and had a series of bunk beds and a very small dining area. Apparently at the start this complex was staffed around the clock, and managed the comings and goings at the Gate. Food was simple. You just said what you wanted and Suzl used a small device in the dining area to create it out of Flux. It also, to her and Matson's delight, materialized beer and cigars.

They all rushed over to Cassie, concerned. She had apparently washed herself off, but she looked weary. ''I'm all right,'' she assured them. ''I'm all right. I heard everyone yelling in here and wondered what had happened and whether I could be of any help.''

''You *sure* you're O.K.?'' Suzl pressed.

She nodded. ''I know he's dead. I can accept that now. What of the children, though, Suzl?''

''They're O.K. A couple of Fluxwives up top took 'em in. I've·been checking on them when I could, but they're in no more danger than we are, which is quite a lot.''

"You—you're running this place?"

Quickly Suzl told her all the details to date. She nodded and sighed.

"You sure you're feeling all right?"

"I'm tired, angry, frightened to death, and on top of that I'm horny as hell."

"Join the club, then," Sondra called from her command chair.

"We're all about to break down and have a real cry, but we can't afford to," Suzl told her. "God! I just wish they'd throw the damned switches and get it *over* with!"

Spirit eased over to Matson and whispered, "Look at them! Even Suzl! They're still just a mass of emotions, wants, and desires."

Matson thought it over. "Yeah, it's the bodies, the hormones, the glands, all that. But I'm not worried about it. It may sound crazy, but I wish I had Fluxgirls with guts in every control when the Enemy comes."

She stared at him. "Why?"

"Suzl's power came from you, remember. I heard about it when we were here trying to take this place back. Cass only held her own against Haldayne until she saw me fall. Don't you see? The key to drawing full strength from that machine is emotion, not reason. You've been there yourself. It might just pay for you to get a little of that passion back yourself. You seem to have lost it the moment you stepped in here."

"I lost my innocence," she responded. "I admit I'm keyed up and more than a little scared, but you have to remember—I saw them all *before* they were like this. I don't like what's become of them."

"Save your hate for the Enemy," Matson told her. "There's far too much hate in this world for the less important things now. Besides, as of now they're only that way because that's how they've been for a while and there's an emergency. What they decide on after this is over will be what shapes their lives."

"Perhaps you're right. You seem fairly confident that we *will* get through this."

"I'm always confident in a battle. It doesn't make any practical sense to be otherwise until you lose. I think they'll be sons of bitches, but I'm not sure the threat hasn't been overblown. We've been held hostage and kept down on World for twenty-seven centuries because of them. I think we either free ourselves or we'll live forever under this."

"You sound like one of the Seven," she said.

"They're no better or worse than Mervyn and the Nine or a hundred Fluxlords, not really. They're the only truly free people on World. Still, any enemy that can hold a grudge for all this time is something else again. Me, I'd prefer some enemy to our own people."

"What!"

"Sure. I don't think our relatives out there are gonna be all that happy to meet us."

"How can you say that?"

"Twenty-seven hundred years ago, on some other planet called Earth which is all Anchor, they discovered Flux and how to use it, and they had their machines to make it jump through hoops. So instead of using it, they established at least fourteen colonies so far away that even *they* didn't know where they all were. Why bother?"

"Exploration? Crowding?"

"Nope. There's more profit in tyranny than in all this, and by number fourteen you're colonizing, not exploring. Now, I read Haller's journal and it's pretty clear that the folks of his time had no idea that people and machines could get mixed up together. They used Flux only by machine—to get from there to here, to do the cooking, that kind of thing. Their aim was to turn this whole planet into Anchor, not use the Flux to do anything but make it Anchor. Why import farmers and shepherds and machinists when Flux would make what they wanted?"

"You tell me," Spirit said wryly.

"I think Flux is probably the most dangerous thing they ever had to deal with. My guess is there was some really nasty accident in the early days that frightened them to death."

"There's nothing in the computer memory on it."

"There wouldn't be, necessarily. Now they wanted what Flux could give 'em, which was the power of a billion wizards, but they didn't want it done close to home. The profits from it in an Anchor society would be tremendous, far more than the cost, but you don't set up a colony and spend all that much to do it and have 'em sit here and make Flux teacups and steaks or even buildings. You want it to do the big stuff, the stuff that costs more to do the hard way no matter what the set-up costs here. And you don't make big stuff with the Flux we got on World. You make it out of the stuff you see out there, beyond the Hellgate."

"O.K.—but what happened?"

"Maybe too much Flux was allowed onto World. Maybe they had new kinds of computers they never used before. Who knows? But all the defensive systems, which are impressive, are Anchor systems. There's really no consideration for Flux power. There's no sign that they used their Flux amplifiers to work individual spells, or programs, or whatever you want to call them. They were intended to work with the stuff in the modules that the computers furnished. They were both frightened and amazed when they discovered that human beings could manipulate Flux through those machines without another machine. It scared the shit out of the army, who went to a great deal of trouble to create those independent programs, the Soul Riders and the Guardians, to limit access to what the big computers had, and to keep the computers from running *them*. Even there they got it wrong through ignorance. The big programs developed independent identities, became thinking beings, because the Soul Riders lived inside humans. They *became* humans—vicariously, anyway."

"But the Guardians didn't."

"No, but they poked into every Anchorite with Flux power because they knew they'd need one when push came to shove. They were limited by their programs, but they also started taking independent action above and beyond their own needs. The Soul Riders only knew that they were to keep the Gates closed, so they went after the Seven. The Guardian, too, got involved in human affairs when it helped us. More than we know, I think. The Guardian couldn't exactly use the computer, but it had to keep the thing repaired—so it learned a lot and got a lot of information which it fed to the Soul Riders when and if needed. They needed humans to get the information, so the Guardian talked to the Soul Riders and the Soul Riders used the hosts."

Spirit nodded. "My Soul Rider was always convinced that it had an unseen master in Anchor. The master was the Guardian, then. It tapped the computer, sent the information needed to the Soul Rider, who then used it. The computers, you see, are nothing more than a collection of data in mathematical form. The Guardian and the Soul Rider are both required to actually get and use it, unless it's in a program module. What you're saying is that it was done that way to keep wizards from accessing the whole thing unaided."

"That's about it. So, think about it a while. They still got it wrong. The machines still used people—but within limits. Now they're a part of you, and Suzl, and fifty-four other people we don't know, and the process is complete. You're not human, Spirit. Nobody in this room is *really* human, not even me. We're all part human and part machine. If you got the power, or know somebody that does, you can be ageless, nearly immortal, just about never get sick, grow back lost limbs, even, under certain circumstances, be brought back from the dead. We—all of us in the top five or ten percent—are the masters of Flux and Anchor. For most of history the people of Anchor were terrified of Flux and its people. Even after all these centuries, I bet our relatives still will be.''

"I—'' Spirit stopped suddenly. "My God! It's nearly time!'' She turned to the others. "Places, everybody! *This is it!*''

On the screens overhead there appeared huge pictures. They weren't true pictures, but rather computer reconstructions of what was happening from its sensing abilities, but they looked real and were for all intents and purposes. Each showed an aerial view of a Hellgate, seven in all, with a small superimposed map of each cluster below with the pictured Gate flashing. All had substantial forces at or near the Gates, although the bulk would still be on the way. There was no way, short of asking specific questions, of telling the nature of those forces, or their origins.

The women were now in chairs and at their posts. Suzl lit a cigar and examined the screens, although with her direct computer link she had far more information at her disposal than they showed. Matson withdrew towards the center of the round room to get an easy view of all screens. Spirit stood silent, eyes half-closed, as if in a trance; Suzl walked back and forth, chomping nervously on the cigar.

Matson called to her. "You set upstairs?''

"Yeah. I rang every damned communicator in the Anchor and told them just what do do—and I used Sligh's voice for it. They're bringing the stuff in now. I've got myself tied in to every damned wizard around the Gate including most of the Seven, would you believe? And I've got beauties and the beast here linked in with the district commanders in clusters three, four, six, and seven, and I can shift them if necessary.''

A tremendous sound suddenly filled the chamber, causing all but Spirit and Suzl to jump. None had ever heard a klaxon horn before. It sounded three long blasts, blasts also sounded by the regulator at the Hellgates.

"MASTER GATE LOCK SEQUENCE KEYED," announced an eerie, unfamiliar female voice at a level that was almost as loud as the horn. "AUTOTRIP INTERLOCK TO INCOMING."

"That's just the Gate computer altering the control room here," Spirit assured them. "It's the *next* message that'll be the story."

"INCOMING, GATES TWO, FOUR, SIX," announced the voice. "VERIFYING GATES CLEAR."

"Three of them!" Suzl yelled. "It's not all seven!"

"BLOCKAGE ON GATE FOUR. SAFETY CHECK. SAFETY CHECK COMPLETED. STAND BY TO PURGE. ALL PERSONNEL STAND CLEAR OF GATE AREAS."

There was a second blast of the klaxon, this time one long and three short, which was repeated after a few seconds.

"Get the word out that it's north and south only!" Matson shouted. "Shift any between-cluster forces north, but keep everybody else on the other Gates. This may only be the welcoming committee, not the main force. Shift Sondra to Gate Two, Jeff to Gate Six. Candy, Crystal—you stand by!"

"VERIFY INCOMING GATES CLEAR OF PERSONNEL. STAND BY FOR PURGE. PURGING. GATES PURGED. INCOMING IN TWO MINUTES, REPEAT, TWO MINUTES. RECEPTION AND SERVICE CREWS STAND BY."

Out at the Hellgate, the enormous crowd had moved back at the ghostly warning and watched as the Hellgate turned from its emerald green color to a brightness that was impossible to look at. The cable leading down glowed briefly, then faded into nothingness all the way to the edge of the Anchor apron.

Sligh breathed a sigh of relief. "I guessed right in the connections after all. It didn't blow."

Gifford Haldayne turned and stared at him. "You *guessed*?"

"INCOMING, GATES TWO, FOUR, AND SIX, IN ONE MINUTE."

"Here we go," Matson said in a whisper. He suddenly cursed, seeing that he'd bit clean through his cigar.

"STAND BY GATE TWO. INCOMING IN TEN SECONDS . . . NINE . . . EIGHT . . . SEVEN . . . SIX . . . FIVE . . . FOUR . . . THREE . . . TWO . . . ONE . . . ACTIVATE MAIN REGULATOR. NOTE SHIP HAS PROPER RECOGNITION CODES BUT IS OF TYPE NOT IN MEMORY. LOGGED IN. TIME IN 14:01:41."

On the screen and at the Gate they watched as the great bowl-shaped depression that was the total Hellgate pulsed and throbbed with light and shook the ground nearby with regular vibrations in time to the pulsing.

A fountain of pure Flux came out of the hole and rose high into the afternoon sky, perhaps twenty meters above the ground level. It steadied, then put forth streamers of energy that formed a skeletal framework, as if some giant hand were drawing a detailed blueprint in Flux. This was pure Flux, and could be seen by all, whether or not they had the power, and the sight was awesome.

"It's a *program*," Suzl said wonderingly. "They change the whole damned thing into a Flux program, like the Guardian or the Soul Rider, then squirt themselves through on the strings! When it gets here, enough Flux is drawn out of the Gate to reform it into solids just like it was."

"Then our computers must be working that program!" Matson shouted. "Tell 'em to turn it off!"

"We tried that *seconds* ago," Suzl told him, tense and excited now, as if "seconds" meant "years." "It doesn't work. It's an overriding command, strictly automatic, as a safety feature!"

The four equatorial Gates remained quiet, but at the two Gates to the north the scene in their own cluster was being repeated before an equally awed and extremely frightened horde who didn't have the benefits of computer speed or access.

The process was completing itself now, and in the three Gate bowls sat solid-looking objects of enormous size. To everyone they looked like metal versions of a child's spinning top, although they had a bottom curving to more or less fit the bowl. As large as they were, though, it was clear that they had not been designed for these receiving depressions; the ships were angled and off-center, and had slowly pitched forward to rest on one rounded side a good five meters below the top of the depression, while rising five on the opposite side.

"BERTHING COMPLETED. GATE RESET TO OUTGOING. GROUND CREWS STAND BY TO ASSIST PASSENGERS AND CREW."

"Well, they have smaller ships than we did," Spirit sighed.

"Yeah, well, that's a fact," Matson responded, "but it don't mean anything. If they're the size of cockroaches there could be a million of them."

"They're not. They're all in box-like containers. We saw it as the thing formed, and were able to count them."

"How many?"

"Each box is a hundred and fifty-two point four centimeters long, ninety centimeters high, and ninety-two point seven centimeters across. There's a space between each one, and fifty percent is cargo and machinery for the ship. The computer estimates that there are two thousand three hundred and forty-two such boxes, each containing a living organism."

"Well, that's something," he said. "The others the same?"

"Exactly the same," she responded, eyes shut.

"O.K., we outnumber them but probably don't outgun them. That means that either they think they have all the power they need or they're only the first wave."

"The external area is being computer scanned in extreme detail," she told him. "The nature and language of the scan are incomprehensible, but the actions are clear and deliberate.''

''How far?''

''Apparently to the horizon. The computer says that the top section is a separate machine with its own power source and can be detached. Because of its shape, it almost certainly flies. Our own scans indicate a capacity of no more than four box occupants.''

''Scouting, then, not troop transport. That means the initial group is there to secure the landing site and scout out the terrain. They're the leading wave, and that's bad. Keep those forces at the equator. Is it safe for our boys to move?''

''We've energized the two forward sections of the tunnel. The rest is safe.''

''The temple access gates are open,'' Suzl added. ''Get 'em started, I'd say. Nothing remotely alive as we know it is going to get down that tunnel from the ship right now.''

''They'll be alive as we know it,'' Matson assured her. ''Otherwise they wouldn't be here.''

''Power's on in the ships,'' Spirit announced. ''We detected a slight trembling. It's Flux power—they're stepping down to normal Flux levels and drawing a string from the Gate itself. Harmless to humans, but enough for them. The computer believes that it is recharging its energy cells.''

''That figures. We must have done it the same way, and Haller and his people came back down through the tunnel and over to here.''

''The computers agree. There is a ring of power collectors around a hatch of some directed at the tunnel. Because their ships weren't designed for our Gates, but because it seems you have to do it just this way or it doesn't work, they've sacrificed stability inside their ship to keep their collector over that tunnel entrance. The computer now agrees entirely with your speculation, you might like to

know, except that they have a way to store it before use. Just cutting power won't stop them.''

"Sure it will, and they'll know it. It'll get 'em out in the open.''

"Sligh is trying a broadcast on every frequency known to him,'' she told him. "The usual welcome and assurances of peace and friendship and all that. So far no response.''

"*Whoa!*'' Suzl called out, almost falling down. "There was a sudden big power surge there!''

Out at the Gate, a huge and partly visible wall sprang up, looking like a giant inverted glass bowl. It covered the area around the Gate for a distance of more than five kilometers, trapping the welcoming committee and all nearby forces inside.

"It's a *shield*!'' Cassie shouted. "It's a wizard's shield in Anchor!''

"In Anchor, yes, but its source is Flux from the Gate itself,'' Spirit told them.

"They are the demons of Hell come now to keep us from finding the true path,'' Cassie whispered so low that none of the others clearly heard.

"The shield's a good one,'' Suzl reported. "About the only thing getting through it is air.''

"Where's its power coming from, though? The ship or the Gate?'' Matson asked her.

"Definitely the ship.''

"That's a hell of a lot of power to drain. Any way to find out just how much of a drain it is?''

"We can figure the power required to maintain it, and it's very close to the amount of power coming in from the Gate. We don't know their storage capacity, though.''

"Any attempt at communications on *our* part?''

"The Commander's been trying, but so far nothing. Nothing for Sligh, either, by the way. They don't like the fact that they're trapped, and they're trying to put as good a light on it as they can. They sure didn't expect *this*, though."

Spirit was grimmer, yet firm. "The probilities are great that they know about us—where we are and what we have if not *who* we are. They haven't even *tried* to use the tunnel. The Commander's made her decision. She is now transmitting what is essentially an ultimatum. If they do not immediately open contact, she will act upon them as a hostile force."

"Good girl. Can you give me an estimate on whether or not we have sufficient force to move that thing?"

"We don't know its exact composition so we don't know its weight. If it's greater than a million tons, no. If it's somewhere around there, it depends on just how far we have to nudge them. It doesn't much matter. If it doesn't work, they will have to make the next move."

"If it doesn't work," Matson responded, "the living may envy the dead before we're through."

20

MISTAKE IN TIMING

The Anchor Luck computer had first become aware of Matson's unorthodox reasoning when he had explained some of his theories to Mervyn and to Adam Tilghman. As defense installations, they were preprogrammed with basic strategies and methods; as self-aware devices, although not in a way humans would understand that term, they were also aware that certainly their standardized methods would probably fail by themselves as they must have in the other colonies. And, as self-aware devices, they were capable of learning even from such a slow-thinker as the stringer colonel, and then following up on his plans. They were basically programmed to defend against hostile human attack; otherwise, they were maintenance computers, established primarily to form the new world and keep it stable. Their programming also required that all major decisions must be approved or requested by humans. They could recommend, but needed Spirit and Suzl to act, and they awaited the order of their Commander.

But a message was received from the strange object. It

came from the southern ship only, indicating that it was in fact the command ship of the fleet, and it came not at computer speed but in the English of their ancestors.

"We are *Samish*," it said, although that last word was subject to a great deal of interpretation. It was in no known tongue or inflection. "We wish no fight, no death of your people. Resistance to us is evil. Resistance to us is against the Plan. Those who do what is righteous and what is their destiny will be as gods. Only those who are evil will be destroyed."

"Sounds like the Holy Mother Church," Jeff commented, listening to it with the rest of them.

"Definitely machine-generated speech," Spirit told them. "Doubtful it's a translator. Probabilities are that they can't naturally talk our way."

"Missionaries!" Matson spat. "Missionaries with power. Damn! The worst combination!"

The Commander proceeded cautiously, and on the open voice band they were using, allowing the computer to suggest and guide her comments.

"We also do not wish any loss of life, but we do not comprehend your initial statement. Please clarify."

"It is the order of things," the Enemy replied. "To *Samish* was given the power. *Samish* was anointed Lords of Creation. We now are exploring our domain. The First Lord has raised up others to serve *Samish*. *Samish* must root out all evil to achieve perfection of the universe. You are not the first of your kind *Samish* has been guided to by the First Lord. Within the past—year—we have come upon you three times. The first was righteous, and gave over to *Samish*. The second was evil, and fought *Samish*. *Samish* destroyed them and remade them in the image decreed by the First Lord. The third had both good and evil. *Samish* set the good over the evil. It is the way of things. *Samish* brings the truth and the power to the under-races."

"Now it sounds like a Fluxlord," Sondra noted.

"That's pretty much what the computers think it's offering," Suzl told them. "If we surrender, it'll give us all Flux power. If we fight, it'll destroy us. And if we're mixed, it'll create Fluxlords out of the ones who go along and Fluxlings out of the rest. Of course, the computers supporting them will be *Samish* computers, so it'd be hierarchical. However, the computers believe that three in the last year is beyond the bounds of probability. It believes the odds are even that either the *Samish* year is very, very long, or else they still believe it's twenty-six hundred and eighty-two years ago. The computer is inclined for a number of reasons to the latter belief."

Matson laughed and clapped his hands. "Sure—now it all makes sense! Nobody, but nobody, waits that long just to invade. No culture, no civilization, is *that* static, not an expanding, militaristic one with a missionary complex. And even if they did, they wouldn't show up just five minutes after the Gates were opened. They'd leave some kind of sensing device to signal them if and when and go on their way."

The computers took a nanosecond or so to decide pretty much what Matson was doing in a far longer period. They had taken the first three colonies they'd hit after intersecting the human string, then set off the next—World. The three leading ships of the attack force had been sent ahead to negotiate and determine conditions, scout out the land, and make contacts. The main force would follow. But they were converted into energy and then shot as energy along the string in that alternate universe, and when they got here the Gates were locked. They couldn't get in, they couldn't back up, and they couldn't in energy form even get a recall. They might even have blocked the entrance. They had been just outside in that energy swirl all this time—as energy. No time had passed for them.

Considering the span of time, World had simply outlived them. And because of World's unique culture and traditions, it had changed the least in all that time, while civilizations rose and fell, messianic campaigns were waged and then ebbed, great discoveries had been made. Only World, and its lonely invaders, had remained stagnant.

The Commander's computer suggested a confirmation question. "We assume the Soviet world was the evil one."

"We do not know that world. The evil one was the People's Republic Expreditionary Force," responded the *Samish*.

Confirmation! That was the Chinese colony.

The probability, then, was quite small that the horde behind them was even now rushing to World. The problem was boiling down to getting rid of six thousand and a bit more of the *Samish*, whatever they were.

"We regret that we must refuse your offer," the Commander told them. "You cannot offer as a reward that which we already possess."

"You do not know what you say," the *Samish* replied. "We have the power to give you control of the energy of the First Lord's universe. We ask only for the worship we are due."

Matson needed no computer to guess the "recent" (to them) history of the *Samish*. An egocentric race, like humanity, believing it was the center of all creation, had discovered the Flux universe and developed its technology to use it, and apparently not that much differently than humanity had, no matter what the difference in the two races. There was only one way to do it without getting smeared all over creation and they'd done it. Only their method of manipulating Flux differed, and probably only in detail. Somehow they had come upon, the first time, what had happened here on World, a merger of mind and machine. In their case, theology and science had not conflicted. They searched for their god's heaven, and saw it in the Flux universe, one of brilliant and limitless energy and light.

Then they had come upon others out there, on the worlds the strings took you to. They found intelligent life, but life very different from their own—and life which did not have the power over Flux that they did.

The first was righteous, and gave over to Samish.

How human of them, Matson thought. He remembered when Coydt and the New Eden Brotherhood had attacked and seized Anchor Logh. By the time the liberators had arrived, the population had been willing to endure whatever indignities and horrors the new government could and would administer to save their own lives and those of their children.

The Chinese, whoever they were, had fought to the last one, although they had lost. That, too, was human. They had chosen death, and a courageous one, to deny their conquerors the spoils of war.

The third, which had split into two camps, was the most human of all. There the Company directors, or their counterparts, had outargued or outmaneuvered the army until it was too late to seal the Gates. The resulting civil war, with the Company on the *Samish* side, had placed the directors as Fluxlords of that world over the vanquished.

Near the Gate, Onregon Sligh gnashed his teeth and pounded his fist in frustration. He could listen in on the conversation, but the power on both sides was so strong that even if he could break in he'd be ignored. And he had no idea who the hell the *Samish* were bargaining with.

"I told you there was somebody else," Gifford Haldayne said accusingly. He looked around at the others. They were all there, crowded around the small transceiver: Rosa Haldayne, Chua Gabaye, Ming Tokiabi, Varishnikar Stomsk. . . . All but Zelligman Ivan.

"They're offering us nothing at all," Gabaye snapped. "We *already* control the whole damned planet! All we did was get suckered into being trapped in Anchor."

"I wonder," said Gifford Haldayne, staring at the transceiver, "if we've been kidding ourselves about *that* all these years. *We* opened the Gates, but they sure as hell aren't talking to us."

"Whoever they are, they will soon attack," Sligh predicted. *"Then* we will attempt to strike whatever deal we can."

Sligh was certainly correct in at least the first part of his statement. Clearly further conversation was getting neither side closer together.

"You may go in peace," the Commander told them, "or you may put down your shield and we can attempt friendly relations. The choice is yours. But we will not subordinate ourselves to another race. We have had quite enough of that among ourselves, thank you."

She still *sounded* like a librarian, Matson thought, but she was also playing it cool, calm, and correct and she clearly had the guts for this business. Those Soul Riders picked well, it seemed.

"It is unnatural, against the grand scheme of the universe," the *Samish* responded. "Under-races which deny the primacy of the First Lord also deny the Divine Scheme. Such is corruption, such is evil. Even now there are forces within our shield poised to strike us. We will demonstrate our power."

The small pinched-top section of the main ship began to glow, then with a sound of connectors snapping back it freed itself of the main ship and lifted slowly and dramatically into the air.

"Stand by to place first thrust attack into operation!" came the Commander's message to the operations officers at the northern and southern Anchors. *"The loss of weight of the vehicle may have tipped things in our favor."*

They had packed the tunnels nearly solid with every type of explosive known that they could lay their hands on. The Guardians now dropped the safety shield just ahead of the regulator and pumped highly compressed air into the gaps in the massive load. In effect, it was Matson's great cannon, aimed at the massive but exposed underbelly of the ships.

The small flying vehicle made a humming sound as it

took off from the Gate and headed out towards the largest New Eden force within the shield. Similar ships took off almost simultaneously from Gates Two and Six, but this time in Flux.

The computers shifted their estimates, and through the district commanders instructed and briefed the wizards in the north about what was to happen. The Nine had been reduced to the Five, but because of their abilities to travel Flux at great speed, Talanane and Serrio were at Gate Two, and the other three were at Gate Six. Their strong powers, combined with that of the local wizards and Fluxlords, was considerable.

The small ships were obviously Flux amplifiers of some sort, but they were within the greater shield and did not have a great deal of shielding themselves. The wizards of the north watched them come, waiting until the last moment to erect their own shields. Mervyn, alone, had once beaten an amplifier; no one in Flux was alone, and the Nine had amplifiers of its own, used up to now to guard the Gate and pulled back when that had proven useless.

The New Eden defenders were more constrained, but so was the ship. In an Anchor environment its amplifiers were very limited, and they tried to pick up power from the city electrical lines and grids. Suzl was able to pretty much block this, leaving the ship to other armaments.

The *Samish* were about to discover that they had picked a unique offshoot of humanity, primitive though it was culturally and technologically. This was a hard, nasty race, who'd practiced on itself what the *Samish* alone believed they possessed. When the feared demons had proven to be no more than strong wizards, the Fluxlords felt themselves right at home.

The New Eden ship rose into the air and hovered there a moment, then shot a series of devastating rays into the main body of troops about a kilometer from Anchor. There was tremendous loss of life and materiel where the rays struck, but hard-bitten commanders who'd conquered three

Anchors ordered a return fire with rockets and sweeping heat rays.

In the north, the Fluxlord's shields went on. It would not stop the ray weapons, but it sure as hell stopped the ships well short of the main body. Wizards who had conquered other powerful Fluxlands knew well to disperse their troops and their most powerful wizards, but they would have to take some losses from the rays until the commander made her move.

"*Now!*" came the order from Holy Anchor, and simultaneously small sparks of Flux flew from the firewalls into the explosive. The projectile was not shot or shell, but air—compressed air, which would go through the shield, propelled by the mighty force of the giant explosions which had no place to go but out the tunnel.

All three ships shuddered, and for a brief moment their shields flickered, but then reformed. For New Eden it was not enough, but for the northern defenders in Flux it was the opening they waited for. Power from the Fluxlord's shields reached out like a living thing and struck and engulfed the tiny ships in the few precious seconds of power cuts. Mighty fingers of force gripped the ships and squeezed them, compressing them more and more into dense balls of metal glowing with great heat. Now the commanders, using their Soul Rider connections, concentrated everything they had on the master shield. It wavered, and broke several times, reforming as a smaller and yet more powerful shield. They smashed it again and again, and did manage to restrict it to the area just around the Gates, but from that point the alien shield held. They kept the pressure on, but knew they would have to find an alternate way to the Enemy's heart.

In the south, the alien's flying craft was faring better. Capable of instant bursts of great speed and near supernatural maneuverability, it was having no trouble keeping out of the way of the weaponry being hurled at it, and its ray projectors definitely had a far better range.

"We taught them respect in the north," Spirit said glumly, "but those ships were too heavy for what we had to explode. They still have their power and their equipment."

Matson looked over the small company in the control center. "Other than Suzl and yourself, who has the greatest Flux power in this room?"

"In practical terms, the twins," she responded, "although Mom has greater potential. She can't use it herself, but with spells fed to her, her past experience will make them the most effective. Why?"

"Because I think there's a power big enough to budge that ship, if she's willing to go along and if you're willing to do the dirtiest thing you've ever done in your whole life."

"The computers can't divine your meaning. Explain."

"The key to what you said is *potential*. Do me a favor. Ask your computer who was stronger in absolute terms, Coydt or Cassie."

Spirit looked surprised. "Why—in relative access ability, she's *much* stronger. But—she lost to him!"

"That's the point. Your Mom overall has had a pretty unhappy life for somebody always at the top. She took on Gifford Haldayne with almost no training and beat him as easy as you'd step on a bug. Then she totally remade an entire Fluxland and stopped massed armies from fighting in a matter of minutes. In the backwash, without even knowing it, she restored me to life. I understand how it was done now, but she doesn't—and I don't think it'd ever been done before. It wasn't intellect, although the intellect's there, that made her so powerful, or Coydt, either. It was emotion—raw, burning, overpowering feelings. It strengthens the link to the computer and acts like a massive amplifier. The computer here will deliver whatever it takes."

"But she lost to Coydt!"

"Deep down she *wanted* to lose. She'd had two decades of living a life of terrible responsibility and near total deprivation as the head of the Church. She knew I was there, and it damn near killed her because she wanted me and couldn't ever have me. All she needed to do was to keep Coydt occupied until I blew that amplifier. She didn't need to beat him to defeat him, and she knew it.''

Spirit shook her head sadly. ''Oh, my God!'' she whispered. She looked over at her mother and felt the onset of tears. She understood, too, the truth of what he was saying. The Soul Rider had not understood it, merely tapped it when it was present, but it knew. Under the height of passion in the Hellgate, Suzl had assumed her powers and gained sufficient computer access, at least for a time, to sense the presence of the control room and to break the unbreakable spells that had bound Spirit. The key was always there, but the computers did not think as humans thought, and what was not quantifiable was not truly real to them. Even now they resisted, granting his point but also noting that such a level cannot be deliberately reached, and that was to be regretted. With the power of raw Flux to tap just behind her, and the regulator to keep it in bounds, the amount of force that she could potentially generate could indeed do the job—could, in fact, do almost anything.

''There is a possible way,'' Matson told her, ''although it's a gamble. It might work, it might not. If it does, though, you and I will feel a little bit filthy for the rest of our unnatural lives.''

''Side hatches are opening!'' Suzl shouted. ''They're coming out!''

''Tell eveyone to hold their fire!'' Sligh ordered. ''At least we're going to see just who we are dealing with.''

The hatch opened inward on the upper portion of the ship, then a long ramp of the same metallic substance as the ship extended, correcting for the ship's list, and reached all the way to the Gate apron. Within moments, the first of the *Samish* troopers began coming out. Onregon Sligh felt the hair on the back of his neck straighten and rise. Many in the crowd screamed, and a number began to run.

The control room personnel all watched the viewer. Only the New Eden ship was opening; the two in the north had been badly stung and weren't about to risk anything yet.

The creatures were like nothing ever seen, even in the most terrible of nightmares. They were shaped somewhat like rounded hourglasses on their side, with the rear section a bit thicker and more elongated. The front half contained two stalked eyes that were huge, unblinking, with blood-red irises and heart-shaped pupils of deep purple which seemed oddly dull and segmented, like those of insects. There was really no up or down to the creatures; their bodies were covered with thin, snakelike tentacles each resembling hard steel wire, and these seemed to spring out of the body, or retract, at will and as needed, and with blinding speed. Just how many tentacles they had was unclear, for their bodies were completely covered in thick, matted black fur. The tentacles moved in some cases so fast the human eye couldn't follow them, yet they never tangled. They walked on them, and used them as a nearly infinite set of fingers. The tips apparently could secrete some sort of substance that allowed perfect traction in any eventuality, but left an ugly slime where they touched.

The first *Samish* to emerge were armed with unfamiliar devices that had to be weapons, and they went *up* onto the polished metal surface of the ship, taking the high ground. Observers could see on some of these a sac-like opening on the rear body section that seemed to open and close in regular, undulating motions. Whether it was a mouth, an anus, some sort of reproductive sac, or something no human could understand was unknown.

The defensive computers observed, analyzed, and made their informed speculations. The eyes were independent and the motion of the creatures was equally exact forwards backwards, or sideways. There were tentacles waving about over various parts of the body, serving no apparent function. Since there was no physical difference in the spindly things, it seemed obvious that these were multi-purpose organs, not merely arms and legs but possibly delivering all the senses except sight.

Their extreme precision in large numbers spoke of exceptional organization and training, or what the computers suspected from the conversation at the start. Their English, although ancient, had been quite good, yet they had never referred to themselves as a group or race—not "the *Samish*" or "we *Samish*," but always simply as "*Samish*."

"Based on available data," Spirit told them, "the computers believe that we are seeing a collective organism totally bonded to its computers. Each ship is an entity, not each *Samish*."

"That fits," Matson replied. "The army obviously had a great fear of that, right here when it discovered wizards and spells and figured out what was happening. That's why it created the independent units and the limited access. It must have happened to the first *Samish* to successfully handle Flux."

She nodded. "They programmed their computers, which included their beliefs and their oddities. To them it must have been a religious experience. By now they must simply breed each colony matched to the colony's central computer."

"Explains why they're unbeatable in a head-on battle. No human army could match that degree of precision, coordination, and suicidal dedication. We must take out their computers or we lose. Given enough time, all they need is a standoff. Who knows how many eggs or whatever they're carrying, or can produce?"

Spirit approached Cassie, who was sitting there, spellbound and horrified, watching the spectacle on the screen. With Spirit's link to her mother's mind through the computer, she was appalled at what she found there. Shock, horror, revulsion, fear and hatred all churned irrationally in Cassie's mind. Her old and new religious training had overridden her pragmatism, aided and abetted by the unrestrained emotion her Fluxgirl body allowed. To Cassie those were not alien invaders but the demons of Hell up there, the very horror she had always pictured in her nightmares since she'd been a child. In a very basic way she had regressed through all the shocks and horrors she had experienced in the past day to that little girl, seeing monsters in the darkness after the horrors of Hell were explained to her. And in her current body, with over sixteen years of letting *it* be in control, she had no way to damp it down from within.

But Spirit could be damped, and hardened, by the cold pragmatism of the machine to which she was wed. She could easily damp down her mother's state, but she did not. Instead she took hold of it, fed it, enhanced it, and edited it.

"Mother, only you can defeat them," Spirit told her firmly. "Only you can save our souls. Will you do it, for whatever Gods there are and for your children?"

She looked up at Spirit and her expression was painful for the human part of her daughter to look upon.

Suzl came over and gently eased Spirit away, then took Cassie's hand. "Come on, Cass! We have to serve the purpose we were born to."

Matson started to object as it became clear that Suzl was going to accompany Cassie all the way to the Gate itself, but Spirit cut him off.

"Suzl's purged the tunnel and freshened the air from Anchor. She can handle her basic job from there. The *Samish* aren't anywhere near Anchor yet." She swallowed hard. "In a way, Suzl is doing a tougher thing to herself than to Cassie. And I've got to do it to both of them."

Matson took his daughter's hand and squeezed it gently. Until this time he had barely known her, but at this moment, she felt every bit his daughter. By her acceptance of his plan, they shared a terrible bond that would always be present.

Cassie remained pretty much in a state of shock as she and Suzl entered the Gate. There was no immediate danger to them there; Suzl controlled the mechanism jointly with three other Guardians who were watching from their own control centers. She issued the commands that opened computer access to them, fed as well by the other three controllers, and other commands that would place the basic maintenance and routine operations of the center on automatic. She then blocked the command structure from her mind, surrendering command and control to the other three Guardians. She no longer had any more command power over the great computer. She and Cassie had equal and open access to the command files, but not on a rational basis.

She began to be afraid.

At the other end of the tunnel, the *Samish* continued to disgorge their horrible bodies and much materiel and equipment from the ship. Sentries kept the humans near the tower under constant surveillance, weapons at the ready, covering the build-up.

Sligh was on the transceiver on the frequency the *Samish* had used, trying to reestablish contact. He was all mind—cold, hard intellect, and he was thinking fast and furious.

"The installation at the tower is no threat," he assured them. "The people in and around the tower and its buildings are not your enemies. We wanted you here. We opened the Gates for you. We wish only to learn from you. Do you understand this message?"

Finally, there came a reply. "You can access the power?"

"Some of us, yes, but not where we stand."

"Those of you who can will approach the installation with no weapons or other implements. Those who cannot must remain exactly where they are. Do this now."

The Haldaynes, Gabaye, Tokiabi and Stomsk all crowded around inside the small communications shack.

"I'm not going to walk alone and unarmed into the monster's nest," said Chua Gabaye firmly. "We're not even sure what they *eat*."

"We remain here as common prisoners, lowest of the low, or we go down and take our chances," the always impassive Tokiabi noted flatly. "We always knew that death was a possibility, but it is no more certain now than before."

"But there's no *profit* in it," Gifford Haldayne complained.

"How do we know?" Sligh responded. "How can we be certain? Regardless, the stakes have been raised. As Ming so nicely put it, we either take our chances down there or, when they're ready for us, we'll be made into their mindless, worshipping slaves."

"There is no other choice," Stomsk put in. "You saw with what ridiculous ease they crushed the best trained and equipped Anchor army on World. Soon they will be able to drain off whatever power they require and take on the others. They're probably already in control of the north. In this instance, the odds say to be good, not evil. I will go down."

"Everyone can make up their own mind on this," Sligh told them. He turned back to the transceiver. "We are coming down. Your friends are coming down to you." Then he picked up the radio and smashed it against the wall before any of the others could stop him.

"What'd you do that for?" Haldayne asked angrily.

"No separate deals, no funny business. We play it their way as long as it is our only choice."

They went outside and looked across to where, on the apron, the creatures were swarming all over, building things whose purpose was not yet known with astonishing speed and using tools made for them.

"Funny," said Gifford Haldayne. "That's just where

we trapped Tilghman last night. I kind of wish now I'd let him win."

Suzl's mind had become almost a complete blank. Like Cassie, she knew where she was and what was at the end of that tunnel, but overpowering contradictory emotions, urges, and impulses crowded out reason. They embraced, trying to draw some strength, some comfort, from each other's presence, to shut out the fear and fend off the isolation. It turned, oddly, into a session of passionate lovemaking on the tunnel floor between the great swirl of the Gate and the solid mass of the regulator.

The computers, drawing upon their past experience and partially directed by Spirit, orchestrated the scene.

Cassie loved Suzl, Suzl loved Cassie, that was all that mattered, that was all there was in the world. The fires of the Hellgate glowed in response and were drawn to them in a warm rush. Their minds were a sea of emotion without thought, and bathed by the glow and strength of the Gate forces they became as one.

But there were images. . . .

Suzl as a deformed freak, with breasts longer than her arms and a male organ longer than her breasts, begging, pleading . . . "Make love to me. . . ."

Matson on his great horse, laughing as he directs artillery and rocket fire, then, suddenly, a mass of blood and falling, falling. . . .

Spirit, young, naked, and innocent, unable to communicate, unable to understand, held in a cage for laughing and jeering onlookers as she screams uncomprehendingly. . . .

Adam, falling, four bullets in him, coughing out his life and pleading for the life of a dream as his blood coats their naked bodies. . . .

Horrible, tentacled creatures with blood-red eyes and matted hair doing something disgusting, something they don't want to look at, something they don't want to look at, something they cannot avoid. . . . They are eating the children alive, and the children are screaming and pleading, "Mommy! Mommy!"

Fields of death after a great battle; the patron of the Reformed Church walks among a field so littered with dead that the blood stains her robe and she cannot avoid stepping on what had so shortly before been young men and women, the future of world. . . . "No more . . . ! No more . . . !"

Countless Fluxlands filled with transformed people worshipping their Fluxlords and being happy, obedient slaves, while they travel through them marveling at how pretty things look and how nice it all seems, ignoring the faces, the minds, the horror because it isn't theirs. . . .

"No building can be built upon an existing site until the old one is demolished," Mervyn says matter-of-factly. "We must destroy World in the name of the Empire in order to save it. . . ."

"No more! No more!"

A world ruled by tentacled monsters, the Demons of Hell itself, their foulness owning and controlling everything, while a subject human population lives in soulless misery without hope, only with evil, even giving their children over to their Demon Masters as toys. . . .

Above, the *Samish* checked all systems, as power suddenly seemed flickering and intermittent. It switched to full battery power as an emergency and called back the scout ship. That there was a problem was undeniable, but all checkouts came back with "Undefinable error."

Below them the regulator clicked and whirled and fed what was necessary to the two tiny figures between it and the Gate. They could feel the power; it was all around them, a living, massive entity.

They're up ahead, at the end of the tunnel. The Monsters. The Demons of Hell. With them there is no hope. Under them there is no salvation. They are evil. They will devour you. They will devour love. No love, no joy, no dreams, no hopes. . . . No more . . . No more . . . !

Cassie's mind reached back into the computer and it fed her what she most wanted, the only thing she wanted. And with it flowed the continuing stream of images.

She saw Adam's dream, a land of beauty and love and peace and joy. She saw the land torn asunder by giant black tentacled shapes dripping foul slime and crushing the land and the dream.

Above, the *Samish* checked out its erratic lines and sent probes down along the Flux string to check the source of the difficulty, but they could not reach beyond a point of absolute brilliance, an energy wall that was unbelievably raw and churning.

Inside Cassie, the tension became unbearable; the massive force coalescing around the two bodies into a great ball of pure Flux was a part of herself and could not long be held in check. The visions continued, even multiplied in horrifying intensity.

This time the Guardian supplied the mathematics and the timing.

"No more!" she screamed, the tension unendurable. *"NO MORE!"*

The force shot up the tube at the speed of light and struck the bottom of the *Samish* ship. It blew right through the shielding and then blew in the lower hatch, and still it went on, burning through all the levels of the ship, shorting out all electrical systems. But the primary load was on the Flux receptors around the hatch, which opened full, carrying the bulk of the energy directly to the storage batteries, now still mostly full. They overloaded and ruptured almost immediately, and the entire bowl was suddenly filled with terrible heat and the sound of massive explosions. At the same moment the shields collapsed, the great ship actually rose into the air from the force of its internal throes, like some great beast in mortal agony, then flipped over back down to rest almost on its side, pierced by a gaping series of holes surrounded by boiling liquid metal.

The energy surged into the Gate apron, making it crackle with electricity, frying the *Samish* and their works. With one exception it did not extend beyond, for its target had been the Enemy and the same computer control that focused it now damped it. The only exception was the exposed end of heavy cable, cut at the very edge of the apron by the initial purge and still just at it. The cable had been built to conduct Flux, and conduct Flux it did, straight to the great tower and from it through all the electrical lines. The tower began to melt, and when it reached structural instability it collapsed on the groups of people below, most of whom were already dead or in agony from the massive surge of electricity.

Near the edge of what had been the shield, the small craft of the *Samish* suddenly became unstable. It started wobbling in the air, then stopped dead, poised for a moment, while the few surviving military men watched and held their breaths. Then it dropped like a stone to the ground, hitting it so hard it actually bounced three times before coming to rest on its side.

Outside the shield boundary, the reserve troops watched and cheered as loudly as they could, then moved in towards the Gate to pick up the pieces.

Deep in the tunnel, Jeff, Matson, and Sondra huddled over two still figures lying sprawled near the regulator, Jeff checking Cassie and Sondra checking Suzl. Both nodded, and the two men each lifted a small, frail-looking woman and stepped back through the now-reopened Anchor access Gate.

21

SOME UNSETTLING SETTLEMENTS

In the two northern clusters, the *Samish* had first been deprived of their remote eyes and ears and then, with the destruction of the southern ship, their command. The two northern *Samish* "brains" could not agree on what had happened in the south—things had been going along quite well, quite normally, when suddenly all communication had ceased. What they *did* know, eventually, by some sort of monitoring devices, was that the southern ship had exploded and that it had proven vulnerable, despite their computations, from the tunnel beneath. They had gotten word that there was a problem in the Flux power linkage before it blew.

There had been initial fear on the part of the defenders that one or both of the northern ships would leave to get help or reinforcements or merely to report the problem. They couldn't be stopped from doing so, and once out there, even after all these centuries, it was unknown just *what* they would find and what might come calling as a result.

The *Samish*, however, were prisoners of their own strange culture as much as the humans were. A defeat, even a strategic retreat, was simply unthinkable. To move in that direction would be to admit that they were not the godlike superiors of this puny under-race. A faulty transformer, bad batteries, even unworthiness in the First Lord's sight they could accept as reasons for the southern defeat, but they could not accept, or perhaps were not programmed or permitted to accept, any thought that their theology might be wrong or their god might be false.

The northern military command centers immediately received and analyzed the methods and the reasons for the success of the southerners. When the *Samish* retracted the bulk of their shield to concentrate on protecting the immediate area around their ships and then began feverish building activities, there was no question as to what they were up to. Mobile ground amplifiers were obviously being constructed in preparation for a methodical breakout. Right now they were totally dependent on the ship's power, but clearly they were working to draw not only on the ship but on World's own Flux. If they did that, they would weaken the Soul Rider and the wizards while still having the ship's power for protection and reinforcement.

Having both the advantage of Flux and the advantage of a successful program run in the south, the wizards of the north concentrated on creating and molding similar personalities and similar powers among their own. It took more of them, but one try was successful, and then there was one *Samish* vessel remaining.

That one analyzed that indeed this population was so infused with evil that it had found a way around their defenses. Instead of retreating, this *Samish* apparently considered it an honor to be put to such a challenge. It moved its entire population out of the ship and away from the apron, and proceeded to build what it needed to implement a total breakout.

Ultimately, the fanaticism of the *Samish* with *their* amplifiers met the angry and frightened wizards of Flux with *their* amplifiers head to head. The carnage was terrible, yet somehow the two were evenly matched. The unitary nature of the *Samish* made them dedicated, nearly suicidal fanatics—but so were the minions of the Fluxlords, who willingly fought to their deaths for their deities. As Flux wielders, the *Samish* were fully as expert as they claimed to be, but they were now fighting wizards with minds of their own and the full programs of their own master computers to tap. But in one respect, each side had something going for them. The *Samish* ground weapons were far superior to anything that World could offer, and the resulting body count was very much in the aliens' favor, with a ratio of five hundred humans killed for every *Samish*. It cost over a million human lives, enormous by World's scale.

But there were a lot more human beings than *Samish*. With more flocking there from the other clusters every hour, the *Samish* were ultimately outnumbered by more than fifteen hundred to one.

Without *Samish* bodies and *Samish* minds, the shields could not hold. While this one had outguessed and outmaneuvered its attackers from below, it was now alone, a bare computer with considerable local power but no way to implement it. Faced with retreating or being destroyed by the forces now converging on it, it chose to destroy itself in one huge blast.

With no reinforcements coming, no *Samish* at the equatorial Gates, the battle was finally over.

Despite the horrible cost in lives, most of World breathed a sigh of relief when, after waiting a decent interval, nobody else showed up in any of the Gates. Considering how many people on the planet had been raised from the cradle to believe that the opening of the Gates was tantamount to the end of the world, the whole thing actually seemed somewhat of an anticlimax. The fact that it had been neither easy nor cheap was not a factor; except for a very few, nothing had ever come easy or cheap on World except slavery and death.

It seemed ironic to many that the ancient army of their ancestors that had come to World from some far-off place had made all the right decisions, even if it could never guess the timing or the type of people who would finally make it all pay off. They had closed and locked the Gates just in time; the enemy had been right there, and would have walked all over that first generation with its total dependence on its machines and its ignorance of true Flux power. They had severed direct contact with the computers when they first encountered this sort of powerful link, and by that move almost certainly saved humanity on World from becoming one with their computers and, perhaps, a version of the Enemy they eventually faced and defeated.

There was no indication in the records that the early scientists, engineers, and mathematicians who acquired the Flux powers were actually executed; instead, they were driven into Flux by the army and the odd church it supported for its own ends, there to breed, pass on the talents to new generations, and learn to perfect what they had. They destroyed the existing amplifers and other advanced terraforming and weapons systems primarily to safeguard and secure Anchors against attack—and until the Empire had arisen to destroy the rigid division of Flux from Anchor and Coydt van Haas had rediscovered how to build some of the ancient machines and use them, it had worked. Worked, probably, for far more years than those who'd created the plans and the society dreamed it would.

Ultimately, they and their computers had come to the same conclusion as Matson would tens of centuries later: that the existing technology and defense systems had not stopped the unknown enemy. Flux power might, if that technology were not allowed to interfere with its growth and development. But it was Matson who realized that raw, unbridled emotion was the method by which the maximum amount of power would be collected in a single individual. The computers were the epitome of pure reason; this sort of thing was beyond them, and even the reasoning human-machine interfaces, the Soul Riders and the Guardians, fell back on logic and reason no matter what their feelings. The Ancient men and women who created the system had human emotions, but tried very hard to filter them out and allow reason and logic alone to remain when doing their jobs.

Matson's plan had created an unthinkable mixed marriage, in which reason stood back and waited until all was right, then coolly fed the mathematics and controlled the results of highly complex physics, fed to, and through, human beings reduced to raw unbridled emotion.

Why this was so, and why Flux power worked at all, was unknown and perhaps could not be known by these people, with these machines, in such isolation. The computers themselves had solid, convincing theories—about eighty thousand of them, in fact, almost all contradictory. Earth, if it still existed, might know by now.

All of World's actions and activities in this area had been aimed at what to do when and if the Gates were opened; there was no thought at all of what to do after the Enemy was disposed of, for nobody, in ancient times or on World, had really believed humanity could win—except Matson, and even he wasn't as sure of things as he'd let on. He simply had seen no profit in believing otherwise.

The first conference on the future of World was held not too long after victory was assured, but only fifty-six people were involved. At that point, they were the only ones who counted.

The first question the Guardians and Soul Riders discussed was whether to retain their interfaces with, and control of, the computers. There was vast knowledge there, and almost unlimited power, and that finally decided them. The system would be reset. The Guardian and Soul Rider interfaces would be disengaged from the existing humans and reset to their original forms so that they, too, would be ignorant once more of their purpose. They were surrendering their heritage from Earth and their ancestors, but by doing so they chose to remain human. The logic was inescapable: if one were to defeat an enemy, only to become just like him, then who wins?

They had seen creatures who looked monstrous, but who still at one time had been a race of curious individuals who'd probably told dirty jokes and laughed and faced tragedy and died, who'd known joy and sorrow, fear and pain, and also pride and love. In surrendering their animal selves to the machine, they had become machines, and in doing so had lost far more than they had gained.

The decision was not unanimous, but was sufficiently large that the others had no choice but to agree or be forcibly restrained and disengaged by the collective might of the others.

The coldly logical and reason-dominated computers, interestingly, not only did not argue against this but supported it. Considering the human viewpoint and the alternative they themselves had just seen, they could see no logical alternative.

The next questions were on the kind of world they would re-enter. The Church was through as any sort of effective institution; despite Guardian and Soul Rider moves to lift all binding spells, the truth had shattered its foundation. World would change, now—perhaps radically so, without a cohesive cultural force to bind it—but that was the price of truth, and it was not necessarily bad. Perhaps it was time for a dynamic rather than stagnant civilization to emerge.

No attempt would be made to extend landscaping and terraforming beyond New Eden; clearly Flux had been the margin of victory in the war, and clearly it should not be weakened further. On the condition that all ancient writings and records, both the Codex and New Eden's library, be available to all the governments of Flux and Anchor,

New Eden would not be tampered with, so long as it obeyed the rule that the building and use of amplifiers was now banned. What they did with their philosophies, or even their armies, was their affair; Flux, however, must remain Flux.

The Gates would not again be locked. The combinations were known, of course, and there was no way known to change them, but there was another way. The alien ships were to be left the wrecks they were in the dishes. They could be studied, probed, and analyzed, even gutted, but they must remain. At least equal mass of some kind would be placed in the four other dishes. The computers assured them that this would prevent any more "incoming" due to the safety systems; however, "incoming" would be announced and would activate the defensive systems once more. Removing that mass from any of the Gates would now be an additional criterion for activation. The defensive system in each tunnel was reset, this with a new bypass code known only to the Soul Riders and Guardians. The computers picked and encoded it themselves; no human would ever be able to find a place to look it up. Access to the Gates and regulators, then, by wizards or researchers, would be only through Anchor, which gave a measure of control.

New Eden's disposition was left to the four Guardians of its quadrants. The Soul Riders served a military function in crisis but were chiefly concerned with Flux; the Guardians were supreme in Anchor if they wished to be. While the Soul Riders had been equally split between males and females, there were three female Guardians to one male, he a supply sergeant in Mareh and formerly a foreman in a textile mill. All were natives of their respective Anchors; all three of the women, like Suzl, were Fluxgirls now and had been at least since their Anchors had fallen. All were products of the old Church-dominated Anchor system, which was important. All believed that a culture had to have a unifying faith to bind it as a practical matter, and all were somewhat uneasy at the collapse of it elsewhere.

The only confidant Suzl would accept from outside the circle was Cassie, because of their closeness and Cassie's great experience in such matters. At the start, Suzl had a vision of New Eden that was logical but not to her friend's liking at all.

"We should just turn the tables on them the way we turned it on those monsters," Suzl said flatly. "I wonder how these guys would like it if *they* couldn't read or write and were only good for sex and the shit work?"

"No!" Cassie shot back, looking alarmed. "Don't you see, Suzl, that would just keep things going in the same old pattern? Is it less a crime, less wrong, if *I* murder you than if *you* murder me?"

"Well, I'd rather not have either one, but I'm selfish enough to admit I'd dislike being murdered more."

"But that's just the point! New Eden's injustices, even Coydt's crazy view, came from doing just what you're talking about doing. Even Adam admitted that they were turning this place into just another giant Fluxland kingdom. Oh, maybe you'll get some temporary satisfaction out of a reversal, but in the end it's the same crime. If it was wrong for them to do it to women, it's equally wrong for us to do it to men."

Suzl sat down, sighed, and chewed on her cigar. She did look a bit disappointed. "So what would you suggest we do? We have a mess here, you know. All the top dogs are dead, the younger ones were brought up in this system and believe in it, and most of the women have big families."

"I've been giving that a lot of thought, and I can't see any way we can be perfectly fair and create something wonderful out of what's here. People are going to suffer, as usual, but we've got to accept that and try for some sort of balance."

"I'm listening."

"First of all, considering it's Anchor and there's the master program, just how much physical change in people is possible?"

"With individuals, a lot. With large groups, like millions, only basics. Cassie, disengagement of computer interfaces is only a few weeks away, maybe sooner if they can get their other messes cleared up. There's no time to process everybody individually."

"Maybe not, but maybe we can get a compromise that won't be a hundred percent right but will give some people a fighting chance. First of all, a certain measure of restoration should be made just in the interest of the innocents. We can't change this system, Suzl, we can only give everybody the chance to make their own hard choices. Let's start with the intellectual part. Can we arrange it so there's no longer a barrier of literacy or mathematical skill?"

"Sure. The program simply took a short cut and shorted one small area in the message paths of the brain. It's a common birth defect, in fact, that was just duplicated. I've known other folks who were never here that had it."

"Well, that puts all the women back on an equal footing, so to speak. If they knew how before, they'll know again, and the children can be taught. It's been my experience that even if the system conspires to keep a kid from learning to read, she'll do it anyway if she gets the chance. But what about this 'body rules the mind' business?"

"Well, hormones are hormones and glands are glands. Everybody's different, really, as to that. You can't suppress one thing without doing it to everybody. I don't know about you, but I did all this in *this* body and it hasn't really affected my performance. It's more a matter of *believing* that stuff and going with it than anything else. I can suppress it if I need to. I don't feel I'm in any way unqualified to run this Anchor with the body I've got."

Cassie nodded. "It's a shame we can't allow them the choice of new or old bodies, since the very fact of looking like this tends to reinforce that body-mind business. I know it does for me. We acted like fools right here in the control room during the crisis just because we looked that way and for years acted that way."

"Yeah, but we snapped out of it and did our jobs perfectly when the push came," Suzl pointed out. "When we had to suppress it, we could and did. When we needed to let it all out, like in the tunnel, we did that, too."

"Yes. The tunnel. All that forced me to look hard at my whole life and attitudes, and I'm not at all happy with what I saw." She sighed. "Still, you're right. We were acting the way New Eden expected us to act because we'd been just that way for so long. Well, then, we leave it as it was. If their minds can triumph over their bodies they deserve to lead. Can you adjust it so that the bodies could be individually redone in Flux?"

"The formula was an add-on to the master program in the cluster, but not in Anchor, remember. All the Anchor girls are no different in Flux than anyone else, including the two of us, since we've removed all the binding spells. Still, something taken out of Anchor into Flux should be transmutable, just as something made in Flux and brought in is fixed. Yes, they could reach equality but not on their own. Any good wizard could fix it, though, one-on-one. But there are *millions* like that. Nobody will ever be able to cover them all."

"It'll have to do."

"If we do it this way, it's gonna make for a real rough period," Suzl warned. "You'll still have New Eden boys and Fluxgirls and the basic system but now the Fluxgirls will have their smarts and their past knowledge back. At the start it won't be much, but after a while those women aren't gonna take being kept down, not all of them. Conditioning, like we said, may hold the majority, particularly the older generations, but the foundations will be shaky. Smart, knowledgeable women won't be kept out of power and influence forever. That'll threaten the men. There'll be beatings and violence and rapes and stuff again, like in the old days.''

''Maybe. If there's anything to Adam's dream and ideas, though, they'll work out a compromise and build their new society. It there isn't, it'll fall apart, but there are far too many people here now and it's far too big a land to exercise the kind of control they worked on Anchor Logh. The men would need Flux to do it, and odds are the women have a lot more power in Flux than they do. They won't chance it. They'll adjust or the system will fall apart. They have to.''

''Maybe. I'll try and sell it to the other Guardians and I guess they'll buy it. Nobody else has come up with anything that sounds better, mess though it is.''

''All we can do is give the women the chance to be whole human beings again. Anything else, no matter how long it takes, will be up to them. We inherited this, we didn't create it.''

Suzl looked at Cassie thoughtfully. ''And what about us? You, me, the kids?''

''What do *you* want to do?''

''Well, I was down in that tunnel, too, remember. First time in years I had to face myself, old and new. I've been in this body almost half my life. I think that if I had the mental freedom I had then, like I have now, it and I can live pretty happily together. I'm not the old Suzl—I'm the collection of the old and the new. I like parts of both. I'm gonna keep myself just this way, I think, except I might get rid of this damned tattoo. What about you?''

''I've been thinking a lot about that. I've been topside and I know what'll happen if I go back and pick up from here. What I want is something I never had or had the chance to have. I had a part of it with Adam, but it was flawed by the system. In a way, Adam was too much like I used to be, when *I* headed the Church, and I got to take a good hard look at myself in that as well as in the tunnel. I took a gamble when I accepted that spell at the wedding, and I won part and lost part. Maybe it's time for me to take one last gamble.''

22

VISIONS AND SPIRITS

A lone rider sat atop a black horse on the apron outside the ancient gate of Anchor Logh and looked momentarily back, deep in reflection. The old gate had plenty of holes in it now; it never had been much good to those who'd built it to keep out the horrors of Flux, but it had made the inhabitants feel safe and secure. He felt a great deal of kinship with that old gate and its old attitudes. Both of them had shared a lot of experiences and both were rather old-fashioned and out of date in the world today.

Another rider, coming hard, emerged from the gate and rode up to him, halting expertly. "I hoped I'd catch up with you," Spirit said to him. "It would be hell finding *you* in the void."

"Well, you made it," Matson responded dryly. "I can't say I'm really surprised to see you, daughter."

"What were you doing that slowed you down here, if I might ask?"

"Just—remembering. Wondering if an old fossil like

me is going to be able to survive in this new world of ours.''

"You'll always survive," she assured him confidently. "Besides, you're a hero to World. Even Fluxlords who hate everybody and everything, even themselves, and Anchors suspicious of their own, call you a hero—the man who saved World. Even New Eden will build statues to you, maybe as big as the ones they're building of Adam Tilghman.''

He laughed dryly. "Well, that's what the old boy wanted. And, sure, I'm safe enough now—anybody who'd draw down on me would be killed by his best friends. The thing is, I'm not any hero. I'm the same crusty old hellbound son of a bitch I always have been, no different. There were hundreds of people on World who came up with the same ideas I did. The fact is, I stole all those ideas and all those plans from other folks. Mostly women, too. Didn't figure out a one. Only I mouthed them off around a Soul Rider, a Guardian, and big-shot wizard so the computers knew my name and let me in where I could talk 'em up.''

"It doesn't make any of it any less true. Shall we go into Flux a ways? I want to be well away from here when disengagement comes.''

He nodded, and both figures eased their horses through the reddish-gray curtain of the void. They were in no hurry, and he, at least, hadn't decided just what to do next. He wondered about her, and asked her about her plans.

"None, really," she told him. "I have a lot of hard decisions to make myself. I figured a little time out here would help me make them.''

"I gather that one of them wasn't to stay in New Eden and see now it all comes out.''

"Hardly. Dad, I may be old in years, but the fact is that I'm really just going on eighteen, so to speak. I've never really been out here in full possession of my wits, as a real human being. My entire adult life, except for the brief period in the takeover days of Anchor Logh, is a total blur. I could relate to some people and some specific incidents, but it seemed entirely like a dream. Now, suddenly, I wake up, and I have to take up a real life again. I like it, but I'm as jittery as any schoolgirl.''

"You ought to travel around a bit, see the place,'' he told her. "It's interesting, if a little depressing. Even when you lose your friend you'll still have enormous power and that beautiful fine-tuned machine of a body.''

"I'd like to, but that's one of the hard choices to make. Dad, I'm pregnant.''

He and the horse stopped dead in their tracks. *"What!"*

She nodded. "When that terrible change came over Pericles and Jeff, and I was forced to run, I grew terribly depressed. I didn't have much of anything, but I *did* have a son I loved, and I felt I'd lost him. Oh, I know it was a silly, emotional action, but it's done.''

"How far along? And who's the father?''

"Barely three months, if I guess the timing right. And the father's Mervyn. Oh, don't look so shocked. He was very kind to me and pretty good looking near the end.''

"It don't look like Mervyn's coming back. You've got a fatherless kid holding you down. You've got the power. It doesn't have to be that way.''

"I know—for some. But this is the last of the Hallers in direct lineage, and that's a responsibility, I think. And to use the power to transfer it and walk away—not even my mother did that with me, under her circumstances. And if I have it, I'll bring the child up. It'll be the great-great-grandchild of a founder, the child of a great wizard, and the grandchild of Matson and Cass. That's quite a proud line.''

"Sounds like you've already decided.''

"On that, anyway. Where and with whom I'm not so sure of. You said it yourself, though—we're practically immortals. I have time. I can't just have it and abandon it, like I was abandoned. Oh, don't look so guilty! I know you didn't know about me, and I know the reasons for it all, but this is different. It's a matter of choice.''

They rode a while more in silence, each deep in their own personal worlds. Suddenly Matson said, "The *Samish* could have been us, you know. I think about that a lot.''

She nodded. "Yes, I know. No matter how horrible they looked, or what hellish world spawned them, they were in many ways only one step further on than us. That, the time lag they never did seem to know about, and our sheer numbers were all that saved us, even with what we had to fight.''

"It could *still* be us, if everybody hadn't agreed to disengage.''

She shook her head. "Not now. We'll be free to laugh and cry and love and hate and be our own petty selves. Still, it wasn't unanimous.''

"So I heard. I wonder if we're not seeing it start all over again. The overwhelming majority for disengagement and blocking the Gates, a small but passionate minority saying, 'No, stop—the price is too high. We can handle what they couldn't.' The Nine versus the Seven. The army versus the Company. It's all there, just as they must have faced it long ago.''

"Oh, I hope not! *God!* I hope not! I hope we've learned this time, and that the technology and knowledge we *do* have will keep us in perspective, at least. There's nobody lurking at the Gates any more that we can't prepare for.'' She sighed. "It'd be different if we knew how to build and use ships of our own and go out there ourselves, but for security reasons that wasn't in the computer files, and the three ships of the enemy are too melted down and burned out to figure out. Even if they were perfect, it still wouldn't help. We don't have the programs, the cosmic stringers, to keep us riding out there to a destination or get in anywhere else with the proper entry codes. So all we can do is close the Gates, shove the garbage in there, wipe clean the memory records of the Guardians and Soul Riders so they're back to their command shell states, and disengage. Unless human beings show up and give us the stars, our future has to be made right here."

"Unless some new wave of religion and knowledge suppression knocks us back again. New Eden still has that potential. Changes in that system will come slowly, and with much suffering. The system that ultimately emerges may be something entirely new, but maybe not anything we'd like. Whether it's just another Fluxland variation or something really radical and new remains to be seen." He paused a moment. "You've talked with your mother?"

She nodded. "She's changed. She's really changed from the person I knew."

Matson gave a sardonic smile. "No she hasn't," he said. "With the possible exception of me, she's the most consistent person I've ever known. You know she expects me to come back and marry her, and Suzl." He sighed. "I'm surprised and my ego's a bit bruised that she let me get away so easy this time."

"I don't know. I don't think I'll ever understand either one of you. You, for example, have been so busy practically running New Eden the past few weeks I'm surprised you didn't stay. Maybe she expects you to come back and protect New Eden from the re-emergence of the worst elements of the old leadership."

"Most of Coydt's bad boys were at the Gate when the ship blew, which was mighty convenient. They didn't trust anybody, not even themselves, to be anywhere else. The junior officers, most of which grew up in this sort of system or spent most of their lives in it, are shocked by the evil of their leaders. They really believed in the dream and feel betrayed. Using Tilghman as a model and a martyr was simple because of that, and the officers proceeded to do their own purging. They'll be the power brokers now, the men who make the decisions, and they'll do it from the framework of this master program. None of them considered leaving for a moment."

"That's another depressing thing, I think. Even on the borders with Flux, most of the women chose to remain there even knowing what they do now."

"Yeah. In fact, more men left than women. Remember, almost all of the women are Anchorfolk with a long-standing and deep-seated fear of Flux. It's the old Anchor Logh proposition all over again. Better the devil you know than the hell you don't. Most of 'em certainly don't understand the full ramifications of what they're choosing, but that's par for the course. Many had young kids and no alternatives for them or themselves. Most of the ones who *did* understand knew they'd probably just wind up slaves of some Fluxlord, and there were quite a bunch that really bought the new faith's line. You know, as bad as the new system sounds, when you consider the alternatives for most folks it's really not that awful, and now that the women have their pasts, their skills, their self-control back they'll gamble on changing the system from within. It may be a bad gamble, but who knows for sure?"

"I gather you don't put much stock in their new faith."

"I put great stock in it as a driving force for a new culture, but if you mean believe in it, no. I believe in machines and people. I believe that machines will keep on doing any dumb thing they're told even if it doesn't work, and I believe that people, when faced with critical choices in their lives, will always do the safest and easiest thing— and it's the wrong thing ninety percent of the time." He took out a cigar and lit it. "I gather Suzl never told Cassie that Tilghman could be ressurrected if you went along."

"No. Suzl is a competent and sometimes smart person, no matter what she seems to be. She knows I'll never do it, and she knows she can't talk any of the others into it, and she sees no reason to drive a permanent wedge between Mom and me. And—she understands. She admired Tilghman, that's clear, but she loves only her own children, Mom, and me." She sighed. "You know, if Suzl had ever had any goals, any ambition in her, she could have done or been anything she wanted to be. She doesn't, though. She just always makes the best of what she's stuck with. She didn't even care what happened to New Eden—she let Mom decide that.''

"Well, most folks are that way," he said philosophically. "I never had any real goals, except personal and temporary ones. I doubt if you do, either. I don't judge and condemn, like Mervyn did, and I don't want to change the world like your Mom. I'm too old and cynical to believe people can be fixed up to the good. I'm satisfied if it leaves me alone.''

"Even if it's New Eden and its computer-derived religion?''

He chuckled. "I don't know where religions get their pedigrees. Certainly I kind of believe in some God someplace, if only because I just can't believe all this is an accident—it's irrational. I kind of suspect that the reason women are more religious than men is that they get to see it start with a good screw, then develop as a lump, come out a baby, and see that baby turn into a complicated human being. I just can't take the idea seriously that it's the way the science fellows say, that it was all chance and good luck, and neither have a lot of other smart folks. But going from that to any one true religion is just as bad to me. In those records old Tilghman studied there were dozens of religions back on old Earth, and a good many here. All disagreed and all were sure they were right. He tried to reconcile them and give the result direct application to World. It's not as crazy as it seems.''

"What he came up with was.''

"No sillier than praying to a planet that's nothing but a big ball of gas, I don't think. He started with the notion that we were part animal and part thinking creature, and he decided we were maybe sixty percent animal and forty percent think, which might be generous. He looked at World from his own background, and decided that all the animal urges could be covered but one—sex. Gender, actually. He decided that this was at the root of our real headaches. Maybe it wasn't for the ancient folks, but it was for us. He came from a society that had a female empress-goddess who dominated all the males, remember, and he was liberated by Coydt, who sure as hell had sex as his reason for doing everything he did. The Anchors were dominated by a women-only clergy. But the old religions had men running the society. Women could get high up by exceptional ability or accident, but mostly it was a male-oriented society. That got him to thinking. The fact is, the way us humans are made up, women are superior to men and men know it, deep down. The male strut and roar covers a basic inferiority complex."

She stared at him. "Come again?"

"Yep. Men only exist at all on the biological level to serve one purpose, and one man can serve that purpose to a lot of women. Other than that, men aren't really necessary. Women think as sharp as men, can do just about anything men can do, and can run a church, a society, a government, an army—you name it. Because of child-bearing, you actually have a better tolerance for pain and better reactions. Left alone in Anchor with no spells, you naturally live longer than men. Not that you're any better at governing or running a business or a church or even a battle, but you're no worse, either. And, deep down, most men know this. You see where it leads?"

"I think you're making too strong a case against your own sex."

"Nope. It's clear. Oh, I got more arm muscles and bigger chest muscles, but two or three women can lift what I can or use a rope and pulley just like I would. That's why human society went the way it did. Men had to be the boss, had to run things, had to have all that responsibility—otherwise, they had no reason for being at all. Just screw a lot until they made a bunch of babies, then curl up and die. In the old days, Anchor men committed suicide ten times more than Anchor women. They were sick and lethargic and only running the play government and playing soldier on the walls gave 'em any feeling of worth. That's why most of the male Fluxlords are so devoted to women being sex objects or slaves.''

"Is this you—or Tilghman?"

"Both of us. But old Adam, now, he was an intellectual and it drove him nuts. He finally decided that it was illogical for men to live past procreation at all unless society *had* to be male dominated. Since this didn't seem fair, he took from one of the old religions the idea that sexes alternate, that we live as both before going on to the great reward. Believe that, and the rest is logical. It gets rid of the moral problem.''

"So his male ego, his inferiority complex, led to the subjugation of women in New Eden?"

"You might say that. He didn't see it that way. He started with the woman. She had to have the children, because men couldn't, and he felt kids needed a full-time parent to turn out right. Now since the man was always number two in that situation, it was his job to earn the living and provide the other basic needs—food, shelter, clothing, whatever—and protect his home and family. He was also expendable—we could lose a lot of men and still have the same number of kids, but we couldn't lose a lot of women and do that. So he saw them as complements, and opposites, in every way imaginable. To make it even fairer, he wanted every girl to be shapely, sexy, and pretty, and every guy to be tall, muscular, and handsome. He believed that system would produce a balanced world of peace and plenty.''

"You don't think so, though."

"Well," he said, thinking it over, "I don't know. I kind of doubt it. But for me, the worst part is that it won't get a fair chance unless all of World is brought under the system, and I don't like that idea any more than you do. The system they eventually export won't be the one that's there now, but it's still going to be one I wouldn't like to

live under, and no matter how the male-female relationships wind up it'll be a technological powerhouse.''

"Do you think they'll win?"

"No. Tilghman and New Eden unleashed a force that
won't be stopped on World now, but it isn't their system.
Their system's pretty tame, when you think about it. They
broke down the Church, they broke down the unifying
culture that kept us pretty much the same for all those
centuries, and they introduced science and technology and
a lot of the ancient philosophies. Their system has no
chance of filling the void, but even now all over World
others are thinking of *their* perfect societies and perfect
forms, and learning to use what we've rediscovered. These
will all study how New Eden did it and they'll form their
own radical systems and try and extend them. There'll be a
lot of conflict and eventually through war and alliance
other systems will emerge that make New Eden look like
Tilghman's heaven.''

She shivered a bit. "You sound like we're going to lose
our humanity and turn this place into a Hell.''

"The possibility's there, along with a thousand Adam
Tilghmans, female as well as male.''

Spirit changed the subject because it was getting
uncomfortable. "What do you think of Sondra's choice?''

"Sondra has seen and heard just about everything there
is on World. She's had a hell of a life so far. Now she's
discovered that the Soul Rider fooled around with her Flux
power and she's a much better wizard than she thought and
it's brought back the self-confidence. Her mind and abilities are completely restored. She kept the body because
she has young children now and didn't want to wrench
them, but she can look any way she wants in Flux so it
makes staying the same easy.''

"I still don't like her settling down with the kids in
Flux, though, power or not.''

"Settling down with Jeff, you mean. He'll be working
off his guilt complex about her for years, maybe forever

He's a powerful and trained wizard, and she's got him wrapped around her little finger. They'll do all right. Sondra says that Flux might be a real nice place for a Fluxgirl who's a wizard, and a nice place to raise kids."

"I still think it's like, well, *incest*. She's my half-sister."

"She's no genetic kin to either of us anymore. Jeff didn't like to see his Mom rolling in the hay, and you don't like your son settling down with her. As long as she retains the body and spell that the master program gave her, there's no physical relation to anyone. She's been pretty much lost since giving up the trail, and now she's got something new. Beats hell out of running a basic training class for new stringers, anyway. She was ready for a big change and this is it. In a way, you might call their new relationship inevitable."

"I couldn't stop it, that's for sure. I know you're heading out now to that new Fluxland they created. I've been—hesitant—about going there myself right away, considering my feelings, but, damn it, I want to get to know my son a little, too."

Matson nodded. "Mostly I have to be *somewhere* where I won't be made into a saint or a statue. Besides, I have to go by there. The twins went with them to learn how it's all done."

"Dad! I didn't know that! I thought that when all marriages were declared invalid—well, they didn't seem the type to choose independence over New Eden."

"They don't *need* New Eden. Give 'em a few years to learn Flux wizardry and they'll be more dangerous than New Eden. Only the fact that I've kind of grown fond of 'em and they seem to really like me gives World any real hope for the future. They're already starting to loosen up on their cultural roots, too. Once they tear into reading and math—watch out!"

"Then you're not going back to New Eden."

"Sure. For visits. To give some advice and nudges where I can. But not if I have to accept their system. Not unless I get a few thousand acres and some cows and horses and total ownership including a guarantee of being left alone.''

They camped for a while, to feed themselves and give their horses a rest. It was simple for Spirit to conjure up whatever was required, so they needed no pocket. While Matson was drinking the last of his beer, in fact, he looked over and saw his daughter shudder.

"What's the matter? Morning sickness?"

"It's done," she said quietly, and with a trace of sadness. It was the first time since she'd been conceived that she was totally alone inside her mind and body, and she didn't realize until it was gone how much of a hole it would truly leave. Still, she felt a measure of peace as she sensed the Soul Rider leave her body and fly up and away into the mists of the void. "The Soul Rider is free once more to roam. I wonder how long it'll be before it learns how to think again?"

"Not long enough to suit me," Matson responded. "Well, let's get going. It's only a few more hours to the place. If you want to tag along, that is. You're hung up enough about this business that maybe you need some time alone."

"No, Dad. Just the opposite. I was alone for a very, very long time, and I've never felt more alone than now. I never want to be alone again. I'll come—for a visit, anyway. As you said, I've got to be *somewhere*, and I have to live a very long time in this new world. If I can't start with my own family, I don't know how I can cope with the outside."

"You know your big trouble? You really got it in the head with your parents. The more I listen to you the more I hear myself, only contaminated a little with your mother's idealistic streak."

They rode along, getting to know each other better as they did so. She liked him a lot, and felt a growing pride and inner glow at being his daughter. If she had only a fraction of his magnetism, his wise pragmatism, and his incredible inner strength, she felt lucky indeed. Yet he wasn't perfect. He was an ornery, stubborn man who could be warm to her yet cold and callous to injustice—and to many people. As he said, he wasn't a saint or a monument, he was a human being—and that was what made him great.

The sidebar string to Jeff and Sondra's new land was well concealed even for an expert, but Matson had no trouble in finding and following it. He had a lifetime of experience doing just that.

Like most Fluxlands, this one had no permanent shield to drain the reigning wizard's power, but the moment the void began to clear and form itself into vague shapes, then turn into clear landscape, both Jeff and Sondra would know who had arrived and where. Any enemy or stranger crossing that boundary would meet a firm shield soon enough.

"It's *big*," Spirit remarked, both amazed and impressed. "You know, in a way, that deep blue sky and the forests and glades and streams remind me of . . ."

"Pericles," Matson completed. "Yeah, it's a new New Pericles in a way. It figures. He worshipped the old man, and I arranged to have Mervyn's people and records moved over here since their temporary got shaky. Some nice touches, though. Lots of flowers, and the hills over there; I think I see a lake off to the left."

"I see it! It's *beautiful!* Looks even better without all the marble buildings."

"Well, I'll kind of miss the naked statues, but that's not much of a price to pay. I wonder how far we got to ride into this place before we find a human being?"

It was, in fact, almost four hours before the solitary dirt path led them to the settlement. The great lodge, made apparently of hardwood, was set on wooden stilts up high against a hill and partially in it. The place was multistoried and enormous, yet it retained a genuine rustic air, and it was framed by two waterfalls cascading down into a pool below and then running off as a river. The noise of the falls was obtrusive at first, but you quickly got used to it.

Below, on either side of the river, they could see smaller buildings—cabins, mostly, although some seemed rather large—going off into the woods. There Mervyn's surviving staff of probably no more than thirty or thirty-five lived and worked.

There were stables below, and several horses were in them, but they were able to see to their own mounts and then head for the redwood stairs under the house that led up to it. Matson stuck a cigar in his mouth and went up with Spirit—there was room for more than two on the stairway.

When they reached the top they found themselves on a broad deck, or porch, leading to the first floor. There were mats and recliners around, allowing anyone to relax in the warmth of the outdoors without going far, or just to enjoy the magnificent view.

Sondra came out and greeted them warmly with hugs and kisses. "We were wondering how long it would take you to get here," she told them.

"How're you doing?" he asked her seriously.

"*Wonderful!* How do you like the place? Jeff and I designed it together." She meant the Fluxland, not merely the house.

"It's beautiful," Spirit put in. "You may have two freeloaders here for quite a while."

"Everyone's welcome," Sondra responded, obviously delighted that Spirit had come. "I have to go back in and check on things. That noise you hear that sounds like the second invasion of the *Samish* is the kids. Come on with me, Dad. I've got a lot to say to you."

Together they entered the house. Spirit started to follow then heard all the commotion and decided she'd stay outside a bit and just relax and admire the view. The sound o the waterfall might be intrusive to some, but she found it soothing, almost carrying her back to a different existence.

A screened door opened behind her, and she turned and saw a small, slight, yet very familiar figure there. She was taller than any Fluxgirl although still far shorter than Spirit, of very slight build, thin and somewhat plain-looking, but still a little cute. It was, in fact, a familiar boyish figure from the past, still looking nineteen or twenty, with only a few subtle changes. She had sandy-colored hair now, fluffed up and curled and reaching to her shoulders, highlighting her face. Her skin was a coppery bronze, her eyes brown. She wore small, dangling earrings and had a touch of makeup on, which seemed just right to highlight her features. She wore a tight-fitting dark brown body stocking and a pair of dark brown leather boots with thick high heels. The outfit showed such small breasts that they would be totally concealed with anything looser fitting, but her figure was firmly curved and athletic.

Spirit gaped. "Mother? Is that *you*?"

Cassie smiled. "Who else?"

"But you're back to normal—sort of."

That brought a laugh. "Sort of. Actually, except for the hair and skin color this is just the body I had before being tossed into Flux that first time so long ago."

"But—I've seen pictures! You looked like a boy! That figure isn't the original, is it?"

"Yeah, it's hard to believe, but it is. The truth is, the way you see yourself sometimes—most times—is reflected by your appearance. I was never very conscious of my figure because I didn't think I had much of one; I always dressed like a boy, kept my hair real short, never wore makeup or jewelry, always loose-fitting clothes to conceal what I thought of as my lack of a body. It's sure as hell not the body I *did* have for a while there, but I finally had a chance to see myself from one of those glamour girl perspectives and I found that it's more a matter of how you present what you have than of trying to crawl in a hole.

That goes for men, too, if they want to take the trouble. I had my fling as a sex object; now I thought it was time to stop the fantasy stuff. I don't *need* it any more. I just decided I was going to be what I really am, and not run and hide anymore. I finally decided it was time for me to grow up.''

''But—what are you doing *here*? I thought you and Suzl would be back in Anchor Logh for disengagement!'' Spirit persisted.

She shrugged. ''Why? We sure as hell didn't need to be there, and there was nobody we had to come home to. I talked it over with Sondra and Jeff, and some of the staff here moved me and the kids in three days ago. Suzl will be along when it's all over, which I guess should be any time now. She kept her Fluxgirl body, but she's got all her wizard's power again. For me to come back to myself I had to pay a price.''

''What?''

Cassie nodded. ''We had to leave those millions of women in New Eden looking like they had since they became Fluxgirls, and there was a general feeling among the Guardians that it should be a hard and fast rule, just to be fair about it. Particularly for me. But if I stayed that way I'd stay in New Eden forever, and I'd be expected to remarry and to serve as some kind of example or living monument. I couldn't take that. So to appease both the Guardians and the government that would want to use me I had to pay a big price. I agreed to it. I'm totally disengaged, totally cut off from Flux power. I can't ever see strings. I'm not a wizard any more, not even a false one. That way, I'm not threat now or in the future to New Eden or to anyone else.''

''That's *terrible*! It's unfair!''

''No, it's perfectly fair. Any other way I'm a threat to them. If I can no longer live under their system and endorse and be a shining example of it, I become a threat. I have a hell of a track record, remember, for upsetting the established order. Without Flux power of any kind, I'm safe. They can all rest and so can I. With that power they would always be nervous, like New Eden was at the start, and they'd be out hunting me down. They locked me into the master program—the absolute master. I won't age, they agreed to that much when I agreed to surrender all power, and I'm not only totally without Flux power but totally immune to it as well. No wizard can alter my body or my mind, because to do that they would have to go through the computers, and the computers are instructed to keep me just this way. It was a nice gesture.''

"Nice! I think it's *awful* what they put you through!''

Cassie sighed and took her oldest daughter aside for a moment, never more conscious than now of the gap separating them. "I've lived a very long time,'' she said seriously. "I've been three or more different women in that space. Now this is the fourth and last incarnation. I'm going to look like this and feel like this and be like this until somebody kills me or I fall off a cliff or something. Sure, they took the power, and I have to admit that it's a lonely and frightening thing to be in Flux dependent on someone else, but it's no different than I started, and certainly Suzl coped with that condition for years until you linked her up. No, after you've been a genuine Fluxgirl for fifteen years or more this is a pure delight, and, in a way, I'm happier without the power.''

"I don't think I'm ever going to understand that one.''

"Well, they're *right*, Spirit. I *would* always be a threat to them. When I think of what I *did* do with the power— well, it wasn't much that was positive. I fought a lot of wars, defeated a lot of Fluxlords, transformed a lot of bright-eyed girls into slavish devotees of a religion that was totally false, and built an empire. When Coydt took that away from me, I discovered something terrible about myself, something I really couldn't deal with. I didn't know how to be anything else. I was a professional warrior-priestess at a time when warrior-priestesses were out of date. Thinking about it now I realize that *that* was the real reason I accepted Adam's spell and married him. I'd been a failure at everything except the warrior-priestess role—a failure as a lover, mother, even, in the end with Coydt, as a wizard. My self-confidence was shot to pieces. I needed some role, *any* role, that would let me just run away. You see, Spirit, in all that time I never really grew up. I never had the chance.''

Spirit shook her head in confusion. ''I don't think I'm going to be able to follow this.''

''Well, now I'm through. I'm trapped as you see me, and I don't mind a bit. I'm no less a mother to the kids, who seem to approve of this new look—after a lifetime around nothing but Fluxgirls *I* am the one that looks exotic!—and I'm no less a human being for it, either. I really don't want anything more from this life than the teenage Cassie long ago did. I think I finally earned the right to be a person, not a symbol or somebody's tool. I might still get the urge now and then to save the world or mount a revolution, but I can't—and no wizard or Soul Rider would want to have anything to do with me. For the first time in my life, I'm really free, and I understand myself better than most folks ever will.''

The daughter looked at her mother, and for the first time there seemed to be a glimmer of, if not understanding, at least respect passed between them.

''So what will you do now?'' Spirit asked her.

''That depends on how things work out. I've still got the kids, and I'm not necessarily out of that business if I don't want to be. Who knows? Maybe I can't really grow up. Maybe I'll always think on the grand scale no matter what. I mean, there's a possibility in this new land here to start one hell of a dynasty. Just think of the pedigrees alone.''

''*Mother!*''

The door opened again with a crash and Matson came tearing out, saw her, stopped, and stood there for a moment.

Then suddenly, he felt an urge rising in him, and he simply couldn't repress it.

"Matson!" Cassie yelled sharply. "Stop laughing yourself sick and kiss me!"

AUTHOR'S AFTERWORD

The Soul Rider saga was conceived as a single novel and then broken into three parts because of its length. At the end, I had intended to include appendices with much of the technical data and background on the physics involved, but in going over it and in particular the "history" leading up to World's founding, I found that there was enough material to do a novel on it alone, a prequel of sorts which will involve the discoveries and construction of World and will, I hope, be a pretty good independent novel in its own right. Thus, in a year or so, expect to see Birth of Flux and Anchor *from Tor Books, who also thought it was a pretty good idea.*

Also, in concluding this novel, I discovered that we've raised a lot more questions about the dynamics of revolution than we've solved, and that there is a lot of World we haven't really seen, trapped as we've been in Anchor Logh and New Eden. New Eden is obviously a bankrupt system and a failure, but it has certainly taught all of the power-mongers of World just how empires and revolutions are

*built. We have left World in ferment; as New Eden dies,
and so too the fear of the Gates, we have a political system
as much in Flux as Flux itself. I find I have more to say
here, and I hope you would like a return trip as well. Tor
has also agreed to a (hopefully single volume) sequel for
the future, to come after our prequel.*

*My thanks to Tom Doherty for allowing this book to be
the length it needed to be, and whether you liked or
loathed the ideas we played with here, if it made you think
then I'm happy. For those of you absolutely ill at New
Eden's methods and philosophy who don't already know
what we were doing here, I should warn you not to be
complacent. New Eden was firmly based on a real theocratic
government and its own writings, one alive and well in our
own world as the book was written, needing neither Flux
nor new technology to exist and even gain adherents
elsewhere. Sleep well.*

Jack L. Chalker

POUL ANDERSON
Winner of 7 Hugos and 3 Nebulas

KEITH LAUMER

Buy them at your local bookstore or use this handy coupon:
Clip and mail this page with your order

TOR BOOKS—Reader Service Dept.
49 W. 24 Street, 9th Floor, New York, NY 10010

Please send me the book(s) I have checked above. I am enclosing
$_____ (please add $1.00 to cover postage and handling).
Send check or money order only—no cash or C.O.D.'s.

Mr./Mrs./Miss _____
Address _____
City _____ State/Zip _____
Please allow six weeks for delivery. Prices subject to change without
notice.